From the Pen of Surgeons

DR B.K.S. SANJAY
DR GAURAV SANJAY

PRABHAT
PRAKASHAN

Published by
PRABHAT PRAKASHAN PVT. LTD.
4/19 Asaf Ali Road,
New Delhi-110 002 (INDIA)
e-mail: prabhatbooks@gmail.com

ISBN 978-93-5562-837-4

FROM THE PEN OF SURGEONS
by Dr B.K.S. Sanjay and Dr Gaurav Sanjay

Edition
First, 2024

Price
₹ 700 (Rupees Seven Hundred Only)

Printed at
Sita Fine Arts, Delhi

Dedicated to well-being of the society

You perform your prescribed duty; for action is superior to inaction. Desisting from action, you cannot even maintain your body.

– From Gita 3: 8

Humans are mortal, so are the ideas. An idea needs propagation as much as a plant needs watering. Otherwise both will wither and die

– Dr B. R. Ambedkar

Change is a universal law. We believe that if there is a need to bring change in the individual, society then there is a need to change their thoughts because thoughts are the primary source of all actions. Communication plays an important role to transfer the thoughts and to transform an individual and the society.

– From this book

Foreword

'From The Pen of Surgeons' by Dr BKS Sanjay and Dr Gaurav Sanjay is an eclectic collection of 102 short essays by the father son duo – both of whom as the name suggests are prominent surgeons of Dehradun, where in addition to their professional commitments as distinguished surgeons, they have also made a name for themselves as Good Samaritans and engaged citizens who have also put their best foot forward for all social causes – be it road safety or gender empowerment, substance abuse or issues concerning the demographic future of the country.

These essays have been written over a five year period – from August 2018 to July 2023, and cover the very difficult Covid years when India faced, and surmounted a major challenge, and one in which medical professionals did their best to alleviate the sufferings of humankind.

However, the real strength of this 447-page collection of essays is their views on issues which are normally beyond the ken of doctors. There is, for example a tribute to Dr Ambedkar, the architect of India's Constitution, a column on reading and appreciating literature as well as the importance of education in the transformation of lives of young people.

The writing style is elegant and simple: the subjects covered are varied, and each topic can be read in five to seven minutes. In fine, I recommend this book for the general reader for it will raise awareness not just about living, but about taking responsibility for our health and well-being – whether it be through Yoga, or better diet and a healthy life style.

Dr BKS Sanjay has shown his mettle, not just as a doctor, but also as a poet and litterateur: no wonder then that he was awarded the Padma Shri, and it is good to see his son, Dr Gaurav follow the footsteps of his worthy father on the path of professional excellence as well as public life. More power to them – both for their surgeon's scalpel as well as their fountain pen!

– **Sanjeev Chopra,**

Ex Director, Lal Bahadur Shastri National Academy of Administration
Historian, Policy Analyst and Festival Director of Valley of Words

❑

पी.सी. मोदी
P. C. MODY

महासचिव, राज्य सभा
SECRETARY GENERAL, RAJYA SABHA
29, संसद भवन, नई दिल्ली-110001
29, Parliament House, New Delhi-110001
Tel.: 23017355, 23034695, Fax: 23792940
E-mail: secygen.rs@sansad.nic.in

Message

I am happy to know that Dr B.K.S. Sanjay and Dr Gaurav Sanjay, two outstanding orthopaedic surgeons in our country, have compiled their articles on enduring and contemporary public health and social issues and the same is being brought out in form of a publication titled 'From the Pen of Surgeons".

The publication captures the enormous knowledge and depth of understanding of the authors in their professional field besides their ability as public health practitioners and communicators to create the right public health awareness in the country, especially at a time when the COVID pandemic posed humongous challenges in the field of public healthcare.

The subjects covered in the publication are indeed exhaustive. These range from road safety to education, environmental sustainability to public health, yoga to inclusive development and many more. But the overriding narrative has been to flag the national loss arising out of growing fatalities and falling health standards of the people due to road accidents, smoking, alcoholism, growth of population, etc. and to address the growing public health concerns for ensuring good health and happiness of the people. The reflections of the authors in their analysis of chronic and emerging health challenges such as cancer, diabetes, tuberculosis, hepatitis, infectious diseases, and COVID-19 have been as incisive as their thoughts on broader social issues having impact on quality healthcare, like literacy, education. nutrition, women empowerment and population control. The authors have been able to present their professional knowledge and advice in a lucid language while making the rigour and nuances of the public health issues more pronounced not only for the healthcare administrators but also for other stakeholders including the general public.

I hope the publication with its distilled wisdom will serve as an important guide to all those who wish to see the country emerging stronger on the bedrock of good health and happiness of our people which is inherent in the pursuit of holistic healthcare.

I wish authors of the publication all success in their noble endeavours.

(P.C. Mody)

23 September, 2022
New Delhi

❑

Message from The Pioneer

We were aware of Dr BKS Sanjay being an experienced and illustrious orthopaedic surgeon. However, his concern for social welfare, especially in aspects he has directly experienced and resolved, enhanced our interaction with him. A busy surgeon who takes out the time to spread awareness through his writings and other modes is someone who also meets our aim of doing our bit for the welfare of society. Dr Sanjay and his son, orthopaedic surgeon Dr Gaurav Sanjay have been writing guest columns in The Pioneer, Dehradun since 2018. The issues they raise in their columns are pertinent for the citizens and the establishment alike. We believe that the messages the father-son duo spread through The Pioneer have and will continue to benefit the society.

– Ajit Sinha
Managing Director,
The Pioneer, Dehradun

❑

Author's Note

Health, education and nutrition are the fundamental needs of every individual. There is need of awareness of importance of health, education and nutrition in the life. Being the orthopaedic surgeons we have seen the all kind of suffering not only the victims but the relatives, friends and family of road traffic victims.

90% of the road traffic accidents are due to negligence of the drivers. Therefore there is need of knowing the bad effects of road traffic accidents and awareness about the importance of knowing and following the traffic rules. The goals and the basis of writing these columns were to spread the awareness to the masses with a hope that people will learn and share these experience which were depicted in these columns. The writing are based on our personal experience that have been from starting of our orthopaedic education till date.

The purpose behind compiling all these columns in the form of book is to further spread awareness and reference. In a book to concerned citizen and professional in the medical health and the other fields.

We both of us have been writing guest columns in the pioneer Dehradun since August 2018. The columns are focused on raising awareness and informing the public on important health and other social issues.

– Dr B.K.S. Sanjay

– Dr Gaurav Sanjay

Sanjay Orthopaedic, Spine & Maternity Centre
20/3, Doon Vihar, Lane No. 2, Jakhan, Rajpur Road,
Dehradun, Uttarakhand - 248001
Email: soscentredoon@gmail.com
Phone No.- +91-9412051155

Acknowledgements

It is a matter of great pride and immense privilege for us that Dr Sanjeev Chopra, a former Director of the Lal Bahadur Shastri National Academy of Administration, Mussoorie, a historian and a prolific writer along with Mr. P. C. Modi, Secretary General, Rajya Sabha, New Delhi graciously agreed to write foreword and message for the book respectively. We are grateful to both of them.

We are thankful to our family members, Mrs. Bhavna Sanjay, Dr Pratik Sanjay, Dr Sujata Sanjay, Nandita and Nashita, colleagues, readers, patients and their families for their valuable contribution in supporting us in every possible way and even giving us their suggestions and ideas from time to time. We would like to acknowledge the feedback given by various readers from time to time. The feedback has given us tremendous encouragement to write these many columns. We would also like to thank the whole team of 'The Pioneer', Dehradun newspaper specially to Mr Ajit Sinha, Hariom Singh and Paritosh Kimothi for giving us an opportunity and an excellent platform to express our ideas on pertinent issues facing the society regularly.

We would also like to thank Sonia, Laxmi and Karishma who have helped us in writing these columns and in editing, compiling and creating this book by providing their invaluable assistance. We are also thankful all those who over the years shared their experiences and ideas and contributed in our joint efforts in making this world a better place to live.

❑

Contents

❑

1

Impacts of Road Traffic Accidents in India

– Dr BKS Sanjay,
Thursday, 23 August 2018

As our country is growing economically, so are the road traffic accidents. Apart from the obvious damage, the increase in these road traffic accidents is also creating hurdles in the economic growth of the nation. This author believes that human resource is the biggest resource. Every year the nation is losing 1.5 lakh people and a similar number of them are being disabled permanently, if they survive such accidents. Road accident does not spare any section of the society whether a person is poor or rich, unskilled or highly skilled. Majority of them are in the age group of 20-40 years and are usually the bread earners of the family.

I also believe that health, education and nutrition are the fundamental needs of any person. As we know, our nation is struggling to meet the basic needs like health, education and nutrition. The road traffic accidents are depleting the resources meant for these basic needs. The injuries caused by road mishaps are not only causing physical disability but also causing economic disability.

After the road traffic accidents, everybody becomes poorer than what he or she was earlier. Fifty per cent of the families are either borrowing money from someone or selling their assets like land, house, cattle, vehicle, ornaments etc. for the treatment of their beloved. But unfortunately, in spite of the best available treatment in our country one-fourth to a half of accident victims remain temporarily or permanently disabled and unfortunately but practically become a liability to their family.

A study conducted in 2016 by the UN Economic and Social Commission for Asia and Pacific (UNESCAP) revealed that India loses $58 billion annually due to road accidents which is worth about three per cent of the GDP. If we consider only the estimated monetary loss which is spent by the patient and his/her family in the hospital it adds up to about `2,000 crore annually.

One will recall a major bus accident took place at Pauri district in Uttarakhand recently in which 48 out of 60 people died. Similarly, in a recent Himachal Pradesh accident 52 out of 98 passengers died and in Maharashtra, 32 people out of 33 died. In a recent police report, it was found that about 15,000 accidents are occurring annually in Uttarakhand out of which 10 per cent fatal accidents are leading to death of the driver and passenger. Of those who survive, 25 to 50 per cent become handicapped.

In the last 10 years, the numbers of road traffic accidents have doubled in India whereas they have decreased by one-third in China. Among the major reasons behind the road traffic accidents are sleep deprivation and alcohol intake while driving. The existing mental, social and financial pressure on the drivers give them a kick to over speed even on congested roads which leads to road traffic accidents.

Over speeding, overtaking and over loading are also responsible for increasing number of road traffic accidents. It has also been scientifically proven that when speed increases the number of accidents tend to increase. According to a police report three-fourth of vehicles on the

Yamuna expressway had been found to be over speeding. According to a police survey conducted in the Mountain State of Uttarakhand, the major causes of road accidents are over speeding or over loading. The people are trying to save time by over speeding and over taking to waste the time on the social media instead.

The increasing desire to stay connected on social platforms has become so addictive in recent years that people have the urge to use it even while driving vehicles. This is very dangerous as has also been published in many reports that state that mobile phones are the cause of fatal accidents with the number of such mishaps rising day by day.

In a 2017 Government report published, it was found that the risk of fatality is 40 per cent in case of people who are driving and simultaneously using mobile phones resulting in an accident. Some time ago in Kushinagar (Uttar Pradesh), 13 children died because the driver was using the mobile phone with earphones while crossing a railway line and he could not hear the horn of the train and the shouting of the school children who were trying to alert him about the incoming train.

A visual experiment was conducted in Hong Kong where it was shown that the 5-6 seconds it takes one to take out a mobile phone, unlock it and read the messages, are enough to cause fatal accidents. No message or call is so urgent, attending which can't be deferred by a few minutes. If they are so important, one should stop the vehicle at the side of the road and only then respond to them. Driving safely and staying safe while driving is more important rather than trying to stay connected 24×7 on the social media.

Road traffic accidents are on the increase all over the world but the incidence of accidents is more in India where there is a need for comprehensive measures to prevent them, treat them at a proper time and at an optimum cost. There should be a national mission to make the general public aware about the road safety rules and regulations. Contributing its bit, this author's organisation too has been conducting such awareness programmes since 2005.

As part of such efforts, one shares his experience with the students of schools and colleges who are the target population-also stressing that a single accident can change physical, mental, social and financial status of the injured person.

According to a study, 90 per cent of accidents are due to driver carelessness and only 10 per cent are due to other causes like ill maintained roads and vehicles. If we follow the traffic rules honestly the chances of accidents can be reduced significantly. I believe that nowadays one cannot complete formal education, go to their place of work or go to other places without driving a vehicle or being driven by someone else to reach the place of learning or work.

Just by knowing the above facts, one should realise the importance of driving in our day-to-day lives. Our country is having many hundreds of thousands of educational institutions but not even a few hundred driving schools. Driving schools could have played a big role in decreasing the number of road traffic accidents.

The students should be made to use helmets while using two-wheelers and use seatbelt while in four-wheelers. Human resource is the biggest resource and we should try to save it. For this, whenever you are using the roads always think about road safety and your safety.

http://www.pioneeredge.in/impacts-of-road-traffic-accidents-in-india/

❑

2

Back Pain: A Serious Modern Household Medical Problem

– Dr BKS Sanjay,
Friday, 28 September 2018

The importance of our back can be gauged from the commonly used adage about a particular person being the backbone of that organisation or society. The backbone plays an important role in maintaining and functioning of our body.

The human spine is a complex structure spanning from the head to the tailbone. The spinal column protects the spinal cord and the nerve roots. It allows the body movements in three dimensions and also maintains the balance of the head, the trunk and the pelvis through the various intervertebral discs, facet joints, muscles and adjacent ligaments.

A backache is the second most common problem a person experiences after a headache. It is estimated that everyone will have back pain at least once in his or her lifetime. The mountainous terrain exerts more forces on the back and makes the people in the mountains more prone to back pain.

Back pain could be due to falling from a height, carrying too much of heavy loads, lack of exercise, wrong posture while driving, while sitting or while carrying loads. The people having a sedentary lifestyle are more prone to develop back pain due to weakness in the surrounding muscles.

Among the florid symptoms of back pain, slipped intervertebral disc is a common cause. The intervertebral disc material slips from its place and compresses the spinal cord or the exiting nerve root. The prolapsed intervertebral disc is becoming a common problem in young age because of wrong workouts in the gymnasium.

The slipped disc gives rise to pain in the region supplied by the compressed nerve or the typical radiating pain in the legs (sciatica). The disc pain is characterised as radicular pain which has a nature described as shooting, burning or an electric current like the pain in one or both legs. Continuous disc pressure on the nerve root causes the progressive decrease in the efficiency of the muscles and long-standing compression may even present with the variable degree of paralysis.

Treatment modalities of slipped disc depend upon the degree of compression of the nerve. These vary from medications, physiotherapy and injection epidural steroid to surgical removal of the slipped disc. It is worth mentioning here that not all cases of the slipped disc, can be treated with only exercise or medications and neither do all such cases need surgery. A moderately or a grossly slipped disc can never revert back to its place and it has to be removed surgically.

The elderly patient usually presents with spinal canal stenosis (narrowing of spinal canal) due to overgrowth of the surrounding structures which is characterised by neurological claudication in lower extremities, numbness and occasionally with urinary retention, dribbling and/or constipation. Just like a slipped disc, a vertebra can also slip either due to fracture of the parts of the vertebra or due to degeneration of the facet joints. If the bony spinal canal is unstable at any level then it may require surgery.

Another common cause of back pain is facet joint arthritis. As other joints of the body degenerate with an advance in the age so do the facet joints. The back becomes stiff in the morning on while getting up and pain is relieved after the increase in the movements as the day progresses. Facet joint arthritis is treated with NSAIDs, physiotherapy, exercises, local steroid injections and rarely with surgery. Spinal cord tumours are a rare presentation among the causes of back pain.

Spinal tumours can occur in any age group and are usually associated with back pain at night and neurological symptoms of numbness or paralysis. Spinal tumours are usually treated with surgery. Though spinal cord tumour surgery is technically difficult comparing to the other spine surgeries the results are gratifying in properly selected cases.

As minimally invasive surgery has become popular among surgical specialities, it has followed even so in spine surgery. Minimal invasive spine surgery has reduced the comorbidities associated with open surgery like the incidence of infection, prolonged hospital stays and postoperative pain after surgery. Injection therapy has been found to be quite effective in treating various back pain pathologies. Steroid injections, anaesthetic drugs and other agents are used for treating various causes of back pain. The rationale for using steroid injection is that it works as an anti-inflammatory around the injected area, hence, reduces the pain. Epidural steroid injections are usually given for radicular pain caused due to the slipped disc. Steroid injections are also given for the pain due to facet joint arthritis and fibro fasciitis pain at the lumbosacral junction. This fibro fasciitis pain is quite common in young ladies.

Local steroid therapy is also quite effective therapy in such cases.

Tuberculosis infection of the spine is quite common in our country. However, with the current TB drugs available, TB infection can be controlled in 90 per cent of the cases with anti-tuberculosis drugs. Only 10 per cent of the patients require surgery, if the infection is not controlled with drugs or if the patient develops paralysis during or before treatment.

Spinal needle biopsy is a simple, effective and cheap procedure to diagnose the pathology of the spine. It can easily differentiate between infection and tumour of the spine. The author believes that if the culprit is to be punished or killed, then first he should be properly identified before commencing the punishment. It is a terrible mistake if an innocent person is killed in the place of a culprit. In the same way, if a patient of infection is being treated for cancer or vice versa then it is a grave mistake. The same principle is to be applied in case of disease as in the case of the culprit, first, the disease has to be identified and then treated accordingly. One can appreciate the outcome of such a mistake which can be made on empirical treatment started on the basis of clinical judgement only.

Lack of awareness, neglect of pain, poverty, lack of trained doctors and the shortage of good hospitals accentuates these simple problems to a serious problem in about 20 per cent of back pain patients. Spine surgeries are difficult and risky but its success completely depends on the skill of the surgeon and standard of medical facilities available in the hospital. Spine surgery, like any surgery, has very good results if done on time and before landing up in the complications due to the neglect of treatment. After the surgery, the patient has to follow a definite protocol for a certain time to get the ideal result. The author himself has done more than a thousand surgeries, varying from simple to most complicated high risk spine surgeries in the past 20 years and none of them has resulted in paralysis after surgery. In fact, the author's name was recorded in the Limca book of records for spine surgery.

http://www.pioneeredge.in/back-pain-a-serious-modern-household-medical-problem/

❑

3

No New Patients, but Numerous Old Patients Struggle

– Dr BKS Sanjay,
Monday, 22 October 2018

Health is not only an asset but a resource too. The physical, mental and social development depends upon good health. If every person is developed, then the country too will definitely be developed. Any goal of majority of the people can be achieved only if the people are physically fit. If hands and feet are not functioning well, then it becomes difficult to achieve various goals in life.

Polio and cerebral palsy (CP) are the common causes of paralysis and disability in children all over the world but particularly in developing and poor countries like India. World CP Day is observed on October 6 and world polio day is observed on October 24 every year all over the world. The awareness campaign is being organised all over the world during this month and India is not an exception. This article, too, is part of an awareness campaign to reduce the disability in polio and CP afflicted children.

The author strongly believes that health is not only an asset but a resource too and any kind of disability not only reduces the efficiency of a disabled person, but indirectly affects the society and the nation as a whole. Being an orthopaedic surgeon and seeing the personal, social and financial suffering of victims of post-polio residual paralysis and cerebral palsy in last 40 years of his career, this author has taken a resolve to increase awareness among the affected and general public about the impact of polio and CP on personal and social front in India. One regularly gives his services through free camps and public awareness lectures for these disabled patients and has done 1526 operations on such children and made their life better through his surgical knowledge and skills.

Polio is a highly infectious disease caused by polio virus. The polio virus spreads through faecal oral route that means polio virus contaminates food and water consumed by affected child. Therefore, hygiene is vital to prevent the infection.

Since the introduction of extensive use of polio vaccine, the incidents of the polio have been drastically reduced all over the world and ultimately, most of the countries have become polio free except few countries namely Pakistan, Afghanistan and Nigeria. Last polio infection was seen in India on January 13, 2011. WHO has declared India polio free country on 27 March 2014.

Polio is a crippling disease which mainly affects the children of up to five years of age. It affects the anterior horn cells of spinal cord and rarely the brain cells. It, usually, affects the lower limbs. It is a flaccid type of paralysis and is non-progressive. Maximum recovery of paralysis occurs within two years of infection, if not, it gives residual paralysis. This residual paralysis results into deformity and contracture of the joints which makes the gait abnormal. These days, we are not dealing with any new case of polio infection but with the old affected polio patients.

Polio virus affects the paralysis of certain group of muscles which cause the imbalance of the muscle power that usually gives the angular fixed deformity around the joint due to growth potential of the epiphysis in the children. Joint is deformed usually in multiple plain which makes normal walking either difficult or even impossible. The deformities are progressive initially but usually they become static at a later stage.

The principle of surgery in polio is correction of deformity, balancing of the muscle power, stabilisation of joints and lengthening of the bone. This can be achieved with physiotherapy by strengthening of the weak muscles, manipulation of contracted joint, correction of deformity by repeated use of passive force, use of splint, orthosis or calliper etc.

Most of the mild deformities can be corrected with the above-mentioned means. If they cannot be corrected and deformities are gross then patient require surgical intervention. In polio multiple muscle and multiple joints are involved hence it requires multiple surgeries at multiple sites depending upon the power of muscle and severity of deformity of the joint.

Tendon transfer is indicated when dynamic muscle imbalance results in a deformity that interferes with ambulation or function of the upper extremities. The basic principle of tendon transfer is to balance the power of muscle around the joint by transferring the powerful muscle to the weak muscle. When a relaxed or flail joint cannot be stabilised by the tendon transfer then it should be stabilised by fusing the range of motion of the joint. It is rarely required nowadays, if it is done then it is usually on the foot joint.

The aim of treatment, in simple words, is that the deformity should be prevented, if existing-it should be corrected and corrected position should be maintained forever. If deformity cannot be corrected by the tendon surgery, then bone surgery has to be done to correct the deformity and corrected position to be maintained by the internal fixation like plate or external fixation by fixator or by plaster for the period till the bone is healed which usually take approximately three months' time. Patients should use the brace or splint for another nine months to a year.

The shortening of the limb is the rule in the polio rather than exception. If the shorting is of half an inch to an inch, then the heel of the shoe can be raised. Ilizarov external fixator has been a boon in the polio and CP surgeries particularly to correct the deformities of the joint and to lengthen the limb simultaneously.

If shorting is more than one inch then bone should be lengthened. About two to three inches lengthening of bone can be easily done. The bone can be lengthened up to 8-10 inches by the experienced and skilled surgeon with Ilizarov external fixator though it takes up to a year for complete healing and recovery.

The polio surgery is very rewarding. The simple surgery can change the gait of the polio patient and ultimately the life of the patient. They can be self-reliant rather than being dependent on others after successful surgery.

http://www.pioneeredge.in/no-new-patients-but-numerous-old-patients-struggle/

❑

4

The World Day of Remembrance for Road Traffic Victims

– Dr BKS Sanjay,
Monday, 19. November 2018

Roads and streets are more than just connections from point A to point B. They tell stories, some of them tragic but worth learning. They are bitter yet important. These stories could be lessons for others. On this day I wish to share my experience with you. The World Day of Remembrance for Road Traffic Victims (WDR) is held on the third Sunday of November each year to remember the millions of those who died or were injured in road traffic accidents and the plight of their loved ones who have to come up with the consequences of their deaths or injuries.

It is also a day on which we thank the emergency services and reflect on the tremendous burden and cost of this daily continuing disaster to families, communities and countries, and on ways to halt it. WDR was started by the British road crash victim charity, Road Peace, in 1993 and was adopted by the United Nations General Assembly in 2005. In 2008 events were held in 28 countries including India.

Road deaths and injuries are sudden, violent and traumatic events. Their impact is long lasting, often permanent. The cumulative toll is truly tremendous. This author believes that human resource is the biggest resource. The road traffic accidents are depleting not only financial resources but the human resources as well. These injuries are not only causing physical and financial disability but social disability too. As our country is growing economically, so are the road traffic accidents. Every year, the nation is not only losing 1.5 lakh people, but also an equal number of them are being disabled permanently, if they survive. Road accidents do not differentiate between the sections of the society, rich or poor, skilled or unskilled, old or young.

However, statistics show that majority of those who are affected are in the age group of 20-40 years and are usually the bread earners of their families. As we all know, a major accident took place in Uttarakhand in the recent past in which 48 out of 60 people died and in similar accidents in Himachal Pradesh and Maharashtra 52 out of 98 and 32 people out of 33 died, respectively.

The grief and distress experienced by this huge number of people is all the more agonising because many of the victims are young and because many of the crashes could have been prevented if proper precautions were taken. The governments and society's response to road death and injury and to the bereaved and injured victims is often inadequate and inappropriate in commensuration to a loss of life or quality of life.

It can be prevented if everybody cares about safety first while on the road. The number of road traffic accidents can be brought down significantly it proper road safety guidelines are followed. In a recently published 2017 Government of India report, it was found that if those people who are driving and simultaneously using mobile phones, meet with a road traffic accident, then 40 per cent of them die.

Recently in Kushinagar, UP, 13 children died because the driver of the school vehicle was using the mobile phone while crossing the rail way line. The victim may not be our friend and our family member but he could be friend and family member of someone else for sure. One can only imagine the suffering of parents and grandparents of the kids killed in an accident.

Being an orthopaedic surgeon for about 40 years. I came to know many such stories, but would like mention two such stories. In one incident, a young man was killed in a road traffic accident while he had gone out to distribute his marriage invitation cards two days before his marriage. Now his widow mother is dependent and living alone though she has a daughter because according to popular tradition, the mother does not live with her married daughter's family.

In another incident, the teenager daughter was going to drop her mother who was a teacher to her school one morning. On the way, they met with a road traffic accident. They were a family of four-- father, mother, brother and sister. The father and son already had long standing mental illness. The mother sustained fracture of hip bone and the daughter had fractures of thigh and leg bones. The daughter succumbed to her injuries. Parents lost their only daughter and the brother lost his only sister.

However, the problem is far from over, the mother is having persistent lifelong fear of developing loss of blood supply of fractured hip which is a known complication in these types of fractures in spite of the best possible treatment. This special day of remembrance is therefore intended to respond to the great need of support for the road crash victims, for public recognition of their loss and suffering.

It has also become an important tool for governments and for those who works to prevent crashes or respond to the aftermath. It offers the opportunity to demonstrate the enormous scale and impact of road deaths and injuries and the urgent need for action. Road traffic accidents are on the rise all over the world but such accidents are more in India not only because of inadequate road safety measures but also due to lack of willingness and awareness in the masses to follow traffic rules as well.

There is an urgent need for comprehensive measures to prevent them, treat them at a proper time and at optimum cost. The World Day of Remembrance for Road Traffic Victims has become an important tool in global efforts to reduce road casualties. It offers an opportunity for drawing attention to the scale of emotional and economic devastation caused by road crashes and for giving recognition to the suffering of road crash victims and to acknowledge the importance of the work of support and rescue services. A national awareness programme should be launched to make the general public aware about the road safety rules and regulations. And to be a small of part this magnanimous task, the author's organisation has been conducting such awareness programmes since 2005.

I have been sharing my experience with the students of schools and colleges, keeping in mind the fact that even a single mishap during road accidents can change physical, mental, social and financial status of the injured person for a generation to come. According to our study, 90 per cent of accidents are due to driver's carelessness and only 10 per cent are due to other causes like ill maintained roads and vehicles. If we follow the traffic rules honestly then the chances of accidents can be reduced significantly.

http://www.pioneeredge.in/the-world-day-of-rememberance-for-road-traffic-vitims/

❑

5

World Observes the International Day of Disabled Persons Today

– Dr BKS Sanjay,
Monday, 3 December 2018

According to the World Health Organisation (WHO), disability is an umbrella term, covering impairments, activity limitations, and participation restrictions. Impairment is a problem in body functions or structures; an activity limitation is a difficulty encountered by an individual in executing a task or action and a participation restriction is a problem experienced by an individual involving the day-to-day life situations.

Disability is thus, not just a health problem but rather a complex phenomenon, reflecting the interaction between features of a person's body and features of the society in which he or she lives.

Overcoming difficulties faced by people with disabilities requires interventions to remove environmental and social barriers as well. People with disabilities have the same health needs as physically fit people. They might experience constraints in health care, both because of poverty and social exclusion, and also because they may be vulnerable to secondary conditions. The International Day of Disabled Persons (IDDP) was decided to be celebrated internationally on December 3 every year and later promoted as an international observance by the United Nations 1992 onwards.

The major emphasis during the annual observance is given to promote the awareness about the people with disabilities as well as to encourage such people by providing a lot of training and assistance in their day-to-day activities to enhance their quality of life and remove the social stigma towards them.

Since 1992, it has been observed continuously every year with a lot of success all over the world including India. It also looks to involve all the persons with disabilities in society in various walks of life such as the political, economic, social and cultural spheres. Every year, the celebration of the International Day of Disabled Persons focuses on the different issues of the disabled persons across the world.

Being an orthopaedic surgeon, I will restrict myself to the orthopaedic disabilities, their causes, and remedies. The potential causes of orthopaedic impairments include genetic abnormalities, birth trauma, cerebral palsy, rickets, polio, various infections, bone tuberculosis, arthritis, fractures, and amputations.

The main causes of orthopaedic disabilities are cerebral palsy, clubfoot and polio in children, fractures due to road traffic accidents in adults and degenerative arthritis and osteoporosis in old age.

Our ancient Indian scriptures state that, if there is birth, there is development, disease, degeneration, and death. If we analyse the causes of disability, then all the four stages of life are vulnerable to disabilities depending upon the age of the individual. Most of the causes of disabilities like infection and other diseases can be and have been prevented with the advancement of medical technology and skill, but ageing cannot be. Ageing and the degenerative changes associated with age are themselves the causes of the disability.

Main causes of disability in old age are senile degeneration, arthritis and osteoporosis. Osteoporosis is a silent disease. Osteoporosis is caused mainly due to disturbed calcium metabolism. Osteoporosis during old age cannot be halted completely but its pace can be reduced by keeping an active lifestyle as much as possible and supplementing the diet with calcium and vitamins.

Wrist, hip and spine fractures are commonly seen in osteoporotic bones. People become disabled for the rest of the life if these fractures are not treated well in time. Disability is a subject you may read or hear about, but not think of as something that may happen to you. However, your chances of becoming disabled are greater than you realise today. More people live with disabilities than ever before due to our ageing societies, as well as improved medical treatment.

Over a billion people of the world's population, about 15 per cent have some form of disability. According to the Government of India census report of 2016, out of the 121-crore population, 2.7 crore persons are disabled which amounts to about 2.2 per cent of the total population.

It is increasing at an astonishing rate of about 25 per cent in each decade. However, the absolute numbers have started coming down all over the world, including in India, due to better education, health and medical services.

If the road traffic accidents are treated well in time, then firstly the patient will not at all be disabled and even if he or she becomes disabled, in spite of the best possible treatment, then the level of disability will be significantly less.

I strongly believe that surgery has played an important role in the lives of persons with disabilities. Their lives have been changed significantly and they are not only developing or improving themselves but also contributing to the growth of society.

I once read in a book that in a particular region of Tunisia, there is a water well which the local sages believe is connected to another well in the holy city of Mecca. But ordinary people like me believe that every well is interconnected underground.

Therefore, I and my organisation are making our best efforts to spread awareness by organising free health camps and lectures to reduce the disabilities and to make disabled people able through prompt surgical interventions.

I sincerely believe that it is my duty to serve the society because we all are a part of it. There is a Zulu proverb "Umuntu Ngumuntu Ngabantu" which means that a person is a person through/because of other people. The deformities and disabilities caused due to any reason whatsoever should be corrected at the earliest. Hence, this author always advises the patient and the patient's family that if surgery is needed, then, the sooner the better because plants can be straightened, not the trees.

http://www.pioneeredge.in/world-observes-the-international-day-of-disabled-persons-today/

❑

6

Tackling Diabetes with Lifestyle Changes

– Dr Gaurav Sanjay,
Monday, 14 January 2019

Much of the diabetes burden can be prevented by making lifestyle changes. The complications of diabetes are of significance also in terms of socioeconomic costs. Diabetes is a chronic disease which occurs when the pancreas does not produce enough insulin or when the body cannot effectively use the insulin it produces. This leads to an increased concentration of glucose in the blood, known as hyperglycaemia.

Type I Diabetes Mellitus earlier known as Insulin Dependent Diabetes Mellitus, childhood onset or juvenile Diabetes Mellitus, is characterised by a lack of insulin production. Type II Diabetes Mellitus earlier known as Non-Insulin Dependent Diabetes Mellitus or adult-onset diabetes is caused by ineffective use of insulin by the body. Gestational Diabetes Mellitus is hyperglycaemia that is recognised during pregnancy, it can lead to serious health risk for both mother and child. Diabetes is a growing challenge in India with estimated 8.7 per cent diabetic population in the age group of 20 to 70 years.

The rising prevalence of diabetes and other non-communicable disease is driven by a combination of factors like sedentary lifestyle, rapid urbanisation, increasing life expectancy, unhealthy diet, consumption of tobacco and alcohol and sudden increase in per capita income and increased consumption of processed foods. Obesity is the most important risk factors responsible for diabetes. Much of the diabetes burden can be prevented or delayed by making lifestyle changes favouring a healthy diet and regular physical activity. According to the Indian Heart Association, India is projected to be home to 109 million individuals with diabetes by 2035.

The number of Indians with diabetes is likely to be doubled in the next decade. Diabetes was India's seventh biggest cause of early or premature death in 2016, according to the data shown by Institute of Health, Matrix and Evolution. According to the same report around 47.3 per cent of India's 70 million diabetics are undiagnosed. There is a general perception that diabetes is a disease of the rich and affluent society, however, data has shown that there is evidence of an epidemiological transition with the prevalence of diabetes being higher in low socioeconomic group of urban areas of more economically developed states.

According to a research by Indian Council of Medical Research (ICMR), Asians have a 2-4 times higher risk of acquiring type II diabetes than Europeans. Studies have shown that diabetes in Asians develops a decade earlier than in Europeans, at lower weight and those with pre-diabetes progress to diabetes at a faster rate. Being an orthopaedic surgeon, now I will focus on the related orthopaedic complications. The pathology behind the orthopaedic complications can be mainly attributed to neuropathy and angiopathy. Nerve damage (neuropathy) is a complication of diabetes that leads to a loss of sensation in the feet. Decreased sensations can lead to a wound as small as the size of a pinhead which can progress to a serious infection in a matter of days as they often go unnoticed.

Diabetes also damages the blood vessels (angiopathy), decreasing the blood flow to the feet. Orthopaedic complication of diabetes include: foot ulcer, gangrene of toes, plantar fasciitis, tendonitis, avascular necrosis of femoral head, Charcot arthropathy, diabetic foot in the lower limbs and frozen shoulder, carpal tunnel syndrome and Dupuyptren's contracture in the upper limbs. In the upper extremity carpal tunnel syndrome and frozen shoulder are the most common problems. In such patients the pain increases during night time. Carpel tunnel syndrome is due to compression of nerve at the level of the wrist. If the patients are hypothyroid then there is an additional risk of it.

Diabetic patients are also more prone to frozen shoulder. Diabetes also causes premature osteoarthritis, delayed bone healing and increased chances of infection after open injury or any surgical intervention. It is also associated with poor wound healing because of narrowing of the arteries and damage to the nerve. Poor circulation weakens bone, and can cause disintegration of the bones and joints in the foot and ankle. As a result, people with diabetes are at a high risk for breaking bones in the feet. When a diabetic patient fractures a bone in the foot, he or she may not realise it because of the pre-existing nerve damage which causes loss of sensation and lack of pain. Hence, patients continue to walk on an injured foot which results in more severe fractures and joint dislocations. Sharp edges of a fractured bone within the foot can point downward toward the sole, increasing the risk of chronic foot sores from the abnormal pressure.

The easiest measures to lower the risk of diabetes is to keep your blood sugar level under 100 mg/dl, HBA1C below 5.7 per cent and blood pressure below 130/90 mmhg. The chances of lowering the risk factors can be enhanced by brisk walking, running, swimming or playing sports. In our country, swimming or community recreation centre facilities are not available widely. We can follow the principle of doing any recreational activity that makes you sweat and breathe harder for at least one hour a day for seven days a week. This will significantly reduce the chances of diabetes in the future.

There is common slogan "wider the waist line, shorter the life line." Keep a healthy weight with waist size below 90 cm for men and 80 cm for women. For general screening, the approximate weight can be calculated with a simple formula of height in centimetres minus 100. The remaining number in kilogramme is roughly the approximate weight. The other standardised formula is Body Mass Index (BMI) which can be calculated as: - weight in kg divided by height in metre square multiplied by 100.

It is interpreted as underweight <18.5, normal weight 18.5 – 24.9, overweight 25-29.9, obese class I 30-34.9, obese class II 35-39.9, obese class III > 40. Other simple measures used to lower the risk are to use the stairs rather than the lift, stop smoking and reduce your alcohol consumption, do your daily household work. It could be cleaning your utensils, room or clothes and arranging your wardrobe or bed. These complications are of significant clinical concern in terms of morbidity, mortality and socioeconomic costs. The yearly cost to treat diabetes is estimated to be Rs 27,400 per capita, which if constant would reach an annual Rs 1.95 lakh crore over six times the 2018 health budget by 2025, according to a report by a global consulting firm.

http://www.pioneeredge.in/tackling-diabetes-with-lifestyle-changes/

❑

7

Deadly Cancer Can Be Nipped in Bud

– Dr Gaurav Sanjay,
Monday, 4 February 2019

World Cancer Day is observed on February 4 to raise awareness on cancer and to encourage its prevention, detection and treatment. Cancer is the second leading cause of death in the world. It can be defined in simple words as uncontrolled growth of cells. The second character of cancer cells is to survive on the normal cells of the body. In general, the cells in a multi-cellular organism are programmed for collaboration but many diseases occur because these specialised cells failed to perform their assigned task. Cancer takes this malfunction one step further, not only is there a failure of cells to maintain their specialised function but the growth of cancer cells is unregulated.

The most significant risk factor for cancer is prolonged longevity. The other common risk factors for cancer include tobacco, alcohol consumption, sun and radiation exposure, use of certain chemicals and hormones etc. Lifestyle changes like poor diet, lack of physical activity and overweight, adulteration and pollution are also being blamed for rising incidence of cancer. The definite diagnosis of any pathology can be made with tissue diagnosis (biopsy) only.

It is truer in the case of cancer, because the treatment modalities for cancer are expensive and have more complication than other common diseases. The tissue diagnosis or biopsy not only defines the origin of the tumour but it also grades its invasiveness to the surrounding tissue. The approach of the treatment depends upon all these above-mentioned factors. The curability from a tumour is usually inversely proportional to the tumour margin. Hence sooner the diagnosis better the outcome. However, in our country where the health services are not at par with developed nations, the results are not always so.

Many patients consult the doctors with a delayed presentation because many times at early stage these tumours are painless and hence neglected by the patients as they don't consider it worth consulting a doctor. I presume that this is one of the main factors that in our country people are going for cancer treatment at a delayed stage to the available health facilities. Another feature of cancer is recurrence of tumour in addition to the distant spread.

The cause of recurrence is usually residual tumours which are not visible to the surgeon during removal of the tumour however with the invention of newer modalities like bone scan, CT scan, MRI and PET scan the incidence of residual tumour has decreased as better pre-operative planning can be done. In addition to the tumour burden and residual tumour, the other major determinant of treatment outcome is the physiological response of the patient to treatment.

A patient who is already having poor health status is more likely to suffer, more than a healthy and a fully active patient. The treatment modalities in the cancer patients are based mainly on whether the treatment is palliative or curative. Cancer treatment nowadays is multidisciplinary approach because cancer is such a disease which affects not only the involved site but it also spreads to nearby organ and to distant sites. The multidisciplinary approach includes surgery, chemotherapy and radiation therapy alone or in combination. This approach helps to eradicate or cure the cancer from the affected organ or prevents spread in distant organ.

However, this combination of approach increases the chances of morbidity and sometimes mortality, because most cancer therapies are toxic. These patients are already fighting with the cancer and are in a systemically compromised state due to which they become unable to fight with the treatment induced toxicity. The common side effects of chemo therapy and radiation therapy are nausea, vomiting, alopecia (loss of hairs) and low grade fever which can be managed with certain effective drugs. These patients usually have decreased body weight, anorexia and many psychosocial problems. In addition to the above the patient needs empathy and supportive care not only by medical and paramedical staff but by the patients' friends and family members.

The common causes of death in these patients are infection and distant spread leading to circulatory, respiratory, hepatic and renal failure ultimately to multi-organ failure. Being an orthopaedic surgeon now I will restrict myself to the treatment of orthopaedic cancer related to bone and soft tissue. The bone cancer constitutes 1 per cent all body cancer, 3 per cent of bone cancer are seen in children. The common bone tumours in children are Osteosarcoma and Ewing's sarcoma. Osteosarcoma is a malignant bone tumour and it commonly involves bones around the knee. In order of frequency, proximal end of tibia and distal end of femur and proximal end of humorous are involved. Osteosarcoma is a fast-growing tumour.

A patient can succumb to death as it often spreads to the lungs. Ewing sarcoma mainly involves the pelvic bone and flat bones. Whenever Ewing sarcoma involves the long bone than it is usually involves the mid shaft of the bone. These tumours usually give progressive pain and swelling around the involved bone. Pain in bones in tumours usually does not get relief from commonly prescribed pain killers and at a later stage pain does not get relieved even with narcotic drug. Sometime when the tumour becomes large, so do the intensity of the pain and the range of the motion of involved joint decreases and the patient become bedridden. Bone tumours are usually treated with the combination of surgery, chemotherapy and radio therapy. Earlier these cancers were treated with the amputation of limb but nowadays with the advent of CT, MRI, bone scan and PET scan, the limb saving surgeries are being done frequently. MRI can tell the extent of the tumour.

The bone scan and CT scan can show the distant spread of the tumour. After knowing the extent of the tumour, surgical removal can be planned before surgery and better results can be achieved. The well-planned meticulous surgery can remove the cancer completely but if it is left in local area because of any reason or the tumour has spread in the other part of the body then in such situation chemo therapy and radiation therapy can control the cancer cells. A surgeon should keep a margin of normal tissue around the tumour mass. In conclusion, I would like to emphasise that like any other cancer treatment, the bone cancer treatment should be done by well-trained and experienced doctor in a well-equipped hospital to save the limb and life of these patient.

http://www.pioneeredge.in/deadly-cancer-can-be-nipped-in-bud/

❑

8

Time to Act; TB is Preventable and Curable

– Dr Gaurav Sanjay,
Sunday, 24 March 2019

Tuberculosis is preventable and curable. It is time to act, to find, treat and end this disease at a time when a quarter of the world's tuberculosis patients live in India. TB have lived in symbiosis with mankind since prehistoric time. TB is recorded in Indian, Egyptian, Greek, and Roman civilisation as far as 5000 years ago. Each year, we commemorate World Tuberculosis Day on March 24 to raise public awareness about the devastating health, social and economic consequences of TB and to step up efforts to end the global TB epidemic. The date marks the day in 1882 when Dr Robert Koch announced that he had discovered the bacteria that causes TB.

TB remains one of the world's deadliest killer infections. Each day, nearly 4500 people lose their lives to TB and close to 30,000 people fall ill with this preventable and curable disease. According to National TB statistics India 2016 report, it is estimated that about 40 per cent of the Indian population is infected with TB bacteria, the vast majority of them have latent TB rather than active TB disease. The theme of World TB Day 2019 was - 'it's time' – to find, treat and end TB to ensure no one is left behind.

According to a WHO report, one-third of the population of the world is infected with TB. Out of this, 95 per cent of the mortality due to TB occurs in developing nations. Twenty-five per cent of these deaths can be reduced with proper and timely treatment. The main symptoms of TB are general malaise, weakness, loss of appetite, loss of weight, low grade evening fever and can be associated with cough, bowel disturbances, lymph nodes swelling, pain in joints and back with difficulty in walking etc.

I strongly believe that if the culprit is to be killed then first, he should be caught and then be properly identified after investigation. As for identification of the culprit a photograph is needed, it is also required for identification of the diseases. Photo of the disease can be taken with simple test. As every bacterium has a specific character so does the TB bacterium. A drop of TB pus is required to identify TB bacteria or a tiny bit of appropriate tissue is required to find TB granuloma. These tests can be done in most of the labs. The treatment of TB should be started only after confirming its diagnosis. This ensures better treatment of the disease.

Thousands of people were dying all over the world before 1947 because there were no drugs available against TB bacteria. But after the invention of anti-tubercular drugs, the numbers of deaths have been significantly reduced. The anti-TB drugs are very effective. The perceptible results can be seen within three weeks. Many patients get symptomatic relief due to which they get a false impression that the diseases have been fully cured and many a time the patients do not re-visit their doctors and stop their medication themselves. However, it is advised that patient should take medication for the entire period (six months to 1.5 years) as per doctor's advice and should follow up at the required intervals.

If patients break the treatment regime in between, the infection can reoccur and then the same medications are not effective due to drug resistance. They then have to be prescribed secondary line drugs which are more expensive, more toxic and have to be taken for a prolonged time.

In addition to medications, operations are also needed in some TB cases. If operation is needed, it is desirable to consult an experienced surgeon. Surgery is not necessary for every patient. It is needed only in those patients who are on anti TB drugs but are not improving or have deteriorated during treatment, or the patients have the pus formation in spinal TB and have subsequently developed paralysis during treatment.

If a hump has developed in spinal TB, then operation is needed to aspirate the pus and clean the bone and to correct the hump with the help of spinal implants. For correction of the hump, the author has developed a technique in which half of the diseased vertebra is removed and two separate vertebras are converted into one and a half vertebra into a single block. After a proper surgery and completion of tuberculosis treatment the patients can achieve their pre-operative status.

In my opinion inadequate investigation, delayed or wrong diagnosis and improper treatment are the main cause of failure of treatment. Doctor can be blamed for empirical treatment / wrong diagnosis but patients are to be blamed for irregular and inadequate duration of treatment.

Inadequate dose for inadequate duration is main cause for multi-drug resistance tuberculosis (multi-drug resistance (MDR)-TB) or extensive drug resistance tuberculosis (XDR-TB). MDR/XDR-TB is a major problem not only in our country but in the whole world. This is a manmade catastrophe. The reason for the inadequate dose could be poverty, non-availability of TB drugs, non-availability of trained paramedical and medical staff and dis-continuation of TB drugs abruptly.

Some physicians in our country or in the other countries are influenced by whims without any fact which makes them think that every infection in the spine is a TB infection but it is not so. Because of this misunderstanding they treat all patients of spine infections with the anti-tubercular drugs. It was found in research that nearly 20 per cent of the spine infections are due to pyogenic or non-tubercular bacteria.

Empirical anti tubercular treatment not only cause unnecessary financial burden to the poor patients but rampant use of TB drugs in non-tubercular infection and has caused the incidence of MDR/XDR-TB to rise in our country.

As we know, most of the anti-tubercular drugs are metabolised in the liver and at times this unmonitored drug toxicity can lead to drug induced liver injury which can even lead to the death of the patient. Tubercular infection is considered to be social stigma in our country.

According to the first national anti TB drug resistance survey 2014-16, India recorded more new TB patients annually than any other country, contributing to 27 per cent of the world TB burden. More than a quarter of TB patients in India have drug resistance to one or other anti TB drugs. The treatment success rate among MDR-TB in India about 46 per cent and death rate is around 20 per cent as against the global level of treatment success rate of 52 per cent and death rate 17 per cent. It is said that MDR-TB is 6.19 per cent among all TB patients with 2.8 per cent among new and 11.60 per cent among previously treated TB patients. The incidence of XDR-TB was 1.3 per cent.

http://www.pioneeredge.in/time-to-act-tb-is-preventable-and-curable/

❑

9

High Toll of Road Accidents in India – Human and Economic Loss

– Dr BKS Sanjay,
Monday, 06 May 2019

The United Nations is observing Global Road Safety Week from May 6 to 12. The UN's ongoing campaign: Save Lives # Speak Up campaign provides an opportunity for civil society to generate demand for a strong leadership for road safety and evidence-based intervention which could save many lives. More than a million people die worldwide every year on the roads and 20 to 50 million people suffer from road traffic injuries. This situation is quite serious in our country. Almost 5,00,000 accidents are happening in India resulting in the deaths of about 1,50,000 people. One-fourth of them who survive are becoming permanently disabled and only one-fourth of them are achieving their pre-injury status in spite of the best treatment available in our country.

Road traffic accidents are the leading cause of death among young people aged 25 to 29 years. Our country is economically losing the worth of one to three per cent of the GDP. Almost 90 per cent of these fatalities worldwide occur in low income and middle-income countries even though these countries are having only approximately half of the vehicles of world. In research conducted by the author, 90 per cent of these accidents occurred due to the driver's negligence. The main causes of accident in India are over taking, over speeding, drunken driving and recently, use of mobile phones while driving.

The seriousness of fatalities increases in drivers and passengers those who are not using helmet on two wheelers and not fastening the seat belt while in four- wheelers. In a recently published 2017 Government of India report, it was found out that those people who are driving and simultaneously using mobile phones, if they sustain a road traffic accident, about 40 per cent of them die.

If you see the current scenario of road accidents, the things are quite similar almost everywhere in India as the author has travelled through nearly the whole country and scores of other countries in the world. I think that aggression on the road is a common scenario on Indian roads and it seems that Indians take pride in breaking the existing traffic rules while travelling on the roads. The road traffic accidents can result in injuries ranging from scratches to the death of the individual and knowing very well the consequences of road traffic accidents, the people are more adventurous on the road in India than anywhere else.

Because of this aggressive behaviour and violation of the traffic rules, the nation is losing a lot in terms of human and economic resource. Here I would like to cite an example of a patient who was driving a bike and had a head-on collision with another bike in which the other biker died. The impact of the collision was so high that five-inch broken piece of thigh bone of the patient penetrated into the thigh of the opposite biker. One of his upper limbs is still paralysed and even after treatment he will not be able to achieve good upper limb function due to the severity of the injury. The same patient is still under treatment for the last one years.

In spite of the death of his friend and prolonged suffering, to my surprise and probably yours as well that the patient was requesting me to make him fit as soon as possible so that he can drive another bigger bike more powerful than the one he was riding earlier. This is not a unique example but one of the hundred such cases I have come across in my 40 years of orthopaedic experience. This patient or the other patients like him, do not repent what they have done to themselves and to their family, friends and relatives. Human resource is the biggest resource and country is losing it every day on the roads. It is not only the family and the friends who are losing this precious resource but the nation too.

Statics show that 70 per cent of the fatalities are occurring with the use of two wheelers and remaining involve four wheelers or public transport like buses. A lot of the burden is borne by the pedestrian on the narrow roads. Though the numbers of accidents of the public transport vehicles are the least but they are fatal particularly on the well-maintained highways in the plain area and they are more fatal in tortuous roads on mountains.

The numbers of accidents are less in mountains but the fatalities are more in Uttarakhand. According to state transport department's report of 2018, about 1,500 accidents occur yearly and about 1,000 people die in these accidents.

If we follow traffic rules than we will not only save the lives of these people but save a significant amount of the money which is unnecessarily being wasted on the treatment. According to the recent UN and World Bank reports, in our country almost one-fourth of the people are still living below the poverty line. Those who cannot afford three meals a day cannot be expected to afford costly medical treatment.

In India health facilities are not comparable to those of a developed nation. In India, 50-70 per cent of the hospital expenses are borne by the patient even in government funded hospitals and almost 100 per cent in private hospitals. It is not only in our country that medical treatments are becoming expensive as in developed nations it is even more expensive. In India, many of the people are getting the treatment after selling their assets like jewellery, land, vehicle, animals and house. Once it is sold it is difficult to buy back especially if the person is poor and unemployed.

These road traffic accidents are becoming a hurdle in the growth of nation. It should be the duty not only of the government but also of the public and social organisations to spread awareness on society and nation losing a lot in terms of human and financial resources.

The numbers of public transport vehicles are not increasing with the same pace as private vehicles. It is the need of the hour to increase the number of public transport buses to reduce the overcrowding of the private vehicles on the road and to develop new modes of mass transportation.

As the nation is growing, so is the number of vehicles. At present India has only one per cent of vehicles but 10 per cent deaths from road traffic accidents. All of us should spread awareness to prevent these accidents because they have taken a form of an epidemic. If something is not done soon then it is bound to go out of control. The public should learn the traffic rules and follow them; the government should teach the traffic rules and should enforce them to prevent the road traffic tragedies. Prevention is always better than cure.

http://www.pioneeredge.in/high-toll-of-road-accidents-in-india-human-and-economic-loss/

❑

10

Negative Impact of Smoking on Health

– Dr Gaurav Sanjay,
Friday, 14 June 2019

The World No Tobacco Day may have been observed nearly a fortnight ago but its message remains very relevant irrespective of when the occasion was marked. Smoking, dhumapana (literally "consuming smoke"), has been practiced for at least 2,000 years in India and also finds mention in the Atharva Veda. The practice of inhaling smoke was employed as a remedy for many different ailments and it was recommended to promote general health and is prescribed in Ayurveda.

Before the advent of modern times, smoking was done with pipes with stems of various lengths, Hookah or chillums. Today the means of dhumapana have been replaced almost entirely by cigarette smoking. Beedi, the hand rolled tendu (Diospyrosmelanoxylon) leaf herbal cigarette filled with dry crushed tobacco is a modern descendant of the historical dhumapana. Tobacco was introduced to India in the 17th century. It later merged with existing practices of smoking (mostly of cannabis).

Tobacco smoking affects the health of blood vessels. Smoking causes narrowing of the arteries. These arteries carry oxygen to various tissues and organs by binding with haemoglobin. Nicotine reduces the capacity of haemoglobin to carry oxygen from lung to peripheral tissues. Once narrowing of the vessels occur due to any reason, the healing capacity in any tissue of the body is disturbed. Due to this, there is impaired healing of any tissue such as skin, muscle or bone in smokers.

From the orthopaedic point of view, fracture healing is one major issue with such people and the other common issues are back and leg pain. The back pain is usually associated with claudication and smokers can have both, vascular and neurological.

The smokers initially walk without pain but gradually they start feeling pain radiating to their lower limbs and this pain forces them to stop walking or they have tendency of developing some subjective weakness of muscles after walking and sometimes they feel that they will fall if they keep on walking or standing. Even if they undergo surgery for such a cause they usually do not get same amount of relief as a non-smoker would get. They are at increased risk of recurrent back pain and/or persistent back pain even after spine surgery.

Smoking is known to cause increased chances of osteopenia and osteoporosis. The incidence of fractures increases in smokers in old age and it is directly related with the increasing time of tobacco exposure. Smoking can also adversely affect the longevity of joint replacements. The leg fractures are known for more complications in comparison to other long bones due to its subcutaneous nature. The complications of wound healing, fracture healing and infections are more in a smoker than in non-smokers. The result of soft tissue coverage if required in such patients like flap surgery is not as successful in smokers as in non-smokers. Smoking also causes peripheral arterial disease. Fifty per cent of it is attributed to smoking. It is more marked in lower extremities. It is more common in cigarette smokers than in smokers of beedi.

In advanced cases of peripheral arterial disease, if there is a small wound on the toe or foot then such wounds usually do not heal because the blood supply to the tissues is compromised in such patients and ultimately it can also lead to complications such as infection and gangrene rather than healing in the usual way.

Such situations often need to be treated medically in early stages and they usually also require surgical intervention in late stages like repeated debridement, prolonged antibiotic administration and prolonged hospitalisation which increases the cost of treatment. Sometimes in spite of spending time and money, the patient ends up losing a limb or at times even life. Nowadays, amputations are mainly being done due to complications of smoking induced peripheral arterial diseases.

It has been proven in many scientific studies that smoking is in important risk factor for development of postoperative respiratory complication after major surgical procedure. The incidences of complications are more after general anaesthesia but they are seen with regional anaesthesia too. The surgeons should motivate the patients to quit smoking as soon as possible prior to surgery so that they can get better surgical outcome and also till he achieves good wound healing after surgery.

The overall numbers of smokers have reduced in India due to the efforts of the government and non-governmental organisations. Education is also playing an important role in reducing the number of new smokers. According to a WHO report of 2015, there are almost 12 crore smokers in India which amounts to nearly 10 per cent of the population. More than a crore people die every year in India due to smoking related diseases.

There are many campaigns which are run throughout the year where the general public are told about the risks associated with smoking. The general public perception is that the smoking causes only lung cancer but it is also an important factor in causing oral cancer, oesophageal cancer and cervical cancer in females.

Smoking not only affects the survival of a smoker but that of others as well who are exposed to second hand smoke. The incidence of smoking related diseases is increased almost in 25 per cent in the passive smokers. Smoking reduces the life expectancy by almost 10 years in comparison to that of a non-smoker.

All kinds of habits whether good or bad, usually start in teenage years of individuals because this is a transitional phase due to new hormonal surge. The teenagers start having tendency to take risks to try out new things and this makes them more vulnerable.

Nine out of 10 smokers smoke their first cigarette well before the age of 18 years. The awareness programme is most needed at this age to convince them not to indulge in the habit of smoking. The smokers above the age of 35 should be motivated to quit the smoking because in a study it was found that if smoking is stopped before the age of 40 years, it reduces the risk of dying from smoke related disease by 90 per cent.

Many such smokers will require a multidisciplinary team approach for smoking cessation, including group counselling or behavioural therapy. Doctors are having a special social status in society all over the world but in India, traditionally, the doctors are considered to be next to God by many. A doctor can have the unique opportunity to initiate a conversation with patients, their family and their friends to make them aware about harmful effects of smoking during their consultations. The interaction within self-help groups is also an effective tool to motivate the smokers to quit smoking.

http://www.pioneeredge.in/negative-impact-of-smoking-on-health/

❑

11

Yoga and General Wellbeing

– Dr BKS Sanjay,
Thursday, 20 June 2019

Health, as defined by the WHO, is "a state of complete physical, mental and social wellbeing and not merely the absence of disease or infirmity." Yoga is a physical, mental and spiritual practice to maintain good health. The United Nations General Assembly adopted an India led resolution declaring June 21 as International Day of Yoga which is commonly referred to as Yoga Day.

Though Yoga originated in India, it is not meant for people of any one religion or region but for whole mankind. Lord Shiva considered to be Adiguru, is the father of ancient Yoga while some historians claim that Patanjali is a father of modern Yoga. Last year's Yoga event was held in the ground of the Forest Research Institute of our green city Dehradun. Nearly 50,000 volunteers took part in that event which was led by Prime Minister Narendra Modi.

It is the universal law of nature that everyone wants to seek pleasure and get rid of pain. It applies not only to the humans but to the animals as well. Yoga could be one of the means to achieve it. The importance of Yoga is becoming known in various spheres now. The scenario of orthopaedic practice has changed in last 40 years.

Earlier the patients were coming in OPD mainly for treatment of developmental deformity, paralysis due to infection like Polio and, TB and for fracture related complications. But nowadays OPD attendance is usually the patients of chronic musculoskeletal pain, complication of the road traffic fractures and degenerative problems.

After recent advancement in medical field, the problems caused due to infection and fractures had been reduced significantly but not that of degeneration. As it is said if there is birth, there is development, disease, degeneration and death. Degeneration is a part of life. We cannot stop the degeneration but with conscious and unconscious effort we can reduce the pace of degeneration. Yoga can play an important role in this.

Stress is a new health problem. Around 70 per cent of the diseases are stress related. Stress has been reported as a cause not only of diabetes, hypertension, heart diseases, asthma, and many musculoskeletal problems but also of cancer as well.

Breathing exercise and meditation techniques have been proved to reduce the stress which has been proved by many bio feedback studies. The practice of Yoga not only helps to maintain better physical health but it can also be a tool for stress management. By changing our lifestyle, we can change our health and ultimately our life.

The WHO has reported that the worldwide burden of musculoskeletal problems is increasing day by day. Most of the musculoskeletal problems are self-created which are caused due to changes in lifestyle. The modern change in lifestyle has created problems like obesity, diabetes, hypertension, hypercholesterolemia, heart problems and stroke among others.

The habit of alcohol and smoking in sedentary work life style is working as fuel in the fire. It is not difficult to change the lifestyle. But it needs a change of the mindset. If we want to bring change in the society then target people should be children particularly adolescents and teenagers.

As it is said, it is easy to make any habit in childhood but difficult to leave that habit in adulthood. Therefore, the goal should be to target the children to give them good habit. A scientific study from JIPMER Puducherry showed that Pranayam at the rate of six breaths per minute reduced heart rate and blood pressure in hypertensive patients within five minutes of practice.

In another study, the practice of Yogasan and Pranayam for three consecutive months reduced the blood sugar level in diabetics. Regular practice of Yogasan and Pranayam also reduced the blood cholesterol. It is reported that Yoga practice can take care of more than three dozen diseases. Multiple scientific studies proved that the Asanas, breathing and relaxation techniques used in Yoga are very effective.

In addition to Yoga, if an individual can abstain from lifestyle habit of alcoholism and smoking then result will be much better. If one does his or her household work and avoids sedentary work, does Yoga exercise and takes balanced diet then there is fair chance that one will have healthy and longer life.

The exercises are usually of three types-- aerobic, anaerobic and flexibility. All kinds of exercises help different organs of the body. Physical exercises do not need any kinds of tool to perform. Aerobic exercise consumes more oxygen. As other organs of body need exercise so do the heart. But heart cannot do any exercise itself but any exercise of the body will force the heart muscle to work more proportionately. As heart rate increases, so does the strength of the muscle which maintains the health of the heart muscles.

Indirectly it reduces of chance of heart attack, hypertension, diabetes, obesity and insomnia. Aerobic exercise releases endorphin which reduces the stress and restlessness. Anaerobic exercise can be performed in the absence of oxygen. They are usually fast activities for short duration. It increases the strength and endurance. The third is a flexibility exercise. All Yoga exercises are good examples of the flexibility exercises.

Pranayama is the formal practice of controlling the breath, which is the source of our prana, or vital life force. Pranayama is an excellent breathing exercise for good health. It is the perfect breathing exercise which increases the positive energy level in the body and removes toxins. Pranayama is of the three breath-exercises.

It refers to a particular system of breath control with three processes as purak (to take the breath inside), kumbhak (to retain it), and rechak (to discharge it). Pranayama supplies more oxygen to the body and is the key to a healthy body. Sometimes Yoga alone cannot solve the problem but Yoga therapy can be complementary to the other therapy.

Yoga can improve strength of the muscle, flexibility of the joint and calmness of the brain by controlling the respiration, heart and metabolic rate and blood pressure which are the important parameters to know the health status of any individual.

Not having the time to indulge in such exercise is a common excuse. But we should realise that the benefits of the exercise are manifolds in terms of time and labour spent in Yoga exercise. The advantages of Yoga are many. It does not need any extra equipment or extra space as most of the exercises need.

The habit of Yoga exercise, breathing and meditation should be part of the day-to-day activity of an individual to maintain one's physical, mental, social, psychological and spiritual health. Yoga needs little bit time and little bit physical exercises at regular internal to improve the general health of an individual. The Yoga practice of half an hour to one hour on daily basis is enough to maintain good health.

http://www.pioneeredge.in/yoga-and-general-wellbeing/

❑

12

Violence Against Doctors: A Significant Public Health Problem

– Dr BKS Sanjay,
Monday, 01 July 2019

Doctors Day is celebrated to recognise the contribution of doctors to individual life and communities. The date may vary from nation to nation. In our country it is celebrated on July 1 which is birth and death anniversary of the most famous physician of India Dr BC Roy.

The annual celebration is to spread awareness about the contribution of doctors to the society. Although Doctors Day is supposed to be celebrated by patients to thank them but in reality, it is usually celebrated by doctors themselves in India.

The medical profession is one of the riskier professions. Knowingly doctors are taking risks of getting infected with dreaded infection like TB, AIDS and Hepatitis etc. from patients and getting post radiation cancer from radiation exposure in performing their duties.

But taking that much risk and working in odd conditions and hours, they are being rewarded with verbal and physical violence. Verbal aggression or violence is so common that none of the doctors can claim that he has not encountered verbal abuse from the patient's side for no fault. "No physician, however conscientious or careful, can tell what day or hour he may not be the object of some undeserved attack, malicious accusation, blackmail or suit for damage."

This paragraph from a reputed journal from the USA, written 135 years ago shows that violence against doctors is not new, and that it has been reported from all over the world, but the trend of violence against medical doctors is rising rapidly in our country, which is alarming. In 1996 the 49th World Health Assembly declared violence a major and growing global health problem. Several such incidents have been reported from India in the past however, this menace has not been highlighted adequately earlier.

The recent violent act done in Kolkata has elicited the attention of mass media and also of the political system. Being an orthopaedic surgeon with an experience of 40 years and dealing with simple to life threatening accidents, I have yet to see the patient, friends and family of road traffic accidents victim who own the responsibility of an accident.

On the contrary, they blame others for the cause of accidents and blame doctors for any complication if it occurs during treatment even knowing very well that the complication occurred due to his or her own mistake. I would like to cite the example of one my patients who was being treated for old infected non-union of thigh bone fracture.

Infection was controlled, fracture was healing and patient was walking for past four months with a plaster. However, he sustained a fracture again and blaming me, started to threaten me with dire consequences. The matter was brought to the notice of police.

Most of these problems are very small in the beginning but they take alarming shape and the outcome of the conflict becomes horrendous. Most of the times, the conflict is not because of the medical negligence. But if conflict is analysed minutely then the reason turns out to be mainly non-medical problem and rarely medical.

If you analyse the incidence of the violence against the doctors, the cause is often monetary-- either one doesn't want to pay the pending hospital bills during treatment or anticipate the hefty monetary compensation after the treatment.

Those who are well to do or well-educated prefer the monetary compensation and will take legal course. However, with it comes to those who are not well to do or well versed with the medical or legal knowledge, then incident escalates to verbal and/or physical violence against the doctors.

The other causes of medical violence are the social and psychosocial problems. In the majority of the cases (60-70%), such violence takes the form of either verbal abuse or aggressive gestures and rest of them turn out to be physical violence. It seems that these incidents are either reactive or hostile. As long as they are reactive, it can be understood easily. Like the death of a younger person having no known medical problem or a medical problem not known to the friends and family.

When deaths occur suddenly in the hospital then the reaction can be understood by the medical staff. But it becomes very difficult to understand when a person dies either after fatal accidental injuries or after the complication of chronic medical problems after many days of hospitalisation.

After the declaration of death, family and relatives become violent and, things go wrong up to such an extent that the people start using verbal and physical force with mob mentality, disturbing the working of the hospital and damaging hospital property or using the force or threatening the medical doctor with death. It looks as if the people are prejudiced or hostile to that doctor.

A study conducted by the Indian Medical Association found that 75 per cent of the surveyed doctors had suffered some form of physical violence while on duty. Most of these assaults were by relatives of very ill patients admitted in Intensive Care Unit (ICU) and emergency.

The medical profession demands hard work almost round the clock. These hard-working hours are already changing the mind set of younger generation, hence not many boys and girls are interested in joining the medical field. Now even the children of doctors are not interested to go in the medical field specially after witnessing such experiences of hard work only to face verbal and physical abuse.

It is an apparent and paradoxical situation in our country where significant numbers of patients are not even educated and having no knowledge or experience of the medical field. However, such people are evaluating the knowledge, skill and efficiency of those doctors who are experts in their field to allege that a particular doctor has treated the patient wrongly.

Most of the times, these violent acts are based on the perception of patient's family and friends rather than reality. A hostile attitude of the relatives creates the problem. The moment patients reach the emergency they presume that doctor is not giving any attention to them.

The prejudiced hostile attitude is root cause of the violence against the doctor. This prejudice hostile attitude is increasing day by day in such situation some time the mass media act as a fuel in the fire.

There is hardly any day that we do not hear or read and see some such report in mass media. The problem is prevalent in almost every hospital. The situation becomes quite difficult in emergency patients when patients are being brought by hordes of people. Everybody expects that doctor should attend to their patient and should leave others patients immediately which he is attending.

They get shocked that doctor is not giving importance to them because they think they are VIP in their own way. The issue of medical treatment takes a backseat while their ego takes the front seat. Second thing which annoys such people is the formalities of the hospitals which have to be met. The third issue relates to the payment while the fourth issue is that the patients and all relatives want to know about the patient's diagnosis, prognosis and treatment approach in detail while also wanting everything to be fixed quickly.

None of them can understand how much difficult it is for a doctor to fulfil the various expectations of many friends and relatives of the patients, particularly when most of the smaller hospitals do not have many staff and security personnel to check these people. As Doctors Day was started to celebrate the achievements of the doctors by the patients their family and friends, in the current scenario how can one expect such patients to celebrate the occasion? Many cases of abuse or violence against the doctors are being ignored and rarely reported by most of the doctors especially in busy hospitals or in the reputed hospitals thinking and understanding very well that this will ultimately harm the reputation of the doctor and/or the hospital.

However, I am sure doctors of my standing or experience might have memories of many such abuses in their practice. There should be an understanding that vandalism and violence in a hospital or clinic is a criminal offence and any civilised society should have low tolerance for such heinous acts.

Disputes between patients and hospitals or doctors are not to be sorted out through violence, but in a civilised society, there are avenues for dispute redressal which should be used. I personally feel that the situation is pathetic and this kind of the street justice is commonly seen in the medical practice now. If the situation is not controlled, it will be a serious threat to medical profession. No one can say for sure that he will not need medical help from womb to tomb. The union health minister Dr Harsh Vardan has taken quick action to make a bill for the violence against the doctors a non-bailable offence with minimum 12-year jail.

Once it is passed and implemented, it will be a milestone for controlling this menace. The working of all professions is based on the principle of trust and faith among the service giver and the client. But it is most important in the doctor-patient relation, if we don't have bond of trust and faith between doctor and patient then how can doctors work? Unfortunately, the doctors are always under the scanner of suspicion by patients and their relatives.

Modern medicine is neither cheap nor 100 per cent effective in curing the disease in all cases. Doctors are most of the time working in conditions of many uncertainties because human body is working on dynamic principles not like the other sectors. The doctors are dealing with the living and loving people. The loss of loved one is more traumatising to any person than the loss of other things like money or material.

If you analyse the working of the small private hospitals, they are not having enough medical and non-medical staff proportionate to the types of services hospital renders. The hospital services have many components. One is the medical component and other is non-medical component. Behaviour is first thing which influences the results, irrespective of profession. Most of the problems can be sorted out with the acceptable behaviour itself. As I mentioned earlier, behaviour of an individual is a very important to render the service. That means doctors not only needs medical knowledge but also has to maintain the good interpersonal relation. Communication skill is an important tool of the medical care.

The doctor has to deal with the medical and non-medical problem. Hence doctor should have good behaviour, knowledge and skill to deal with different kinds of problems. But unfortunately, doctors are also human like patient and their relatives and it should always be kept in mind. As there are certain responsibilities of doctors and other healthcare workers, similarly, responsibilities also have to be borne by patients and their relatives.

http://www.pioneeredge.in/voilence-against-doctor-a-significant-public-health-problem/

❑

13

Viral Hepatitis: Leading Cause of Liver Cirrhosis and Cancer

– Dr Gaurav Sanjay,
Monday, 29 July 2019

World Hepatitis Day is observed on 28 July every year to raise awareness about hepatitis and its complication, prevention and treatment. The date of 28 July was chosen because it is a birthday of Noble prize-winning scientist Dr Baruch Blumberg, who discovered the hepatitis B virus and developed a diagnostic test and vaccine for the virus.

Hepatitis is an infection of the liver. Hepatitis can be self-limiting or can progress to liver cirrhosis or liver cancer. The goal of the Hepatitis Day 2019 is to find the missing millions to eliminate viral hepatitis by the year 2030. Hepatitis is most serious public health disease which affects liver which is an important body organ to maintain to almost all metabolic activities. One cannot lead the healthy life without normal liver function. Viral hepatitis is the commonest cause of liver infection. Hepatitis B virus (HBV) is 100 time more infectious than HIV/AIDS.

According to ICMR report, it is estimated that currently about 40-45 million people are HBV carrier and 10 million are infected with HCV in India. Viral hepatitis is leading cause of liver cirrhosis and cancer. Hepatitis virus is of five types, hepatitis A virus (HAV), B virus (HBV), C virus (HCV), D virus (HDV) and E virus (HEV). HAV is the most common cause of acute hepatitis in the world. HBV and HCV are chronic viral infection. According to global hepatitis report 2017, HBV and HCV are the major public health problems. It is more in Asian and African countries probably due to prevailing low socioeconomic conditions leading to poor hygiene and sanitation.

Hepatitis A/ E that spreads mainly through contaminated food and water or hepatitis B/C that spreads by body fluids, blood transfusion, use of infected needle and syringe and through mother to child transmission during early childhood. Most of the person suffering from viral hepatitis do not develop any obvious symptoms in the initial period but later on it can become complicated with serious liver problems like liver damage (cirrhosis), cancer and liver failures which needs liver transplant.

If the patient, in addition to viral hepatitis, is suffering with alcoholic and/or drug induced hepatitis then problem gets exacerbated. The drug induced hepatitis usually caused in our country is due to anti tuberculosis drug, anti-epileptic drug and cretin painkiller drugs which can cause serious damage to the liver.

Hepatitis can reduce the appetite, give feeling of nausea and vomiting, cause low to high grade fever and jaundice. Jaundice is accompanied by yellow discoloration of the eye sclera (white part of the eye), urine and stool and at extreme stage yellow discoloration of skin which is easily seen in light skinned people. Viral hepatitis A, B and C can be diagnosed by your symptoms, physical examination and blood tests. Ultrasound, CT scan and biopsy of liver are also used for making the diagnoses.

Hepatitis A and E usually are acute and self-limiting which resolve within few weeks. It needs no specific treatment but supportive treatment like good nutritious diet and adequate rest. Hepatitis E can sometimes be dangerous especially in pregnant women, and also in men leading to liver failure and eventually, death. Over 90% of hepatitis C can be completely cured within 3-6 months of treatment.

Hepatitis A and E are easily prevented by practicing personal hygiene and public sanitation. In our country where basic hygiene and sanitation is lacking, avoidance of eating food from unhygienic road side vendors will prevent hepatitis infection at a larger scale. Vaccines are available for protection again hepatitis A and B viruses but not against hepatitis C. Unfortunately, there are no specific drugs for treating hepatitis A and E, however there are effective antiviral drug to treat hepatitis B and C infection.

There is no treatment for hepatitis D but can be prevented by hepatitis B immunisation. Hepatitis E is caused by hepatitis E virus (HEV). It can lead to acute liver failure. The infection is caused by contaminated food or water or uncooked or undercooked meat in epidemic areas. Hepatitis B and C virus can spread after sharing of the needle which is quite common practice in drug addicts. It can also spread through the sharing of the infected razor blade. The shaving of hair is a common practice in our country.

Most of the people especially in the rural area get their beards shaved and haircuts from the common barbers, hence during the shaving the customer should demand for the use of clean razor and of new razor blade because it is quite common to get cut in skin during the shaving of hair especially if the barber is not attentive to his job.

As HBV and HCV are found in blood and body fluids, it spread through infected needle, infected blood and blood product and other body secretions. It can be prevented by using single use disposable needle and syringe and transfusing the screened blood from the authorised blood bank and disposing infected material through appropriate medical waste disposal authorities and having safe sex with protective measures.

Hepatitis B is occupational hazard for health workers. Surgeons have ethical obligation to render care to the hepatitis infected patients and same to other patients. The risk of transmission of HBV from patient to the surgeon is greater than that of surgeon to patient. High viral consultation indicated increased risk of transmission. The actual risk of hepatitis B and C are many times more than the HIV infection in health care worker. About 37.6% of HBV, 39% of HCV and 4.4% of HIV in health care worker around the world are due to needle stick injury.

A study by a French surgeon estimated that general surgeons have 6.9% life time risk of contracting HCV and 0.15% life time risk of contracting HIV. Being an orthopaedic surgeon, I can say for sure that orthopaedic surgeons are more vulnerable for getting unintentional injury due to needle stick or sharps than any other surgeon because an orthopaedic surgeon deals with many neglected orthopaedic deformities and many sharp tip instruments and implants in addition to general instruments. The fractures ends are often sharp and surgeon or assistant are at greater risk to get an injury during reduction of fracture. Needle stick or sharps injury can be prevented by using safe practice during work and getting vaccinated against infection. Surgeon should continue to use highest standard of infection control, universal safety precaution and accepted measure to prevent blood exposure.

http://www.pioneeredge.in/viral-hepatitis-leading-cause-of-liver-cirrhosis-and-cancer/

❑

14

Overpopulation Causing Depletion of Natural, Manmade Resources

– Dr BKS Sanjay,
Monday, 19 August 2019

Population in India is rising at the alarming rate. Overpopulation in India is an urgent and important issue. Indians are living with the ticking timebomb of overpopulation. The issue of the overpopulation in India was also addressed by Prime Minister Narendra Modi during his 73rd Independence Day speech from the Red Fort in the national capital.

The Prime Minister urged the citizens to understand the importance of birth control in the nation. Modi said that population explosion in the country will create various problems for the coming generations. There is need of social awareness in the country. This article is a small initiative to emphasise the impact of overpopulation in India.

Human resource is the biggest asset but it is becoming a liability for the nation. According to 1941 Census of India, the population of India was nearly 31 crores. It was estimated to be 33 crores in 1947 after the partition, and has increased almost four times since independence. The current population is estimated to be 135 crores.

The land surface area of Indian land is 2.4 per cent of the world but the Indian population is 18 per cent of the world population. India is the second most populous nation of the world after China. If we compare the current Indian population with combined population of G7 countries which are most developed and rich countries, the Indian population is twice their population. Indian population is almost equal to the total population of whole north, south and Central American countries.

If the causes of over population in India are broadly analysed then the first cause is increasing birth rate and decreasing death rate. With the advent of medical technology, we could reduce the death rate but we could not control the birth rate at the same pace. Main causes of overpopulation are illiteracy and poverty. According to UN reports, one-fifth of Indians are living below poverty line and almost one-fourth of the Indians are illiterate even after 72 years of independence.

Irrespective of the caste, creed, religion and region, in general, the preference for male child is dominant in India. Under the influence of parents and grandparents, the younger couple has to have male child even if they have many female children. Religion plays an important role in shaping the mindset. Followers of a particular religion considers that a baby is a gift from God hence they do not use any means of birth control. The population of Muslims has risen from nine per cent of the total population in 1941 to 15 per cent in 2019. The other cause of overpopulation is hot climate which is supposed to be a cause of increased fertility. The trend of early marriage is still existing in India which prolongs the reproductive period in women.

The overpopulation has ill impact on the growth of the society and nation as well. The ill-effect of overpopulation is being seen in the form of increasing trend of unemployment, overcrowding on infrastructure and depletion of the natural and manmade resources. Overpopulation is making India a more competitive society and the trend of the competition is visible in every field which is the root cause of stress. Stress has been blamed for almost 70 per cent of the diseases. Diabetes, hypertension, stroke, cardiac problem, insomnia and hormonal disturbance are somehow caused due to stress. Overpopulation is indirectly increasing the poverty and illiteracy. Illiteracy and poverty are interrelated. Illiteracy is causing poverty and poverty is causing illiteracy. It is a vicious cycle.

As on July 5, 2019 the world human population was estimated to be 7.717 billion while most contemporary estimate of the earth's carrying capacity is 4-18 billion. Though the country is developing and the current GDP is growing at between seven to eight per cent, the pace of the growth of the infrastructure especially in the fields of education, health, food and housing is not keeping with the pace of the growth of current population which is approximately 135 crores.

The modern automation is also threatening the rate of employment. But overpopulation is playing havoc on employment. Increased demand for resources is also another major issue. Even if you have the money, can you easily buy fresh air, clean water and healthy food on demand supply ratio principle in overcrowded or an overpopulated area? During the world war, richest countries like Britain which import food from overseas had to resort for food rationing. We should understand that most of the problems on our planet are due to either mal-distribution or depletion of the resource.

Overpopulation is the main cause of contamination of air, water and food which are vital for all living creatures. The overpopulation is fuelling climate change and climate change is ultimately affecting not only the longevity and existence of the human beings but of every creature on the planet.

Natural resources like land and drinking water are also limited. Only one per cent fresh water is easily available and only 0.007 per cent of water is available for current seven billion world population. According to a NASA report, India is having serious decline of fresh water due to overuse of water resources for its agricultural and industrial demands. None of the cities in the country has 24-hour drinking water supply.

The situation of water supply becomes worse in summer season all over the country. The production of the food is increasing consistently but still it is not keeping pace with the growth of population. Any effort to improve the infrastructure or to increase food production are unable to meet the needs of the present population, then how can it work for the future population which is increasing at the pace of 1.2 per cent yearly? In a few years, India will be the most populous nation.

Overpopulation is depleting the natural and manmade resources. A message is to be spread to the society that if one is divided by more than one, the dividend will be less than one (1/>1=<1). This point is to be emphasised to the general population that we should act and use science and technology to reduce the birth rate.

The sooner the better. Even with any advancement in science and medical technology, we cannot stop death but can stop birth to change the demography of the nation. If at all something is to be done towards the control of the population, then by any means the birth rate has to be decreased and there should be a mass movement for this. Means of birth control like role of child marriage, use of contraceptive aids, birth spacing are to be known and contraceptive aids should be made available free of cost for all reproductive bearing age group people. The easiest and simple way to control the population is to give free, similar and quality education and health to all irrespective of the caste, creed, class, religion and region.

http://www.pioneeredge.in/overpopulation-causing-depletion-of-natural-man-made-resources/

❑

15

If Punishment Is Not Painful, How It Can Be Punishment?

– Dr Gaurav Sanjay & Dr BKS Sanjay,
Monday, 16 September 2019

According to WHO report of 2018, almost 5,00,000 accidents are happening in India every year. These accidents result in the deaths of about 1,50,000 people. One-fourth of the accident victims who survive become permanently disabled and only one-fourth of them achieve their pre-injury status in spite of the best treatment available in our country. Many a time, optimum results are not possible due to financial constraints with patients and family members and sometimes due to limited resources in the hospitals.

The senior among the authors has an experience of more than 40 years in treating patients of road traffic accidents. Road traffic accidents have become an epidemic in our country and this is taking a high toll on human and financial resources. These road traffic accidents are becoming a hurdle in the growth of the nation. It should be duty not only of the government of the country but there should be contributions from the public, NGOs and other social organisations as well, to spread the awareness that the society and nation is losing a lot in terms of human lives and financial resource.

Road traffic accidents are the leading cause of death among young people aged between 15 and 29 years. In economic terms, the country loses about two to three per cent of its GDP due to road accidents for which we should be collectively concerned but it seems our efforts are not matching in the actions taken to prevent them. The proposed bullet train project from Mumbai to Ahmedabad is estimated to cost almost Rs one lakh crore. If we are able to save the money spent on treating these injuries then our country can execute more than one bullet train every year.

The mass media is full of reports and opinions to the effect that the recently amended Motor Vehicles act is against the general public because they have to pay more penalty if they violate the rules or disobey the law. It seems that the interpretation of most of the state governments of our country and that of the public in general is that the sole purpose of the amendment is that the government wants to earn the money by penalising the traffic rule violations. But contrary to that, on many occasions from different platforms, the current road transport minister Nitin Gadkari has reiterated that the idea of increasing the penalty against the violators is not to earn the money but to save the lives of many stakeholders who can be involved in road traffic accident.

If we go according to the concept of penalty for the offenders, penalty is imposed only on those who break the law. The idea of penalty is to deter the offender from breaking the law in the future and to send a message to the society that if anybody breaks the law then he or she will be penalised.

There are various means of penalising an offender. However, the financial penalty can be easily imposed and executed. Now the question arises as to why there is hue and cry against the amended act. What one can gather from the mass media reports is that many are against the hike in the amount of penalty against the violators.

Here, one must note that the penalty has been raised for violations like not wearing the helmet/seat belt from Rs 500 to Rs 1,000 knowing very well that it will be applicable only if we violate the law. If we are so concerned about saving our hard-earned money then it is surely easier to carry our driving license, vehicle registration certificate and other documents. Is it that difficult to keep our DL, RC in our wallet when every day we also carry money and other documents with us?

Now the second question raised is whether it is so difficult to wear the helmet and seat belt before starting our vehicles and getting on the road. It is to be noted that the chances of fatalities and seriousness of injuries increase in riders who are not using helmet while using two wheelers and not fastening the seat belt while travelling in four wheelers.

The third issue is blocking an emergency vehicle such as an ambulance. The penalty is raised from Rs 1,000 to Rs 10,000 for this offence. We should analyse whether our work is so important and urgent that we block the road for the emergency victims in the vehicle like ambulance, fire brigades and police vehicle chasing the violators or criminals.

The hike of penalty for drinking and driving has been increased from Rs 1,000 to Rs 10,000. The accidents which happen under the influence of alcohol usually happen during the night due to over speeding and overtaking and they are usually fatal. The treatment cost of these poly-traumatised patients cannot be done under Rs 10,000 in any well-equipped hospital in the country. If this hike can prevent even one fatal accident, is it not worth for the individual, family, society and ultimately our nation?

A question was raised during a debate on a national TV channel about a certain segment of society not being in a position to afford the hiked penalties because the penalty is more than their monthly income. Here one would like to ask whether the scope of the penalty should be decided according to the law breaker.

Punishment is defined in legal language as the infliction of some kind of pain or loss upon a person for a misdeed by an authority. Financial punishment is a common form for minor crimes and a common example of a fine is money paid for violation of traffic rules. If the offence is because of ignorance then the criteria of least of penalty is to be considered however when offence is done knowingly and repeatedly then how can one expect not to get punished.

As far as motor vehicle offence is concerned one thinks it should be a national policy rather than a policy which varies from state to state particularly when we know that there is need for following the traffic rules similarly all over the country.

Almost 10 per cent of world road traffic fatalities are occurring in India although we have only one per cent of the vehicles of the world. A research conducted by authors found that 90 per cent of these accidents occurred due to the driver's negligence. The main cause of accident is that that we are violating the traffic rules. Overtaking, over speeding, drunken driving and recently use of mobile phone while driving are the main causes of road traffic accidents in India.

If punishment is not painful then how can it be punishment? The pain must be essential and not accidental to the infliction of punishment, according to the criteria of punishment principle. Where is the question of punishment, if we follow the law? Should it not be suggested that we all should follow the traffic rules honestly and save our money which we can use for our food, education and health of their families?

If you see the current scenario of road accidents, the things are quite similar almost everywhere in India as authors have travelled through many cities in our country and scores of other countries of the world. One has observed that aggression on the road is a common scenario on Indian roads and it seems that Indians take pride in breaking the existing traffic rules while travelling on the roads. Because of this aggressive behaviour and violation of the traffic rules, the nation is losing a lot in terms of human and economic resource.

One wonders that if the money is an important criterion for these law violators and if they want to save the money, then can it not be suggested appropriately that such people follow the traffic rules so that they save their money and probably their life too and the money and lives of the others as well? These violators will not only save their money on penalty but also the money which is going to be spent on the treatment in the hospitals if accident happens.

All of us should spread awareness to prevent these accidents because they have taken the form of an epidemic. The public should learn the traffic rules and should follow them; the government should teach the traffic rules and should enforce them to prevent the road traffic tragedies.

http://www.pioneeredge.in/if-punishment-is-not-painful-how-it-can-be-punishment/

❑

16

The Right to Education Means Right to a Qualified Teacher

– Dr BKS Sanjay & Dr Gaurav Sanjay,
Thursday, 3 October 2019

World Teachers Day, also known as International Teachers Day, is celebrated on October 5 every year. This day provides the occasion to celebrate teaching profession worldwide to take stock of achievements and to address the issues related with this profession. This is an occasion to commemorate the teaching profession's contribution to educating the children of the world. The theme of World Teacher's Day- 2019 is 'young teachers: the future of the profession'.

More than 100 nations celebrate the World Teachers Day globally. In our country, the national teacher's day is celebrated on September 5 every year. Former President of India Sarvepalli Radhakrishnan's birthday falls on September 5. Hence, the nation has adopted his birthday as Teacher's Day since 1962 to celebrate the contribution of Radhakrishnan who was a teacher by profession.

In India, traditionally, Guru Poornima is observed as a day to venerate teachers since thousands of years. In Indian tradition, the teachers are placed socially above the parents and very often equal to the God. As the great Indian saint Kabir said, "Guru Govind dou khare, kake lagoon pay, balihari guru aapno, Govind diyo batay". Translated it means-"Both teacher and God are in front me, whom to honour first? I am indebted to the teacher who showed me God." One can well understand importance of teachers in Indian culture.

But contrary to the above saying, more than three-fourth of contractual teachers failed to get the minimum pass marks in a recruitment test. There was a media report in March 2009 which state that out of 66,736 sanctioned posts of teachers in Delhi Government Schools, more than a third (25,000) of the teaching staff posts were filled by guest and contractual teachers who had been teaching in the school for several years. They were demanding regularisation. The Government asked them to pass a basic written recruitment test to become permanent teachers. Of the 21,135 teachers who appeared in this test, 16,383 (77 per cent) failed. In a report from Bihar, one-fourth of primary teachers tested in class V level subjects failed. These two reports show the dismal state of affairs of education and teachers in India.

Here, it would be apt to cite another media report from the Bihar regarding the examination which has often been in the news for mass cheating, topper-scam and other anomalies. It was noticed by the nation only when the famous case of topper Ruby Rai came into light. Ruby topped in political science, but she was not even able to pronounce the word political science properly, knew nothing about the subject and was equating political science with home science.

Cheating and copying had been sporadic incidence few years back but now it seems that it has become the norm. The situation had become so bad that Supreme Court of India had to intervene and state that students caught cheating during exams deserved no leniency and should be severely punished.

As per the university regulation, a PhD candidate must qualify in entrance test in order to be enrolled to pursue a PhD degree in a university but many candidates who had not even appeared for the test were enrolled and candidates who appeared but did not fulfil the minimum eligibility requirements were also enrolled.

A research scholar for a minimum of three years can be eligible for the degree but degrees were given within one and a half year to many students. Many such irregularities were revealed in the PhD entrance test scam of Uttarakhand Technical University in 2017.Here, one would also like to recall another entrance examination scam which was named as Vyapam scam which was unearthed during 2013 in Madhya Pradesh.

It involved collusion of undeserving students, parents and scamsters including certain politicians, businessmen, bureaucrats, board officials and many middle men who manipulated the exam hall sitting arrangement and managed to employ impostors to write papers and they also tried to forge answer sheets by bribing the officials. This was not manipulated in only one examination but 13 different examinations including premedical test organised in Madhya Pradesh.

The whole issue is being investigated by country's top investigating agency Central Bureau of Investigation on the order of the Supreme Court of India in July 2015 because Vyapam seems to be vyapak (extensive). Many senior intellectuals of the country believed that Vyapam was just the tip of the iceberg and similar scams in education and recruitment examination are operational in almost in all states of India.

There is one more fraudulent incident-Tamil Nadu NEET impersonation scam reported last week in the media. It is alleged that a son of doctor got admission in Theni

Government Medical College in Tamil Nadu by engaging a proxy candidate to simultaneously write the exam for him with same credential from another centre. Tamil Nadu CB-CID hinted at a larger racket that could be spread across the country.

A single national level National Eligibility-cum-Entrance Test for undergraduates (NEET-UG) was introduced recently to get rid of existing menace of capitation fees and other fraudulent activities which were prevalent in medical entrance examinations across the country.

NEET-UG 2019 was conducted by National Testing Agency (NTA) of Government of India this year. The authors were already having the apprehension how long NEET will remain neat. But, after learning of the above-mentioned scam, it seems even NEET will not remain neat as expected by Government of India.

The authors also believe that these incidences are the tip of the iceberg. They show the standard of education and that of the examination as well as the standard of the teachers. After learning of such facts one can imagine what will be the future of the nation because we believe that health, education and nutrition are the three basic pillars of the growth and development of any nation. One appeals to the authorities concerned to check this menace so that future of the nation can be saved.

Education is one of the important pillars of the growth of an individual and ultimately of the family, society and the nation. Living together is itself an education. The children learn from the family and environment. Jean Jacques Rousseau a French revolutionary philosopher who believed that people are born basically good, it is society that corrupts and makes a man evil.

After our parents, the most important role played is by teachers in the process of our learning about life around us. Rousseau states that the teacher should be on standby in this period of child development, ensuring that the child does not acquire bad habits.

Nothing counts as much as school as stated by Horace Mann, an American educational reformer who promoted universal public education and teachers training schools. He also said that where anything is growing a former is worth of thousand reformers.

John Dewey, an American educationist said whatever role is of food and reproduction in existence of physical life of humans, similar role is of education in their social life. The growth of the society or the formation of society is not because of physical closeness of the people but the similarly of the thoughts. Dewey said that the governments elected in a democracy cannot be successful unless the electors who are governed by these governments, are educated.

The role of the teacher becomes very important as a teacher understands that development of every child is equally important and recognises the responsibility and faith that a parent places on the teacher when a child is sent to school. According to BR Ambedkar, an architect of the Indian constitution and educationist, education ought to be brought within the reach of everyone, hence, education should be cheapest in all possible ways and to the greatest possible extent.

In India, the Right to Education Act was made in 2009 and in 2018, the UNESCO adopted the theme, the right to an education means the right to a qualified teacher. However, seeing the current situation in India the right to education cannot be realised without trained and qualified teachers.

http://www.pioneeredge.in/the-right-to-education-means-right-to-a-qualified-teacher/

❑

17

Washing Hands to Avoid Infection & Diseases

– Dr Gaurav Sanjay & Dr BKS Sanjay,
Monday, 21 October 2019

As in every year, the Global Hand Washing Day was celebrated on October 15 just a few days ago. This day is dedicated to increasing awareness and understanding the importance of hand washing. Hand washing with soap is an effective and affordable way to prevent diseases. If water and soap are not available then hands can also be cleaned with ash in some circumstances. The Global Hand Washing Day was observed by many people irrespective of their designation, caste, creed, religion and region they belong to to raise awareness on protection from the spread of diseases caused by hand-to-hand contact. The theme of 2019 Global Hand Washing Day was "Clean hands for all".

Nearly 80 per cent of your exposures to germs occur through touch. Most of the Hospital Acquired Infections (HAI) are commonly transmitted when hospital staff become complacent and do not practice correct hand hygiene regularly. Since medical staff move from patient to patient, they themselves serve as a carrier for spreading pathogens. Essentially, the staff members act as a vector.

About five percent of patients admitted to hospitals in the United States develop hospital acquired infection and five per cent (one lakh) of them die each year. In our opinion, considering the socioeconomic conditions in our country, the situation could be worse. About 25 per cent of these infections can be prevented by healthcare workers themselves, if they take proper precautions during caring for every patient.

A prevalence survey conducted under the auspices of WHO in 55 hospitals of 14 countries representing four WHO Regions (Europe, Eastern Mediterranean, South East Asia and Western Pacific) showed an average of 8.7 per cent of hospital patients had nosocomial infections (originating in hospitals). A scientific review of studies performed also revealed an endemic burden of Hospital Acquired Infection (HAI) in India.

Hospital acquired infection are on rise in our country. Sometimes it becomes impossible to control it in spite of the best efforts of all stakeholders (patient, family, doctor and staff). The age-old dictum of "prevention is better than cure" holds true in case of HAI and it should be endeavour of all stakeholders to tackle the menace of HAI.

New Delhi Metalloid-beta-lactamase (NDM) "Indian Superbug" has already unleashed a New Drug Resistant Epidemic. It had been found in drinking water in New Delhi. It has been spread through the medical tourism in patients in more than 35 countries all over the world. It is very similar to what happens when you accidentally include a red shirt which gives off its colour in a wash mixed with your whites.

Overcrowding in patient's room and personal hygiene of patient and medical personnel are two important causes of infection. There is such a wrong trend in our society that many visitors (relatives and friends) who have not at all met the person for years, but, are coming to meet the patient in the hospital to sympathise act as vectors to spread and acquire HAI, and at certain times it becomes difficult to deal with them by the treating doctor and the hospital administration especially in smaller setups.

Overcrowding by patient, staff and visitors should be avoided in hospital premises particularly in and near high risk areas like Operation Theatre (OT) and ICU, geriatric and paediatric wards. Isolation and personal hygiene of the patient and staff have been proven to prevent infection and ultimately to reduce morbidity, mortality and healthcare cost.

It is best to avoid visiting hospitals except when absolutely necessary to prevent infection. If you do end up in one, refrain from touching other patients, and hospital and medical equipment, and if you do so, wash your hands often, particularly before preparing or eating food, before and after touching wound dressings or bandages and after using the washroom.

The hospitals are also social organisations. Kindly cooperate for youth benefit and that of the hospital, society and nation. At any time, only an authorised person should visit patient. Visitors should be only from immediate family (husband, wife, children, parents, grandparents, brothers, sisters) and close friends.

All visitors must follow the same procedures and precautions as hospital staff to adequately control the spread of infection. Visitors and healthcare personnel are equally to blame in transmitting infection. Moreover, multidrug-resistant infections can leave the hospital and become part of the community flora if steps are not taken to stop this transmission.

Madhya Pradesh government in our country holds the Guinness World Record for the most expansive hand washing programme in which 1,276,425 children in 51 different districts participated on October 15, 2014. But on other hand, country like Ethiopia only 300 people celebrated Global Hand Washing Day in Addis Ababa on October 15, 2013.

Now these incidences show that people are becoming aware of hand washing throughout the world. Although this is a small number of people participating but it proves the Chinese proverb "A journey of a thousand miles begins with a single step".

The habit of hand washing will contribute a lot in the personal hygiene as well as it is service to the society because humans learn by copying each other's habits, especially in the bigger organisation like schools and hospitals. The habit of hand washing is very effective and will spread to the others especially in the younger children and newer recruits in any organisation. The noted cricketer Sachin Tendulkar along with his team joined millions of school children around the country as part of the first global hand washing day in India in 2008.

Hand washing frequently is the single most important measure to reduce the risks of transmitting skin microorganisms from one person to another or from one site to another on the same patient. But across the world more than half (60 per cent) health workers do not adhere to proper hand hygiene. Gloves should not be regarded as a substitute for hand washing in hospital setup.

Millions of children are dying either of respiratory infection or intestinal infection all over the world which is more common in low socioeconomic countries. The simple inexpensive habit of hand washing will reduce death from diarrhoea by almost half and death from acute respiratory infection by a quarter, it was observed in a scientific study published in 2015. The act of hand washing should be a habit which should be taught to the children by the family and in the schools because a habit of good hand washing with soap before eating and after using the toilet can save more lives them any single vaccine or medical intervention.

The main problem found in the practice of hand hygiene in India is connected with the lack of continuous running water, available sinks and time-consuming performance of hand washing. An easy way to resolve this problem could be the use of alcohol-based hand rubs, because of faster application compared to correct hand washing.

In a study conducted in Kenya, research found that students were much more likely to wash their hand when another student is present. Peer influence is only successful if students know that hand washing is desirable action. Any habit formation is easier to make it but it is difficult to get rid of that. Therefore, this habit of hand washing should be inculcated in these school going children.

Hand hygiene and hand washing can play an important and critical role in prevention and control of infection and to achieve universal health coverage as envisaged by World Health Organisation. The simple habit of hand washing will not only increase the longevity of an individual but will also improve the quality of life of an individual. When we, as an individual will be healthy, then our family, society and nation will be healthier and happier.

http://www.pioneeredge.in/washing-hands-to-avoid-infection-and-disease/

❑

18

The Plight of Children in India

– Dr Gaurav Sanjay & Dr BKS Sanjay,
Monday, 25 November 2019

Hunger affects each one of us but it affects the children all the more. Adults need the food mainly for their sustenance but the children need it also for their physiological growth.

Stunted growth or sub-ideal growth of malnourished children is well-known but what is seen apparently is the affected physical growth of the bone and muscles while proportional growth of all organs is affected, which cannot be seen by all.

Hunger not only harms the individual physically and physiologically but emotionally and psychologically as well. When one is hungry then every cell of the body is under stress and their productivity is at the least. It is well-known saying in our country that Bhuke Pet Bhajan Na Hoy Gopala.

There is a paradoxical situation in India. At one hand, over a third (40%) of the food produced in India is wasted according to United Nations Development Programme and on other hand, one-third of the children are malnourished.

According to Global Hunger Index (GHI) of 2019, India is at 102nd position, behind its neighbours Nepal, Bangladesh and Pakistan.

India is currently the second largest producer of food grains globally, hence enough food is available in country despite many odds but because of poor purchasing power, people are unable to buy the available food products in the open market. According to 2011 census, nearly a quarter of population (22%) is living below poverty line.

It has been proven that diarrhoea and respiratory tract infection are two leading causes of death of under-5 years of age children in India. It has been proved scientifically that malnourished children are more prone to all kind of infection including tuberculosis because they lack of adequate body resistance to fight with the infection. Nutrition related factors contribute almost a half (45%) of deaths in children under-5 years of age.

Infection and malnourishment are a vicious circle. If we want to improve the health of the children then we have to educate the parents and the families to give the better nutrition.

According to 2011 the National Census of India, out of total child population of nearly 260 million under-14 years of age group, 10.1 million are working as child labourers. Child labour problem is not only existing in India but all over the world particularly in Asian, African Central and South American countries. UNICEF estimates that Indian has the highest number of child labour in the world, while Sub-Saharan African countries have the highest percentage of child labour.

Though the Child Labour and Regulation Act was passed in 1986 and later on amended in 2016 but in spite of that the practice of child labour has not been abolished completely, though it has been reduced.

About 70% of child labour is involved in agriculture and its related sector. It is not only in our country but this trend exists in almost in all cottage industries in poor and developing countries all over the world. Millions of children are employed by roadside food vendors (dhabas), small hotels and restaurants in India.

The practice of child labour is prevalent all over country but the type of child labour depends upon the geographical area of nation. Child labour is common in small shed operation in unorganised sectors like firework, silk, mining, carpet and bidi industries etc. An official estimate for child labour working as domestic labour is more than 2.5 million while NGO's estimates the figure to be 20 million.

If the cause of the child labour is analysed then the main cause seems to be over population because those family which are having more children are mainly poor and illiterate and ultimately this poverty and illiteracy are forcing the parents to send their children for child labour. It has been seen that parents who are poor but have a single child or two children are unlikely to force their children for child labour.

Sexual assault: The Protection of Children from Sexual Offences (Amendment) Act 2019 seeks to protect children from sexual offence such as sexual assault, sexual harassment, and pornography.

Though the punishment for such offence is imprisonment between seven years to life, and a fine but even this act is unable to control this heinous crime. One out of three girls are facing some sort of sexual offence in form of physical, emotional or verbal in nature in India. Such offences are happening almost daily in our country.

It seems that sexual offence in India by perpetrator is usually due to hostility against the victim or victim family which is more common against poor families and in rural and remote areas. It seems it is done to humiliate the victims emotionally and socially. It was reported in a television programme that a rape has been reported in a 9-month-old girl. It is so painful to hear such incidences.

Health education and nutrition are the fundamental needs of all individual irrespective of caste, creed, region and religion. They are interrelated and are the foundation stones for the growth of the individual as well as the nation.

Long time ago all these three things were available free of cost but in current time one has to buy them and for that one need the money which can be earned only thought the employment which could be formal or informal. This need of the employment is forcing the trend of child labour especially in poor, illiterate and in big families.

The trend of child labour still exists because employers prefer children because they have to pay less to them and children can be forced to do the work for more time and can easily be lured for other undesirable acts from them.

Though right to education to all children between 6 to 14 years and additional incentives like scholarship to underprivileged children are guaranteed by constitution of India, still 32 million Indian children have never been to schools, according to an official report.

According to the International Labour Organisation (ILO) sending children to school is many a time more beneficial to the society and the nation, instead of sending them for child labour. We think the practice of child labour is not only stunting the physical growth of individual but stunting their emotional, psychological, economic and social growth of these children. The practice of child labour is stunting the growth of not only of an individual but of a generation.

Authors believe that human resource is the biggest resource and because of practices of child labour the society and the nation are losing the opportunities to develop the greatest resource on the planet.

In our opinion, over population is the root cause of all ills in these children. To control the overpopulation, vulnerable society should be given a message that if one is divided by more them one then quotient or dividend will be less than one. If people can understand the value of this message, then the result will be far reaching.

Though there are many Acts in India to protect the rights of children but seeing the current plight of children the results of these Acts cannot be realised without the sincere and honest efforts of all stakeholders.

http://www.pioneeredge.in/the-plight-of-children-in-india-on-world-children-day/

❑

19

Negative Impacts of Automobiles on Public Health

– Dr Gaurav Sanjay & Dr BKS Sanjay,
Thursday, 14 November 2019

Many aspects of our lives have been influenced by automobiles since their invention. Neither education, nor employment, nor business and any other social interaction can be done without driving or travelling in a vehicle nowadays.

Air, water and food are vital for our life. The first thing a body demands after birth is air. One breathes for the sake of being alive and if unable to breathe properly then the person is no more alive. It should be our endeavour to maintain clean air to ensure survival of self and of others.

Air pollution in India is a serious issue ranking higher than lifestyle diseases like obesity, diabetes, hypertension, heart diseases, stroke etc. It should be noted here that 13 out of the world's 20 most polluted cities, are in India. Most common cause of air pollution in Indian cities is automobile exhaust.

The Air (Prevention and Control of Pollution) Act was passed in 1981 but in spite of that even after almost 40 years India has been currently ranked 177 among 180 countries in the environmental performance index (EPI)-2018. That's a very dismal record to say the least!

Though there are various other causes too of air pollution in India but we will confine ourselves to the air pollution caused by automobiles. Though India has only one per cent of the world's motor vehicles share, these contribute to almost 10 per cent of air pollution in India. India stands a close third after USA and China in being the most polluted country.

Most of the drivers are not educated hence they cannot assess the grave situation of air pollution problem and therefore, they ignore the practice of blending of fuel which gives more toxic emissions.

The problem is not only the burning of fuel but adulteration of the fuel too which is an even bigger problem. These people prefer the easier way of making money by blending the fuel from lower priced fuels like kerosene and diesel. Usually, diesel is adulterated with kerosene and petrol with diesel. The blending of fuel may be as high as 20 to 30 per cent. As the amount of adulteration increases, so is the amount of pollutants like carbon monoxide, carbon dioxide, nitrogen oxide, sulphur dioxide, nitric oxide and other hydrocarbons in air.

The problem of fuel adulteration is common not only in India but in other South Asian countries as well. The monitoring of pollution of the vehicles is also cumbersome and costly as it is perceived by the drivers and the owners of the vehicle. Another important problem with the increasing number of automobiles in India is the congestion on the roads, that is, the increased number of vehicles per kilometre throughout the country.

The length of roads is increasing in recent times but not in proportion to the number of vehicles. The road network has grown only by a third in the last decade while number of vehicles has risen three-folds resulting in increased road congestion. The total number of vehicles in the year 2017 stood at 252 million while it was as low as 3,06,000 units in the year 1951.

In 2011, road density in India was 142.7 kilometres per 100 square kilometres. Road density is the ratio of the length of the country's total road network to the country's land area. While National Highways constitute 1.8 per cent of Indian roads, they carry 40 per cent of the traffic. The majority of existing National Highways are two-lane roads (one lane in each direction).

The number of expressways and highways are limited hence the roads are congested and the traffic is slow particularly in big cities and in metros. Due to slow speed of traffic the amount of fuel consumption is more and so is the emission of pollutants.

It has been reported that if speed is within 20 to 40 kilometres per hour, then pollutant emission is two times but if speed is on an average below 20 kilometres per hour then pollutant emission is four to eight times more in comparison when the speed is on an average at 60 kilometres per hour. Greenhouse effect caused due to fuel emission is the major cause of climate change and the gradual warming of our planet.

This air pollution caused by automobiles is resulting in significant respiratory health problems in our country. Air pollution is affecting the whole population but it is more marked in children and the elderly. Over a million Indians die prematurely every year due to air pollution. According to a report, half of the children in Delhi have abnormal or disturbed lung functions, according to Delhi Heart and Lung Institute. Quality of air has improved visibly in Delhi after the introduction of CNG driven auto rickshaws and taxis.

The recent introduction of e-rickshaws is also contributing their share to maintain clean environment. Various steps are being taken by our government to phase off the cars which are older than 15 years and vehicles running on diesel which indeed is a promising step to improve the air quality in cities which will have far reaching effects in controlling the air pollution.

The negative effects of automobiles include an increase in the rates of accidental deaths, isolation from community or society, air pollution due to emission of greenhouse gases, noise pollution, gradual warming of planet and decreased amount of physical activity leading to many health problems like obesity, diabetes, hypertension, cardiovascular diseases etc.

In addition to stress of accident and death, stress of finances to repay the vehicle loan, maintenance of vehicle and day-to-day running cost of vehicle are common. If these costs are analysed then they are at times more than the cost of the vehicle itself.

Road travel seems to be the preferred travel choice in India with over 60 per cent of the population using personal or shared vehicles to commute. In comparison to the sources of mass transportation, personal automobile transportation has relatively high cost per passenger per kilometre.

No doubt, the long-distance drive of the car is convenient specially if we are with children or are having some baggage, otherwise for the individual traveller with no or minimum baggage it is never cost effective. The physical fatigue and mental stress are taking a high toll on the health of drivers.

The introduction of mass transportation systems all over the country especially in the big cities will give far reaching effects because the mass transportation will not only reduce the fuel consumption and air pollution but it will be environment friendly as well especially means like the underground rail mass transportation. It will be one of the most suitable means for the clean environment and will be time saving especially in the big cities.

The public bus or rail transportation between two cities should be preferred over the private two wheelers and four wheelers for the short distance. The people should prefer to walk for the shorter distance and should use bicycles more frequently.

The practice of tricycle or the manual rickshaw is also a better physical option for transportation in the cities especially for shorter distances because it is not only clean for the environment but it also provides employment opportunities for the unskilled strata of our population.

http://www.pioneeredge.in/negative-impact-of-automobiles-on-public-health/

❑

20

Universal Health Coverage: An Access to Good Healthcare Services for Poor People

– Dr BKS Sanjay,
Thursday, 12 December 2019

Universal Health Coverage Day is commemorated each year on 12 December. Universal Health Coverage is promoted as an instrument to help advance the more broadly conceived human right to health, which is based upon a number of international agreements, or widely affirmed international documents.

Under the United Nations Sustainable Development Goals, all UN Member States have agreed to try to achieve Universal Health Coverage by 2030.This includes financial risk protection, access to quality essential health care services and access to safe, effective, quality and affordable essential medicines and vaccines for all.

The Theme of World Health Organisation of this year is universal health coverage. Universal Health Coverage Day is celebrated and is promoted by the World Health Organization to provide for their citizens affordable, quality health care by all nations to their citizens.

Every person irrespective of caste, creed, race, region, and religion needs health, education and nutrition for growth. Indian scriptures mention that all should be healthy and disease free and none should suffer any way. A Chinese philosopher once said that health is the biggest right. According to an Arabian proverb where there is health, there is hope and where there is hope, there is everything. The Roman believed that prevention of illness was more important than cure of illness.

Hence good health should be the highest priority of all mankind. Although, progress is being made by countries in all regions of the world but millions of people still have no access at all to health care. Health is not only an asset but a resource too. But our experience shows that the health need is being pushed to a secondary position on several occasions especially in poor and developing countries like India.

It is said that a sensible person never kills the hen, which gives the golden eggs. But our society and the government are killing it. What is HEN? H stands for Health, E for Education, and N for Nutrition. The troika of health, education and nutrition is being driven in a haphazard and in an uncoordinated way in our country.

It is important for government and individuals to look after the health of all people to make them more stable and stronger to complete any task easily and quickly. The WHO is focusing on universal health coverage, so is our government.

It is not only my experience but I am sure it may be your experience as well that in India the health needs of most of the people are competing with the basic human needs like food, shelter and education. In India, we are still not realising the importance of good health and the government is still figuring out how to keep our fellow countrymen healthy. To achieve this goal the Government of India has implemented Ayushman Bharat Yojana. The main aim of this programme is to improve health care service for the poor people of whole country. The money will not be any problem for these needy and poor people to obtain good health care, if the situation arises.

The WHO asserts, following countless studies, that nations which invest in universal healthcare make a sound investment in their human resource. Access to affordable health care will not only truly improve someone's health and life expectancy, but also will reduce poverty, create jobs and drive economic growth of the nation.

The UN has adopted 17 sustainable development goals for eliminating poverty. One of the goals includes providing Universal health coverage. The global coalition of hundreds of organisations in 116 countries has urged the governments to make the policy changes in governance so that everyone, everywhere can access quality health care without been forced into poverty.

Health, education and nutrition are the basic foundation stones of any individual and of the nation. The importance of universal health coverage is been emphasised all over the world by many organisations to give affordable health care services to the all people.

The Government of India has started Ayushman Bharat Yojana, Pradhan Mantri Jan Arogya Yojana or National Health Protection Scheme which will cover 10 crore poor families or approximately 50 crore beneficiaries providing coverage up to 5 lakh rupees per family per year for secondary and tertiary care hospitalisation. This scheme provides cashless benefits from any public or private empanelled hospitals across the country.

After implementation of this scheme, the cost of treatment which usually deprives the poor patients from accessing good affordable health care will not be a problem if situation arises. If this scheme is implemented honestly then it will be a mile stone in health care services of India.

This scheme is accepted and being implemented all over the country accepts four states i.e. Delhi, Odisha, West Bengal and Telangana. Millions of people have been benefited from this scheme till date. However according to many mass media reports, the wide spread misuse of this scheme has been reported particularly by the private doctors and hospitals by generating the fake bills.

Nearly 3000 fraud cases have been detected by November 2019 under Ayushman Bharat Health Insurance Scheme according to a national mass media report.

The bills have been generated either doing the surgeries on ghost patients or doing the multiple surgeries in same patient or showing the fake ICU admissions and in many other ways. There had been at least 697 fake cases under this scheme from our state Uttarakhand alone, where fine of more than Rs one crore has been imposed on these fraudulent hospitals. The health facilities in our country not very well evenly spread all over the country. But in general, the health facilities are more concentrated in urban and in plain areas. There are places in the country especially in hilly and remote areas where one cannot get the average quality health services.

If at all they are available then at far away and they are relatively expensive for these poor peoples. All these three, health, education and nutrition are interrelated. We need money to achieve them but money can only be earned when person is healthy. If you are not healthy then you have to spend all earned money to gain the health. In such a scenario everybody should be health conscious.

In India health facilities are not comparable to any standard of a developed nation. In India, 50-70% of the hospital expenses are borne by the patient even in government funded hospitals and almost 100% from their pocket in private hospitals.

It is not only in our country that medical treatments are becoming expensive but even in developed nations it is even more expensive. In our country most of the people are getting the treatment after selling their assets like jewellery, land, vehicle, animal and house etc.

Once it is sold it is difficult to buy back especially if the person is poor and unemployed. Ayushman Bharat Yojana is a step to improve health care services in India particularly for poor people. Considering the socioeconomic conditions of the nation, all of us stakeholders should work collectively to make the Ayushman Bharat Yojana successful nationwide.

http://www.pioneeredge.in/universalhealthcoverage-access-to-good-health-care-services-for-poor-people/

❑

21

State of Medical Education in India

– Dr BKS Sanjay,
Thursday, 23 January 2020

Troika of health, education and nutrition are the basic needs of each and every individual irrespective of the caste, creed, race, gender, religion and region. All these three are interrelated.

The United Nations General Assembly proclaimed January 24 as the International Day of Education. The right to education is enshrined in article 26 of the Universal Declaration of Human Rights. The declaration calls for free and compulsory elementary education. The Convention on the Rights of the Child, adopted in 1989 goes further to stipulate that countries shall make higher education accessible to all.

The international community recognised that education is essential for the success of all 17 United Nations Sustainable Development Goals. These goals are concerned with poverty, health, education, nutrition and other basic infra structure. There are 104 sub-indicators for these 17 goals. I would like to touch only education. Secret of success of any individual in day-to-day life lies in application of behaviour knowledge and skill. All these three can only be acquired with education only.

The adjusted Net Enrolment Ratio from class I to X in India is 76 per cent while the target is 100 per cent enrolment. Under the universal health coverage, the target is 100 per cent however India could achieve 29 per cent according to the National Family Health Survey (NFHS 4). Tendulkar committee estimated in 2011-12 that 22 per cent of Indian population lives below poverty line while Sustainable Development Goal (SDG) target is 11 per cent.

Hunger is a big problem in India which is causing stunting in children. About 35 per cent of children under-5 years are stunted according to the Comprehensive National Nutrition Survey report 2016-18 of the ministry of health and family welfare. Similarly, mortality under-5 year per 1,000 live births is 50 which should be 25 as per SDG target. Unemployment rate for 2017-18 in India stands at 6 percent which should be 0 per cent.

Being a medical doctor and having worked in scores of medical institutions of India and abroad in last 40 years in different capacities from trainee to teacher and examiner to adviser in various medical bodies, I will confine my views mainly to medical education.

According to a report published in 2018, there are 374 medical colleges. There are 31,385 under graduate seats in Government and 60,105 in private medical colleges. But the ratio of doctor and patient is not matching with WHO standard which is 1:1,000. Over population is diluting this ratio though the country is training the maximum number of the doc tors in the world.

Rupees 300-400 crore is needed to establish a medical college and approximately Rs 50 crore annually to run it. Our medical colleges are mainly located in the rural areas particularly most of the private medical colleges. The cost of the land is exorbitant in urban areas hence the owners prefer to establish the medical college in rural and remote area. But then it becomes difficult to get the patient in such sparsely populated rural areas and to get the well-established experienced doctor, as a full-time faculty in that area.

The younger generation newer teachers do not prefer even well-equipped medical college of rural and remote areas because of non-availability of quality education for their children and other basic facilities like shopping, recreational and entertainment facilities for their children and their families. They rather prefer small and poorly equipped setup in urban areas. The frequent shifting and premature promotion of faculty again leads to the further deterioration in the medical training and teaching and this becomes vicious circle.

Recently, the medical infra structure is becoming more and more expensive and health care services are becoming more and more technology oriented hence colleges are ill equipped. Therefore, they are unable to provide the quality medical education as expected.

There is mismatching of money and merit in India. It is a paradox in medical education sector in the current scenario. The government colleges have well-educated and experienced faculty but they lack newer or advanced technical support. However, many private colleges are well-equipped but they do not have properly educated trained and experienced faculty. Hence in both scenarios the quality of education is compromised.

According to Dr BR Ambedkar, the architect of the Indian constitution and educationist, education ought to be brought within the reach of everyone, hence, education should be cheapest in all possible ways and to the greatest possible extent.

But contrary to above views most of these private medical colleges are run by businessmen on business principles while the concept of medical education is lacking. The owners of the medical education institutions are working as the investors and they want to make more money from these organisations. The medical colleges have become centres to mint money. Fee for full MBBS course in private medical college is ranging from Rs 50 lakh to more than Rs one crore in certain colleges.

Practice of cheating, copying and impersonation was prevalent in Xth and XIIth board examinations but now it seems that these malpractices have come in medical entrance examinations as well. Here I would like to remind you about Madhya Pradesh medical entrance examination scam of 2013 which was named as Vyapam scam.

A single national level National Eligibility-cum Entrance Test by Government of India for undergraduate (NEET-UG) was introduced in 2013 to get rid of the existing menace of capitation fees and other fraudulent activities which were prevalent in medical entrance examinations across the country. Here, I would like to share one more fraudulent incident of Tamil Nadu NEET impersonation scam reported in October 2019 in mass media. It is alleged that the son of a doctor got admission in Theni Government Medical College in Tamil Nadu by managing and engaging a proxy candidate to simultaneously write the exam for him with same credential from another centre.

A report by Reuters in 2015 stated that one out of every six (17 per cent) of medical college in the country has been accused of cheating, according to Indian government records and court filing. These incidents could be the tip of the iceberg. One can imagine the quality of medical education being imparted.

If the status of the medical education is analysed seriously in detail, then it seems that there is problem in our education system. Most of the brain functions are developed in childhood. Interest of the education in any children develops in primary schools. The children not only learn the skill of the reading and the writing but they learn ethical values as well and they themselves develop the skill of further improvement in them. Old habits die hard.

We should try to improve not only the medical education but emphasis should be given to the primary and secondary education. If we improve primary and secondary education then we can definitely improve medical education along with them.

Health, education and nutrition are the three basic pillars of the growth and development of any nation. Education is one of the important pillars of the growth of an individual and ultimately of the family, society and the nation. Health, education and nutrition in modern times have become saleable products which are bought by the money only. Money can be earned by employment especially for those who don't have the funds to start as an entrepreneur and therefore employment can only be achieved by quality education.

John Dewey, an American educationist said whatever role is of food and reproduction in existence of physical life of humans, similar role is that of education in their social life. Horace Mann an American educational reformer said where anything is growing, a former is worth a thousand reformers.

If we analyse overall causes of poor results of medical or surgical treatment then they are mainly attributed to the lack of quality basic medical education, training and the experience of that particular doctor. The quality of the work depends upon the quality of the worker. The aim of the government should be not only to provide the education but equitable quality education. Although this is relevant for all kind of education but it is more relevant in case of medical education as medical doctor with the life of human beings and many times decisions have to be made at an instant which may change the life of the individual.

http://www.pioneeredge.in/state-of-medical-education-in-india/

❑

22

Adulteration, Pollution Preventable and Modifiable Causes of Cancer

– Dr Gaurav Sanjay,
Wednesday, 05 February 2020

World Cancer Day is observed every year on February 4 to raise awareness on cancer and to encourage its prevention, detection and treatment. Cancer is the second leading cause of death in the world. Cancer can be defined in simple words as the uncontrolled growth of cells. The second characteristic of cancer cells is their ability to survive with the normal cells of the body. Cancer is known to spread to distal organs and can also recur at local site after treatment.

This condition has tormented humans for as long of our civilisation has existed. Cancer is not new to the humans as it is being perceived today. It is recorded in Egyptian texts dating back to about 5,000 years and similarly it has been mentioned in Ancient Indian medical texts Charak and Sushruta Samhitas. It was known as "Arbud".

A study published in the Lancet 2017 shows that the incidence of cancer in children is increasing day by day.

A UK based charity; Children with Cancer organisation states that the exposure to external factor such as pesticides, air pollution and dietary habits may have bearing on the increased incidence of childhood cancer. In his professional experience, this author has known the child of a family friend who developed a germ cell tumour at the age of six months. Here, the cause seems to be either genetic or environmental in the womb.

The ICMR 2016 data shows a significant rise in the incidence of cancer among both men and women. Cancer burden in India has more than doubled over the last 25 years. The highest incidence of cancer in women is breast cancer and oral cavity cancer in men. According to a Government of India report breast, cervical, oral cavity and lung cancer together constitute almost 40 per cent of all cancer burden.

Tobacco in any form is known to cause cancer. Tobacco smoking causes lung cancer and tobacco chewing causes oral cancer. The consumption of alcohol is linked with liver and stomach cancer mainly but may cause breast cancer too. It has been found that there is a synergistic impact of smoking and drinking in the risk of developing several types of cancer particularly oral cancer and stomach cancer. Several prominent studies have found an increased cancer risk associated with urban air pollution. Particulate matter present in the ambient air has been found to be a major contributor to increased cancer risk.

It is estimated that up to 20 per cent of cancer cases can be linked to embryonic exposures of toxins which are commonly found in many commonly used household substances most notably liquid detergents and certain cosmetic products. In June 2015, a global collective of medical resources attempted to address the long-standing concerns of chemical exposure in everyday life which estimated that up to 20 per cent of cancer cases can be linked to environmental exposure of toxins. A study published in 2016 found that 90 per cent of the US households had dust which contained chemical suspected to be harmful to human health specifically by interfering with the endocrine and reproductive function.

Free radicals in the body are known to damage the normal cells and these free radicals are linked with the cause of cancer. Antioxidants are important for good health and offer other benefits too. It is good to consume antioxidants through natural colourful fresh vegetables and fruits.

It has been estimated that 30 per cent of all cancer in developed nations and 20 per cent in the developing nations are linked to the diet we consume. Over a hundred studies from around the world have reported a link between red meat intake as a likely cause of developing cancer while the exact pathway of cause of cancer is not clear. Out of all meat, beef has the highest positive correlation with colon cancer.

Diet plays a vital role in maintaining good health. Most of the lifestyle diseases like diabetes, hypertension, coronary artery disease, atherosclerosis, hyper lipoedema and many other diseases are linked with bad food habits. But certain foods like broccoli, cauliflower, cabbage, radish, carrot, beans, berries, tomatoes reduce the chances of cancer and can reduce the growth of the cancer cells significantly. Other foods like turmeric, garlic, cinnamon, citrus fruits, flaxseeds, olive oil and fatty fish are known to reduce the chances of cancer as well. It has become increasing clear that overeating can have a major impact on your risk of developing cancer.

Green tea is the healthiest and probably one of the cheapest beverages on the planet and it is loaded with the hundreds of micronutrients and plenty of antioxidants that have powerful effect on the body. It not only improves the brain function but reduces the body weight and decreases the risk of cancer.

Tea is rich in polyphenols and green tea has about 30 per cent polyphenols by weight. The polyphenols reduce the formation of free radicals in the body which can damage the normal cells. These free radicals are also known to play a role in ageing. The treatment of cancer usually includes a combination of surgery, radiation therapy, chemotherapy and other supportive therapies. The most important factor which influences the outcome of the treatment depends upon the age and, comorbidities of the patient, type, site, size, stage, quality of surgery and doubling time of the cancer.

The price of the anti-cancer drugs is phenomenally high and is hurting the low income people and developing countries the most. The high price of anti-cancer drugs is even pinching the developed nations of the world like USA, UK and other European countries. According to a survey which was conducted in 2014 by National Sample Survey Organisation (NSSO), Ministry of Statistics and Programme Implementation, Government of India, it was found that out of pocket expenditure on cancer treatment is among the highest for any ailment. Cancer can be a major cause of acquired poverty.

The treatment of cancer is very expensive India it is reported that treatment cost can go up to Rs 20 lakh per year. In certain cancers one can imagine how difficult it would be to the patient and their families when 22 per cent of the Indian population is still living below poverty line according to the Government of India data collected in 2011.

Various scientific studies have found that about 60 per cent of cancer related deaths can be prevented by primordial prevention (removing the cause of disease so that exposure to risk is minimal) and early detection by screening (test to detect disease).

In spite of spending significant amount of money for treatment which families are usually unable to afford --but somehow arrange by borrowing money from friends and relatives or by selling their meagre assets-- they ultimately lose the beloved one to the fight against cancer and in such a way the whole family gets devastated.

Improper diet, adulterated food, contaminated and polluted air, water and soil are the common causes of cancer. Recently other factors like lack of physical activity and obesity have been found to be linked with cancer development.

Cancer awareness and early detection should be a priority for all governments and particularly in our country because of the negative socioeconomic implications. It will be worthwhile to educate and spread awareness among the people to take steps to prevent cancer and realise the importance of early detection and adequate treatment.

http://www.pioneeredge.in/adulteration-pollution-preventable-and-modifiable-causes-of-cancer/

❑

23

COVID-19 Pandemic: A Wake Up Call

– Dr BKS Sanjay & Dr Gaurav Sanjay,
Monday, 16 March 2020

Coronavirus has spread across the world reaffirming the fact that health is not only a localised problem to be dealt by one country but a global issue. In the current scenario, the whole world is vulnerable. This viral infection has flu like symptoms which can also lead to difficulty in breathing and ultimately the patient can also die. There is currently no vaccine.

The scientists are still not sure how it spread to humans from bats or other suspected animals. There are two theories- one is that some person has consumed the meat of a carrier bat or was infected through the urine or stool or the carrier.

Coronavirus was previously never isolated in humans and emerged first in China, in the city of Wuhan in December 2019. It has now spread in over 100 countries of the world and has infected more than one lakh people within two months. It has killed more than 3,500 people accounting to 3.5 percent mortality rate. There is apprehension that it may further spread and may affect the whole world.

Health, education and nutrition are the fundamental needs of any individual. Health, out of the three, is important in every stage of life because only a healthy person can achieve the desired goal and make their life better. Infection is not new in the humans. There is scientific proof that the origin of virus and bacteria is noted far before the origin of human species.

Infection is not new to our country too. It is believed that we all are infected with one or other virus or bacteria at some point of time in our lives. The main cause and spread of infection in our country is either ignorance or lack of awareness. We are not giving much importance to personal hygiene and public sanitation as we should.

As India is a tropical country hence there is frequent change in weather. The incidence of common cold is widespread which we see on a daily basis. The rate of infection is directly related to the personal hygiene and public sanitation.

Although, even if we have the highest sanitation and hygiene standards, the bacterial and viral diseases can never finish off but definitely the incidence of clinical infection and spread can be controlled. The operation theatres are disinfected with the aim of reducing the number of bacteria and virus to an almost negligible count so that the possibility of the infection becomes minimum.

It should be understood that we all share the same environment in our family but it is usually one of us who gets the infection, not the others. The body resistance can be improved with good diet. There is no specific treatment for coronavirus yet apart from the general method of increasing the body resistance and giving supportive treatment. Taking a balanced, nutritious diet, maintaining personal hygiene and sanitation can prevent coronavirus infection.

Coronavirus has elicited the attention and response of the whole world. China has proved and world has agreed that the principle of isolation is quite effective in controlling and containing the spread of coronavirus.

The Chinese government has isolated nine million population of Wuhan. If anybody was suspected, then he or she was investigated and if found positive for coronavirus-admitted in the hospital. China has controlled the spread of this infection significantly with this measure. We would like to emphasise the importance of isolation here. Isolation is not a new trend but has been going on in our country for centuries. Due to tradition of isolation, the mother and new born babies were kept in isolation in the cleanest area of the house. Nobody was allowed to meet the mother and the baby but only the designated lady called dai.

The aim of isolation was to keep the mother and baby in a safe and clean area to prevent or avoid any infection, knowing very well that the body resistance of the mother after delivery and new born baby is the least at that time.

If we analyse seriously, that if there is a boundary for each house then why should not there should be a natural boundary for a city so that cities can be separated from each other. Contrary to the above principle, there is significant crowd in our hospitals. There is a social trend in our country, there are many friends and relatives who don't visit the patients' home for years together even for social ceremonies like marriage and death but if that person is admitted in the hospital, then they will definitely visit.

This kind of crowd not only creates problem for the doctor and hospital staff but the patient also unknowingly. Here we would like to emphasise that the incidence of corona virus infection is not the last of such epidemic outbreaks but considering the situation and circumstances of our country then there is fair possibility of similar incidence to occur in the near future as well.

This situation makes one wonder if it would be sensible for policy makers and bureaucrats of our country and that of other countries to focus on the value of a natural boundary of at least of few kilometre either of natural forest or manmade greenery between two cities which can work as the isolation areas and act as a wall between these cities, so that God forbid if there is a similar health emergency like coronavirus epidemic, or manmade tragedy like terrorism at least they can be controlled if needed. This will enable protection of people of affected cities and other cities.

It is said that coronavirus can survive from a few hours to five days on surface of any floor or of any objects like chair, table, door knobs, phone etc. They all should be decontaminated with the commercially available anti-microbial agents as a precautionary measure. The tradition of hand washing has been a practice followed for centuries in our country.

We would like to quote that the tradition of hand washing can be seen at any religious place in our country. Hand and feet washing is quite a common social tradition which is very prevalent in citizens of Asian countries irrespective of religion. As the infection is spread by coughing, sneezing or touching infected objects, all should cover the mouth and nose while sneezing/coughing and wash hands frequently.

Hand washing is the most effective measure to prevent infection and can save many more lives which cannot be saved by any expensive machine and medicine. We all are stakeholders and should follow the dictum that prevention is better than cure.

http://www.pioneeredge.in/covid-19-pandemic-a-wakeup-call/

❑

24

Coexistence With Nature Is the Need of the Hour

– Dr BKS Sanjay & Dr Gaurav Sanjay,
Monday, 06 April 2020

There are many conflicts among humans all over the world, be it in families, neighbourhood or beyond the boundaries. Gradually these conflicts escalate to quarrels, fights and then war, if not managed properly and brought to a consensual solution.

War has been fought to prove one's supremacy over the so-called enemy. Initially humans were fighting with primitive animals and then fought with the other races to increase their influence and to increase their territory of control but recently most of the humans are uniting to fight with nature to have more comfort and security.

On March 24 prime minister of Japan, Shinzo Abe declared the postponement of the summer Olympics to be held in July-August 2020 in Tokyo. There was a significant emphasis in news that in the past only war had cancelled the Olympics. Is it not war which is going on for last three months in the world? The war which is being fought this time is not war among the human armies as it was in 1916, 1940 and 1944.

The war of 2019-20 is like a "Third World War" between mankind and a microorganism named COVID-19 which is thought to have emerged in the wildlife market of Wuhan in China and has spread in almost all countries of the world by the time of this article being written. COVID-19 has infected more than a million people and has killed more than 50,000 of them in a span of nearly three months from its emergence since December 31, 2019. The authors have an apprehension that this number will continue to increase in near future if we analyse the history of novel coronavirus management in Wuhan, Hubei, China.

It is difficult to say at this stage who will win this war, whether the giant army of 7.8 billion humans or the new born microorganism COVID-19. Considering the past experience, it seems this war will also be won by humans but at what cost? It is estimated that financial loss globally will touch nearly $20 trillion, in addition to the human loss. Almost half of the world population is locked down in their houses in efforts to prevent spread of the virus in their community. Anticipating the consequences of COVID-19 pandemic, our Prime Minister Narendra Modi addressed the nation and declared the lockdown of the whole country for 21 days from midnight of March 24 to control the further spread of infection in the rest of the population.

Any infection can kill people in mass numbers as it has been seen with outbreaks of plague, small pox and polio in the past. There is no other known disease or weapon which can kill millions of people of different parts of the world in such a short period of time. War and famine could be within the control of humans but not spread of air borne infection by a bacterium or a virus.

Environmental improvement, scientific and technological advancement would have less effect on such infection as it has been seen in COVID-19 infection. The virus emerged in China which claims to be superpower of the world and it has spread the most in a country -- USA which is supposedly the most developed and current superpower of the world.

Renowned anthropologists, Douglas P Fry and Patrik Soderberg reviewed the documented anthropological studies about organised war between humans and nature and they concluded that some of the most primitive people on earth were actually quite peaceful compared to modern civilised people. It is said that our ancestor chimpanzees are much more peaceful. We have lived in coexistence with plants, animals and nature for millions of years that's why our species has survived till date but we think recently we have forgotten the concept of coexistence.

In recent times, the existence of bio diversity is reducing. Survival is a natural instinct of all living organisms including bacteria and viruses. According to United States Centre for Disease Control, humans always try to find out new means and other alternative to survive, so do the viruses and bacteria which undergo mutations to survive new medicines in order to stay virulent.

Isolation in closed space and social distancing in open space are the key factors to prevent the spread of COVID-19, hence isolation of not only humans but those of cities is also needed. But considering the current scenario of overcrowding in homes, over populations in country and poor planning and designing of the houses and cities, it is almost impossible to maintain isolation and social distancing in most of these houses not only in rural areas but even in big cities particularly in the slum areas. Is it not a wakeup call for our leaders and policy makers to accommodate the current population in both closed and open spaces?

We may somehow be able to contain the current COVID-19 infection which is spread by droplets and then physical contact but what will we do if there is an air borne infection in the near future with a high virulence? After learning from the novel coronavirus pandemic, are our planners going to bring changes in town planning or rethink about a population policy which needs to be strictly in place or think about a national food policy to increase the body resistance to fight with such infection or have a national environmental policy which emphasises on concept of coexistence with nature?

Nowadays on an average, millions of people are travelling daily and some of them are reaching from one end of the world to another within a day. This mode of infection is very alarming and world has seen the consequences of this fast travelling where airplanes have become carriers and vectors of infection. If we analyse, it could be true that COVID-19 has emerged from Wuhan, China but who is responsible for its widespread transmission? Is it not the humans? Bat is still said to be the origin of COVID-19, but now human to human transmission is possible and humans have become a host.

Nature can survive if any species becomes extinct including humans but surely humans cannot survive without nature. Survival of humans depends upon air, water and food which are produced or reproduced by nature. Humans can only transform these natural resources to make them useful or for their trade.

Unfortunately, humans cannot make or generate any new resource without involving any of these natural resources. All human inventions are based on transformation of one resource to another, that being their only credit. This haphazard misuse and transformation of natural resources is the root cause of ecological imbalance. If at all transformation is needed or desired then it should be done in harmony with nature.

The way COVID-19 has infected the whole world irrespective of geographical boundaries, it has proved the Indian dictum of "Vasudhaiva Kutumbhakam" -- whole world is one family. If one member of family is infected, the others are prone to get infected. According to the most accurate scientific census nearly 8.7 million species are living on the earth. A total of 1.3 million species have been identified and described and human species is one of them. Imagine if giant dinosaurs can become extinct, then similarly, humans to can be put at the risk of getting endangered, if we do not live in a symbiotic relation with mother earth. Nature is great and we all should love nature but we can start loving nature only when we are in close contact with it. If we try to explore its beauty then we will spontaneously start loving it the same way we love our family, community and nation.

http://www.pioneeredge.in/covid-19-coexistence-with-nature-is-the-need-of-the-hourse/

❑

25

Ordinance Brings Relief to Saviours Victimised Amid COVID-19 Pandemic

– Dr BKS Sanjay & Dr Gaurav Sanjay,
Thursday, 23 April 2020

Currently as we battle the COVID-19 pandemic, none of the professions is under as much stress as the medical profession. In spite of taking considerable risk, working in odd conditions and at odd hours, some of them are facing verbal and physical violence. Verbal aggression or violence is so common that none of the doctors can claim that he has not encountered such behaviour from the patient and his acquaintance for no fault. In this scenario, the Central Government has brought an ordinance to end violence against health workers with provision for imprisonment of up to seven years for the guilty along with a fine.

Violence against doctors is not new, but manifold increase in is alarming in our country. A study conducted by the Indian Medical Association found that 75 per cent of the surveyed doctors had suffered some form of physical violence while being on hospital duty. Several such incidents have been reported from India in past.

The recent violence faced by a doctor during COVID-19 pandemic has again elicited the focus of the media and the political establishment. The authors being orthopaedic surgeons having experience of dealing with patients after simple to life threatening accidents, have also faced such abuse. Most of the doctors nowadays are working under some sort of fear, be it legal or physical abuse.

How can you expect best services to be delivered to the society in such an atmosphere? It becomes difficult to understand how health workers are at fault while taking risks and performing their duties door to door amidst the COVID-19 pandemic. In one recent case, after reaching the suspected patient's house, the situation escalated to such an extent that the health workers faced the risk of mob violence which could be potentially fatal.

It seems such people are prejudiced and hostile not only towards health workers but the entire government machinery trying to control the pandemic. It is a very dangerous trend for the nation. We personally feel that the situation is pathetic as this kind of the street justice is commonly seen in medical practice nowadays. If the situation is still not controlled, it is and will be a serious threat to the medical profession.

No one can say for sure that he will not need medical advice during his life from womb to tomb. Violence against doctors is a heinous crime. The perpetrators should be penalised and a strong message should to be sent to the society that anybody breaking the law will have to bear the consequences, so that others are discouraged from committing the crime.

The union health minister, Dr Harsh Vardhan, has taken quick action during his tenure to make a bill for violence against doctor or healthcare personnel as a non-bailable offence with a minimum of 10-year jail term and Rs 10 lakh fine. Once it is implemented, it will be a milestone to control this menace.

The Prime Minister Narendra Modi appealed the general public to appreciate the efforts of all the doctors, paramedical staff, policemen and media persons by Tali-Thali programme for five minutes on the day of Janata curfew. This appeal was honoured by most of the people of the country irrespective of caste, creed, class, religion and region to show their gratitude to the frontline workers in the fight against the COVID-19 pandemic.

Contrary to this there have been incidents of abuse against several health workers and frontline workers in India who are exposing themselves and doing their duties to prevent the spread of COVID-19. Though the incidents of violence against doctors and other health workers are few but they are eye opening.

At times, it seems the gratitude shown by the public on March 22 was to make Tik-Tok videos and use it as a photo-opportunity to be posted in the time of lockdown. We can imagine, that had these violent outbreaks not been during the pandemic there would have been nationwide protest by the doctors and the other health workers but the medical fraternity has again shown restrain.

It should be mentioned that medical workers who were victimised forgave the abusers and also visited the same places the next day to help the same abusers. In spite of all the hue and cry about the Indore incident another shameful incident happened in Moradabad, UP where a team of health workers and police personnel were attacked by a mob when they went to screen the COVID-19 suspects.

It is known that this viral infection can be fatal with the virulence of COVID-19 reported to be 10 times more than that of any viral infection. Here, one would like to re-emphasise that more than 20 lakh people are infected and around 1.4 lakh people have died all over the world since the emergence of COVID-19.

In spite of taking all precautions of personal safety including the use of personal protective equipment even in developed nations like Italy and Spain, 10 % of the health worker had contracted the COVID-19 infection and died. Considering the socioeconomic and health infrastructure of India, one can imagine how difficult it would be for health workers directly involved with the COVID-19 patients to give them health care services.

In general, the response from the society had been the same as our Prime Minister, Narendra Modi anticipated in his appeal to the nation to give all kind of support to all health workers and frontline workers to increase their morale in the fight against the fatal COVID-19 virus. But contrary to the PM's appeal, things have gone in very different ways in various instances.

It was painful to learn from mass media about certain neighbours and landlords of the health workers misbehaving and evicting these medical professionals out from their rented apartments citing unscientific reasons. We can imagine how disgusted these hard-working saviours must have felt when after sacrificing so much to save the life of fellow citizens, they were treated like modern day untouchables. It is pathetic and shameful that the saviours are being victimised during this unprecedented health emergency.

The authors hope that the ordinance brought by the Centre will facilitate the desired change in the situation being experienced by health workers. Strict legal provisions and their proper implementation are necessary to safeguard the life of the saviours who are fighting against the fatal virus.

http://www.pioneeredge.in/ordinance-bring-relief-to-saviours-victimised-amidst-covid-19-pandemic/

❑

27

Immunity a Paramount Factor in Preventing Infection

– Dr BKS Sanjay & Dr Gaurav Sanjay,
Friday, 08 May 2020

Humans have a habit of boasting about their power but a microorganism, COVID-19 has forced mankind to kneel down. This novel coronavirus wakeup call could be a sign of impending catastrophe. We share the same environment while living with our family and in our localities, but usually only some of us are more prone or gets these infections more commonly than others. Have you ever thought why this happens? The COVID-19 pandemic has reemphasised that in addition to hand washing, isolation, social distancing, there is something else which matters more than other things to prevent any infection--our immunity.

The immune system is a natural defence system our body possesses against any bacteria, virus, parasite, fungi and any other environmental toxins with potential to make us ill. The environment is full of these pathogenic invaders. Whenever our immune system is weak, these bacterium and virus take over the defence system of our body. In general, low count of haemoglobin, total protein and T lymphocyte count are the common markers of low immunity.

In one of the most comprehensive analysis of immune function performed till date, published in the journal cell in 2015 revealed that our daily habits and environment like the history of past infection, shapes our body's defence and immunity more than the DNA passed down by our parents. An effective and efficient immune system is central to the host's defence against infectious diseases. The immune system has the capacity to respond to millions of antigens. Our immune system is of two types; the innate or natural and the acquired or adaptive.

It is known that individuals with defective immune response are more susceptible to develop infection and are more likely to suffer from infectious morbidity, mortality and improving the immunity reverses and decreases these two parameters. Environmental, scientific and technological advancement has shown less effect on the COVID-19 infection as it also emerged in countries which are viewed as developed. USA, which is one of the most developed countries has in fact got the most number of infected patients and the highest mortality among other countries of the world. It seems that personal hygiene and public sanitation were not very effective factors to prevent the emergence and spread of the virus in the nations which have the highest standards of cleanliness.

As our age advances, the immunity of the body decreases to even fight against a less virulent virus or bacteria which can give rise to an illness. It has been seen in the COVID-19 pandemic that the communities within the affected population with a compromised immunity are at high risk of developing the infection and also have a high mortality. Most of the people, who died due to the current pandemic were above 60 -70 years and had comorbidities like diabetes, respiratory and kidney diseases. There are various ways to strengthen the immune system like good diet, antibody infusion or vaccination.

The idea of vaccination is to give a mild controlled infection in the body which produces antibody to that antigen. Gene therapy and bone marrow transplantation are other costly ways to tackle weak immunity in selected cases. Convalescent plasma therapy has been a recent technique which has been used to improve the immediate urgent need of antibodies against a particular infection or antigen.

According to an article in American journal proceeding of National Academy of Sciences, it was found that 10 patients in China who were critically ill began to show significant improvement after convalescent plasma therapy in which plasma taken from people who recovered from COVID-19 was processed and centrifuged. This convalescent plasma therapy is under trial and also approved by ICMR in selected COVID-19 infections in our country as well.

The means to enhance the immunity mentioned earlier are cost ineffective and cannot be practiced at the large scale in masses. Planned and well enforced steps need to be taken to enhance the general immunity by diet and nutrition in the entire country which will be cheaper and have long lasting effects like the midday meal scheme implemented in 1995 for school children.

Individually, the first step should be to change our lifestyle which should include consumption of more fresh fruits and seasonal green leafy vegetables. We should also try to do more physical work. The third step is to reduce smoking and alcohol consumption to a minimum level. The last and important thing is to get a good eight hours sleep which also reduces and minimises our stress level. Scientific studies have shown that our immune system is made, not born.

The development, maintenance and optimal function of immunity are dependent on adequate nutrition. Immune response can be improved only by nutrition. Our health deteriorates if we become malnourished. Malnutrition is common in our country and is usually of two types- quantitative and qualitative. In quantitative, individuals lack adequate calories in their diet and in other one they have enough calories usually from junk food which lacks enough quantity of all desired nutrients. Proteins are the building blocks to improve and enhance our immunity.

Pulses are the common source of protein. Eggs are the best source of high quality protein, which is almost 100% absorbable by the gut. Micro nutrient malnutrition is very common in our country especially among the poor although it is also seen in affluent society. It is also common in developed countries particularly in the geriatric age group due to lack of appetite and malabsorption of food.

It is known that green vegetables and the fresh fruits are the main and the rich sources of micronutrients but people prefer to avoid them as they usually produce gaseous distension and bloating. The micronutrients which include minerals and vitamins play a very important role in maintaining good health and particularly help in developing good immunity. They are iron, zinc, selenium, copper and vitamins like B6, B12, folic acid, C, D, and E.

There are nearly 30 minerals and a few vitamins which our body cannot synthesise. These micronutrients and vitamins are abundant in nuts, seeds, green vegetables and fresh fruits and can be found in citrus fruits, red bell pepper, broccoli, garlic, ginger, spinach, carrot, yogurt, almonds, walnut, turmeric, green tea, banana, papaya, kiwi, poultry, sunflower seeds, shellfish, and cinnamon.

Population ageing is a global phenomenon. According to 2019 UN report, 9% of the total world population is above 65 years of age. People are now living longer but not living healthier. It is estimated that in India, almost 30 million elderly are above 80 years and require some sort of medical or physical assistance. Health and pharmacy industry are working to make humans immortal. The goal should rather be to improve quality of life so that humans can also live comfortably and independently for rest of their life as other animals are living.

http://www.pioneeredge.in/immunity-a-paramount-factor-in-preventing-infection/

❑

27

COVID-19 Pandemic and Effects of Overpopulation

– Dr BKS Sanjay & Dr Gaurav Sanjay,
Friday, 22 May 2020

The world will not be the same after the COVID-19 pandemic. Health, education and nutrition are the fundamental need of any individual. Considering the socioeconomic and geopolitical status in India, a large chunk of these three things are in the private hands where work is on the principle of business and hence, they are expensive and out of the reach of common citizens.

Employment in India is unplanned and unorganised, because of which the society is facing many problems. If we want to improve the status of health, education and nutrition then first we have to bring the growth of population under control. Over population is exacerbating the competition for availing the resources whether natural or manmade. As such almost all resources are limited and this is making the society very competitive and greedy. This competition is leading to the abuse of natural resources which is causing an imbalance in the ecology. The needs for survival are forcing the humans towards destruction of the forests and depletion other natural resources.

To fulfil the growing demand of the population, there has been rapid urbanisation and industrialisation which are the main cause of climate change and global warming. Climate change is causing multiple natural calamities around the world, the incidence of which is becoming more common every year and causing ecological and human loss. Novel Coronavirus infection has given a wakeup call to the whole world but particularly to the countries which are over populated, over crowed and having poor health infrastructure.

As we know there is no specific treatment for COVID-19 infection but social distancing and isolation has been proved an effective way to prevent it. But is it really possible to maintain social distancing in majority of our families at home or at work in our overpopulated country? It is practically impossible as a significant number of citizens are living in substandard conditions where almost 8-10 people are living in small 10x10 feet accommodation due to poverty.

According to a media report, almost a million people are living in just little over 2 square kilometre area of Dharavi, Mumbai which is one of the most densely populated localities in the world. Dharavi has suffered in the past as well with many epidemics, including 1896 plague, which killed over half the population of Mumbai. Will history repeat itself during the current COVID-19 pandemic?

Maharashtra is one of the most COVID-19 affected states and the task of containing the contagion is proving to be a major challenge for the administration. Reports suggest that the administration is finding it difficult to sanitise the various narrow lanes of Dharavi and facing problems in contact tracing and surveillance in the crowded locality of Dharavi. It is not the only slum in India but there are dozens of slums which have been illegally built up in each metropolitan cities of India which are posing the health threat to the humans living there.

There should be global population policy as efforts of one nation or few nations would not be so impactful. The overpopulation problem should be approached as a global problem. It is time for all countries to control population in order to have sustainable life on earth without violating the rights of others and wildlife.

Over population is the root cause of all ills. We feel that awareness about the consequences of overpopulation needs to be reemphasised to the public, influential policy makers and religious preachers to bring grass root changes in the way we think about procreation. As we know if one is divided by more than one, then, the quotient will be less than one.

This applies to all our resources as well. This message should be ingrained in the citizen's mind that over population is causing depletion of all our natural and manmade resources all over the world. There should be multipronged approach to control the population with government and public participation without any suspicion. As such, many ways are being practiced to control the population.

The concept of one baby norm is good to control over population at the subsequent generations but the drawback with one baby principle is that population will be half in each generation. The population will be one-fourth after two generations as it is being seen in many European countries where the population is in negative growth.

If we analyse the difference between one and two baby per couple norm, then the principle of two baby norms is sustainable and a very effective way of curbing the population and maintaining the population which will be stationary at each generation. Having a girl and a boy in the family will help in maintaining the sex ratio which will help equalising the current imbalance in many states due to which there is disarray in the framework of the society. As our government policy to control the population is based on the concept of voluntary family planning, it has not given the results needed to curb the growth of the population.

There should be a law which should be strictly enforced and monitored to ensure that there are no more than two babies in any family. Once the population is controlled then other things will gradually change as well. There will be progress of both individuals as well as that of the nation.

There should be a law of two child norm not only in our country but all over the world which is likely to improve health, education, nutrition of all individuals irrespective of geographical boundaries. Our Prime Minister should take an initiative to work in this direction and once again prove the Indian dictum of "Vasudhaiva Kutumbhakam" which means the whole world is a family.

http://www.pioneeredge.in/covid-19-pandemic-and-the-effects-of-overpopulation/

❑

28

Road Traffic Accidents No Less Than a Pandemic

– Dr BKS Sanjay & Dr Gaurav Sanjay,
Monday, 8 June 2020

The medical dictionary defines a pandemic as a disease which spreads throughout the whole country or the world, affecting an exceptionally high proportion of the population. A true pandemic causes high degree of mortality.

According to WHO data, nearly 1.35 million people die and almost 50 million people suffer as a result of road traffic accidents every year worldwide. Compared to this the COVID-19 pandemic has killed over a quarter million people and infected little over five million in about five months.

On May 11, 2011, United Nations declared the global plan for the Decade of Action for Road Safety 2011-2020. The UN set a goal to halve the number of global deaths and injuries from road traffic accidents by 2020 but it could not be achieved. After almost a decade, the third Global Ministerial Conference on Road Safety was convened at the request of the UN general assembly by the government of Sweden and WHO in February 2020. The theme of conference was "Achieving Global Goals 2030" and it highlighted the connection between road safety and many other sustainable development goals. Similarly, the second world youth assembly co-hosted by WHO, together proclaimed "enough is enough".

A SDG of a specific stand-alone target in the health goal was adopted to reduce road traffic fatalities. The goal was set to halve the number of global deaths and injury from road traffic accidents (RTAs) by 2030. Our government has also set an ambitious target to save human lives on our roads. The road safety target with global goals is only going to be attained if we seriously work for it.

Human resource is the greatest resource in mankind and our country is losing almost 400 people every day on the roads due to these accidents. More than half of all RTA deaths are among young adults between 15 and 44 years of age and males account for 73 per cent of the fatalities. Most of them are bread winners for their family. Research conducted by us revealed that 90 per cent of these accidents occurred due to the driver's negligence. The main causes of these accidents are overtaking, speeding, drunken driving and use of mobile phone while driving. We think that aggression on the road is a common scenario on Indian roads and it seems that we take pride in breaking the traffic rules. The people are more adventurous on the road in India than anywhere else in the world. All these causes of accidents are due to behavioural problem of the drivers which should be tackled to prevent road traffic menace. Because of this aggressive behaviour and violation of traffic rules, the nation is losing a lot in terms of human and economic resource.

Another major problem with the increasing number of vehicles in India is the congestion on the roads. Though, the length of roads is increasing, it is not in proportion to the increasing number of vehicles. Road network has grown only by a third in the last decade while number of vehicles has multiplied three times exacerbating congestion. The total number of vehicles in 1951 grew by 823 times to 252 million in 2017.

More than a million people are killed and millions are being injured in RTAs each year worldwide. This situation is quite serious in India too. About five lakh accidents occurring annually in India cause 1.5 lakh deaths while one-fourth of those who survive become permanently disabled and only one-fourth of them achieve their pre-injury status in spite of the best treatment available in our country.

According to WHO and Government of India report, in our country, we lost around 50,000 people due to road traffic accidents in the corresponding four months last year while with the COVID-19 pandemic this year in India the death rate has decreased to almost two and a half thousand people only. If we compare the deaths caused by road accidents and COVID-19, the deaths in the latter are almost negligible.

According to road transport ministry report, two-wheeler riders are the most vulnerable lot and as many as one-third (35.2%) of those killed were two-wheeler riders followed by car and jeep drivers. Public transport is the most-safe in current scenario in our country.

If we want to reduce the numbers of accidents in our country then we have to first reduce numbers of vehicles and have to increase mass public transportation. The numbers of accident have drastically been reduced as per Uttarakhand police reports and that during lockdown in April 2020 the numbers of death due to road traffic accidents was almost zero. In another report only 750 people were killed in road crashes across the country between March 25 and May 31. It proves that the road traffic accidents are directly proportional to the number of vehicles on roads.

Following the ministerial conference held in February concluding with the Stockholm Declaration, the new global plan for Decade of Action shifted to safe affordable, accessible, sustainable mode of transport like walking, cycling and using public transport.

In our opinion whether person dies due to COVID -19 pandemic or a traffic accident; it is a loss to the family and ultimately a loss to the nation. The way the government, NGOs, media and society at large have shown enthusiasm and spent resources to spread awareness to contain Covid-19 pandemic has been commendable. If a fraction of it is spent on preventing this road traffic epidemic then the resulting saving human lives will be worthwhile.

The policy makers, administrators and public should comprehend this and all should try to control the RTA pandemic at each level. We all should always remember and remind others that prevention is better than cure.

http://www.pioneeredge.in/road-traffic-accident-no-less-than-a-pandemic/

❑

29

Yoga, A No Cost Natural Immunity Booster

– Dr BKS Sanjay & Dr Gaurav Sanjay,
Monday, 22 June 2020

The immune system is a natural defence system our body possesses against any bacteria, virus, parasite, fungi and any other environmental toxins which have a potential to make us ill. The environment is full of these pathogenic invaders. Whenever our immune system is weak, these invaders try to overpower the defence system of our body.

According to a renowned American immunologist, the complex immune system has a mechanism by which it performs the enormous task of identifying, isolating and killing invading organisms. It has been seen in the COVID-19 pandemic that the communities within the affected population with a compromised immunity are at high risk for developing the infection and also have a higher mortality. Immunity is a paramount factor in the prevention of any infection. Scientific studies have shown that our immune system is built over time, not born.

The development, maintenance and the optimal functioning of our immune system is dependent on our daily habits, nutrition and environment. Poor nutrition, sedentary life, lack of sleep and stress all lead to a weakened immune system which increases our vulnerability to any sickness. Health, as defined by the WHO, is "a state of complete physical, mental and social wellbeing and not merely the absence of disease or infirmity." Yoga is a physical, mental and spiritual practice which can be done to maintain good health.

It is a universal law of nature that everyone wants to seek pleasure and get rid of pain. It applies not only to humans but on animals as well. Yoga could be one of the means to achieve it. The United Nations General Assembly adopted an India led resolution declaring June 21 as International Day of Yoga. Pranayama is the formal practice of controlling the breath, which is the source of our prana or vital life force.

Pranayama is an excellent breathing exercise for good health. It is the perfect breathing exercise which increases the positive energy level in the body and removes toxins. Research published in the Journal of Behavioural Medicine suggests that Yoga can be helpful way to boost our immune system and decrease inflammation in the body. Yoga is one of the most effective and time-tested natural immunity boosters that can lead to a healthy, sickness-free body.

It lowers stress hormones and strengthens the nervous system while also stimulating the lymphatic system, which removes toxins from the body. Yoga calms the mind and can contribute to deeper, regulated sleep, which is crucial for wellness; sleep is one of the most important factors in healing and maintaining a healthy immune system.It is said if there is birth, there is development, disease, degeneration and death. Ageing is an inherent phenomenon.

One of the most important ways we can strengthen our internal defence mechanism and longevity is by boosting our immune system. The less efficient our immune system is the more prone we are to infection, disease and degeneration. We need to create an ageless immune system by boosting our immune system continuously.

There are various natural steps that have been shown to boost our immune system and therefore our longevity. In fact, building our immune system is the frontline of the Revolution against Ageing and Death (RAAD). Individually, the first step should be to change our lifestyle which should include making the habit of eating more fresh fruits and seasonally available green leafy vegetables. Secondly, we should try to do more physical work.

It may be in the form of professional need or recreational. The third step is to reduce smoking and alcohol consumption to a minimum level. The last and important thing is to get a good 8 hours sleep which also reduces and minimises our stress level. Stress is a new health problem which is a constant factor in today's fast paced life that can jeopardise our health if left unchecked. It reduces the body immunity. Stress is a common conditional response to a physical threat or psychological distress that generates a host of chemical and hormonal reactions in the body.

As a part of the adaptive response to stress various body systems such as the autonomic, cardiovascular, gastrointestinal, and immune systems may be affected. Around 70% of the diseases are stress related. Breathing exercise and meditation have proved to reduce this stress, which has been proved by many bio feedback studies. Ample researches have shown that just 20 minutes of meditation a day increases endorphins, decreases cortisol levels and fosters positive states of mind to promote better health.

Planned and well enforced steps need to be taken to enhance the general immunity. Various scientific studies were conducted with an aim to highlight the beneficial effects of Yoga practice on bio-parameters, such as oxidative stress, antioxidant components, immune functions, and secretion of stress hormones. It was concluded that regular Yoga practice remarkably attenuated oxidative stress and improved antioxidant levels in the body. Yoga helps lower stress hormones that compromise the immune system, while also conditioning the lungs and respiratory tract, stimulating the lymphatic system to oust toxins from the body, and bringing oxygenated blood to the various organs to ensure their optimal function.

While the asana makes up the cornerstone of infection prevention, the benefits of Yoga don't stop there. Since both common cold and flu attack the bronchial passages, it makes sense that conditioning the lungs and maximising one's breathing capacity through pranayama would build resistance against the preying organisms.

The means to enhance the immunity mentioned earlier are cost ineffective and cannot be practiced at large scale by the masses. However, Yoga doesn't need any extra equipment or extra space as most other exercises need. Yoga, unlike other forms of exercise, focuses not only on a certain part of the body but works on everything. The habit of Yoga, breathing and meditation should be the part of one's daily activity to maintain physical, mental, social, psychological and spiritual health.

Yoga needs only little time and is to be done at regular intervals to improve the general health of an individual. Practicing Yoga daily for half an hour to one hour is enough to maintain good health. If we want to bring change in society then our target population should be children particularly adolescent and teenagers. As it is said, it is easy to make any habit in childhood but difficult to leave that habit in adulthood. Therefore the goal should be to target the children to give them good habits.

http://www.pioneeredge.in/yoga-a-no-cost-natural-immunity-booster/

❑

30

A Doctor's Advice: You Are What Your Habits Are

– Dr BKS Sanjay,
Thursday, 02 July 2020

Twenty five hundred years ago it might have been said that man understood himself as well as any other part of his world but today he understands least. Physics and biology have come a long way, but there has been no comparable development of anything like science of human behaviour.

According to Buddhist philosophy, our life is shaped by our mind- we become what we think. To succeed, make everything your ally rather than enemy, be it another person or your own brain. We must change our thinking process and behaviour to bring change in anything. American psychologist BF Skinner was famous for seeing humans as no different as animals. Humans should be analysed as animals interacting with their environment. As animals, humans are basically creatures of their environment. Humans change their action according to the consequences of their and others behaviour.

As far as health is concerned, personal and social responsibility can be taught only with behavioural changes. Clinical research conducted by us revealed that 90% of the road traffic accident occurred due to the driver's negligence. The main causes of these accidents in India are overtaking, speeding, drunken driving and recently use of mobile phone while driving. I think that aggression on the road is a common scenario on the Indian roads and it seems that we Indians take pride in breaking the existing traffic rules while travelling on the roads. All these causes of accidents are due to behavioural problem of the drivers which should be dealt accordingly to prevent road accidents. Because of this aggressive behaviour and disobeying of the traffic rules, the nation is losing a lot in terms of human and economic resource.

Hospital acquired infection is another major problem in the hospital. Number of infections is directly proportionate to the number of visitors to the patient and to the hospital which can be brought down significantly in our country by making behavioural changes in society. In the current scenario of COVID-19 pandemic behavioural changes like frequent hand wash, use of mask and keeping social distance have proved very effective to prevent coronavirus infection. The practice of this behavioural change has given satisfactory results which are seen particularly in countries like Japan and Sweden.

Doctors are most of the time working in conditions of many uncertainties because the human body is working on dynamic principles not like the other sectors. None of the professions has as much risk as the medical profession. Knowingly doctors are taking risks of getting infected with dreaded infections like TB, AIDS, Hepatitis and recent addition of COVID-19 from patients while performing their tasks. But taking that much risk and working in odd conditions and hours, they are at times rewarded by verbal and physical violence. Verbal aggression or violence against doctors is so common that none of the doctors can claim that he has not encountered aggressive behaviour or verbal abuse from the patient's side for no fault. A renowned psychologist noted that it was natural to try to solve the world's problems by advances in technology or science. He asserted that real solutions would only emerge when people's behaviour is changed.

What matters the most is better interaction among the humans. We don't need many medical scientists and doctors but we need many social scientists and doctors who can change human thinking and their behaviour. Behaviour is the first thing which influences the results, irrespective of profession. Behaviour of an individual is very important to render the service. A genuine relationship or interaction is one in which you and the other person are comfortable with each other and feel safe to speak their mind and confident to be heard. Most of the problems can be sorted out with acceptable behaviour itself.

Behaviour is defined as an action that is observable and measurable. The observable actions are more descriptive. In psychology, behaviour consists of an organism's external reaction to the environment. In simple words behaviour is the range of actions by an organism with their environment. Behaviour serves two purposes- either to get something or to avoid something. It can be learnt and can be changed at any age and any stage of life, however it is easier at childhood than later on. Human behaviour plays an important role in all phases of human life. The success of any person depends upon the application of a trio of behaviour, knowledge and skill. Behaviour component is nearly 80% of all three.

Habit is something that you do often and almost without thinking, especially something that is hard to stop doing. Habit forming is an endless cycle running every moment you are alive. Highly successful people have learned to develop good habits which they follow daily. A person is a bundle and product of their habits. You are what your habits are.

Every behavioural action is preceded by antecedent trigger followed by a reaction. The process is easily remembered by the acronym ABC. The reaction of any action becomes action and action reaction becomes a vicious circle. Habit formation is the process by which behaviour through regular repetition becomes automatic or habitual. Habit formation has four components; first cue, second craving, third response and fourth reward. Humans can make good habits and can break bad habits. Lab studies have shown that it is never too late to make or break any habit.

The better way is to change behaviour by reinforcing alternative course of action. The cardinal rule of behaviour change is what is rewarded is repeated and what is punished is avoided. Old habits are hard to break and new habits are hard to make but if we want to achieve a certain result from any act then we have to make a habit of performing that act. The popular method to build habits is called the 21/90 rule given by a plastic surgeon Dr Maxwell Malts who states that it takes 21 days to make a habit and 90 days to make it a permanent lifestyle change.

We all make habits in personal and professional life. We want to develop habits which give pleasure and want to avoid those which give pain. The brain is always looking for bigger and better offer but human behaviour follows the law of least effort. If we want to bring the change in the society then our target population should be children, particularly adolescent and teenagers. As it is said, it is easy to make any habit in childhood but difficult to leave that habit in adulthood. Therefore, the goal should be to target the children to give them good habits. Once a habit is formed, it is unlikely to break. It is rightly said that old habits die hard.

http://www.pioneeredge.in/a-doctors-advice-you-are-what-your-habits-are/

❑

31

Overpopulation in India Is An Urgent, Important Issue

– Dr BKS Sanjay,
Saturday, 11 July 2020

Population is rising at an alarming rate in India making overpopulation an urgent and important issue. Indians are ignoring the soon to burst-overpopulation bomb. Our Prime Minister Narendra Modi had urged the nation to understand the importance of birth control during his 73rd Independence Day speech last year from the Red Fort.

Prime Minister Modi emphasised that population explosion in the country has and will create various problems for the coming generations. There is a need for social awareness in the country. This article is a small initiative to emphasise the impact of overpopulation in India on world population day which falls on July 11. According to Paul Ehrlich, overpopulation is a situation where a population is in the process of depleting non-renewable resources. Human overpopulation is when there are too many people for the environment to sustain with food, drinkable water, breathable air etc.

Scientists suggest that the overall human impact due to overpopulation on the environment is causing overconsumption, excessive pollution, and proliferation of technology, and has pushed the planet into a new geological epoch known as the Anthropocene. With the advancement of science and technology, the mortality rate among humans has reduced significantly and within the last two centuries the population has increased manifolds.

Human resource is the biggest asset but it is becoming a liability to our nation. According to the 1941 census of India, the population of India was nearly 31 crore which since then has increased more than four times since independence. The current population is estimated to be 138 crores. The surface area of Indian land is 2.4 per cent but the Indian population is 18 per cent of the world population. India is the second most populous nation in the world after China.

Over population is exerting an ill impact on the growth of the society and nation with an increasing trend of unemployment, overcrowding of infrastructure and depletion of the natural and manmade resources. The recent emergence of COVID-19 pandemic has further exposed not only the health-related problems but other non-health related problems of overpopulation. The densely over populated areas are giving nightmares to the administration to contain COVID-19 infection.

Almost half of the population in the Indian metropolitan cities is living in slums. There are dozens of slums which have been illegally built in each metropolitan city of India which are posing a health threat to the humans living there. Overpopulation is the main cause of pollution of air, water and food which are vital for all living creatures. Overpopulation is causing climate change and climate change is ultimately affecting not only the longevity and existence of the human beings but every other creature on the planet as well. This imbalance is leading to ecological and societal collapse. The impact of overpopulation on mother earth is such that there is a potential risk of mass starvation which may lead to extinction of the human race, as it is believed theoretically.

Modern economics is a competitive economy driven by technological advances where illiterate and unskilled people aren't used due to increased mechanisation or least used due to increased industrialisation as it is evident in many poor and developing countries. The increasing trend of unemployment is causing various socioeconomic problems. Over population is making India a fiercely competitive society and this trend of competition is visible in every field which is the root cause of stress.

Stress has been blamed for almost 70 per cent of non-communicable diseases. Diabetes, hypertension, stroke, cardiac problem, insomnia and hormonal disturbance are somehow caused due to stress. If causes of overpopulation are analysed, then it seems that poverty and illiteracy are the main causes of population explosion.

According to UN reports (2015) one-fifth of Indians are living below the poverty line and almost one-fourth of the Indians are illiterate even after 73 years of independence. The problem of over population is prevalent mainly in poor and developing countries. Illiteracy and poverty are interrelated. Where there is illiteracy, there is poverty and vice versa. The Government is increasing investment in many infrastructure projects.

However, in my opinion the investment should be done to develop a better supra structure that is the human brain. Once the brain is developed, other things will follow. Many poor countries including ours are giving many subsidies in various sectors but in spite of that the desired result is not being achieved.

In spite of spending so much money on such subsidies, India could not achieve what was expected despite 73 years of independence. It is suggested that the Government should provide free education and health to each and every citizen of the nation irrespective of the caste, creed, class, gender, region and religion. If this is not possible then at least these two sectors should not work on the principles of business rather, they should work on humanitarian and social principles.

If it is executed in such a way then the results will be worthwhile and will give far reaching beneficial effects to the nation. Overpopulation is the root cause of all ills. If one is divided by more than one, then the quotient will be less than one (1/>1=<1). This message should be ingrained in every citizen's mind that overpopulation is causing depletion of all our natural and manmade resources all over the world.

A two-baby norm per couple if enacted, with preferably a girl and a boy child, is a sustainable and a very effective way of curbing the population menace and maintaining the sex ratio which will be stationary at each generation. Overpopulation can be contained and controlled. This can be implemented only by humans. There should be global population policy as efforts of one nation or few nations would not be so impactful. The overpopulation problem should be approached as a global problem. It is time for all countries to control population in order to have sustainable life on earth without violating the rights of others and wildlife.

There should be a law of two child norm not only in our country but all over the world which is more likely to improve health, education, nutrition of all individuals irrespective of geographical boundaries. Our Prime Minister should take an initiative to work in this direction and to prove once again, the Indian dictum of "Vasudhaiva Kutumbhakam" which means the whole world is a family.

http://www.pioneeredge.in/overpopulation-in-india-is-an-urgent-and-important-issue/

32

Viral Hepatitis - A Major Public Health Issue

– Dr Gaurav Sanjay,
Tuesday, 28 July 2020

World Hepatitis Day is marked every year on July 28 to raise awareness of the global burden of viral hepatitis. It is estimated that worldwide, 290 million people are living with viral hepatitis, unaware. The theme for this year's World Hepatitis Day is to raise awareness to "find the missing millions".

The liver is located in the right upper quadrant of our abdomen. It performs many critical functions that affect our metabolism, mainly bile production, which is essential to digestion, filtering out toxins, excretion of bilirubin, cholesterol, hormones and drugs, breakdown of carbohydrates, fats, proteins, storage of sugar in form of glycogen, minerals, and vitamins, synthesis of blood proteins and synthesis of clotting factors. Hepatitis refers to an inflammatory condition of the liver. It's commonly caused by a viral infection, but there are other possible causes as well. These are broadly divided into two- infective and non-infective.

Infective pathology is usually due to viral and bacterial infection and the non-infective hepatitis is caused due to excessive alcohol consumption and other toxic material like over use or overdose of certain medication which are mainly metabolised in liver, exposure to poison and rarely hepatitis is caused due to faulty immune system.

The drug induced hepatitis usually caused in our country is due to anti tubercular drugs, anti-epileptic drugs and certain painkillers which can cause serious damage to the liver. People suffering from chronic hepatitis B and C should avoid alcohol because it may accelerate liver disease and liver failure. An auto immune disorder occurs when our immune system attacks and destroys healthy body tissue because of altered programming.

When we have an auto immune disorder the immune system does not differentiate between healthy cells and potentially harmful pathogen. The exact cause of auto immune disorders is still not known.

In acute hepatitis, patients usually have fever and pain in upper right quadrant of abdomen and loss of appetite and weight. In later stages, when the liver is damage significantly then the colour of urine and stool becomes dark yellow just like turmeric. If the colour of eye and skin is changing to yellow then it is a sure sign of hepatitis and liver damage. The diagnosis can be confirmed with blood test, ultrasound abdomen and liver biopsy. Hepatitis deranges the functions of digestive system, metabolism of carbohydrates, fats and proteins. The other serious problem which is associated with hepatitis is altered clotting. The clotting function is essential to stop any bleeding from the body after any injury, be it accidental injury or surgically induced injury.

If clotting function is deranged then there will be excessive bleeding from the all tissues which may lead to excessive blood loss which could be fatal particularly in acute hepatitis and acute liver failure. Here I would like to emphasise that these patients not only need blood replacement but also need correction of clotting factor too. The complication of chronic hepatitis B or C can lead to more serious health problem like chronic liver disease, liver cirrhosis, liver cancer and liver failure.

According to an ICMR report , it is estimated that currently about 40-45 million are HBV carriers and 10 million people are infected with HCV in India. Viral hepatitis is the leading cause of liver cirrhosis and hepatic cancer. Hepatitis virus is of five types, hepatitis A virus (HAV), B virus (HBV), C virus (HCV), D virus (HDV) and E virus (HEV).

HAV is the most common cause of acute hepatitis all over the world. HBV and HCV are chronic viral infection. According to global hepatitis report 2017, HBV and HCV are major public health problems. It is more common in Asian and African countries probably due to prevailing low socioeconomic conditions, leading to poor hygiene and sanitation. Hepatitis B and C virus can spread after sharing an injection needle which is quite a common practice in drug addicts. It can also spread through sharing of an infected razor blade.

As HBV and HCV are found in blood and body fluids, it spreads through infected needle, infected blood, blood product and other body secretions. It can be prevented by using single use disposable needle and syringe, transfusing only screened blood from an authorised blood bank, disposing infected material through appropriate medical waste disposal authorities and having safe sex with protective measures. Hepatitis B is occupational hazard for any health worker. Hepatitis B virus (HBV) is 100 times more infectious than HIV/AIDS. Surgeons have an ethical obligation to render care to the hepatitis infected patients as to other patients.

The risk of transmission of HBV from patient to the surgeon is greater than that of surgeon to patient. High viral load increases the risk of transmission post contact. The actual risk of hepatitis B and C are many times more than the HIV infection in healthcare workers.

About 37.6% of HBV, 39% HCV and 4.4% of HIV in healthcare workers around the world are due to needle stick injury. A study by a French surgeon estimated that general surgeons have 6.9% lifetime risk of contracting HCV and 0.15% lifetime risk of contracting HIV. Being an orthopaedic surgeon, I can say for sure that orthopaedic surgeons are more vulnerable to unintentional injury due to metal sharps than any other surgeon because orthopaedic surgeons deal with many sharp tipped instruments and implants in addition to general instruments. The fractures ends are often sharp and surgeon or assistant are at greater risk of an injury during reduction of fracture even after wearing thick gloves.

Needle stick or sharps injury can be prevented by using safe practice during work and getting vaccinated against the infection. Surgeons should continue to use the highest standard of infection control, universal safety precautions and accepted measures to prevent blood exposure.

http://www.pioneeredge.in/viral-hepatitis-a-major-public-health-issue/

❑

33

The Value of Language and Its Importance in Education

– Dr BKS Sanjay,
Thursday, 20 August 2020

Health, education and nutrition are the basic interrelated needs of every individual irrespective of any distinctions. The international community also recognised that education is essential for the success of all 17 United Nations Sustainable Development Goals. I would like to focus only on education here. The secret of success of any individual lies in the application of behaviour, knowledge and skill. All these three can only be acquired with education.

American educationist John Dewey said that whatever the role is of food and reproduction in existence of physical life of humans, a similar role is that of education in their social life. American educational reformer Horace Mann said that where anything is growing, a former is worth a thousand reformers. Education and learning play a major role in life of not only men but of animals too. Man becomes human only with education. Knowledge is the best resource and we can achieve almost anything with it. The children learn informally from the family and formally in schools. Most brain functions are developed in childhood.

The French proverb goes "a man who knows two languages is worth two men". The use of language is an important part of behaviour as it also contributes to personality development. A child's education starts just after birth and the power of humans grows with education. Children learn from their environment before coming to the school and have already learnt a language at home.

The attempt of education policy makers should be such that the language which children know should give them self-confidence to best express their abilities. It seems that we are not united with each other because for union we need a medium which can help unite us considering the diversity of the nation. One feels that all Indians cannot have the same religion, geographical area, economic status and one culture, but we can definitely have one national language which can be spoken and written by all of us.

In addition to that regional and international needs can be fulfilled by corresponding regional or international language and I feel Hindi can be easily a national language which is spoken by more than a half of India's population.

Many words of Hindi language are prevalent and common in many Indian regional languages. Though on paper, Hindi is the national language but after more than 70 years of independence, Indians could not adopt the national language which is acceptable practically to all.

Primary education is the foundation of development of any child irrespective of any caste, creed, religion and region. If primary education is given in mother tongue, then the quality of education will improve because the basic requirement of communication is speaking, listening and understanding. One can grasp better, express better in his or her mother tongue and others can understand better if they know that mother tongue.

If children are having different media of instruction which is different than mother tongue then it will be difficult to communicate with teacher and other children as well. We don't need the language only for communicating with others but to communicate with self too. Mahatma Gandhi used to say that language is like a mother. Though Gandhi's mother tongue was Gujarati and education in English medium, he wanted Hindi to be our national language.

According to Tamil poet Thiruvalluvar, knowledge can be spread by expressing the thoughts which can be communicated through language only. It is said that he also spoke other languages apart from Tamil. But seeing the recent mass media report it looks the current Tamilian political system does not follow the Valluvar teaching.

Review of literature had revealed that the king ruling over different parts of Tamil Nadu had wide regional and international contact with many countries including Sri Lanka in South, the Himalayan kingdom in the North, Rome in the West and China in the East. It is presumed that without giving due importance to other languages their culture could not have evolved.

The three-language policy is left on the states to decide regarding the choice of languages. The political parties in Tamil Nadu took this act as an attempt by the centre to impose Hindi on them. The three-language formula in the new National Education Policy (NEP) 2020 is "painful and saddening", said Tamil Nadu Chief Minister Edappadi K Palaniswami, as he vowed not to implement the new policy.

This is not the first time that we are changing the language but I presume that language has been changing since the origin of mankind. There is unnecessary hue and cry in a southern state against the NEP which was released recently by the Union Education Minister Ramesh Pokhriyal 'Nishank'. The minister has clarified that the Centre will not impose any language on any state. Is there any harm in learning another language? If Tamils are learning Tamil for local reason and English for global reason then why not

Hindi for national reason because Hindi is the most spoken and used language in India.

It is difficult to understand when India is giving the message of Vasudhaiva Kutumbhakam to the whole world why is it unable to convey this message to one or few of our states?

http://www.pioneeredge.in/the-value-of-language-its-importance-in-education/

❑

34

Aspects of Degenerative Process Escalating With Age

– Dr Gaurav Sanjay,
Monday, 24 August 2020

As it is said, if there is birth, there is development, disease, degeneration and death. Degeneration is a part of life. We cannot stop degeneration but with effort we can reduce the pace of this degeneration. As medical science and technology is improving, so is the longevity of humans. This is also increasing the number of patients suffering from degenerative diseases.

Health, as defined by the WHO, is "a state of complete physical, mental and social wellbeing and not merely the absence of disease or infirmity". It is a universal law of nature that all- both humans and animals- want to seek pleasure and get rid of pain. The scenario of orthopaedic practice has changed tremendously in the last 40 years.

Earlier, the patients were coming in OPD, mainly for the treatment of developmental deformity like club foot and congenital hip dislocation, paralysis due to infection like Polio and, TB and for fracture related complications but nowadays OPD attendance has diverted to treating the patients having degenerative problems, chronic musculoskeletal pain and complications of treatment in complex road traffic accidents. After recent advancement in the field, the problems caused due to infection and fractures have reduced significantly but not that of degeneration. Ageing is among the greatest known risk factors for most human diseases.

Degenerative joint disease which is also referred to as osteoarthritis (OA), is a common "wear and tear" disease that occurs when the cartilage that serves as a cushion in the joint becomes thin and deteriorates. This condition can affect any joint but is most common in knees, hips, hands and spine. Degenerative arthritis presents with swelling, pain, osteophytes (new bone formation) and deformities around the involved bone and joint. We should take a calcium rich, balanced diet and should do more physical work as far as possible on a daily basis. We should exercise regularly and should have regular 7-8 hours of sleep. For good health people should follow this acronym DEWS (Diet, Exercise, Work and Sleep). In addition to that people should do yoga on a regular basis.

Though there are many causes of deformity like fracture, polio, infection, developmental etc. but here I would like to confine myself to the causes, prevention and treatment of deformities caused due to degenerative bone disease. Degenerative process is accentuated if a person is overweight and not taking a balanced and nutritious diet and having mal alignment of bone and joint because of any reason as mentioned earlier. As such any injury in the bone or joint if not treated well can give rise to deformities. To prevent these deformities, one should avoid any injury. But if it happens then it should be treated well. The goal of the treatment should be to achieve anatomical alignment of bone and joint during surgery especially in injuries involving the joint.

Osteoarthritis is a common cause of degenerative arthritis, which increases as the age advances. It is most common in lower limbs in the Indian population. Deformities of knee joints are very common in our population because we Indians traditionally squat or sit cross legged for most day-to-day activities. This habit is now changing to a certain extent particularly in the urban areas.

In early stage, these deformities can be corrected with exercise, splinting and corrective exercise and with physiotherapy; however large joints such as the knee joint can be better corrected by realignment surgery. The other surgery which is very common in osteoarthritis of the knee is total replacement of the joint which is called total knee replacement. Nowadays, knee surgery results are quite predictable and hence it has become a very popular surgery for knee osteoarthritis. The success of any surgery depends not upon type of surgery but on the correction of the mal alignment. If we can achieve a balanced knee then the patient will have a predictable and a long lasting result.

Total hip replacement is usually done for osteoarthritis of the hip. Because of anatomical differences, its results are better in comparison to total knee replacement and here the goal of the surgery should be to have a stable hip with almost full range of motion so that the patient can squat and do cross legged sitting whenever it is needed. In our country none of the activities whether personal, professional or religious can be completed without squatting or cross legged sitting. Joint replacement surgery is quite successful but not that successful in India as in many developed nations. The reasons seem to be late presentation with gross deformities of joint and rarely if the patient develops postoperative infection.

Backache is the second most common problem experienced by individuals after headache. It is estimated that everyone will have back pain at least once in their life time. Back pain is one of the main ailments afflicting the people in general and more so in the hills. Elderly patients usually present with degenerative spine disease resulting into spinal canal stenosis (narrowing of spinal canal) which presents with neurological claudication. Spinal stenosis patients can easily go uphill but it is difficult for them to come downhill. Other common cause of back pain is facet joint arthritis.

The facet joints also degenerate with advance in age. Back becomes stiff on waking in the morning and gets relief after moving certain distance. Arthritic pain aggravates during bending and rotation. When the patients of degenerative bone and joint diseases become symptomatic then in early stage, they can be treated conservatively with the use of heat, massage, exercises and mild painkiller drugs. But when this degeneration progresses these patients cannot be managed conservatively, then these patients are re-evaluated and are often candidates for surgery.

The results of varied types of surgery are quite predictable nowadays. Surgeries are difficult and risky but its success completely depends on the severity of problem, skills of surgeon and the facilities available in the hospital.

http://www.pioneeredge.in/state-of-medical-education-in-india/

❑

35

Literacy – The Cornerstone of Education

– Dr BKS Sanjay,
Wednesday, 09 September 2020

September 8 was declared as International Literacy Day by UNESCO on October 26, 1966. Though it was a subdued affair this year due to COVID-19, it does not diminish the importance of literacy.

Literacy rate is defined as the percentage of people in a given age group who can read and write, understand short and simple statements. Those who can read and write are more powerful than those who cannot, in many aspects of life. Studies worldwide have shown that literacy leads to increased horizon for the human brain and body expression. A Tamil poet Thiruvalluvar said that "letter and number are the two eyes of humans". Acquiring literacy and basic education is the tool for growth of any individual and the nation.

Literacy is crucial to acquiring and learning essential life skills that enables people to address challenges in life. Education can be a prime factor in achieving the UN SDG. Considering the importance of education, many countries are increasing budgetary allocation for education. The developed nations are spending around 5% to 7% of GDP on the education sector, while the poor countries are investing and allocating the least amount to the education sector.

The development of any country can be analysed considering the percentage of budget for the education sector. Though types of natural resources may vary from country to country, education is a resource which can be consistently built and improved. Hence, all governments should give importance to this manmade and acquired resource which is the supreme wealth even written in Indian scriptures.

UNESCO has been mandated to lead the global movement and coordinate the international efforts to provide a framework for ensuring that education reaches out to all. Governments, development agencies, civil society, non-government organisations and the media are some of the partners working towards reaching these goals. UNESCO's coordination with other international organisations allows access to education and growth in diverse communities, allows freedom of expression and enables learning from advancements in technology. The world literacy foundation is working to reach children in remote communities.

According to Valluvar, by birth all men are equal; it is by the differences in their actions that their birth is rendered unequal. Formal and informal education plays an important role in their life. Thoughts are the primary source of all actions which are influenced by the status of literacy and education of an individual. Education is one of the important pillars of the growth of an individual and ultimately of the family, society and the nation.

According to UNESCO figures, India's current literacy rate is 72%- with 80.9% among men and 62.8% among women. If our country wants to progress then our government will have to make a resolve to ensure education for all because education is the prime mover. Overpopulation is the root cause of all ills. Illiteracy and poverty are interrelated. Illiteracy leads to poverty, unemployment and various social and health related problems. The efforts to reduce illiteracy are not at the same pace as the pace of the increasing population. Another significant cause of illiteracy is the perception that education is expensive; hence, poor parents are not sending their kids to school. Illiterate parents do not know the value of literacy and education. As such there is no favourable environment for education in poor families.

Considering the importance of literacy and education India should increase the budgetary allocation for the education sector considerably. The author believes that health, education and nutrition are the foundation pillars of growth of an individual and nation. Though national literacy mission comprised four schemes and teacher training programme were also launched in India, it has not given the results as anticipated by Government of India. It is suggested, that if even a fraction of the amount spent on adult literacy, is spent properly on primary education then things could be very different.

The quality of teachers is also a very strong factor in determining the dropout rate especially in rural and remote areas. Patience and compassion are two important virtues of all teachers. Eventually many kids start hating teachers who lack these qualities and stop going to school. The dropout rate is more than 53% from class I to VIII. To increase the literacy rate and reduce the dropout rates, the medium of instruction or learning will play a crucial role. The medium of instruction or learning should be preferably in mother tongue because the children will learn and comprehend better in their mother tongue. Literacy is the cornerstone of any education. Had we not known or understood an akshar (letter) or an ank (number), how could we have achieved all that we have today?

https://www.pioneeredge.in/literacy-the-cornerstone-of-education/

❑

36

Ensuring Health & Happiness of the Elderly for A Better Society

– Dr Gaurav Sanjay,
Wednesday, 30 September 2020

The United Nations declared October 1 as the International Day for Elderly. On this day UN and its allied groups raise awareness on issues affecting the elderly and our responsibilities towards our elders. It is also a day to appreciate the contributions of the elderly to society. The elderly population is defined as people aged 65 years and above. This year we are still under the siege of the COVID-19 pandemic and it is the elderly who have been afflicted the most by COVID.

Currently the total population of the world is 7.8 billion. It is estimated that there were 703 million persons aged above 65 in 2019. This number is projected to double to more than 1.5 billion people by 2050. One can imagine how seriously this rise in geriatric population will bring changes to the ailing Indian health system.

It is common knowledge that as our age advances, the immunity of our body decreases to fight against even less virulent virus or bacteria which can give rise to illness. Additionally, elderly people usually have other associated comorbidities like diabetes, hypertension, heart, lungs and kidney problems.

Being an orthopaedic surgeon, in addition to these above-mentioned comorbidities, I mainly see two peculiar orthopaedic problems in elderly people—osteoporosis and osteoporosis related fractures. Osteoporosis is a disease which can cause generalised body pain and bending of these fragile bones which is more marked in the lower limbs and the spine. These deformities usually increase as the age advances.

The quality of the bone becomes more porous hence the bones become more bent and more fragile which fracture with trivial trauma. Osteoporotic fractures usually occur in the spine, hip and wrist bone. The common mode of injury is a minor slip in the bathroom in cases of hip fracture and after travelling on bumpy roads, which is quite a common scenario in our country to sustain osteoporotic spine fractures. Wrist fractures usually occur when one falls on an outstretched hand.

Wrist fractures can usually be managed by simple plaster while most osteoporotic spine fractures can easily be managed with brace. But, in the current scenario, there is not much scope for conservative treatment in managing hip fractures. These hip fractures are difficult to manage due to the age of the patients and their comorbidities. These fractures are almost always managed surgically but the results after surgery are also not very predictable.

In my own experience, also supported by scientific studies, a third of the patients with hip fracture who are treated surgically die within a year of the injury irrespective of any surgical treatment and the hospital facilities not only in our country but in developed countries too. Not only do the elderly suffer from physical deformities and problems but also occasionally have mental problems like anxiety, depression, psychosis and Alzheimer's disease or some other sort of neurological problem like Parkinsonism etc.

The UN is promoting the Decade of Healthy Ageing and bringing together UN experts, civil society, government and health professionals to prepare a global strategy and action plan on ageing. This strategy will be integrated into the SDGs especially goal 3 which is to ensure healthy life and promote wellbeing of all at all ages. One of the aims in the present proposal is reducing the health disparities between elderly people in developed and developing countries so as to leave no one behind. Currently, the COVID pandemic has increased the burden on the health system in treating elderly people in a short period of time, hence the policy, planning and the attitude of the public, social workers and policy maker's needs to change.

Ageing and osteoporosis are creating a burden on the already constrained health services in both public and private sectors in India hence, an attempt should be made to prevent osteoporosis and osteoporotic fractures. Primordial prevention by eating a healthy, nutritious and balanced diet containing calcium, vitamin D and the other micro nutrients, daily exercise in any form, any physical, professional or recreational work improves bone strength. This will definitely reduce the incidence of osteoporosis and related fractures. The other preventive measures to reduce incidence of fractures is using a walking aid like cane or walker, keeping the floor dry and turning on the light bulb in the bathroom particularly during the night.

Human resource is the biggest resource but it's worth depends upon the health of the individual. Elderly people can play a critical and an important role through volunteer work and even helping their family with responsibilities and sharing their vast experience. Though elderly people cannot do rigorous physical work they can do many other supervisory works. They can transfer their experience and knowledge to the younger generation which will greatly benefit the family, society and nation. The elderly people particularly the well-trained and experienced professionals should be motivated to make contributions to local communities. This will help both the community and the elderly while boosting their self-esteem and making them feel more dignified as they age.

Ageing is a natural and physiological phenomenon which starts from conception of an individual. This process cannot be stopped but can be modified. According to the 2011 Indian census there are nearly 104 million elderly persons in India and we all should be concerned about their mental, physical and nutritional requirements at large. People are now living longer but not living healthier. Everybody's goal should be to improve quality of life so that all can live comfortably and independently for the rest of their life. For that there is an urgent need to build a stable infrastructure and health care support system for the elderly.

http://www.pioneeredge.in/ensuring-health-and-happiness-of-the-elderly-for-a-better-society/

❑

37

The Link Between Poverty and Road Traffic Accidents

– Dr BKS Sanjay & Dr Gaurav Sanjay,
Sunday, 18 October 2020

Like every year, the International Day for the Eradication of Poverty was commemorated on October 17. Whenever men and women are deemed to live in extreme poverty, human rights are usually violated. We must come together and ensure that these rights are protected and respected. This day is marked to renew the commitment of people from all backgrounds, beliefs and social origins to show their solidity with the poor and downtrodden. The authors being orthopaedic surgeons have closely seen the social and financial suffering of the Road traffic accident (RTA) victims. We feel that road traffic accidents and increase in poverty are interlinked and therefore, we want to highlight the impact of RTA on the society and the nation.

More than a million people die worldwide every year on the roads after suffering from RTA. This situation is quite terrifying and serious in India. Almost 5 lakh accidents occur in our country annually. According to the World Health Organisation 2019 report, low and middle-income countries account for more than 90% of road traffic related deaths, despite having only around 60% of the world's registered vehicles. Although our country is having only 1% of the world's total registered vehicles it accounts for more than 11% of the world's RTAs. One can imagine how grim the situation is likely to become in the near future as number of vehicles is increasing manifold in our fast-growing economy.

As our country's per capita income is rising, so is the number of accidents. Road accidents do not differentiate between the sections of the society, rich or poor, skilled or unskilled, old or young. However, statistics show that majority of those who are affected, are in the age group of 20-40 years and are usually the bread earners of their families.

Poverty and road traffic injuries are strongly interlinked. Poor people are more likely to be involved in a road traffic crash, and the economic impact on people with low incomes can be more significant, pushing people deeper into poverty or limiting their future potential to be economically stable. Given that RTA related deaths and serious injuries are largely preventable, road safety should be considered an issue that can contribute to poverty alleviation at national and household level.

According to a recent UN and World Bank report, almost one-fourth of the people in India are still living below the poverty line. Those who cannot afford food three times a day cannot afford costly medical treatment. In India, 50-70% of the hospital expenses are met by the patient even in most of the government funded hospitals and almost 100% from their pocket if it entails a private hospital.

After the traffic accidents, everybody's financial condition becomes poorer than before. About 50% of the families either borrow money from someone or sell their meagre assets, like land, house, cattle, vehicle, ornaments etc. for the treatment of their beloved. But unfortunately, in spite of the best available treatment in our country one-fourth to a half remain temporarily or permanently disabled and become liability to the family from being an asset at a point of time.

It is necessary for all of us to spread awareness on preventing these accidents, because they have taken the form of an epidemic. If something is not done it is bound to go out of control. We have delivered 193 free public awareness lectures and spread the message among thousands of students and other citizens in Uttarakhand and neighbouring states.

Poor people are more prone to traffic accidents because usually they are pedestrians or using cycles as the mode of their transportation because they cannot afford motorised vehicles. But whenever they meet with an accident they are usually hit by a motorised vehicle and the impact is usually fatal because they don't have any protective shields or safety equipment as the motorised vehicles have installed in them. Once they sustain the accidents then it is difficult for them to get the best medical care due to their financial constraints and the associated poverty. Particularly in India these people usually go to the government hospitals which are mostly not well-equipped to deal with such injuries.

Road accidents push families into the poverty through the loss of money spent on prolonged medical treatment which is common in orthopaedic injuries. We would like to cite an example of a 25-year-old standing on the side of the road when he was hit by an SUV from behind and sustained open fractures of leg and thigh which was treated at multiple hospitals and developed complications. At this stage patient came to us to get treated and became well only after five years of the initial injury. This is not the only one but there are many such examples the authors have seen.

The incidence of RTAs can be reduced significantly if the number of vehicles on the road is also reduced. The COVID-19 pandemic has been a boon to reduce the road traffic fatalities as media report state that the incidence of traffic accidents and resultant fatalities has been reduced by almost 50% from March to September 2020 in comparison to last year.

According to our research, 90% of these accidents occur due to the driver's negligence. The results of Motor Vehicles (Amendment) Act 2019 are visible as informed by Union Minister of Road Transport and Highways, Nitin Gadkari in Parliament in March 2020. If people follow the traffic rules the incidence of road traffic accidents and associated fatalities will reduce significantly and so will the associated poverty.

http://www.pioneeredge.in/the-link-between-poverty-and-road-traffic-accidents/

❑

38

Impact of Alcohol Abuse on Families, Society and Nation

– Dr Gaurav Sanjay & Dr BKS Sanjay,
Monday, 02 November 2020

Alcoholic beverages have been used in human settlements for ages—their consumption was first documented in the Indus Valley civilisation between 3000-2000 BC. The two great Hindu epics Ramayana and Mahabharata also mention the use of alcohol.

Although, the recorded alcohol consumption per capita has fallen since 1980 in most developed nations, it has risen steadily in the developing countries and alarmingly so in India. The pattern of drinking alcohol in India has changed from occasional and ritualistic use to being more frequently used in social gatherings. The use of alcohol is ubiquitous today.

According to a WHO report released in September 2018, the per capita alcohol consumption in India had increased two folds in a span of 11 years between 2005 and 2016.This raised concerns about the health and the social consequences of excessive drinking. India is the third largest alcohol consumer market in the world. A report published by Reserve Bank of India in September 2019 shows that excise and sales tax of liquor is the second or third largest sources of revenue of states and UTs within the country. The studies found consumption in northern India to be between 25-40% whereas in southern India, the prevalence of current use of alcohol varies between 33-50%, with a higher consumption among the lesser educated and the poor.

Alcohol abuse, also called alcohol misuse, is a serious problem. It is a pattern of drinking too much alcohol, too often. It interferes with your daily life. If a male consumes more than 14 drinks per week or more than four drinks per occasion; if women of any age and men older than 65 consume seven drinks per week or three drinks per occasion it is considered to be alcohol abuse. Binge drinking or heavy episodic drinking is a modern epithet for drinking alcohol with an intention of becoming intoxicated over a short period of time which brings a person's blood alcohol concentration to 0.08 gm/dl or above. A study about prevalence of heavy episodic drinking among 15-19 years old in India in 2016 revealed that around 21.1% of males had drunk pure alcohol heavily on at least one occasion in the past 30 days.

Alcohol abuse mainly gives rise to behavioural problems. The people afflicted with alcohol abuse are paying a very heavy price in the form of deterioration of their physical, mental health, family relations, social relation and work related problems. Alcohol is also associated with criminal activities and many crimes are committed under the influence of alcohol. It is also a factor in cases of sexual abuse. On the social front alcoholics usually develop matrimonial discord and other family problems. An Indian scientific study published in 2016 revealed that prevalence of drinking in alcohol abusers varies from 27-37% during domestic violent episodes with married women.

At the work front, such persons usually lack very cordial relations with their co-workers and employer.

Hence, many a time the need to undergo multiple change of jobs frequently especially in the private job sector. Employer and their co-workers perceive that heavy drinkers have lower performance, problems in personal relationships and lack of self-direction, though drinkers themselves do not necessarily perceive these effects on their performance.

The authors have their own experience with an employee who regularly remained absent for two to three days after receiving salary and also used to steal money. In India 30% of the absentia from the duty is related with alcohol abuse. Because of their habit of daily spending on purchasing alcohol, most of them are under financial constraint. Hence, most of the time they are under debt, particularly, people from the lower socioeconomic strata.

Being orthopaedic surgeons, we see many road traffic accidents caused due to drinking and driving. Police must conduct regular checks on the roads to catch these miscreants. We have seen many complications of alcohol abuse in orthopaedic practice.

Avascular necrosis of the femoral head is the commonest orthopaedic complication for which the patient needs to undergo total hip replacement surgery which costs around Rs 2-3 lakh. The hundreds of patients of avascular necrosis (AVN) of femoral head who have been seen and interviewed by us, revealed that most of these patients got habituated to alcohol consumption at a young age. In general, their hips are affected on an average of 10 years after the start of alcohol consumption of more than half a bottle or more.

Chronic alcoholism is the social evil which is the commonest cause of liver cirrhosis (liver scarring) and which had killed around 1.4 lakh people across India in 2016. Alcohol induced liver cirrhosis is the major indication of liver transplant in India which costs around Rs 20-30 lakh.

Drinking alcohol has become a social fashion particularly in urban and semi-urban areas particularly among the youth. Initially, alcohol consumption was common in boys but now a day there is increasing trend of alcohol consumption among girls as well. During a drug de-addiction seminar last year, a senior police officer of Uttarakhand informed, that 16 % of students are affected with alcohol or drug abuse in Uttarakhand. The situation is grim in Dehradun especially in institutional areas where thousands of students are living. Most of these students are living in an unorganised way in small accommodations- hostels or as paying guest where their activities are overlooked.

We all make habits in our personal and professional life. It is an endless cycle running every moment when you are alive. We make habits which give pleasure and want to avoid the habit which gives us pain. Habit is something that you do often and almost without re-thinking. It is something that is hard to stop. If we analyse the cause of alcohol abuse then an important cause of abuse seems to be availability of alcohol, peer pressure and loneliness.

Alcohol abuse is a habit which is formed usually in teenage years. College going students particularly those who are living in the hostels away from their families are more prone to get into the trap of forming the habit of alcohol consumption and drug abuse. During teenage, there is a surge of hormones in the body which induces them in adventurous activities including tasting alcohol either due to peer pressure or trying out new things.

The increasing trend of lavish birthday parties in society in general and increasing trend of fresher's and farewell parties among college going students is a common trend which also is an important cause of giving an opportunity to taste alcohol for the first time in their life. Once the habit of alcohol abuse is formed, it is very difficult to get rid of it, as it is said, old habits die hard. The trend of welcome and farewell party should be conducted within the college campus not in hotels or any other commercial places and supervised by the college authorities, the parents or elder people especially if there is any provision of alcohol.

http://www.pioneeredge.in/impact-of-alcohol-abuse-on-families-society-and-nation/

❑

39

Road Tells Stories, Some Tragic but Worth Learning From

– Dr BKS Sanjay & Dr Gaurav Sanjay,
Monday, 16 November 2020

The World Day of Remembrance for Road Traffic Victims (WDoR) is commemorated on the third Sunday of November each year to remember the millions of lives lost in road traffic accidents. Roads and streets are more than just connections between a point A and point B. They tell stories, some of them tragic but worth learning from.

A national awareness programme should be launched to make the general public aware about the road safety rules and regulations. It is said that health is wealth. But if you get injured then the current socioeconomic status of patient and current health facilities are the paramount factors which modify the course of treatment. We have encountered many such stories, and would like to mention a few.

A 17-year-old boy studying in class XII was not having a valid driving licence but riding his bike on the national highway for the last three years. In a road accident he suffered serious fractures of both his thigh bones. His treatment elsewhere got complicated with severe and virulent infection and then he came to us. An attempt was made to manage and control the infection with certain antibiotics, he developed renal insufficiency. His parents had an altercation with local doctors and also with me during the course of treatment. He was blaming the doctors for everything but not his son who was ineligible to drive a geared bike and was overtaking a bus from the wrong side. This incident shows how ignorant we are about the consequences of road traffic accidents and how often we ignore and break the traffic rules and take life threatening risks on the roads.

Another 39-year-old male came with a painful deformed left forearm. He sustained closed fracture of both forearm bones 14 years back. He was treated with open reduction and internal fixation with plating by an orthopaedic surgeon at that time. Surgery got complicated with infection, since then he was having deformity and disability of his right forearm. His family abandoned him because of his deformity and disability. He was treated for correction of deformity and fracture healing. After surgery he has regained the full range of motion and doing his job as a car mechanic.

Third, a young man in his late twenties was riding a bike with his girlfriend at IT Park Road, Dehradun enjoying the ride with her who was holding his helmet but in the meantime the boy saw the police patrol car. He asked for the helmet from her but the girl in haste put the helmet on the boy's head in the wrong way and in the meantime the bike hit a truck coming from the opposite side. The boy sustained a right knee joint fracture and the girl a complex right elbow joint fracture.

Here we would like to emphasise that the joint injuries are complex in nature and are difficult to treat and it is rare to get full range of motion of affected joint in spite of the best available treatment despite spending a significant amount of money and time. Both have become disabled for the rest of their lives, the boy with a stiff knee and the girl with a stiff elbow. Fourth, a 30-year-old unemployed male, recently married, was standing at the side of the road when he was hit by a car. The man sustained open segmental fracture of left leg and left thigh bone which was treated in local hospital immediately after injury.

During the treatment he developed many complications like exposed and infected bone of left leg, protrusion of nail from thigh bone to knee bone. If we recall the suffering of this young couple, it was enormous. His wife became a mother during the course of his prolonged treatment but was not having even enough money to purchase food. It took almost five years for his fractures to heal and that too after multiple operations. The fracture finally healed and the patient is walking but the knee is stiff. The stiffness will remind him and his family about the tragic traffic incidence he met.

Fifth, a 56-year-old state government employee was going to the office by two-wheeler and sustained injury when he was sandwiched between two cars one noon. He sustained multiple fractures with right hip fracture, right thigh fracture, right proximal arm and left proximal tibia fracture. He was admitted in emergency in hypovolemic shock. Here we would like to mention if such patients do not reach hospital in a couple of hours, then they are likely to lose their life because there is significant amount of bleeding from these fractures which is not visible hence it is ignored by the patient and the family members and often neglected. But on other hand if they sustain an open injury with bleeding then they give a lot of importance and reach the hospital as soon as possible.

Such injuries are also life threatening and the patient should be shifted to a hospital which is well-equipped to deal with poly trauma patient. In spite of such multiple and complex injuries, however, they can be managed successfully and patient can reach pre-injury status in hands of experienced surgeon in a well-equipped hospital and particularly if the patient can afford the expenses of the treatment.

Sixth, a 23-year-old factory employee was going back home along with a friend who was riding. He had road traffic accident on the Haridwar-Dehradun NH 1 one evening. The accident was so severe that bike rider died on the spot and pillion rider sustained head injury and open fractures of both legs. The leg injury was so severe that primary doctor had to amputate the left leg to save his life. Right leg was treated with tibia nailing after 15 days of injury which was further complicated with infection. The infection was uncontrolled. He came to us for further treatment. The limb was saved finally for that he had to undergo more than a dozen operations and spend lakhs of rupees for which he had to sell his agricultural land.

It is worth mentioning here that his mother was a widow whose both children were unmarried and the patient was the only bread earner for the family. After his fracture healed, he got married and is living happily with his family. But in spite of all his treatment he has paid a very heavy price for the accident. These are the few stories which are worth sharing and worth learning from. These are just the tips of an iceberg. According to our study, 90% of accidents are due to drivers carelessness and if we follow the traffic rules honestly then the chances of accidents can be reduced significantly.

http://www.pioneeredge.in/road-tell-stories-some-tragic-but-worth-learning-from/

❑

40

More People Live with Disability Today than Ever Before

– Dr Gaurav Sanjay,
Thursday, 03 December 2020

The International Day of Disabled Persons (IDDP) is held on December 3 every year. Every year, the celebration focuses on the different issues of disabled persons across the world. This is the day to spread awareness, analyse the problems related to disability, prevent the disability, treat the disability, enhance their quality of life and remove the social stigma towards them.

Over 1 billion of 7.8 billion people of the world's population, that is about 15 per cent have some form of disability. The National Sample Survey by the Government of India conducted from July to December 2018 showed that about 2.1 per cent of the total population is disabled in our country due to one or another problem. People with disabilities have the same health needs as physically fit people. Disability is thus, not just a health problem but rather a complex phenomenon reflecting the interaction between disabled person and the society in which he or she lives.

Being an orthopaedic surgeon, I will confine myself to disability related with locomotion and orthopaedic disabilities. I believe health of the limbs and locomotion are as important as health of the heart and the lungs. Whatever mankind has achieved by now is mainly due to locomotion, be it in war or in peace.

Our ancient Indian scriptures state that if there is birth, there is development, disease, degeneration and death. If we analyse the causes of disability, then all these four stages of life are vulnerable to disabilities depending upon the age of the individual. More people live with disabilities than ever before due to our ageing population, as well as improved medical treatment. Some of the causes are clubfoot, hip dislocation, rickets and polio infection in childhood and diabetic foot, Burger disease and Parkinsonism which needs surgery at later stages in old age patients. In my experience, road traffic accidents are the major cause of disability in current scenario in all ages.

Road traffic accidents are causing havoc and producing significant disability in the society. Almost five lakh people are encountering road traffic accident in which more than a fourth are dying and at least a fourth are being disabled for their whole life in spite of the best available treatment in our country. Nowadays, these road traffic accidents are high energy injuries which are fatal and involve multiple bones and sometimes multiple organs. In such scenario, it is very difficult in general to give functional results which match the pre-injury status in spite of the best possible treatment available in the country. If the road traffic accidents are treated well in time, then firstly the patient will not at all be disabled and even if he or she becomes disabled, in spite of the best possible treatment, then the level of disability will be significantly less.

Fractures of the spine (vertebral fracture) are producing serious lifelong permanent disability. Hundreds of thousands of people with paralysis of all four limbs (quadriplegic) or of both lower limbs (paraplegic) are bedridden with none or limited mobility in pathetic situations, in our country. This problem is more accentuated with the poor people in remote areas.

Another common cause of disability is infection which is preventable. The incidence of infection of bone and joint like septic arthritis or tubercular arthritis are getting reduced but the incidence of infection after surgery in patients with fractures after road traffic accidents is increasing proportionately despite taking all precautions before and after surgery including the use of antibiotic. People in general in our country are underestimating the consequences of infection. Bone infection is such a deep-seated infection that it takes years to control. If it is not controlled in time then these non-healing discharging sinuses can also transform into skin cancer which is usually treated with amputation.

Many senior orthopaedic surgeons had taught me that 40-50 years back, that amputation was almost a norm in emergency in the treatment of road traffic accidents. But now, the incidence of amputation has significantly reduced and it is now negligible in road traffic accident-related amputations though the number of amputations after diabetic foot, Burger's disease, atherosclerosis and other peripheral vascular disease has increased tremendously. This can be avoided if we become health conscious because most of the diseases are sedentary lifestyle disease. The awareness about late-stage complications of obesity, diabetes, hypertension, hypercholesterolemia, smoking and alcohol abuse too should be spread among the general public.

Any disability does not cause only physical loss but mental, financial and social loss as well. Here I would like to cite an example of a 39-year-old male presented with a painful deformed left forearm in 2010. He sustained a close fracture of both forearm bones 14 years back. It was treated with surgery which got complicated with infection. Since then, he had deformity and disability. He was separated from family because of disability. After surgery he has regained the full range of motion and is doing his car mechanic job.

Disability caused due to deformity can be reduced significantly with exercise, manipulation, orthosis and/or after undergoing various surgeries. I strongly believe that surgery has played an important role in the lives of persons with disabilities. Their lives have been changed significantly and they are not only developing or improving themselves but also contributing to the growth of society.

Therefore, like government and non-government organisations, I and my organisation are making the best efforts to spread awareness by organising free health camps, public awareness lectures and by writing such articles to reduce the disabilities and to make disabled people able through prompt surgical interventions. The deformities and disabilities caused due to any reason whatsoever should be corrected at the earliest. Hence, this author always advises the patient and the patient's family that if surgery is needed, then, the sooner the better because a plant can be straightened but not a fully grown tree.

http://www.pioneeredge.in/more-people-live-with-disabilities-today-than-ever-before/

❑

41

Eat Less Work More for Healthy and Happy Life

– Dr BKS Sanjay,
Wednesday, 30 December 2021

Happiness is defined in general as the state of ardour you feel on getting what you desire. Happiness is the state of wellbeing, the feeling of contentment and joy or in other words a pleasure with a positive emotional feeling. We all look for happiness in our all daily activities.

An American psychologist, Professor Daniel Gilbert said that human beings are the only animals which are able to think about their future. He pointed out that happiness is subjective. The brain does not differentiate between virtual and real stimulus to it. In both cases, the brain creates an interpretation of reality, it is so good and realistic that we don't grasp that it is only an interpretation. The emotional reactions are almost the same in both situations. There is a neurological reason for these mistakes in perception.

What makes us happy, colours all our perceptions of what happiness is. But even our own perceptions of what happiness is will change at different times in our lives. How do we know what will make us happy after 20 years? Human brain is set up to imagine the future quite well but not perfectly, and this difference is the one we often experience as what we thought would make us happy and what actually does.

What could make happiness more reliable? The answer to it is to find out how you will feel about a particular future course of action for example after achieving money, a career, a choice of city, spouse and children is to ask people who have already gone through the process and how they felt about it. As humans are creatures of belief, in our uniqueness we are naturally averse to relying on the experience of others. However, such a strategy, while not particularly exciting is the best available method to deliver us satisfaction in life and wellbeing. Whereas the happiness from relying purely on ourselves is only able to be stumbled on. Due to the way our brain works, our predictions of how we will feel in the future are not always accurate and that includes what will make us happy.

It is not only my experience, but I am sure it may be yours experience as well, that in India the health needs of most of the people are competing with the basic human needs like food, shelter and education. In India we are still realising the importance of good health, knowing very well that only a healthy person can complete any task easily and quickly and the government is still figuring out how to keep our fellow countrymen healthy. Hence, good health should be the highest priority of all mankind. But our experience shows that health which is an asset is being pushed to a secondary position on several occasions especially in poor and developing countries like India.

Irrespective of caste, creed, region and religion, everybody needs health, education and nutrition. They are interrelated and are the foundation stones for the growth of the individual as well as the nation. A sensible person will never kill the hen which gives him the golden egg but our society and the government is killing it. What is HEN here? H for Health, E for Education and N for Nutrition. The troika of health, education and nutrition is being driven in a haphazard and in an uncoordinated way in our country. The WHO asserts, following countless studies, that nations which invest in universal healthcare, make a sound investment in their human resource. The Ayushman Bharat health scheme 2018 introduced by the Government of India will be a milestone in improving the health care services to the poor and needy.

Whatever we achieve whether natural or manmade can be used and enjoyed only when we are healthy. Hence everybody should strive to remain as healthy as possible during their lifetime. How can we achieve good health is the important and pertinent question. We can be healthy only when we eat nutritious food. For better health, we should eat only when we are hungry and when we are eating then we should keep in mind to eat only a nutritious and balanced diet. We all should take a cup of green tea which is rich in antioxidants, eat a banana which is the best source of energy and magnesium, a lemon which is rich in vitamin C, an egg which contains almost all the important elements needed for the body, a green leafy vegetable which is rich in iron, calcium, magnesium and a fresh fruit which has fibre, folic acid and vitamin C.

An American professor of Harvard Medical School, Dr David Sinclair advised that we should eat plants that have been stressed and grow under harsh conditions. It is found that those who eat less and work more, live a healthy and a longer life. Everybody desires to be happy. Health and happiness are interrelated and directly proportionate to each other. If you are healthy, you are happy. If you are happy, you are healthy. Health is a fundamental need of any individual and everybody should be health conscious. For that we need food, which can be bought by money and that is earned by employment. The goal of the government should be providing the employment to all eligible people or help them set up small business which can generate money.

If we are healthy then we can achieve our desirable goal and enjoy our life, as it is said by an ancient Indian Rishi Bhrighu that we all are products of pleasure and to achieve pleasure is the goal of every individual. One should always take care of themselves in order to remain healthy. To achieve good health one can follow this acronym DEWS: Diet, Exercise, Work and Sleep. One believes that health is not only an asset but a resource too. It should be nurtured by all.

http://www.pioneeredge.in/eat-less-work-for-healthy-and-happy-life/

❑

42

Motor Vehicle (Amendment) Act 2019: A Fruitful Step Towards Road Safety

– Dr Gaurav Sanjay,
Monday, 18 January 2021

Road safety week in India 2021 was observed from January 11 to 17. During road safety week every year, thousands of government, non-government and private organisations take part in activities to highlight the consequences of road traffic accidents and spread the awareness to make our roads safer. Safety from road accidents focuses on the goal that people should safely drive their vehicles on the road, while also keeping in mind the safety of co-drivers and pedestrians. Road safety continues to be a major public health concern and a leading cause of death across the world, killing more than 1.35 million people annually in the world as reported in the Global Status report on Road Safety 2018. About 90 per cent of these casualties are taking place in the developing countries with 11 per cent being accounted for by India.

As per the report on road accidents in India 2019, the accident-related deaths in India in 2019 were 1,51,113 in number. National highways which comprise two per cent of total road network, continued to account for a disproportionate share—35 per cent of the deaths in 2019. The state highways which account for three per cent of the road length accounted for 25 per cent of these deaths. It seems the numbers of accidents are inversely proportional to the vehicular congestion on the roads and are attributed to factors like over speeding, drunken driving and using mobile phone on the national highways.

According to the Government of India data, under the category of Traffic Rule Violations, over speeding continued to be a major killer in 2019, accounting for 67 per cent of the persons killed followed by driving on the wrong side of the road which accounted for six per cent of the accident-related deaths.

Road traffic accidents are a global problem resulting in deaths, physical injuries, psychological problems and financial losses. These financial damages have immediate and long-term consequences on the victims and their families. Road traffic accidents are forcing the people into poverty and disability. Many times, we see in our society that poor individuals cannot pay for better treatment, sometimes this also leads to permanent disability. Many victims of road traffic accidents are the only bread earners of the family. Hence the family gets financially weak as well as mentally weak and they get helpless and sell their house, land, jewellery etc. It should be the duty not only of the government but the public, NGO and the other social organisations to spread the awareness that our society and nation is losing a lot in terms of human and financial resources. Our country is economically losing the worth of one to three per cent of the GDP on financial losses incurred due to road traffic accidents. The current GDP of our country is almost Rs 200 lakh crore.

Some of the reports which appeared in segments of the media in September 2019 showed to general public that the amended Motor Vehicle Act was against the general public because they have to pay more penalties if they violate the rules. It seems that the interpretation of most of the state governments of our country and of that of the public in general was that the sole purpose of government, to amend the law was to earn money from traffic rule violators. But contrary to that, the current Union Road Transport minister Nitin Gadkari had reiterated many times that the idea of increasing the penalty against the violators was not to earn the money but to save the life of many stakeholders who could be involved in road traffic accidents.

The number of accidents from April to June in 2020 (50,336) was 55 per cent less than the corresponding number in the previous year (1, 12,215). In terms of fatalities in road accidents, 56,288 people died in the first six months of 2020 compared to 79,678 in the same period the year before that, a drop of about 30 per cent. During April to June 2020, the number of fatalities in road accidents dropped by nearly 51 per cent compared to the same period in 2019, which is about 20,000 less fatalities. The above data has shown that the number of accidents had decreased significantly after the implementation of Motor Vehicles (Amendment) Act. The contribution of the COVID-19 lockdown cannot be ruled out too.

If we go according to the concept of penalty then penalty is imposed only on those who break the law and the idea of penalty is to deter the offender from breaking the law in the future and to send a message to the society that if anybody breaks the law, then he will be penalised. Punishment is defined in legal language as the infliction of some kind of pain or loss upon a person by an authority for a misdeed. The pain must be essential and not accidental to the infliction of punishment, according to the criteria of punishment principle. If punishment is not painful then how can it be punishment? Where is the question of punishment if we follow the law? The financial penalty works as a deterrent to an individual that the violator will not commit similar crime in future because of fear of similar or worse punishment in future. It also sends a message to the general public that they may get a similar punishment if they violate the law.

Almost 11 per cent of world fatalities are occurring in our country while India is having only one per cent of the vehicles of the world. A research reported by the author found that 90 per cent of these accidents occurred due to the driver's negligence. The main cause of accidents is the violation of the traffic rules. All of us should spread awareness to prevent these accidents because they have taken the form of an epidemic. The public should learn these traffic rules and should follow them; the government should teach the traffic rules and should enforce them to prevent the road traffic tragedies.

http://www.pioneeredge.in/more-people-live-with-disabilities-today-than-ever-before/

❑

43

Pvt & Govt Sectors Should Complement Each Other in Healthcare

– **Dr BKS Sanjay,**
Sunday, 07 February 2021

Noted orthopaedic surgeon and Padma Shri recipient expresses his views in Pioneer Talk

The private sector and government sector should not act as competitors but work to complement each other to provide quality healthcare services especially to the poor and downtrodden sections of the society. Prominent orthopaedic surgeon and recipient of Padma Shri, Dr BKS Sanjay said this while interacting with Paritosh Kimothi and Gajendra Singh Negi of The Pioneer during an online interaction on Saturday.

He opined that though healthcare is a cost intensive sector and needs a lot of capital, the private players should not extract disproportionate profits from their enterprise. "I personally believe that the health and education sectors should not be made as mainly business units and elements of service to the society should be there in any venture in these fields. The profit models should be made while keeping the motto of societal service at the central position," he said.

On the status of the health services in remote and mountainous areas, he said that different yardsticks should be there for the areas located in plains and mountains. On the vaccination drive for COVID-19 and misconception in people regarding vaccination, Dr Sanjay said that the vaccines are safe and there should be no doubt in mind of anyone about the vaccine. He said that dreaded diseases like smallpox and polio which had a very high mortality were eradicated only by the vaccines. On COVID-19 pandemic, Dr Sanjay said that the manner in which government doctors, healthcare workers, police and sanitation workers worked to combat the disease deserves praise from society.

Narrating his experience of holding free healthcare camps in different parts of the state especially in mountainous areas, Dr Sanjay said that he received tremendous love and support from people and never had any problems related to logistics and other issues. The orthopaedic surgeon who holds many records and finds mention in Guinness world book of records and the Limca book of records recalled that he removed a tumour as big as 16.5 kg from the thigh of a patient to save his life. He even had put a tumour affected portion of a bone of a patient in an autoclave to kill tumour cells and then transplanted it back to the patient's body, a feat which received wide acclaim in the medical fraternity.

He said that the innovations should be logical and the practitioner should have faith in his ability, knowledge and training to perform innovative tasks. On his campaign to follow road safety rules to prevent accidents, Dr Sanjay said, "Accidents not only break bones but also break families and relations". Road safety should be included in the curriculum of the schools. The wearing of helmets, tying seat belts and driving rules should be observed religiously by everyone," he said.

On maintaining bone health, the senior orthopaedic surgeon said that the calcium in the bones is like a bank balance which increases till the age of 30, remains constant till 50 years of age and then starts decreasing. He said that the children should be given calcium rich food for their bone health. Dr Sanjay said that physical activity is the key to maintaining good health and proper condition of bones.

When asked to comment on the ongoing controversy on promotion of 'mixopathy' and allowing the Ayurveda practitioners to perform some surgeries, Dr Sanjay said that every medicinal system has its qualities and uniqueness and they should be used for treating patients. He added that the expert of one field should not dabble in the domain of another as sometimes it can have disastrous consequences.

https://www.pioneeredge.in/pvt-govt-sectors-should-complement-each-other-in-healthcare-dr-sanjay/

❑

44

Education – The Way to Empowerment, Financial Independence & Nation Growth

– Dr BKS Sanjay,
Monday, 15 March 2021

Education is the prime mover for the growth of an individual, society and nation. It provides knowledge and skill. Behaviour, knowledge and skill are the tripod for mobility of an individual from the lower strata to the higher strata.

Money is an important resource to buy anything needed for the betterment of an individual which is best earned from employment. Education of an individual makes him employable. A life without a job leads to poverty. The uneducated, poor individuals are working mainly in the unorganised work hours they put in is not proportional to what they are earning and is not enough even to feed themselves and their family in the current scenario. They therefore, cannot or do not send their children to any school, forget about quality education and therefore the children are at high risk of entering the vicious trap of poverty and unemployment.

The current society is market driven. All employers desire to get a highly educated and skilled employee at the minimum salary within the current standard of wages. The situation of education and employment is better in urban areas than the rural and remote areas like the hilly and tribal areas. The situation is pathetic in some regions as seen in many mass media reports now and then. I must say that education is not only the need of an individual, a society or a nation but it is needed for the growth of whole mankind. Whatever the human race has achieved, education has played an important role for the progress of mankind from stone-age to the modern age.

The epics and holy books like the Ramayana, Bhagavad Gita, Mahabharata, Quran, Bible and many more are the gifts to mankind by the people who had been formally or informally educated by their teachers. Now, I would like to confine myself to the problems related to education. There are many mismatches in the field of education not only in our country but in many countries around the world. There are not enough schools, or if there are schools then there are not enough teachers and if there are teachers then many are mostly untrained. Sometimes there are good schools, good teachers but the students do not enough money to pay for the inflated fees of these schools. One feels that the quality of the work depends upon the quality of workers this is all the more important in education particularly for the teachers.

The situation is not bad in India as in many Africans countries where a third to a half of children are still uneducated and the most affected among them is the girl child. In Yemen, a country in the Middle East, more than 80 per cent of the girls have never gone to school. Health, education and nutrition are the basic interrelated needs of every individual

Irrespective of any distinctions. The international community also recognised that education is essential for the success of all 17 United Nations Sustainable Development Goals. Health and education should not work on the principle of commerce because even the rich people cannot live comfortably and peacefully if they lack this trio, then imagine how the poor people can live without these three essential needs.

Education should be the primary goal of every nation. The UN lists the right to education in the universal declaration of human rights. Getting a proper education is the birth right of everyone and restricting education is a crime. Education plays a very important role in our life. Hence in order to live a better and peaceful life we need to be educated. It is education which broadens our horizon. It transforms us completely by changing our mind and thoughts, thereby changing our deeds.

Whatever we are, similar or different it is the education which has brought changes in us. A person having good education becomes a good citizen for the society and we all reap the fruits of good and proper education. As our country has a lot of diversity in geography, ethnicity, caste, creed, language and religion, I strongly believe that it is the education which has united this diverse nation and will further play an important role to keep it united. If we all get the similar, high quality basic education then, we all will work in a synchronous way for the common goal of building our nation.

John Dewey, an American educationist said whatever role food and reproduction has in the existence of physical life of humans, a similar role is that of education in their social life. The growth of the society is not only because of physical looseness of the people but also because of similarity of the thoughts. Educated people work along common lines, with a common spirit and with a common aim, which leads to growing unity. On the other hand, people having different education have differences in motive, spirit and in deeds.

There are many people in India who are poor and uneducated. There are many social, financial and political problems in our country but most of them can be sorted out with the proper quality education and employment. The secret of success of any individual lies in the application of behaviour, knowledge and skill. Whatever we are today, me as an author and you as a reader, the credit goes to education. Education has brought tremendous change since independence in our country and I am sure whatever is left can be achieved or changed with good quality education.

https://pioneeredge.in/education-the-way-to-emloyment-financial-independence-national-growth/

❑

45

The Challenges Faced in Eradication of Tuberculosis

– Dr Gaurav Sanjay,
Wednesday, 24 March 2021

World Tuberculosis Day is held every year on March 24 with the aim of making the common man aware of the serious consequences of tuberculosis (TB) and to try to gather new ideas and scientific developments on how to make the world TB free. According to the data of 2018, about one crore people are infected with TB worldwide, in which about one and a half lakh people die in India every year.

India is a developing nation and it has been able to eradicate diseases such as smallpox and polio while controlling malaria and cholera to a large extent. But in the same way, there has not been as much success in preventing TB infection as was expected after the major success of eradicating polio. For the elimination of TB in India, in March 2017, Prime Minister Narendra Modi had announced a national strategic plan 2017-2025 set out to eliminate TB by 2025, stating that it requires new thinking and innovative ideas on how TB can be eradicated.

According to the World Health Organisation, the definition of abolition means that the number of TB patients in a population of one lakh people should be less than one person, whereas, the number of TB patients in India is 193 per lakh. A quarter of the world's TB patients live in India-according to a 2018 report, the number of total TB patients were about 26,90,000. The problem faced in primordial prevention of TB is not only one but many hurdles are there as in India as about one-fifth of the country is still living below the poverty line-finding it difficult to eat food two times a day. The second reason is the unhygienic conditions for which the Government of India is running a cleanliness campaign but the results of which are not yet as required.

The third reason is the lack of proper and adequate homes for the whole population. Here I would like to tell you that TB could be a fatal disease if it is not treated well in time. The TB bacteria are spread from one person to another by sneezing, coughing and touching with infected hands. In cities where there are densely populated areas or houses where many people are residing, especially in the slums of big cities, all these people are more likely to have TB infection.

After assessing all these reasons, if we think about the infection and prevention of TB, then the increasing population in the country is one of the root factors because the increasing population is reducing the proportion of all resources. If a law is enacted to curb the population it will give good results for the entire population and it will not only be useful in the prevention of TB but also in improving the economic, social and political standards of the entire country.

As an orthopaedic surgeon here, I would also like to mention that the primary TB infection is either in the lungs, in the gut or in the neck lymph nodes. TB infection in the bone or the joint is secondary infection. The incidence of bone and joint TB has reduced significantly compared to the past because today the disease is detected and diagnosed early and the treatment is much more effective than 50 years ago.

It is common perception that TB infects mainly poor people but it is not so. It is infecting rich and affluent people too. The cost of the TB treatment may not be a problem for the rich people but it is becoming very difficult for the poor patients to get treatment for prolonged time as it is required especially in drug resistant TB. Many poor patients ignore the doctor's advice and do not take the full course of prescribed treatment and leave the treatment in the middle, due to which the number of drug resistant TB cases is increasing day by day.

India is facing the highest burden of drug resistant (DR) TB worldwide. If we look deeply at the problem of MDR, it is a big problem in our country though the government is giving free medicines in government hospitals. In spite of all this, these patients are either borrowing money or selling their property to treat it especially in surgical and complex TB cases. Drug resistance is a formidable obstacle to TB care and prevention globally, making it harder and longer to treat, often with poorer outcomes for patients. It becomes somewhat difficult to treat TB infection, especially when it is MDR (Multi Drug Resistant), XDR (Extensively Drug Resistant), TDR (Total Drug Resistant) Tuberculosis in these patients. TDR TB is defined as a form in which none of the drugs available till date is effective against it.

I believe that lack of awareness about TB still exists today, which is making it very difficult for the society and country to control TB. The principle of prevention is better than cure should be understood very well in order to prevent any infection but particularly in case of TB infection. In the end, I would like to say that TB is a treatable disease with cheap and very effective drugs available. Apart from medicines, TB patients require nutritious diet, cleanliness and regular exercise. If the patients take medicines as prescribed and for the duration advised, the infection of TB can be cured. The TB treatment should not be discontinued midway without appropriate medical advice. If there are any side effects of the Anti-Tubercular Drugs, then the advice of a trained doctor should be taken and followed accordingly.

http://www.pioneeredge.in/the-challenges-faced-in-eradication-of-tuberculosis/

❑

46

Health Is Not Only An Asset But Also A Resource Which Must Be Nurtured

– Dr BKS Sanjay,
Wednesday, 7 April 2022

The World Health Day is commemorated on April 7 each year. The occasion is aimed at creating awareness of a specific health theme to highlight a priority area of concern for the WHO. This year WHO theme is to build a fairer, healthier world.

The troika of Health, Education and Nutrition (HEN) are the basic pillars of development and it is unfortunate that both the government and society are ignoring these basic principles, hence the country is paying a heavy price. Health is not only an asset but also a resource which must be nurtured. The people associated with this sector should not work with the sole purpose of commercial benefit, their action should be based on human ethos.

Health, as defined by WHO is a state of complete physical, mental and social wellbeing and not merely the absence of disease or infirmity. Every person has a desire to be happy and I believe that only healthy person can be a happy. A healthy person can do not only his work but the work of others as well. The ability of any healthy person will be higher than the unhealthy person in every way.

Stress is the new health problem—around 70 per cent of diseases are stress related. Stress has been reported as a cause not only of diabetes, hypertension, heart disease and many musculoskeletal problems but also cancer. Breathing exercise and meditation techniques have been proven to reduce stress by many bio feedback studies. The WHO has reported that the worldwide burden of musculoskeletal problems is increasing day by day.

Most of these are self-created which are caused due to change in lifestyle. It is not difficult to change the lifestyle, it needs a change of mind set. The habit of alcohol, smoking and sedentary lifestyle is working as a fuel in the fire. If an individual can abstain from habits of alcohol, smoking and the sedentary work then the result will be much better. Abstaining from these three can result in better health. If one does his or her household work and avoids sedentary work, takes balanced diet and does regular yoga exercise and meditation then there is fair chance that one will lead a healthy and happy life.

If we want change in our self then we should learn the Buddhist philosophy about our life being shaped by our mind—we become what we think. As animals, humans are basically creatures of their environment- humans change their action according to the consequences of their and others' behaviour. As far as health is concerned, personal and social responsibility can be found only with behavioural changes. A clinical research conducted by me revealed that 90 per cent of the road traffic accidents occurred due to the driver's negligence. The main cause of accidents in India is overtaking, over speeding, drunken driving and recently the use of mobile phone while driving. All these are behavioural problems.

Currently, road traffic injuries are the main cause of deformity and disability in our country. The numbers of road injuries are increasing day by day. According to WHO report there are five lakh road traffic accidents in India every year. Out of them almost 1.5 lakh people are killed and a similar number of patients end up with deformity and disability in spite of the best available treatment in current health scenario.

I think that aggression of the road is a common scenario on the Indian roads and it seems that we take pride in breaking the traffic rules while travelling on the roads. We should change our mind set and take pride while following the law. Many psychological studies have shown that the brain does not differentiate between the right or wrong action, but, any action which you like can give you the same kick and adrenaline rush whether it is right or wrong in other words lawful or unlawful.

In my opinion, it is the responsibility of the society and the nation that we should be taught what is right and what is wrong in childhood. Had we all learnt the habit of following the law in childhood then things would have been different in India today as it rightly said that you are what your habits are. An American educationist Horace Mann said that "a former is worth a thousand reformers". The concept of good health should be given in the childhood rather than in the later stages of life.

Infection is another major problem. The country was already facing many infections existing for centuries in our country like malaria, TB and others bacterial or viral infections. The recent COVID-19 pandemic has exposed not only our health system but the mindset of the public too. People are still not giving importance to primordial prevention of infection even after experiencing the COVID pandemic. Whenever the people forget to follow the precautionary measures, these incidences of infection have increased as seen in the resurgence of COVID.

It seems that COVID infection came under control and everyone was very happy that the vaccination will eliminate the infection but in the last week the number of new cases of COVID-19 surged over one lakh cases and the number is increasing at an alarming rate. It has been scientifically proven that the 50 per cent of the lung infection and 25 per cent of the gut infections can be reduced just by washing the hands properly. Here I would like to emphasise that we all should take precautions to prevent infection and take steps to improve the immunity in case of any infection.

Sleep is a fundamental need of every living being just like eating. No person can do without sleep for more than 48 hours. The former prime minister of Britain, Harold Wilson has even said that the prime minister who succeeds, is the one who sleeps for eight hours at his will. Those who do more work have a better sleep cycle, those who do not work as much suffer from insomnia. The lack of sleep and the influence of liquor are the main reasons why night accidents are mostly fatal.

https://pioneeredge.in/Health-is-not-only-an-asset-but-also-a-resource-which-must-be-nurtured/

❑

47

On Benefits of Reading Books – the All - Weather Friends

– Dr BKS Sanjay,
Friday, 23 April 2021

The World Book and Copyright Day is celebrated every year on April 23 to promote the reading of books. Events taken place each year across the world to recognise the importance of books—a link between the past and the future, a bridge between generations and across cultures.

British philosopher Sir Roger Scranton wrote that people with depression feel isolated and that a book can sometime decrease it. A study found that a session of 30 minutes of reading a book lowers your blood pressure, heart rate and psychological distress. It is also established that the beneficial effect of reading books equals to that of yoga and humour. Researchers at Mayo Clinic, USA advise their patients to inculcate reading as part of regular pre-sleep routine. For better results, one should choose print book rather than reading on a screen / tablet/ mobile.

Now, the question is what should you be reading? The answer is, whatever you like and whatever book you can get in your hands. It is especially important for children to read as much as possible because the effects of reading are cumulative. The parents and teachers should set the examples so that children make a habit of reading which enhances their knowledge. The more the knowledge they have, the better they are equipped to deal the challenges they will face. Reading books can help them to learn from masters who have already been through certain situations and also learn how to tackle them. Books are a good way to educate them.

As exercise helps your body to stay healthy and fit, books keep your brain fit. Character is formed from childhood and books play an important role. Reading a book can change your thinking process and ultimately can bring changes in you. Esko Valtaoja had said, you are what you read.

I believe that the origin of language must have occurred only when humans were born because life cannot be developed, or even be maintained without communication with others. A language is needed for communication. Languages and scripts probably were developed millions of years ago, but the making of books in any form is a comparatively modern concept if compared to origin of human civilisation. Knowledge has been passed from one generation to the next through books.

The importance of propagation of knowledge was well understood by our forefathers, so they wrote their knowledge and experience and compiled them in the form of books and also kept it safe so that future generations can gain that knowledge themselves and spread it to others.

Preservation of the books and construction of the libraries had been a part of Indian society since centuries ago. The ruins of universities of Nalanda near Rajgir, Vikramshila near Bhagalpur in Bihar and Takshashila near Islamabad, Pakistan and their grand libraries are the testimony of the past. Nalanda University, was one of the oldest universities in the world in the 5th century. There were 10,000 students, 2,000 teachers and a nine-storey grand library which had more than three lakh books covering almost all subjects. Nalanda and Vikramshila universities were destroyed by invader Bakhtiyar Khilji in 1200 CE and Takshashila by the Huns in 500 CE. Takshashila was designated as a UNESCO World Heritage Site in 1980. The ancient Nalanda University has been resurrected by Government of India, with an act passed by the Parliament in 2014.

There had been hundreds of examples of Rishi, Munis, poets and courtiers who had preserved books, their knowledge and experience for centuries. These books had been spreading that knowledge and experience to only a few in the ancient time but now, the masses are being benefited. The books written and kept in libraries by these intellectuals has been the base on which the ancient Indian was given the privilege of Vishwa Guru. It is the contribution of these books and the libraries that not only Indians but the whole world has gained the knowledge and is being able to use it.

The importance of the books and the libraries had been understood very well by the Indians in past and that is the reason that you can see smaller or bigger libraries in almost every small or big cities of our country even now a days. This is the era of digital technology and the impact of it is being seen clearly. There has been decrease in interest in printed books with the advent of e-books and electronic devices. But I believe that the books will always exist in some form and will never disappear completely. Cicero once said, a room without books is like a body without a soul.

The role of books is not hidden from anyone, in the transformation of the human civilisation the role of books has been important in the formation and flourishing of civilisations of the world. BR Ambedkar had said that cultivation of mind should be the ultimate aim of human existence. If we talk about India, Vedas, Purana, Ramayana, Mahabharata, Gita, Quran, Bible, Guru Granth Sahib, Tattvarthasutra, Tripitaka and many more scriptures are the books which have transformed the ideology of the whole society not in only in ancient times but in current time as well. Books work as a medium between the writer and the reader.

The English writer Stevenson and Hindi writer Rahul Sankrityayan were known to abandon the books after reading them, irrespective of the cost of the book. Both believed not to keep the burden of books and knowledge but to give to the others. Whosoever gets the book, he will read it and will be benefited. Having books and reading them shows your love for them, but after reading it and then giving it to someone else further increase your love for that book.

The habit of keeping the book is good, reading books is better and giving it to someone else after reading is the best. The habit of sharing books will make you a medium of sharing knowledge. Whatever is written in books, it is written very thoughtfully. Make a habit of buying, reading, sharing and gifting books so that you will inspire others to do so. Romain Rolland once said that the friend who understands you, creates you. I have gone through hundreds of books and the books have contributed a lot in shaping my life. I believe that books are one's earnest friends, so love them.

https://pioneeredge.in/On-benefits-of-reading-books-the-all-weather-friends/

❑

48

Hand Hygiene – A Cheap, Simple and Effective Means to Prevent Varied Infections

– Dr Gaurav Sanjay,
Wednesday, 05 May 2021

The WHO has declared May 5 as Hand Hygiene Day. This year the theme of world hygiene day is "seconds save lives-clean your hands". It is the day to raise awareness on making soap and water available globally especially in public places. The patients and their family members are encouraged to join health workers in their effort to practice good hand hygiene.

According to WHO, every year millions of patients around the world are dying due to infection. More than half of the infections can be prevented by proper cleaning of the hands specially before eating food, after using the toilet and before and after touching the patient. Hand hygiene is the act of cleaning the hands with water and soap or any other cleaning agent. The purpose of cleaning the hands is to clean the soil, dirt and/or pathogens and chemicals stuck to the skin which can make us and others ill. Hand hygiene is very important for food handlers, medical staff and the patients too.

The importance of hand hygiene has been known in Indian culture for centuries, therefore, there had been arrangement for washing the hands and feet at homes and religious places. The importance of hand hygiene has been emphasised vigorously worldwide by government and non-governmental organisations during the COVID-19 pandemic. Practice of hand hygiene is more relevant in the current scenario when more than 150 million have been infected and more than three million people have died worldwide. More than 18 million have been infected and more than 2,00,000 have died in India as of today due to COVID-19 viral infection. The COVID pandemic has elicited tremendous attention on hand hygiene which has gained social and political recognition worldwide during this period.

There are some problems with the practice of hand hygiene like availability of continuous running clean water and a cleansing agent. The adequate infrastructure for hand hygiene should be provided and maintained at the all-public places like railway stations, bus stands, religious places, schools and hospitals.

The habit of hand hygiene should be inculcated in homes and in schools. It should be an essential part of the primary education curriculum. Once any habit is formed it is difficult to change. The importance of hand hygiene and technique of hand washing should be taught to children in simple words and simple way. If the cleaning of hands is done in a group and in a play mode, then, children will acquire it faster.

The quality of care and patient safety is an important aspect of the health care services. Infection is detrimental to good health and especially after surgery. Hospital Acquired Infections (HAI) are the life threatening infections which are causing significant human and financial loss. Hundreds of thousands of people are dying worldwide from hospital acquired infection. Sadly, this number is many times more in developing and poor countries including India. Nearly 80 per cent of your exposures to germs occurs through touch. Most of the HAI are commonly transmitted when hospital staff become complacent and do not practice correct hand hygiene regularly. Since medical staff moves from patient to patient, they themselves serve as a carrier for spreading pathogens.

Essentially, the staff members act as a vector. About five per cent of patients admitted to hospitals in the United States develop hospital acquired infection and five per cent (one lakh) of them die each year. Considering the socioeconomic conditions in our country, the situation could be worse. A scientific review of studies performed also revealed that hospital acquired infection are on rise in our country. Sometimes it becomes impossible to control it in spite of the best efforts of all stakeholders (patient, family, doctor and staff). The age-old dictum of "prevention is better than cure" holds true in case of HAI and it should be the endeavour of all stakeholders to tackle the menace of HAI. Hand hygiene is of paramount importance to prevent hospital infection.

Overcrowding in patient's room and poor personal hygiene of patient and medical personnel are two important causes of infection. Isolation and personal hygiene of the patient and staff have been proven to prevent infection and ultimately to reduce morbidity, mortality and healthcare cost. It is best to avoid visiting hospitals except when absolutely necessary to prevent infection. The hospitals are also social organisations. Kindly cooperate for your benefit and that of the hospital, society and nation. At any time only authorised person should visit the patient. Visitors should be only from immediate family and close friends, who play an important role in taking decision for the treatment.

The habit of hand washing will contribute a lot to the personal hygiene while also serving society because humans learn by copying each other, especially in the bigger organisations like schools and hospitals. Good hand washing with soap before eating and after using the toilet can save more lives than any single vaccine or medical intervention. Hand hygiene and hand washing can play an important and critical role in prevention and control of infection and to achieve universal health coverage as envisaged by World Health Organisation. This year WHO calls on health workers and facilities to achieve effective hand hygiene action at the point of care. The point of care refers to the place three elements come together- the patient, the health care worker and care or treatment involving contact with the patient and their soundings. There are five specific moments- before touching the patient, before clean/ aseptic procedure, after body fluid exposure/ risk, after touching the patient and after touching patient's surroundings.

Hand hygiene is one of the most effective actions to reduce the spread of COVID-19 virus. The simple habit of hand washing will not only increase the longevity of an individual but will also improve the quality of life of an individual. When we, as an individual will be healthy, then our family, society and nation will be healthier and happier.

https://pioneeredge.in/Hand-hygiene-a-cheap-simple-&-effective-means-to-prevent-varied- infections/

❑

49

COVID Pandemic: An Opportunity to Augment Health Services in India

– Dr BKS Sanjay,
Monday, 10 May 2021

As we know if one is divided by more than one, then the quotient will be less than one. This applies to all our resources as well. This message should be ingrained in the citizen's mind that overpopulation is causing depletion of all natural and manmade resources all over the world.

Overpopulation in India is an ongoing problem which is becoming a big hurdle in the pace of all kind of developments. Overpopulation and overcrowding in any area are known to cause poor sanitation, poor personal hygiene and improper ventilation. In such an environment, if an infective agent is too virulent, then the chances of the spread of infection increase proportionately.

The common observation is that the incidence of spread of COVID-19 infection is more in the urban areas than the rural areas. Urban metropolitan cities like Mumbai, Pune, Chennai and Delhi have been hotspots for the COVID-19 infection. Though the metropolitan cities have facilities than the rest of India but still, they are not proportionately enough to even cater the current population of these cities. Due to the unevenly distributed health services in India particularly, the rural areas, there is an influx of these patients into metro cities for their medical care especially in critical condition like COVID-19 infection. This exponential influx is further compromising the already compromised health services in these metropolitan cities.

There have been the reports in the mass media that in some cases the whole family has succumbed to COVID-19 infection. The COVID-19 strains are sometimes so virulent and contagious that even if one family member is infected then he may have the potential to infect the whole family. This problem becomes more so in a joint family which is still a common tradition in our country.

The world data shows that five per cent of the population of any country is being infected and one to two per cent of them die due to COVID-19. The pandemic has exposed our poor preparedness for disaster management. By April 27, 2021 more than 180 lakh people were COVID positive and nearly 2 lakh people had already died in India. I think many more are infected in our country but they are not getting tested due to various reasons like ignorance, poverty and fear of isolation.

On analysing the currently available data of COVID-19 pandemic in India, the statistics shows that the current population is almost 140 crores. Out of this, if five per cent are getting infected it means almost 7.5 crore population and 15 per cent of them– nearly one crore needs some sort of supportive treatment in the hospital. Out of seven crore infected patients five per cent- almost 3.5 lakh people will need the ICU services.

The new wave of the COVID-19 pandemic has exposed our poor infrastructure like non-availability of general bed, oxygen and non-availability of ICU beds which are the just the tip of the iceberg. A country may be able to import or arrange a number of ventilators but how can we have instant supply of manpower like intensivists, nurses, ICU technicians and other paramedical staff which is not possible to generate overnight.

If we want to give all the services to the needy people then we have to develop a long-term strategy to have the enough manpower and infrastructure so that the supply chain can be maintained smoothly. The data obtained from the National Statistical Office (NSO) 75th Round Report estimated that India has approximately 19 lakh hospital beds, 95,000 ICU beds and 48,000 ventilators. That means five per cent of the beds are allocated to the ICU ventilators. Ventilators are the main vital support for critically ill patients.

Mapping and training of the medical and paramedical staff to run the ICUs needs to be done. Currently, there are not enough ICU beds. So the number of trained medical and paramedical staff has been limited. Many private doctors and hospitals are having the capacity to buy the ventilators and other machines needed for the ICU patients at the snap of the fingers. But can they arrange or appoint medical or paramedical staff with that ease? Surely not. Our policy makers should make future policy, a stringent plan to deal with COVID-19 pandemic and other medical problems our country may face in near future with a vision to deal with them in a better way to avoid the current chaos we all are in.

As a doctor, I know that the people working in the health sector be it physician, surgeon or nurses or paramedical staff are relatively more knowledgeable and more skilled than other employees. Here I would like to suggest the government and the private hospitals to take the initiative to train the existing health workers with some short-term training to run the ventilators and manage the patients at time of disaster and augment the current health services.

However, one must understand that overpopulation is root cause of all ills in India. I feel awareness about the consequences of overpopulation needs to be reemphasised to the public, influential policy makers and religious preachers to bring grassroots changes in the way we think about procreation. As we know if one is divided by more than one, then the quotient will be less than one. This applies to all our resources as well. This message should be ingrained in the citizen's mind that overpopulation is causing depletion of all natural and manmade resources all over the world.

The recent emergence of COVID-19 pandemic has further exposed not only the health related problems but other non-health related problems too. The second surge of COVID-19 pandemic is giving nightmares to the administration to contain the COVID-19 infection. It seems that the bubble has burst and state governments are forced to keep people at home by enforcing lockdown which itself is not the cure.

The concept of one baby norm is good to control overpopulation in the subsequent generations but the drawback with one baby principle is that population will be half in each generation ultimately the population goes in negative growth. The two-baby norm per couple-preferably a girl and a boy- if enacted is sustainable and a very effective way of curbing the population and maintaining the sex ratio. As our government's policy to control the population is based on the concept of voluntary family planning, it has not given the results needed to curb the growth of the population. Our Prime Minister should take an initiative to work in this direction and once again prove the Indian dictum of "Vasudhaiva Kutumbhakam" which means the whole world is a family.

https://pioneeredge.in/Covid-pandemic-an-opportunity-to-augment-health-services-in-India/

❑

50

Greater Risks from Tobacco Use During COVID-19 Pandemic

– Dr Gaurav Sanjay,
Monday, 31 May 2021

Each year World No Tobacco Day is observed on May 31. This day serves as a reminder to raise awareness about the dangers of smoking and to encourage smokers to quit the habit of smoking around the world. The habits of smoking and chewing tobacco have been prevalent in the society since hundreds of years, across all civilisations and cultures in different forms. Smoking, dhumapana (literally "drinking smoke"), has been practiced for at least 2,000 years in India and has been first mentioned in Atharvaveda.

Although, the overall smoking rate worldwide has decreased but the number of smokers has increased due to increased population. There are more than a billion smokers worldwide, over 80 per cent of them live in developing countries. According to WHO, India is home to 120 million that is 12 per cent of the world's smokers and more than 10 million of them die each year due to tobacco consumption. Another global adult tobacco survey India (India GATS2) showed that India is home to over 27 crore tobacco users. Globally it is the second largest producer and consumer of tobacco products. This is preventable and can be prevented only with the effort of both government and society.

The ill effects of tobacco are known to cause respiratory disorders such as COPD, oral and lung cancers. Smoking precipitates hypertension and cardiac problems. The negative impact of tobacco smoking on health are well-established and known to the society. There is a statutory warning on each pack of cigarette or tobacco pouch reminding the consumer the negative effects of smoking.

COVID-19 virus usually affects the respiratory system. Think of your respiratory tract as an upside-down tree. The trunk is your trachea, or windpipe. It splits into smaller and smaller branches in your lungs. At the end of each branch are tiny air sacs called alveoli. This is where oxygen goes into your blood and carbon dioxide comes out. The novel coronavirus can infect the upper or lower part of your respiratory tract. If it travels down your airways, the lining can become irritated and inflamed. In some cases, the infection can reach all the way down into your alveoli.

COVID-19 is a still a new condition and scientists are learning more every day about what it can do to your lungs. They believe that the effects on your body are similar to those of two other coronavirus diseases, severe acute respiratory syndrome (SARS) and Middle East Respiratory Syndrome (MERS). As the infection travels in your respiratory tract, your immune system fights back. Your lungs and airways swell and become inflamed. This can start in one part of your lung and spread. About 80 per cent people who have COVID get mild to moderate symptoms. You may have a dry cough or a sore throat. Some people have pneumonia, a lung infection in which the alveoli are inflamed.

There are not many scientific research papers on the effect of smoking on the COVID-19 infection. A review of literature has revealed that 34 peer review studies have shown that smokers constituted 1.4 to 18.5 per cent of the hospitalised adults. In another study it was found that a there is a statistically significant association between smoking and severity of COVID-19 cases. The available evidence suggests that even passive smoke exposure is harmful.

Tobacco smoking is known to increase the heart rate and blood pressure and increase of carbon mono oxide level in the blood stream. WHO recommends quitting tobacco use in every way and suggests that within 20 minutes of quitting the elevated heart rate and blood pressure drops, within three months of quitting, blood circulation improves and lung function increases and after 3-9 months coughing and shortness of breath distress improves. Quitting will not save the patients but also their loved ones, especially children from exposure to passive smoking. Tobacco is a known risk factor to predispose to infection like TB of lungs and cancer of oral cavity and the lungs.

In addition to that nicotine can causes hypertension, heart failure, cancer and blindness. The habit of smoking is injurious to health. Considering the role of smoking which increased the severity of illness in COVID the Ministry of Health and Welfare, Government of India issued a warning on May 11, 2020 against the use of any tobacco products during COVID-19 pandemic and took measures to reduce tobacco use given its potential to increase likelihood of virus infection while exhaling respirators droplets, spitting and sharing of the bidi or cigarette etc.

The COVID-19 pandemic is an opportunity to increase awareness to quit tobacco use in every form. Tobacco contains nicotine which is responsible for constriction of peripheral arteries which leads to gangrene usually of the limbs. A noted Indian cardiologist, emphasised in a recent webinar that hypertension, COVID-19 and tobacco are a deadly triad. The author has an experience of treating many patients of peripheral vascular disease and gangrene and in these patients whenever there is a need of painkillers, they do not give them as much relief as to the general populations.

Smoking itself decrease the tolerance of pain and nicotine blunts the effect of painkillers. This becomes a challenge especially after any surgery in these patients. The management of pain in these patients becomes difficult because pain is usually ischaemic and these patients are usually advised to stop smoking. As is known, smoking is an addiction and because of that smokers suffer physiological and psychological impacts on the body and brain. The problem should be understood not only by the patient and the treating team but the family as well.

Any kind of tobacco consumption predisposes a person to many diseases. The habit of smoking and chewing tobacco usually starts in teenage. Hence, there should be strict ban of tobacco sale in or around schools and others education institutes. All forms of advertisement about tobacco sale should be prohibited in mass media, merely statuary warning that smoking is injurious to health is not enough in cases of children and people those who are ignorant and illiterate.

https://pioneeredge.in/greater-risks-from-tobacco-use-during-covid-19-pandemic/amp/

❑

51

Deformity & Disability Correction – the Sooner, the Better

– Dr BKS Sanjay,
Monday, 21 June 2021

Disability is any condition of the body or mind that makes it more difficult for the person with the condition to do certain activities and interact with the world around them. According to WHO, disability has many dimensions, such as impairment (loss of body part), limitation of activity (walking) and restrictions in participation (any kind of social restriction). Over one billion of the 7.8 billion world's population- about 15 per cent have some form of disability. The National Sample Survey conducted by the Government of India from July to December 2018 showed that about 2.1 per cent of the total population is disabled in our country.

Being an orthopaedic surgeon, I will confine myself to orthopaedic disabilities which are defined as loss of motion in which there is disability of the bones, joints or muscles leading to substantial restriction of movement of the limbs. People with disabilities have the same health needs as physically fit people. Disability is thus, not just a health problem but rather a complex phenomenon, reflecting the interaction between disabled person and the society in which he or she lives.

Locomotor disability means problem in moving from one place to another, that is, disability in the legs. According to the 2011 census, 26.8 million population was disabled and 20.3 per cent had movement disability. I believe health of the limbs is as important as that of the health of the heart and the lungs. Whatever mankind has achieved so far is mainly due to locomotion, be it in war or in peace, on earth or beyond. Our ancient Indian scriptures state that, if there is birth, there is development, degeneration, disease and death. If we analyse the causes of disability, then all these stages of life are vulnerable to disabilities depending upon the age of the individual.

Polio, cerebral palsy (CP) and club foot in childhood are the main causes of disability in India. India is polio free since March 2014 that means there are no new cases of polio. But there are lakhs of old polio cases which are causing major social and other problems to the patients and the nation. The main cause of disability in polio is due to muscular paralysis which has to be corrected during surgery. Cerebral palsy is one disability which can be prevented with timely intervention of medical advice during the perinatal period.

The road traffic accidents have become an epidemic in our country, causing havoc and producing significant disability in the society. Almost five lakh people are encountering road traffic accidents in which more than a fourth are dying and at least a fourth are being disabled for their whole life in spite of the best available treatment in the current scenario in our country. Nowadays, these road traffic accidents are high energy injuries which are fatal and involve multiple bones and sometimes multiple organs. In such a scenario, it is very difficult in general to give functional results which match the pre-injury status.

The fracture of the shaft of the long bones are not as dangerous as the fracture of the joints because invariably they result in premature degenerative arthritis. The back bone is considered to be the benchmark of anything. If the back bone is injured then the body below that injury becomes paralysed. There has been a lot of progress in surgical tools, technology and techniques but even then, once the spinal cord is transacted then there is no possibility of repair, regeneration and recovery. This usually leads to serious lifelong permanent disability.

Lakhs of people suffering from paralysis of all four limbs (quadriplegic) or of both lower limbs (paraplegic) are living in a pathetic situation on the bed with no or limited mobility in our country. This problem is more accentuated with poor people, especially in remote areas. Another common cause of disability is bacterial infection which is mostly preventable. Infection can occur at any age. The incidence of infection of bone and joint like septic arthritis or tubercular arthritis is getting reduced but the incidence of postoperative infection in patients with fractures after road traffic accidents is increasing proportionately in spite of taking all precautions before and after surgery including generous use of antibiotics.

The management of open fracture is a challenging problem. These fractures may get complicated after surgery resulting in early infection, mal union or non-union. People in general in our country are underestimating the consequences of infection. The bone infection is such a deep-seated infection that it takes years to control. If it is not controlled in time then these non-healing discharging sinuses can also have cancerous transformation in select group of patients which is usually treated with amputation.

The incidence of amputation has significantly reduced and is nearly negligible in road traffic accident-related amputations. But the numbers of amputations in diabetic foot, Berger's disease, atherosclerosis (narrowing of arteries) and other peripheral vascular disease have increased tremendously in recent times. This can be avoided if we become health conscious because most of these diseases are a result of a sedentary lifestyle. The awareness about late-stage complications of obesity, diabetes, hypertension, hypercholesterolemia, smoking and alcohol abuse too should be spread among the general public.

Anything which causes irreparable damage to bone, muscle, nerve, artery, even skin can lead to amputation which can give rise to serious disability. Impact of disability depends upon the age of the individual for example if the child is affected or disabled then his educational development will suffer while if an adult is affected then his employment is affected and if older people are affected then they usually suffer from social and mental problems.

Any disability, not only results in physical loss but mental, financial and social loss as well. Disability caused due to deformity can be reduced significantly with exercise, manipulation and orthosis and/or after undergoing various surgeries. I strongly believe that surgery has played an important role in the lives of persons with disabilities. Only an hour-long, well-done surgery in these disabled people has changed their lives significantly and they are not only developing or improving themselves but also contributing to the growth of society and nation.

The impact of disability increases proportionately with the time laps of correction. Governments, non-governmental organisations and society should strive to prevent disability of any kind and if it happens then it should be treated as early as possible. Therefore, like government and non-governmental organisations, me and my organisation are also doing our bit to spread awareness by organising free health camps, public awareness lectures and by writing such articles to reduce the disabilities and to make disabled people able through prompt surgical interventions. The deformities and disabilities caused due to any reason whatsoever should be corrected at the earliest. Hence, this author always advises the patient with deformity and the patient's family members that if surgery is needed, then, it should be done at the earliest as a plant can be straightened, but not a fully-grown tree.

https://pioneeredge.in/deformity-disability-correction-the-sooner-the-better/

❑

52

Complexities of Healthcare Services and the Need for Holistic Medical Care

– Dr BKS Sanjay & Dr Gaurav Sanjay,
Thursday, 01 July 2021

Health, Education, Nutrition (HEN) are the fundamental needs of any individual but both our government and society are ignoring these facts as exposed amidst the COVID-19 pandemic. Unlike other services, healthcare services are complex services which have many inherent variables which are usually not cognisable to the common person. There are many steps in providing healthcare services to a patient. The work ranges from small steps like administering an injection, to performing a specialised surgery and handling sophisticated expensive equipment.

Democracy has deeper roots in the mind-sets of all citizens and hence, probably they prefer to get multiple consultations for any problem particularly if they have been advised surgery for a particular problem. Most of the patients and attendants think that a majority vote favouring or against surgery or advice is better to guide them. But this is usually not true. Particularly in situations where there is significant difference between skill, training, experience and current infrastructure available to the practicing doctor even in the same specialty. One thinks this trend is because of lack of trust between patients, their relatives and the doctors. They would initially go to a nearby doctor, get his 'emergency opinion' and then get it re-checked by another doctor. And many times if there is a conflicting view, they end up with a third consultation and ultimately confuse themselves the most.

Here we would advise any patient to go to the doctor he trusts the most based on the doctor's professional education and result oriented treatment. We see it routinely that nowadays decisions for surgery are being made as we make while buying a packet of chips. It is often thought that a surgery done by any surgeon, at any hospital will yield the same results. This is often untrue and in case of a poorly performed index surgery leads to a complicated treatment in the future which is much more expensive with unpredictable results. Often multiple consultations cause accidental over ingestion of the same drugs when communication between the physician and patient is not clear due to non-availability of previous prescriptions and a busy OPD with many leading clinicians. Apart from this over prescription of drugs is also a major problem. At times, the doctor may succumb to the current Indian mind-set that if the doctor has prescribed none or few medications then he is unsure about the diagnosis. We think there is a general perception in the public that if a doctor is not prescribing a bundle of medication then either he is not concerned about the patient's disease or lacks knowledge of the subject.

Everyone is afraid of infections. It is not only the patient and his relatives but the doctor too. Many times, the doctor is afraid about the reputation of his practice, and hence he opts for prolonged and excessive use of antibiotics as an over-precaution especially when he does not know the exact diagnosis or cause of infection. Nowadays patients have become so over enthusiastic and are ignorant that they too demand for 'high power' /wide spectrum antibiotics even though there is no need for it.

Many quacks are prescribing medication just on their previous knowledge rather than evidence-based clinical research. We have come to know from a medical representative that a quack will prescribe only new generation or recently introduced antibiotics in any case of fever with the understanding that the cause of the fever could only be bacterial infection and that the causative microorganism will definitely die as the new drug will not have any resistance compared to those which have been in practice for many years.

COVID-19 pandemic has again proved that health is the most important asset for an individual which every one of us should strive to maintain. Data shows that 80% of COVID-19 deaths occurred in patients who had pre-existing comorbidities like diabetes, hypertension, hyper-cholestereolemia, chronic respiratory disease, cardiac disease, atherosclerosis, cancer and smoking and alcohol abuse etc. There shouldn't be an issue of one-upmanship of any doctor / allopathy/Ayurveda/homoeopathy. It is suggested that the goal should be to uplift the healthcare services of the country with all-out effort which includes all healthcare workers of all pathies. All pathies should be complementary to each other rather than being confrontational.

Here, we would like to emphasise certain basics of treatment. If you need any immediate relief then of course allopathy is helpful and on other hand in chronic diseases like diabetes, hypertension and arthritis etc. medicines developed by any other pathy may work up to certain extent and can be used based on evidence. Thirdly, surgery is usually needed in many mechanical problems like fracture, acute block of a vessel, presence of stone or acute obstruction of intestine, deformities, transaction of limbs etc. In such cases, medicine can't correct the mechanical problems instantly and effectively.

Patient expectation should be rational and based on the state at which he arrives for treatment. Our ancient scriptures state that if there is birth there is development, degeneration, disease and death. If anything goes wrong by chance during treatment in hospital then family, friends and relatives of the deceased person should understand the truth- human beings are not immortal. Cause of death does not need to be apparent to the patient. Like a diabetic patient may die from a silent heart attack or a severe crushing injury may cause acute renal failure. A layman may not understand how a muscle injury can cause kidney failure and such a person experiencing emotional upheaval may instigate violence in a hospital.

Being orthopaedic surgeons, we would like to quote an example of a road traffic accident in which two people died on the spot, third one was on the way to the hospital and the fourth admitted in the hospital and only one was un-injured. In such a scenario, family and friends should understand that the result of treatment depends upon the severity of the accident, available facilities at the hospital, economic status of the patient and of course the skill of the surgeon.

In our country in every case at least one factor exists or sometimes even more than one factor. These facts are never considered by the attendants before they take an emotional decision to assault the doctor and vandalise the hospital property. This behaviour often gives nightmares to healthcare workers and the hospital owners. It has been observed that seeing the incidents of vandalism, not many people are interested in medical profession as their career. The authorities are requested to check it legally and enforce the law lacking which the future of healthcare services will face serious problems.

https://www.pioneeredge.in/complexities-of-healthcare-services-the-need-for-holistic-medical-care/

❑

53

Overpopulation Leading to Undue Stress, Competition and Conflict

– Dr BKS Sanjay,
Sunday, 11 July 2021

World Population Day is observed on July 11th each year. This day was established by the United Nations and is dedicated to focusing on the importance of the population issues. This year the theme is, "Rights and Choices are the answer: Whether baby boom or bust, the solution to shifting fertility rates lies in prioritising the reproductive health and rights of all people." Many scientists think estimating all available resources, the earth has a maximum carrying capacity of 9-10 billion population. The current population of the world is about 7.8 billion and if it is not controlled then by the end of the century it is estimated to rise to 10.8 billion.

There are many causes of overpopulation like high birth rate, low death rate, better medical facilities, rise in the number of immigrants, agricultural and industrial revolution and lack of family planning facilities, especially in rural areas. India has all these factors which result in overpopulation thereby causing other problems like exhaustion of natural resources, climate change, pollution, overcrowding, unemployment and many others. I will confine myself to the issue of unemployment.

Overpopulation is the root cause of all ills. Health, education, nutrition are the fundamental needs of every individual. Nowadays all these needs can be bought or acquired with money which can be generated from employment. It is not easy to get government employment for each and every body. As such there are almost 2.15 crore central and state government jobs in the whole country and the same number of jobs could be in the organised private sector.

In our country many people are employed in various unorganised sectors. Agriculture and farming is the major unorganised sector which employs almost half of the population. According to the economic survey (2018-19), 93 per cent of the total workforce of 45 crore people of India is from the unorganised sector. According to a report by a private economist, one-third of the workers in the country are daily wagers. The census of 2011 revealed that almost 22 per cent of the total population of the country was considered below the poverty line whose daily income was about Rs 142 or less.

Though the share of Indians working in agriculture is declining, it is still the main sector of employment. It was estimated that 80 per cent of the population was engaged in agriculture sector at the time of independence. In 2020 nearly a half (42%) of the workforce in India was employed in agriculture while the other half was almost evenly distributed among the two other sectors-industry and services. The types of employment in agriculture sector are for those who are unskilled in most of the cases and semi-skilled in minority of the people.

Skilled and highly skilled people are rarely interested and employed in this sector. This influx of overpopulation has fuelled disproportionate amount of competition in general in all sectors. This competition has not only given stress to the candidates but to their parents and grandparents as well. Stress of unemployment is increasing day by day due to mismatching of the merit and the desire of the individual. Happiness comes only when whatever you desire is gained.

The impact of that stress is being reflected in the form of deterioration of physical and mental health of all age groups. It is estimated that 70 per cent of all diseases are caused due to stress. People are carrying many kinds of stress like non-availability of food, shelter, security, education and healthcare needs etc. In my opinion most of the Indians are under stress due to overpopulation, even those who are having one or two children- because they all have to share with others the common resources which are limited in the current scenario.

Poor quality education is compromising the quality of work hence employers are not keen to hire such poor-quality candidates. In other words, education and employment are interrelated. The number of seats for any employment is limited though the country is overpopulated. As people are not getting enough employment hence their mental status is not as stable as it should be. I think the number of incidents of crime are increasing day by day because of overpopulation because everybody wants to earn the money for sustenance. If an individual does not get the enough money for living from the legal means then such individuals indulge in illegal means which becomes vicious circle to generate crime and corruption. If we want to improve the situation in the country then the government should make policies to provide the employment opportunity proportionately to the need of increasing population.

Awareness should be spread about the ill effects of overpopulation. If it is not done there will be more and more conflict to control the natural resources. The quality of employment will improve the quality of education and ultimately the quality of understanding. The people will understand the meaning and value of the fact that if one is divided by more than one, the quotient will be less than one which applies to all resources whether natural or manmade. Overpopulation is causing depletion of all our natural and manmade resources across the world. A two-baby norm per couple if enacted, with preferably a girl and a boy child, is a sustainable and a very effective way of curbing the population menace and maintaining the sex ratio which will be stationary at each generation.

Overpopulation can be contained and controlled. This can be implemented only by humans. There should be global population policy as efforts of one or few nations would not be so impactful. Depleting supply of vital non-renewable resources will be issues of future conflicts like terrorism and war. The policy makers are appealed to enact the law to curb the ever-increasing population. The sooner, the better.

https://www.pioneeredge.in/overpopulation-leading-to-undue-stress-competition-and-conflict/

❑

54

Osteoporosis – A Serious Orthopaedic Disease

– Dr Gaurav Sanjay,
Monday, 09 August 2021

Osteoporosis affects both men and women of all races but Asian women especially, postmenopausal are at high risk. Certain medications like steroid and anti-epileptic drugs and certain diseases like hyperthyroidism, diabetes, unhealthy diet, and sedentary work increase the chance of osteoporosis. Osteoporosis can be diagnosed by taking medical history, physical examination along with blood, urine and x-rays. But the gold standard test nowadays, is to measure the Bone Mineral Density, which can be measured by DEXA Scan and can help to confirm the diagnosis of osteoporosis.

Osteoporosis is such a serious health issue that being an orthopaedic surgeon I see at least one new or old fracture in a day in my clinical practice. It maybe by chance or it may also be the true picture of osteoporosis that some time I have seen three different patients of osteoporosis having fractures of spine, hip and wrist which are the common osteoporotic fractures.

I had three successive patients, one a 91-year-old male- have gradual onset of back pain. He had fracture of D 12 vertebra without any obvious injury in the back. Another patient, 97-year-old female sustained left hip fracture due to slip from bed at night. And the third patient came with right wrist fracture who was 50-year-old postmenopausal female. I would like to mention here that this is the common scenario of osteoporotic fracture not only in my OPD but in all orthopaedic OPDs.

The fracture alone is itself a problem but because of their increased age they are having comorbidities like diabetes, hypertension, cardiac ailments and asthma which further increase their morbidity and make the anaesthesia and surgical procedure riskier. Surgical complication which often needs to be dealt in spite of using good quality implants, is loosening and breakage of implants along with cut through of the implant through the bone like "a knife through soft butter". There postoperative recovery is often unpredictable when they have a bag of comorbidities with them. Hence these patients and attendants need good understanding about osteoporotic fracture and its rehabilitation which is often long.

Here I would like to mention that in spite of the best treatment, even in developed nations, one-third of hip fracture patients die within a year despite receiving the best surgical procedure.

Osteoporosis is more common in people who have deranged hormone levels in their bodies. The reduction of oestrogen level in women at menopause is one of the strongest risk factors for developing osteoporosis. Similarly, in men, the gradual reduction in testosterone level, increases the chance of osteoporosis which usually occurs after 70 years. In males, prostate cancer reduces the testosterone level. Hyper activity of thyroid gland or over prescription of thyroxin medication can enhance the osteoporosis. Over activities of other glands like parathyroid and adrenal glands can induce premature osteoporosis.

Uterus removal (hysterectomy) is a common procedure in gynaecological practice done in women for abnormal uterine bleeding. The pre-menopausal uterus removal is associated with subsequent long-term reduction of progesterone secretion. If it is accompanied with removal of ovaries as well then oestrogen levels are also bound to decrease. Therefore, after hysterectomy, these women experience greater, gradual bone marrow density reduction and more bone density loss than women with an intact uterus. The patients are more prone for developing osteoporosis and subsequent osteoporotic fractures too. These patients need the hormone supplementation.

It is suggested that women should retain the uterus until unless they have developed the disabling or life threatening problems. A scientific study reported a twofold increase of osteoarthritis also in these patients. Hysterectomy not only induces bone osteopenia and osteoporosis which weaken the bones, these patients subsequently also develop premature osteoarthritis along with knee deformity, which further progresses to osteoarthritis. It is also noticed that these women developed premature senile changes which are more prominently seen as skin changes.

Prevention is better than cure. This proverb is more relevant in osteoporotic fracture. Hence, efforts should be made to prevent these fractures with a balanced and a nutritious diet which is rich in calcium and vitamin D. Routine physical activities should be undertaken to maintain bone health and achieve peak bone mass density by 35 years. Consumption of alcohol and smoking should be avoided in all ages.

There are medications which are available in the market, which reduce the pace of resorption of the bone. However, these medications should be taken after physician's consultation only. The most common drugs used to treat osteoporosis are called bisphosphonate like alendronate and injectable zolidronic acid and teriparatide. Calcitonin is available as a nasal spray, which reduces the bone resorption. Certain suggestions are made to the general public like keeping the floor dry, particularly of the bathroom. They should have the good visibility at night and not only a night bulb.

Provision of hand railing support at public places and even at home around toilet seat must be there to assist the old and frail patients as they often slip in wet bathrooms during the night due to poor vision and poor balance which is a physiological problem at this age. These old patients should be advised to avoid sudden twisting and turning because both these movements are precipitating factors for fracture of hips. In case of a fracture, then it should be treated by early treatment and fixation should be secure so as to mobilise the patient early. The mobilisation of these patients often requires some sort of support in the form of a walking aid.

https://www.pioneeredge.in/osteoporosis-a-serious-orthopaedic-disease/

❑

55

The Need for Awareness on Duchenne Muscular Dystrophy

– Dr Gaurav Sanjay,
Monday, 06 September 2021

Each year, World Duchenne Awareness Day takes place on September 7. The Duchenne Muscular Dystrophy (DMD) gene, encoding for the dystrophin protein, is the longest human gene known. It consists of 79 exons. This is why 7/9 is the date for World Duchenne Awareness Day. On this day, many government and non-governmental organisations from around the world raise awareness for Duchenne and Becker Muscular Dystrophy (DMD/BMD). Every year, the World Duchenne Organisation sets a special theme to the day that deserves more attention. This year it will be 'Adult Life and Duchenne'.

I believe that the health of the limbs is as important as the health of the heart and the lungs. Locomotor disability means a problem in moving from one place to another, that is, disability in the legs. Common causes of locomotor disabilities in children are CP, polio and myopathies. Out of these the number of disabilities caused by new cases of polio has not been seen from January 2011, however old cases are still prevalent. The disability caused by CP can be prevented with adequate perinatal care.

However, contrary to the incidence of CP and polio, the incidence of myopathies cannot be reduced easily. This is because myopathies are a group of hereditary disorders of skeletal muscle that produce progressive degeneration of skeletal muscle which result in progressive weakness. The common muscular dystrophies are Duchenne Muscular Dystrophy (DMD) in childhood and limb girdle muscular dystrophy (LGMD) in adulthood. The X-linked myopathies or dystrophy are more common and include Duchenne, Becker and Emery Derfuss muscular dystrophy. Limb girdle muscular dystrophy and congenital muscular dystrophy are the two most common autosomal recessive muscular dystrophies.

Now considering World Duchenne Day, I will confine myself to Duchenne Muscular Dystrophy which is a rare disease. I have seen only five cases in a span of almost 20 years of medical experience in some of the largest medical centres of India and abroad. DMD is a sex linked recessive inherited trait, which occurs in males while the carriers are female. It is reported to occur one in 3,500 live births according to western literature. A more recent large study done in India revealed that 27.4 per cent of all myopathies were muscular dystrophies, 30 per cent having DMD and 29.2 per cent LGMD subtypes. In a tertiary neuromuscular centre in Mumbai, DMD formed the main myopathy of childhood while limb girdle dystrophy was the most common diagnosis of adolescent and adulthood myopathies.

There is a family history in 70 per cent of patients and the condition occurs as a spontaneous mutation is about 30 per cent cases. DMD is the result of a mutation in Xp21 region of the X chromosomes which encodes 400-kd protein dystrophin. Dystrophin is important to the stability of the cell membrane cytoskeleton which results in progressive muscle degeneration and loss of function.

DMD usually becomes evident between 4 and 8 years of age. The patients present with large, firm calf muscles and the tendency of toe walking. Clinical examination revealed a waddling Trendelenburg gait and a positive Gower test indicative of proximal muscle weakness. DMD is confirmed with elevated levels of creatine kinase (ck) or creatine phosphokinase (cpk) which varies from 50-100 times of normal value and DNA analysis confirms the diagnosis.

The treatments of DMD include medical, orthotic and orthopaedic treatment. DMD is usually treated medically with the steroid which preserves or improves strength of the muscles and reduces the pace of progression of the disease. However, in spite of the steroid, progress and condition of disease worsen. The role of gene therapy and stem cell therapy are still under investigation.

Orthopaedic treatment is aimed at preventing the joint contracture and to maintain functional ambulation as long as possible. Prevention of contracture of lower extremities can be done with the use of manipulation and with the use of splint. However, if the progression of deformity is not prevented which is often, in such situations patients need surgical intervention in the form of correction of contracture and lengthening of the tendons and maintaining that.

If surgery is indicated then the foot and hip contracture should be released simultaneously, usually through percutaneous incisions then followed by cast application. Prolonged immobilisation must be avoided to prevent further progression of muscle weakness. Other procedures like tendon transfer can be done but they are also not very effective on a long-term basis. Usually, these patients succumb to DMD by 18-20 years of age.

The parents of DMD patients should be subjected to genetic counselling if it is available. In India, due to lack of awareness of muscle diseases, parents of affected children often do not know where to seek help. Illiteracy is also an issue which makes counselling difficult. The social structure in India is also not kind to the physically challenged with no availability of ramps for public modes of transport. Home rehabilitation programmes, designed for those patients who cannot come for regular visits, have proved to be more successful than clinic-based programmes.

The author has an experience seeing not only one boy but both male siblings in a family suffering from DMD. Genetic counselling can offer several benefits like education about inheritance, chances of recurrence and family planning options for affected individuals and possible carriers. It will also cover to explore emotional issues. Genetic counselling for individuals with a known or suspected diagnosis and carrier testing for women at risk will also help considerably.

https://www.pioneeredge.in/the-need-for-awareness-on-duchenne-muscular-distrophy/

❑

56

Quality of Education Depends Upon Quality of Teachers

– Dr BKS Sanjay,
Saturday, 18 September 2021

This author owes a lot to all his teachers because they have shaped his life, otherwise he would not have been in this position and writing this column. Education plays an important role in developing all our human potential. It helps to develop both our inner and outer power. The teachers play an important role in shaping the life of all children and indirectly all citizens.

The teacher-student relationship has changed a lot from the old time to the current time. It has now become very complicated, formal and codified. There has been a tremendous shift in how the teachers used to be in the older generation to that of now. Traditionally the teachers never used to work on the principle of business but rather on the tenets of charity or service.

Mahatma Gandhi had said that the earth provides enough to satisfy every man's needs, but not every man's greed. But unfortunately, the health and education sector are being run in our country on the motive of financial profit. Gandhi had also said what is really needed to make a democracy function is not knowledge of facts, but the right education. I believe the right education can be given only by qualified teachers. "Nothing counts as much as school," as stated by Horace Mann, an American educational reformer who promoted universal public education and teachers.

The good teachers have the eye that can spot the uniqueness of every child. Each teacher can develop that uniqueness in due course of time. Here I would like to cite Rajguru Dronacharya, Maharshi Gautam and founder of Super 30, Anand Kumar. It is being seen very well in the field of sports that the quality of the athlete changes tremendously once the right coach tunes him to excel.

BR Ambedkar, the architect of the Indian constitution regarded education as a critical instrument to raise the overall status of all citizens. He believed that through the acquisition of education, especially higher education, socioeconomic equality can be promoted. Ambedkar said that the cultivation of mind should be the ultimate aim of human existence. He not only promoted education but reflected it in his ideology and said that my final words of advice to you are, "To educate, agitate and organise; have faith in yourself."

NR Narayana Murthy, founder of the Infosys mentions in his book 'A Better India, A Better World' that he sees the colonial attitude of the Indian elite society every day with a glaring difference in ruled and rulers. Indian elite send their children to English medium school while forcing the children of the poor into vernacular schools, extol the virtues of poverty while living in luxury and glorify the rural life while they sit comfortably in cities.

The former president of India, APJ Abdul Kalam indicated that the communication of good values by reputed people was an important first step in changing the mind set of youngsters. The eminent people should participate on social platforms to speak to the young people and they should be invited in the colleges and universities in academic functions as much as possible. The author has an experience of Mayo Clinic, USA where there was a trend to invite almost every Nobel laureate to deliver a lecture for the staff and students. American universities currently employ 70 per cent of the world's Nobel Prize winners.

If we have a dream to make India a developed nation and a super power of the world then we have to follow the simple principle of all developed nations which have invested a lot on education, starting from primary to higher education and reaping the fruits for the nations. Here, I would like to mention that we do not need only the primary education centres for the children but there should be multiple centres of excellence for higher teaching and training of the teachers as well. John Dewey, an American educationist was the first to start the concept of teacher's training schools because he thought that only well-educated and trained teachers can transfer their knowledge and skill to the children.

When the former President APJ Abdul Kalam was asked what makes a country develop he replied that the obvious indicators are the wealth of the nation, prosperity of its people and its standing in the international forum. Any progress based on dreams requires changes, which require learning. Education is one of the important pillars of the growth of an individual and ultimately of the family, society and the nation. Being educated means you are assuming responsibility towards society. Education will give equal opportunity to everybody. Our nation's goal should be to give every child food, shelter, healthcare and education. Education should teach that duty comes first. Each generation has to make sacrifices to make a better life for the next generation.

The education field should be given its due importance in the development of any individual, any society and any nation. It influences an individual's behaviour, knowledge and skill which are the tripod for mobility of an individual from the lower strata to higher strata. Hence, in order to live a better and peaceful life we need to be educated. It is education which broadens our horizon. It transforms us completely by changing our mind and thoughts, thereby changing our deeds.

It is said, a former is worth a thousand reformers. It is suggested that irrespective of profession we should follow a principle of DRAFT- Do Right at First Time because repair and redo are costly affairs. Be honest and true to your profession. Create excellence in whatever you do. The policy makers should ensure that quality education should be given to all, which should be cheap and similar for all citizens. The quality of work depends upon the quality of the worker hence the quality of education depends upon the quality of teacher.

https://www.pioneeredge.in/quality-of-education-depends-upon-quality-of-teachers/

❑

57

Back Pain: One of the Most Common Health Problems

– Dr BKS Sanjay,
Monday, 18 October 2021

World Spine Day is held with the aim of motivating people and creating awareness about the burden of spinal pain and disability and it also recognises the lack of access to quality spine care and rehabilitation in under-served communities, which results in chronicity and permanent spine deformity. The day also aims to increase awareness for the prevention, diagnosis, and treatment of back pain and other spine issues.

The importance of our back can be gauged from the commonly used adage about a particular person being the backbone of that organisation or society. The backbone plays an important role in maintaining and functioning our body. The human spine is a complex structure spanning from the head to the tailbone. The spinal column protects the spinal cord and the nerve roots and allows the body movements in three dimensions. It also maintains the balance of the head, the trunk and the pelvis through the various intervertebral discs, facet joints, muscles and adjacent ligaments.

Backache is the second most common health problem a person experiences after a headache. Low back pain is the leading cause of disability all over the world and it prevents many people from engaging in their domestic and office work and this makes them seek help from healthcare providers. Back pain can affect people of all ages from adult to the elderly. In my personal experience I have noticed more than half the number of patients are related to back pain. The main causes of back pain are muscular spasm, slip disc in young patients and degenerative spinal stenosis and facet joints arthritis in elderly patients.

The worldwide data shows that disability caused by back pain is increasing. This disability is more relevant and the impact is more in low income and middle-income people. The social impact of back pain is tremendous on society. Because of back pain the families are getting indirect mental stress. The psychological and social impact on the patients' health leads to depression, insomnia, anxiety and various psychosomatic disorders.

In pre-industrialisation times the main cause of back pain was lifting or carrying of heavy loads but in recent times, people having sedentary lifestyles are more prone to develop back pain due to weakness in the surrounding muscles.

If we consider the degenerative problem related to the back and its disability. Then the spine joints which are called the facet joints are similar to the synovial knee joints. It is to be understood that as age advances so does various joint arthritis.

The symptoms and signs of facet joint arthritis are similar to that of joint arthritis. Arthritis of any joint presents with pain and stiffness of the joint particularly in the morning time or after prolonged rest. Swelling of the knee joint can be appreciated easily because the joint is superficial and large. But in contrast to the knee joints, the facet joints are smaller in size and deep surrounded by strong and thick ligaments. The facet joint bears the stress bearing forces, many times more per capita area in comparison to the knee joints. Sometimes due to degeneration of facet joints and break of the pars inter-articularis. The body of one vertebra slips over the other vertebra, causing spinal canal compression and leading to spinal cord and spinal nerve compression which presents with the radicular nerve pain with symptoms of dull pain in the calf, around the back, numbness in the legs, difficulty in proper walking and standing. Sometimes even any change of posture, particularly rotational, twisting, or bending can increase the pain.

Mechanical back pain can be managed with the rest, heat therapy, physiotherapy, use of analgesic, chiropractic manipulation. If the problem doesn't subside, then the patient should consult a qualified spine surgeon and should go through the investigations like X-ray, CT scan and MRI of the spine. If the patient is having only back pain but no other comorbidities like diabetes, hypertension, hypothyroidism, varicose veins of the legs then problems can usually be managed simply. Patients who smoke tobacco and consume alcohol are tougher to deal with.

If the pressure on the spinal cord or on the nerve roots remains for a prolonged time, then patients may develop difficulty in passing the urine and faeces. These symptoms show that the problem is very serious and patients often need the emergency surgical intervention like decompression or fixation of the spine as the condition exists.

If in any case surgery cannot be performed because of any reason, especially in non-traumatic spinal cord compression then injection of epidural steroid, or transformational nerve blocks are better options. In the author's experience, injection epidural steroids gives reasonable and acceptable results especially in high risk patients.

Bad posture can cause pain and can increase the existing back pain. Lack of awareness, neglect of pain, poverty, lack of trained doctors and the shortage of good hospitals accentuates this simple problem to a serious problem in about 20 per cent of back pain patients. Spine surgeries are difficult and risky but its success completely depends on the skill of the surgeon and standard of medical facilities available in the hospital. Spine surgery, like any surgery, has very good results if done in a well selected patient, on time and before landing up in complications due to the neglect of treatment. After the surgery, the patient has to follow a definite protocol for a certain time to get the ideal result.

The author himself has done thousands of spine surgeries, varying from simple to most complicated high risk spine surgeries in more than 20 years in the past and none of them has resulted in paralysis after surgery. In fact, the author's name has been recorded in the Limca book of records for doing spine surgery on an 88-year-old male.

https://www.pioneeredge.in/guest-column/

❑

58

Higher the Speed, Steeper the Risk, Greater the Fatalities

– Dr BKS Sanjay & Dr Gaurav Sanjay,
Sunday, 21 November 2021

As every year, the objective of World Day of Remembrance (WDoR) for Road Traffic Victims is to provide a platform for road traffic victims and their families to remember all the people killed and seriously injured on the roads, acknowledge the crucial work of the emergency services team, draw attention to the generally trivial legal response to culpable road deaths and injuries, advocate better support for road traffic accident victims and their families, promote evidence-based actions to prevent and eventually stop further road traffic deaths and injuries.

WDoR 2021 marks the start of the new Decade of Action for Road Safety 2021-2030, during which the WDoR will play a very important part – by highlighting the very reasons for all the necessary actions during this coming decade. WDoR 2021 puts the spotlight and emphasises on the reduction of vehicular and traffic speed. Low speeds have the potential to prevent many deaths and serious injuries, in particular among those like pedestrians and all other vulnerable road users– children, elderly and the disabled. The authors have taken a lifelong resolution to spread awareness for road safety through free health camp and free public awareness lectures.

A study conducted by us revealed that 90 per cent of the accidents are caused due to driver negligence. The main causes of road traffic accidents are over speeding, overtaking, overloading, drunken driving and recently using the mobile phone while driving. An important factor affecting the speed of the vehicle are driver related aspects like age, gender, alcohol intake, number of people in the vehicle and concomitant use of mobile phones etc. Most of the fatal accidents occur due to over speeding.

Faster moving vehicles are more prone to accidents and the risk, and severity of accidents is directly proportional to the speed of the vehicles. Higher the speed, steeper the risk and greater the fatalities. It is observed that younger the driver, the faster the speed of the vehicle. Over speeding was a factor in 26 per cent of the all traffic fatalities in 2019, according to a police report. The incidence of fatalities also increases with simultaneous use of mobile phone and driving. A report cited 40 per cent fatality in such a circumstance.

In addition to that, accidents which occur during night time are also fatal because drivers are usually exhausted due to their hectic day work and even professional drivers are over worked especially in tourist season. It is a common practice in India for drivers to manage their fatigue by consuming alcohol and under its influence they seem to feel that they tend to reach to destination earlier. The reaction time to avoid an accident is usually a fraction of a second. This usually gets delayed after consuming alcohol.

Though we may feel that all our senses are intact, that delay can't usually be quantified after consuming alcohol. While travelling at night, the roads are relatively empty which tend to encourage over speeding. The food and lodging are usually expensive which forces many families and drivers to save money and to reach home at any cost. If any accidents happen at night, then usually they are unnoticed especially in the hilly and the remote areas.

Over speeding not only causes mortality but increase in the morbidity too. An increase in average speed of one km/h typically results in a three per cent higher risk of a crash involving injury, with a 4-5 per cent increase in the speed the crashes can result in fatalities. On other hand studies suggest that one km/h decrease in travelling speed would lead to 2-3 per cent reduction in road crashes. Over speeding is even more dangerous in hilly areas because the roads are narrow and have many hair pin bends due to geographical restrictions. There is a common observation that the accident happened because the driver could not control the vehicle.

It may be the experience of all drivers that if suddenly a T turn comes on straight road and the driver is over speeding then it becomes very difficult to turn suddenly. What usually follows is that the vehicle goes off road and there is vehicular dis-balance which often results in an accident. If the same situation is in the hilly areas which do not have metalled roads then vehicle often goes into the gorge. The use of convex mirror, speed camera and of speed limiting alarm devices are simple means to restrict over speeding.

Newton's third law states that when one body exerts a force on another body the second body exerts an equal force. This principle of action and reaction explains why a force tends to deform a body. This deformation of a body usually appears in road traffic accidents with fractured bones or injury to other vital internal organs of the body. High speed of the vehicle reduces the possibility to respond in time when necessary. The brain needs time to process information, to decide whether or not to react and finally to execute an appropriate reaction. The breaking distance is proportional to the square of speed (v2). Therefore, the possibility to avoid a collision becomes a smaller as the speed increases. A one km/h increase in speed causes three per cent increase in chances of an accident but in practice the relationship is more complex. The exact relationship depends upon many other things on the level of speed and quality of road, type of traffic, area of driving etc.

A principle of physics states that force is directly proportional to the mass. Over loading is another important cause of accidents especially in heavy vehicles like trucks and buses. We usually see many media reports of accidents caused due to over loading. The reason of fatalities is that drivers of such vehicles are not able to respond to emergency condition and unable to control the over loaded vehicle. An over loaded vehicle takes longer to stop and in an emergency situation the driver may misjudge the situation. The over loaded vehicle shifts their load particularly during the acute turns on the roads and also on the highway where they are at a fast speed.

Because of this aggressive behaviour and non-observance of the traffic rules, the nation is losing a lot in terms of human and economic resource. If we follow traffic rules then we will not only save the life of these people but save a significant amount of the money which is being spent on the treatment of injuries sustained in these accidents and can also be used to fulfil their other important needs. All of us should spread awareness to prevent these accidents because they have taken a form of an epidemic. The public should learn the traffic rules and follow them; the government should teach the traffic rules and should strictly enforce them to prevent these road traffic tragedies.

https://www.pioneeredge.in/higher-the-speed-steeper-the-risk-greater-the-fatalities/

❑

59

Conducive Environment Needed for Disable to Develop

– Dr BKS Sanjay & Dr Gaurav Sanjay,
Friday, 03 December 2021

The International Day of Disabled Persons is celebrated on December 3 by United Nations to promote an understanding of disability issues and mobilise support for increasing dignity, the rights and wellbeing of persons with disabilities.

Disability is any condition of body or mind that makes it more difficult for the person with the condition to do certain activities and interact with world around. According to WHO, disability has many dimensions including impairment (loss of body part), limitation of activity and restrictions in participation (any kind of social restriction). About 15 per cent of world population has some form of disability. The National Sample Survey conducted by Government of India from July to December 2018 showed that about 2.1 per cent of total population is disabled. Polio, cerebral palsy (CP) and club foot in childhood are the main causes of disability in India. India is polio free since March 27, 2014.

This means there are no new cases of polio since then. But there are lakhs of old polio cases which are causing major social and other problems to patients and nation. The road accidents have become epidemic, causing havoc and producing significant disability in society. Almost five lakh people are encountering road traffic accidents in which more than a fourth are dying and at least a fourth are being disabled for life in spite of best available treatment in current scenario.

We all need conducive environment to grow and develop in existing environment and circumstances but disabled people need more. We would like to quote few examples of disabled people who have not only helped themselves but have done exemplary work like Homer, Surdas, Ashtavakra in past and Helen Keller, Stephen Hawking, Sudha Chandran, Ravidra Jain, Arunima Sinha, Satendra Singh in recent times. Homer was an ancient Greek author and an epic poet who composed the Iliad and the Odyssey, two epic poems that are foundational works of ancient Greek literature. He is regarded as one of greatest and most influential writers.

Ashtavakra is a revered Vedic sage in Hinduism. His name literally means "eight bends", reflecting eight physical handicaps he was born with. His maternal grandfather was sage Aruni, his parents were both Vedic students at Aruni's school. Ashtavakra studied, became a sage and a celebrated character of Hindu Itihasa epics and Puranas. He is author of Ashtavakra Geeta also known as Ashtavakra Samhita. Surdas was a 16th century blind devotional poet and singer who was known for his works written in praise of lord Krishna. He was a great Vaishnava and is respected and revered by all Hindus.

Helen Keller was an American author, disability rights advocate, political activist and a lecturer. Born in Alabama she lost her sight and hearing after a bout of illness at age of nineteen months. She then communicated primarily using signs until age of seven when she met her first teacher and lifelong companion Anne Sullivan, who taught her language, including reading and writing. Keller was a prolific author. She travelled to 35 countries around globe advocating for those with vision loss.

Stephen Hawking was an English theoretical physicist, cosmologist and author who was born in 1942 in Oxford into a family of physicians. At age of 21 years, Hawking was diagnosed with an early-onset slow-progressing form of motor neurone disease (amyotrophic lateral sclerosis–ALS) that gradually paralysed him. After loss of his speech, he communicated through a speech-generating device initially through use of a handheld switch, and eventually by using a single cheek muscle. He died on March 14, 2018 after living with motor neurone disease for more than 50 years.

Sudha Chandran, Indian actress and classical dancer needs no introduction. Born in Kerala, this artiste met with an accident when she was just 16. Doctors missed a small wound in her ankle and plastered it, which later got infected and there was no alternative left but to amputate her leg. She overcame her disability by getting a prosthetic 'Jaipur Foot' and became one of most popular and acclaimed classical dancers of country. Having received many awards for her amazing talent, Chandran is an inspiration for many.

Born visually impaired, Ravindra Jain started singing at a very young age and took his passion to a new high when he joined Indian music industry, becoming one of most notable music directors of 1970s. Apart from composing various super-hit songs for Hindi movies, he also launched several albums which were praised by many. Arunima Sinha lost her leg when some robbers pushed her out of a moving train. Two years later, she became first woman amputee to climb Mount Everest. She has proved that a strong determination and will is far more important than a strong body. Even with a prosthetic leg, she overcame her challenges and made history. Satendra Singh, an acclaimed doctor contracted Polio when he was just nine months old. He is also a prominent disability activist and works extensively to make public places more accessible to persons with disabilities. His efforts made ATMs disabled-friendly with ramps. Similar initiatives were taken for post office, medical institutes, polling booths, etc. He is also founder of Infinite Ability–a medical humanities group on disability.

The impact of disability increases proportionately with time lapse of correction. Governments, non-governmental organisations and society should strive to prevent disability of any kind and if it happens then it should be treated as early as possible. The deformities and disabilities caused due to any reason whatsoever should be corrected at earliest. Hence, we always advise patient with deformity and patient's family members that if surgery is needed, then it should be done at earliest as a plant can be straightened but not a fully-grown tree.

https://www.pioneeredge.in/conducive-envirment-needed-for-disable-to-develop/

❑

60

Key to Success - Trio of Behaviour, Knowledge and Skill

– Dr BKS Sanjay,
Friday, 31 December 2021

According to a Buddhist philosophy, our life is shaped by our mind-we become, what we think. To succeed, make more allies rather than enemies, be it people or your own brain. We must change our thinking process and behaviour to bring about a change in anything.

American psychologist BF Skinner was famous for observing that humans are no different than animals. Humans should actually be analysed as animals interacting with their environment. Like animals, humans too are basically creatures in their environment. Humans change their action according to the consequences of their and others' behaviour.

As we know from own experience and by observing lives of others, raw intelligence doesn't equate with success. There are many other factors which come into the success equation. Genetic intelligence is only a part of the intelligence equation, the rest is the environment, another American psychologist Carol Dweck noted.

What matters the most is having a better interaction amongst the humans. We don't need many medical scientists and doctors but we need many social scientists and psychologists who can change human thinking and their behaviour. Behaviour is the first thing which influences the results of an interaction, irrespective of profession. Behaviour of an individual is very important to render any service. A genuine relationship or an interaction is one in which you and the other person are comfortable with each other and feel safe to speak their mind and are confident to be heard. Most of the problems can be sorted out with acceptable behaviour itself. Behaviour is defined, as an action that is observable and measurable. The observable actions are more descriptive.

In psychology, behaviour consists of an organism's external reaction to the environment. In simple words, behaviour is the range of actions by an organism with their environment. Behaviour serves two purposes—either to get something or to avoid something. It can be learnt and can be changed at any age and any stage of life. However, it is easier to mould during childhood than later on. Human behaviour plays an important role in all phases of human life. The success of any person depends upon the application of the trio of behaviour, knowledge and skill. Behaviour component is nearly 80 per cent of all these three.

As far as health is concerned, personal and social responsibility can be found only with behavioural changes. Clinical research conducted by me revealed that 90 per cent of the road traffic accidents occurred due to the driver's negligence. Seventy per cent of modern health issues are related to lifestyle changes. These all are the behavioural problems.

Human resource is the greatest resource on planet earth. We all should try to develop this resource of each other. In my opinion, the behaviour, knowledge and skill of any individual are the key to success. The application of behaviour, knowledge and skill in day-to-day life of anyone leads to success.

In general, we choose a specialist of a professional for his knowledge and skill, but in reality, we choose his behaviour. In fact, it is the perception about the person along with his behaviour that acts as subliminal advertisement for his knowledge and skill. Behaviour plays an important role in shaping not only our own life but others life too. Importance of behaviour comes first which is most important, followed by knowledge and skill in same order in any action. Knowledge and skill of any person can be transferred with good behaviour only.

The education sector should be given its due importance in the development of any individual, any society and any nation. It influences an individual's behaviour, knowledge and skill which are the tripod for mobility of an individual from the lower strata to higher strata. Hence, in order to live a better and peaceful life we need to be educated. It is education which broadens our horizon. It transforms us completely by changing our mind and thoughts, thereby changing our deeds.

https://www.pioneeredge.in/guest-column-key-to-success-trio-of-behaviour-knowledge-skill/

❑

61

Education – The Key to Empowerment for Everyone

– Dr BKS Sanjay & Dr Gaurav Sanjay,
Monday, 24 January 2022

The United Nations General Assembly proclaimed 24 January as International Day of Education which was celebrated under the theme "Changing Course, Transforming Education" this year.

Macaulay of the British Raj introduced the English education system in India. The aim of the British education was to get clerks for their offices, to help in various administrative services and propagate the English culture which was suitable for the colonial rulers. The English education system deprived the Indian masses and produced an elite group among Indians themselves. This division of the society created the further alienation among various groups of Indians who were already divided on the basis of various castes and religion.

Gandhi emphasised that the medium of instruction should be the mother tongue of all children. Rabindranath Tagore pointed out that when Indians receive their education through their mother tongue the process of education would be as natural as the process of eating food, digestion starts as soon as food goes into the mouth.

Tagore had often said that the responsibility of education is to see that the growth of the body and mind take place in a balanced manner. The main purpose of education is not only to improve our knowledge but also to develop the ability of the body and the mind to express it to the fullest in any situation to deal with the problems faced in day-to-day life.

Dr BR Ambedkar, the main architect of the Indian constitution, gave prime importance to education. He understood well with his experience and gave his key message of "educate, organise and agitate" to the masses. The basic theme of his philosophy of education is to inculcate the values of liberty, equality, fraternity and justice to all citizens. It is education which will enlighten the human beings and fulfil the dream of every Indian.

Uttarakhand, particularly Dehradun is a leading centre for education and learning in India. In fact, it has been a learning centre from the time of Mahabharata which is why it is also known as Dronanagari. Uttarakhand has many institutions starting from schools to universities giving both primary and higher education. A few of them are The Doon School and Wenham's School, FRI Dehradun, IMA Dehradun, IIT Roorkee, AIIMS Rishikesh, LBSNAA (IAS academy) in Mussoorie etc. Uttarakhand has eight institutions of national importance, 31 universities (three deemed, 12 government, 16 private), six medical colleges, 12 Ayurveda colleges, 38 para medical colleges, 38 nursing colleges (14 government, 24 private), 40 degree colleges and hundreds of schools. Are all of them really fulfilling the purpose which they are supposed to?

Schools in Uttarakhand are affiliated to CBSE, CISCE and UBSE. According to the 2011 census, Uttarakhand had a literacy rate of 80 percent. However, the status of primary education is so dismal that five per cent of class III students cannot identify the numbers 1-9 and 20 per cent of them cannot do subtraction, according to a government report. Another instance of irregularity recently reported in higher education in the media last week showed that a private B.Ed. college was functioning from a three-room house for the last 10 years in Uttarkashi. It is worth pondering whether this is a failure of students, teachers or the government.

The goal of primary education should be to enable children to read, write, speak, calculate and express their feelings and experience through their eyes, hands and other parts of body. In our view, to improve the quality of education, there is a need for good quality teachers. They should not only be good in teaching, transferring knowledge and skill but should also possess quality and behave like responsible guardians of the students. If the situation arises, the teachers should counsel the children and the parents as well.

The quality of work depends upon the quality of the worker. Similarly, the quality of education depends upon the quality of the teacher. American educationist Horace Mann rightly said that "A former is worth a thousand reformers". The goal of education must be to develop the interest of the child in reading, writing and learning. The goal of learning should be to Do it Right at First Time (DRAFT) because repair and redo is a costly affair. In our view nothing in the market should be substandard be it material or man power.

What makes a great teacher is the ability of the teacher to help the students learn for himself. For that the motto of the policy makers should be to have not only good quality schools for the children but also good quality schools for training the teachers. It is suggested that the main thrust should be given to improve the quality of primary education and primary education should ideally be given in mother tongue irrespective of the type and place of school.

A Chinese poet of the Sung dynasty had observed that one of the three most wasteful and disturbing things in the world is to witness poorly educated youth. Another study published in the journal Nature revealed that 52 per cent of IQ depends upon education and environment. Education plays the most important role in shaping the life of any individual. Education transforms a person to live a better life in almost all spheres of life.

It is a fundamental requirement for employment. Employment gives a person financial independence. Money is an important resource to acquire anything in life and money can be earned only by those who are physically and mentally able. It is education which broadens our horizon. In fact, education is the key factor leading to empowerment. We hope if our new education policy is implemented honestly, it will change the whole scenario of education in our country.

https://www.pioneeredge.in/guest-column-3

❑

62

Early Detection of Cancer Leads to Better Outcome

– Dr Gaurav Sanjay,
Saturday, 05 February 2022

As done every year, the World Cancer Day was held on February 4 to raise awareness on cancer and its prevention, detection and treatment. World Cancer Day originated on February 4, 2000, during the world cancer conference in Paris, France. The awareness programme conducted on this day is to remove the stigma which is associated with cancer.

Cancer is the world's second leading cause of death. It is a preventable disease and is mainly caused due to adulteration of food and presence of pollution in the environment. After the industrialisation era, there has been an increased incidence of cancer in almost every organ of the body. Industrialisation has increased the use of many chemicals in the industries. The body is directly exposed to some of these chemicals as it is seen in the colour and paint industries. Similarly, the use of chemicals like pesticides and fertilisers in agriculture and horticulture has contaminated the groundwater.

Adulteration in food products, the pollution of water and air has increased tremendously after the industrialisation age. Hundreds of carcinogens are spread all around us. It usually takes almost 10 years of close contact with any carcinogen to cause cancer. The third most common cause of cancer is change of lifestyle associated with increased incidence of smoking, consumption of alcohol and chewing of tobacco. Tobacco chewing is the main cause of mouth cancer and alcohol is main cause of liver cirrhosis leading to liver cancer in our country.

We know that prevention is better than cure. We all should try to prevent getting affected by cancer. Improper diet, contaminated and adulterated food, and pollution of air, water and soil are the common causes of cancer. Diet plays a vital role in maintaining our good health. Bad food habits, inadequate physical activity, obesity and lifestyle diseases like diabetes are also linked with cancer. Green vegetables and fresh fruits are known to prevent cancer because these contain many antioxidants and polyphenols which reduce the formation of free radicals in the body which are known to damage the normal cells and to cause cancer. Green tea is the healthiest and probably one of the cheapest beverages on the planet which is loaded with hundreds of micro nutrients and plenty of antioxidants which not only improve our brain function but also reduce the body weight and decrease the risk of cancer.

Cancer is usually defined as uncontrolled growth of cells which is clinically presented with gradually increasing pain which is usually not relieved with the ordinary painkiller, gradual increase of any lump or swelling in any part or organ of the body. The lump or swelling are easily visible in the superficial parts of the body like breast, oral cavity and extremities but it takes more time to become palpable in internal organs or internal parts of the body like intestine, liver, uterus etc. The third presentation of cancer would be dysfunction of an involved part or organ of the body. If any one of the symptoms is noticed by an individual then in such a situation one should consult a qualified doctor to rule out cancer.

The diagnosis can only be confirmed by tissue biopsy. Biopsy is a small procedure in which a small quantity of representative tissue or fluid is taken from the suspected area to be examined by the pathologist. If cancer is confirmed, then the treatment should be started as soon as possible.

Another characteristic of cancer is to spread distally and to other organs and recurrence of tumour, both these things usually occur when cancer is diagnosed late and treated late or inadequately. The recurrence is usually caused if tumour cells are left at the time of surgery inadvertently or cancer cannot be removed if it involves the vital structure like arteries, nerves or any other vital organs. The distal spread of cancer can be controlled with chemotherapy and radiation therapy.

The most important factor which influences the outcome of the treatment depends upon the age, comorbidities of the patient, type, site, size, stage and quality of surgery and the doubling time of the cancer. Many patients consult the doctor with a delayed presentation because many times, at an early stage, these tumours are painless and hence neglected by the patients as they don't consider it worth consulting a doctor. In rare cases, it may be missed by a doctor also specially in a poor health infrastructure setup.

The increasing prevalence of cancer is a major public health concern across the world—a big problem for developing countries like India with poor socio-economic condition and poor health infrastructure. Cancer awareness and early detection should be a priority for all governments particularly in our socioeconomic scenario because cancer treatment is specialised and usually very expensive. It will be worthwhile to educate and spread awareness among the people to take steps to prevent cancer and realise the importance of early detection and adequate treatment because early detection of cancer leads to a better outcome.

https://www.pioneeredge.in/early-detection-of-cancer-leads-to-better-outcome/

❑

63

The Importance of Mother Tongue in Primary Education

– Dr BKS Sanjay & Dr Gaurav Sanjay,
Monday, 21 February 2022

The International Mother Language Day is celebrated by UNESCO every year on February 21. Parents are the first teachers of their children and these children then become the foundation stones of a nation. The stronger the base, the stronger is the nation. Every child has the right to learn, to be a useful member of society and to develop individual abilities to deal with any problem faced in day-to-day life.

Humans started communicating with a language almost a hundred thousand years ago. Every country in today's time has its own national language for communication and administration. India being a diverse country, it is said that it has always been a multilingual country since the times of undivided India. Each region has its own language but none of the regions is considered to be truly unilingual. Sanskrit was the most prevalent language in ancient India. However, since 712 AD many Muslim invaders came into India, became rulers and introduced their own language. Since the early 17th century, due to British invasion, English had taken over Persian and other Indian languages.

Under Article 351 of the Constitution of India, the Union is duty bound to promote the spread and development of Hindi language, so that it may serve as a medium of expression among all Indians. Though officially, Hindi is our national language but in practice it is not so. Education is a lifelong learning process but the learning done in childhood has much more significance because the brain is flexible in childhood and it can be moulded appropriately with much more ease during that time rather than adulthood.

The learning process for a child should be in the language which he or she can understand and easily comprehend. Every child learns his first words spoken in his mother tongue. In childhood whatever is taught, the child usually grasps it easily and retains it forever. It is pertinent to mention that American educationist, Horace Mann has said that a former is worth of a thousand reformers. That is why it is very important to give quality education to the children.

It was one of the challenging problems for the founding fathers of our constitution to come to a consensus regarding which language should be our national language or even an official language of the Union. Finally, under a compromise formula embodied in article 343, Hindi and Devanagari script were accepted as the official language of the union with the international form of Indian numerals.

In view of the First Official Language Commission and under Article 343, in1963, the parliament enacted the Official Language Act, 1963 and even after 15 years of it, English continued to be used along with Hindi for all official purposes of the Union and also for transaction of business in parliament. Besides Hindi, our constitution also recognises 21 other Indian languages listed in the eighth schedule. The articles 343, 344, and 351 would show that the ultimate goal is to spread, develop Hindi and the gradual switchover to Hindi and use it for official purposes and as a link language but unfortunately Hindi language could not gain popularity over English language even after 75 years of independence.

Article 350A inserted by seventh amendment provides for local authority in every state endeavouring to extend adequate facilities for instruction in the mother language at primary stage of education to children belonging to linguistic minority groups in a state. There was unnecessary hue and cry in southern states against National Education Policy 2020 which has given due importance to mother tongue stating- "wherever possible the medium of instruction in schools until Grade-V, preferably until Grade-VIII, should be the mother tongue or the local or regional language". This is not the first time that we are changing the language but I presume that language has been changing since the origin of mankind.

Any change cannot be realised until we succeed in transforming our society into one, in which equality, liberty, fraternity and spirituality will flourish in harmony with each other and it is only education which can transform the society gradually and easily. Quality of the work depends upon the quality of the worker which depends upon the quality of education. The goal of education must be to develop the interest of a child in reading, writing and learning.

The medium of instruction in school plays an important role in guiding and modifying a child's personality because language is one of the basic needs for communication. Mahatma Gandhi used to say that language is like a mother. BR Ambedkar emphasised that it is education which will enlighten the human beings and fulfil the dream of every Indian.

There has been a false notion that the students of English medium schools do better and mastery of English language ensures success in life. The problem is not the medium of instruction but the quality of teaching. According to the

Annual Status of Education Report put together in 2019 by Prathama, an education NPO, it was found out that only 16.2 per cent of children enrolled in Grade-I could read a grade-I level text, while only 39.5 per cent could add one-digit numbers orally in rural India.

Primary education is the foundation of development of any child. If children are having different mediums of instruction which are different than mother tongue then it will be difficult for children to learn and for teachers to teach. If primary education is given in mother tongue, then the quality of education will improve because a child can grasp better, express better in his or her mother tongue and others can understand better if they know that mother tongue. It is suggested that the main thrust should be given to improve the primary education and it should ideally be given in mother tongue irrespective of type or place of school.

https://www.pioneeredge.in/guest-column-the-importance-of-mother-tongue-in-primary-education/

❑

64

Equal Opportunities to Women, A Social Investment

– Dr BKS Sanjay,
Wednesday, 09 March 2022

International Women's Day was celebrated as every year on March 8. It offered an opportunity to reflect on progress made, to call for change and to celebrate acts of courage and determination by ordinary women who have played an extraordinary role in the history of their countries and communities. The theme for International Women's Day 2022 (IWD 2022) was "Gender equality today for a sustainable tomorrow", recognising the contribution of women and girls around the world, who are leading the charge on climate change adaptation, mitigation and response to build a more sustainable future for all.

Article 15 of the Indian constitution gives the guarantee of equality to every citizen irrespective of gender. I do not state that the conditions have not improved for the female gender but overall, gender gap has not been able to catch up with the pace as the opposite gender. The concept of equality cannot be brought only with legislation. It requires transformation of thinking in the male dominated society. We are proud that our nation even had a woman Prime Minister in the past, but in spite of that the changes or the impact has not been reproduced in all the other spheres of life, in all religions and communities as it should ideally have been. In my opinion, whatever change appears in today's era which has been achieved in the condition of females is mainly confined to the affluent and highly educated society.

There was always a hue and cry whenever the issue of women reservation was raised. It seems to be correct to some people that a particular section of the society equates their women as the true representatives of all women. Rather, if that section of the society really wants to improve the status of female gender as a whole then they should in a real sense, consider the concept of equality to all women irrespective of caste, creed, region and religion. If it is diligently considered, then the status of all women will change.

It is pertinent to mention that even after seven decades of independence majority of the sexual abuse, molestation and rape incidents are still happening with the downtrodden, underprivileged girls and women. I would like to mention that most of the time even women of the affluent society do not give due importance to raise their voice against the perpetrators especially if the accused or perpetrator belongs to the affluent section or their community.

There have been incidents and reports in the mass media that the women of the affluent and influential society are becoming a party with the perpetrators, to commit the crime with women of poor and downtrodden society. The incidents in the recent past like incident of Unnao, Kathua and Hathras are the glaring examples of the discrimination within the same gender. It is suggested that when whole society practices the motto of Vasudhaiv Kutumbakam then things will change otherwise it will remain the same or could even worsen in the coming time.

I would like to raise the issue of domestic violence which is prevalent even today not only in uneducated and poor families but also in well-educated and rich families.

But contrary to that, there are many instances of harassment by the female gender of the opposite gender as well as that against the whole family. Whosoever is at fault, it is not only destroying the life of husbands or wives but also of their extended families.

If we really want to improve the status of women, we need to change the mindset of the whole society. An all-out effort should be made against the female infanticide, to give quality health, education and nutrition to the female gender as provided to the males. Prime importance should be given to education. I believe if equal opportunities are given to the females then the situation will be different and very soon they will have the same life as other females are having in the developed society.

Equality of opportunity in the matter of public employment is guaranteed in article 15 and freedom of speech and expression is guaranteed in article 19. In fact, equality is the fundamental right of every citizen- for example not to be discriminated on the grounds of religion, caste, sex or place of birth which is granted by article 15 to all citizens.

Education is the prime factor to give employment and employment is based on the quality of education. I believe that only if education is given to all girls either free or at subsidised rates then the ability of these girls will be changed and they will be able to deal with any problem faced in the life whether physical, social, economic, political or emotional. Our current government has taken many steps to give opportunity to girls to lead in many fields which were unheard earlier.

Though Article 15 states there should not be any discrimination on grounds of religion, caste, sex, place of birth, clause 3 and 4 of article 15 embody exceptions to the general principle of non-discrimination. They respectively empower the state to make special provision for women and children and for the advancement of any socially and educationally backward classes of citizens for scheduled caste and scheduled tribes.

In my opinion, if the nation wants to improve the status of the female gender then the nation should prioritise giving employment and a law should be made to give job preferably to the women of the families particularly if such families have never got the opportunity to get a government job in past.

Another suggestion is that considering the scarcity of job particularly in the government sector, only one person per couple should be given the government job with preference to the women. I am sure such arrangement will not only increase the chances of employment for other people as well as but also give an opportunity to empower the women too.

https://www.pioneeredge.in/guest-column-equal-opportunities-to-women-a-social-investment/

❑

65

Tuberculosis is Preventable and Curable

– Dr Gaurav Sanjay,
Thursday, 24 March 2022

World Tuberculosis Day is held every year on March 24 with the aim of making the common man aware of the serious consequences of tuberculosis (TB) and to focus on new ideas and scientific developments on how to make the world TB free. The theme for this year's World TB Day is "Invest to End TB- Save Lives."

TB is an ancient disease and it has also been mentioned in the Vedas and Ayurveda Samhita. The TB burden in India is staggering. TB is a contagious disease caused by mycobacterium tuberculosis. If left untreated, then every active infected patient of chest TB can transmit and infect 10 to 15 people every year.

India is a developing nation and it has been able to eradicate diseases such as smallpox and polio while controlling malaria and cholera to a large extent. But in the same way, there has not been similar success in preventing TB infection as was expected after the major success of eradicating polio.

It is a common perception that TB infects only poor people but it is not so. It is also infecting rich and affluent people. The cost of the TB treatment may not be a problem for the rich people but it is becoming very difficult for the poor patients to get treatment for prolonged time as is required especially in drug resistant TB. Many poor patients ignore the doctor's advice and do not take the full course of prescribed treatment and leave the treatment midway, due to which the number of drug resistant TB cases are increasing day by day.

The first United Nations high level committee on tuberculosis directed four new global targets, one of these targets was diagnosis and treating 40 million people with TB in the five-year period from 2018 to 2022. To prevent the Drug Resistant TB (DR-TB), WHO's end TB strategy calls for the early diagnosis of TB and universal drugs susceptibility testing.

India is also taking part in the recent global initiatives to find the missing cases. In 2018, Prime Minister Narendra Modi had given a clarion call to end TB in India by 2025, five years ahead of SDG target of 2030. Under the National Tuberculosis Elimination Programme (NTEP), in combating the disease of TB, all patients, irrespective of where they seek care, received free of cost, high quality TB care to realise the goal of TB- free India by 2025.

This kind of programme can be implemented easily through public awareness by mass movement, encouragement of healthcare seeking behaviour and the de-stigmatisation of TB. The case for investing to end TB is first and foremost financial, however the investment of hard work and determination are as essential as the financial resource needed to end this preventable and curable disease.

NTEP is based on the daily DOTS (Directly Observed Treatment, Short-course) chemotherapy strategy. The Uttarakhand programme has introduced daily drug regimen for the treatment of drug sensitive TB since 2017. Under the new daily regimen, TB patients will be given fixed drug combination (FDC), three or four drugs in specific doses in a single pill on a daily basis. These drugs will be administered according to the weight of the patient.

After assessing these aspects, if we think about why the infection is so prevalent and about the prevention of TB, then the increasing population in the country is one of the root causes. Overpopulation is depleting the natural and manmade resources. A message should be spread to the society that if one is divided by more than one, the dividend will be less than one. If a law is enacted to curb the population it will give good results for the entire population and it will not only be useful in the prevention of TB but also in improving the economic, social and political standards of the entire country.

As an orthopaedic surgeon here, I would also like to mention that the primary TB infection is either in the lungs, in the gut or in the neck lymph nodes. TB infection in the bone or the joint is secondary infection. The incidence of bone and joint TB has reduced significantly compared to the past because today the disease is detected and diagnosed early and the treatment is much more effective than 50 years ago.

India is facing the highest burden of drug resistant TB worldwide. I believe that lack of awareness about TB still exists today, which is making it very difficult for the society and country to control TB. The principle of prevention is better than cure should be understood very well in order to prevent any infection but particularly in case of TB infection.

In the end, I would like to say that TB is a treatable disease with cheap and very effective drugs available for it. Apart from medicines, TB patients require a nutritious diet, cleanliness and regular exercises. If the patients take the medicines as prescribed and for the duration advised, the infection of TB can be cured. The TB treatment should not be discontinued midway without appropriate medical advice. If there are any side effects of the anti-tubercular drugs, then the advice of a trained doctor should be taken and followed accordingly.

Not all orthopaedic patients infected with TB need surgery, however if it is needed particularly in case of joint and spine TB then the results of surgical treatment are predictable and effective. In spine tuberculosis if the infection is not being controlled in spite of the anti-tubercular treatment and if a patient develops paralysis while being treated with oral drugs then such patient needs urgent surgery along with high suspicion for drug resistant tuberculosis which needs drug sensitivity.

https://www.pioneeredge.in/guest-column-tuberculosis-is-preventable-and-curable/

❑

66

Open Secret of Atmanirbhar Bharat - Health, Education & Nutrition to All

– Dr BKS Sanjay & Dr Gaurav Sanjay,
Thursday, 07 April 2022

World Health Day is celebrated annually on April 7 to commemorate the anniversary of the founding of the WHO in 1948. In view of the current pandemic, a polluted planet and increasing incidence of diseases, the theme for World Health Day 2022 is 'Our Planet, Our Health'.

Health, as defined by WHO, is a state of complete physical, mental and social wellbeing and not merely the absence of disease or infirmity. Every person has a desire to be happy and we believe that only a healthy person can be happy. A healthy person can do not only his work but the work of others as well. The ability of any healthy person will always be higher than that of an unhealthy person in every way.

Health is not only an asset but also a resource which should be nurtured by all. Health and happiness are interrelated and directly proportional to each other. If you are healthy, you are happy. If you are happy, you are healthy. Health is a fundamental need of any individual and everybody should be health conscious. One should always take care of themselves in order to remain healthy. To achieve good health one can follow the acronym DEWS: Diet, Exercise, Work and Sleep.

A healthy lifestyle can be attained by maintaining a balanced diet and taking all the essential nutrients required by the body. A proper meal plan helps to attain an ideal body weight and provides the energy you need to keep active throughout the day and reduce the risk of various diseases. A balanced diet supplies the nutrients your body needs to work effectively.

In quantitative calorie deficiency, individuals lack adequate calories in their diet and in qualitative deficiency, they have enough calories usually from junk food which lacks adequate quantity of desired nutrients.

Proteins are the building blocks to improve and enhance our immunity. Pulses, dairy products and meat are the common sources of protein. Eggs are the best source of high-quality protein, which is almost 100 per cent absorbable by the gut. Micro nutrient malnutrition is very common in our country especially among the poor, although it is also seen in affluent society. It is also common in developed countries particularly in the geriatric age group due to lack of appetite and malabsorption of food. It is well-known that green vegetables and fresh fruits are the main and rich source of micronutrients but people prefer to avoid them as they usually produce gaseous distension and bloating.

It is suggested that we all should take a cup of green tea which is rich in antioxidants, eat a banana which is the best source of energy and magnesium, a lemon which is rich in vitamin C, a green leafy vegetable which is rich in iron, calcium, magnesium, a fresh fruit which has fibres, folic acid and vitamin C and an egg which contains almost all the important elements needed by the body.

About 70 per cent of all diseases are due to the change in lifestyle which has increasingly become sedentary. The main culprits are overeating, less physical work and consumption of tobacco and alcohol. It is suggested that we should eat less and work more. This is the secret of a healthy and a happy life.

Any activity lasting for a half an hour to an hour which makes the body sweat is enough to maintain good health. If we all do our personal and domestic work daily then one won't need to go to a gym. Unfortunately, in our culture, work has not been given due importance.

Sleep is a fundamental need of every living being just like eating. No person can do without sleep for more than 48 hours. Those who do more work have a better sleep cycle and those who work less suffer from insomnia. Lack of sleep and the influence of liquor are the main causes of road traffic accidents in our country and night time vehicular accidents are often fatal. It is observed that fatigue is a proven cause of accidents. In private sector due to the greed for money drivers are forced to drive nonstop for longer hours creating mental fatigue and in public sectors due to non-availability of enough trained drivers the available staff is asked to drive for longer durations.

It is not only our experience as we are sure that you may have experienced it too that in India the health needs of most people are competing with basic human needs like food, shelter and education. In India, we are still not realising the importance of good health and the government is still figuring out how to keep our fellow citizens healthy. It is important for government and individuals to look after the health of all people to make them more stable and stronger to complete any task easily and quickly.

WHO is focusing on universal health coverage, so is our government. In our opinion Ayushman Bharat Health Scheme 2018, Ayushman Bharat Health Infrastructure

Scheme 2021 and Swasth Bharat Yojana launched by the Government of India under the leadership of Prime Minister Narendra Modi is a major factor in improving health services not only for the poor and needy but for the entire country. If these projects are implemented honestly then they will prove to be a milestone.

Human resource is the greatest resource on earth. If we want to realise the dream of self-reliant India then the government should make arrangements to provide quality health, education and nutrition to all citizens preferably at subsidised rate. As it is said by ancient Indian Rishi Bhrighu, we all are products of pleasure and to achieve pleasure is the goal of every individual. If we are healthy and happy then we can achieve our desired goal and enjoy our life.

https://www.pioneeredge.in/guest-column-open-secret-of-atmanirbhar-bharat-health-education-nutrition-to-all/

❑

67

Books are the Best Friends, Love Them

– Dr BKS Sanjay & Dr Gaurav Sanjay,
Monday, 02 May 2022

As every year, the World Book Day was recently celebrated on April 23. This occasion was declared by UNESCO to attract the attention of people all over the world. There are many stories behind the celebration of World Book Day. For the first time in the year 1923, the date of April 23- World Book Day and the relationship between books was established by various book sellers in Spain to pay tribute to the famous author Miguel de Cervantes. This day is also his death anniversary.

World Book and Copyright Day is specially celebrated by teachers, authors, publishers, librarians, all private and government educational institutions, NGOs, working people's groups, mass media etc.

Change is a universal law. We believe if there is a need to bring change in the individual, society and country then there is a need to change the thoughts to bring any change. It is written in our scriptures that "Vicharh Param Gyanam, Gyanam Param Balam" which means that thought is the ultimate knowledge and knowledge is the greatest power. BR Ambedkar had said that just as a plant needs water, similarly an idea needs propagation or else both die. Books are a good, cheap and permanent medium for propagation of any idea.

Books are running our entire social ecosystem whether Manusmriti, Gita or Ramayana in the past or the Constitution of our nation in the modern era. Books are the source of prosperity of any nation.

Thousands of years ago, the right to teach belonged to the Guru. Due to which the spread and dissemination of knowledge was limited. You must have read and heard the parable of Guru Dronacharya who refused to give education to Karna and Eklavya. Today, anyone can get knowledge and progress to the highest level with their passion to study, as is the example of today's Super 30's manager Anand Kumar.

Books are such friends that whenever you want them with you, they are with you and fulfil their full duty and responsibility. There is no constraint like time and circumstance with books. Books are not only our friends, but they act as teachers, gurus and guides to all of us.

The books are the treasure for the future generation. Selection of the books for reading is an important aspect. The habit of reading is done by the readers but selection of the books for reading is done either by parents or by teachers particularly in younger children and teenagers.

Children who have the habit of reading books from childhood progress in their respective fields because their books and teachers contribute to shaping their life. We are orthopaedic surgeons and have made it a habit that before every operation, we read the book about that operation, from which we learn something new every time and we feel that in this way not only the quality of the operation improves but so does the patient's clinical outcome.

The importance of education and books was understood by many of our wise men, politicians and many enlightened people of the society. The main architect of Indian constitution Ambedkar understood the importance of education and gave its due importance in the framework of the constitution. One of his three basic mantras is to be educated.

Writers die but their books remain immortal like our books Ramayana, Gita, Quran, Bible, Guru Granth Sahib, Agam and Pitik etc. When we read a book, it seems that we are having a personal connection with the author and this feeling is what makes the authors immortal.

Books are not only to be bought and be kept in the book shelf but should be read on a daily basis. A survey revealed that the television is watched by people in general for 35-45 hours in a week which is almost equal to the working hours and people pretend that they don't have the time to read a book.

Hardly anyone will deny that the habit of reading books is not a new one, rather we all have this habit since childhood. Perhaps those who could not make this habit in childhood could not reach new heights in their careers like those of their peers who were avid readers. In our opinion, we should not make the habit of reading books only, but make it a habit of reading good books.

Groucho Marx said that a book is a man's best friend, apart from a dog. We think that a book offering would be the cheapest and best durable gift, especially on the occasion of birthday. Reading a book costing a few hundred rupees brings a big change in people's life. The texts in Ramayana, Gita, Quran and Bible not only change people's thoughts but also change the way they live. We are seeing this not just now, but for centuries in the past. The religious books have been shaping the humanity for centuries and the constitution of countries recently.

https://www.pioneeredge.in/books-are-the-best-friends-love-them/

❑

68

Smoking – The Leading Cause of Amputation in India

– Dr Gaurav Sanjay,
Tuesday, 31 May 2022

Each year World No Tobacco Day is observed on May 31. This day serves as a reminder to raise awareness about the dangers of smoking and to encourage smokers around the world to quit the habit of smoking.

According to 2021 data, there are almost 267 million tobacco users in India. Among adults (age 15+), 28.6 per cent of the population currently uses tobacco products (men 42.4 per cent; women 14.2 per cent). Tobacco use is a major risk factor for development of many chronic diseases including cancer, lung disease, cardiovascular disease and stroke. It is one of the major causes of death and disease in India and accounts for nearly 1.35 million deaths every year. Smoking also increases risk for developing tuberculosis and problems of the immune system including rheumatoid arthritis.

The negative impacts of tobacco smoking on the general health of humans are well-established and known to the society. There is a statutory warning on each pack of cigarette or tobacco pouch, reminding the consumer about the negative effect of smoking but despite these tonnes of tobacco are being consumed every day in our country. In fact, India is second in the world in terms of consumption of tobacco.

Tobacco smoking is known to increase the heart rate, blood pressure and increase of carbon monoxide level in the blood stream. The elevated heart rate and blood pressure drops within three months of quitting smoking, blood circulation improves and lung function becomes better after three to nine months with decreased symptoms of coughing and shortness of breath. Quitting will not only save the patients but also their loved ones especially the children from exposure to passive smoking.

Smoking itself decreases the tolerance of pain and nicotine blunts the effect of painkillers. This becomes a challenge in surgical patients especially during the postoperative period. The management of pain in these patients become difficult because the operative pain is compounded with the usual ischaemic pain these patients have. For elective surgeries these patients are usually advised to stop smoking. Smoking is an addiction and because of that a smoker suffers from the physiological and psychological impacts nicotine has on the body and brain. This problem should be understood not only by the patient and the treating medical team but by the family as well.

The habit of smoking and chewing tobacco usually starts in teenage. Hence, there should be strict ban on tobacco sale around schools and others educational institutions. All forms of advertisement glorifying tobacco should be prohibited in the mass media. Merely a statuary warning that smoking is injurious to the health is not enough especially in the case of children and people those who are ignorant and illiterate.

In addition to chronic respiratory disorder and lung cancer, tobacco also causes hypertension and arteriosclerosis. Smokers arrive in the orthopaedic OPD mainly due to ischaemic pain and in delayed cases with gangrene in the lower limbs. The author has an experience of treating many patients of peripheral vascular disease and gangrene. In these patients whenever there is a need of painkillers, they do not give them as much relief as to the general population.

Because of the narrowing of the blood vessels, there is decreased perfusion in the distal tissues which causes ischaemia resulting into the ischaemic pain and frequently gangrene of the distal part in the limbs. The organs like the toes and hands which are having hair pin like arrangement of the blood vessels are more prone to ischaemia and gangrene. Gangrene due to smoking is usually dry gangrene but whenever these patients have associated diabetes and if they become secondarily infected then it becomes wet gangrene.

Pain at times gets relieved by increasing the dose and consumption of tobacco at an early stage but becomes refractory to even high doses at the later stage. Due to this problem these patients indulge in other substance abuse. This causes further problems to the patients who then get trapped in multiple substances abuse practice.

Author had the experience of treating a middle-aged patient who was having a habit of consuming bhang, smoking beedi, cigarette and drinking alcohol almost on regular basis since teenage. He had already got his right below knee amputation due to blockage of the arteries, due to the habits of smoking and drinking. In spite of that, the patient has not stopped any of his habits. Last week he reached my OPD with severe pain and gangrene of the third toe which was not getting relief with the common painkiller and even with the narcotic drugs. Ultimately, he was subjected to mid foot amputation in an attempt to salvage his only weight bearing limb to maintain his mobility.

Due to the narrowing of blood vessels, there are high chances of poor wound healing and further necrosis of the incisional wound and even sometimes precipitation of gangrene of the operated site requiring revision amputation at a higher level. It is pertinent to mention that such patients should not blame the doctor, as it is common practice in our country, but should blame their body and themselves as a result of their prolonged substance abuse. This problem gets further accentuated if a patient is elderly, diabetic, hypertensive, having poor immunity because of any reason and taking steroids or immunosuppressant drugs for any pre-existing diseases.

Such patients should be given counselling before surgery and they should be informed about the possibility of such complications. If these patients develop infection and have poor pre-operative poor general condition then they can also succumb to these complications. Most habits whether good or bad are mainly formed in teenage. Therefore, it is the responsibility of the parents, society and the government to do everything to prevent the habits of smoking, tobacco consumption and alcohol drinking because prevention is better than cure.

https://www.pioneeredge.in/guest-column-somikng-the-leading-cause-of-amputation-in-india/

❑

69

Increasing Number of Road Accidents A Cause for Concern

– Dr BKS Sanjay & Dr Gaurav Sanjay,
Wednesday, 08 June 2022

Road traffic accidents have become an epidemic with the nation losing almost one and a half lakh people and 3-5 per cent of GDP. About 90 per cent of the accidents are due to drivers' negligence.

Fatal road traffic accidents in India are a common scenario. The recent accidents in Uttarakhand at Uttarkashi, Tehri, Champawat and Chakrata are glaring examples of the negligence of drivers and impact of these accidents on the society and nation. Six accidents occurred on February 22, resulting in the deaths of 21 people in Uttarakhand. This exemplifies the tragic loss of human resources the greatest resource on earth.

A GMVN bus carrying 28 pilgrims from Madhya Pradesh fell into 200-metre-deep gorge on the evening of June 6 while on the Char Dham Yatra. According to Uttarkashi district disaster management officer speaking to the media, the mishap occurred at 7:15 PM after the driver allegedly dozed off. The cause of sleep seems to be driver fatigue. It was said that this trip was his third trip without a rest.

The Champawat accident killed 14 people out of 16 who were returning from a marriage ceremony on the night of February 22. The pick-up vehicle which was supposed to carry 10 people was carrying 16 people. According to Newton's third law, whenever objects A and B interact with each other, they exert forces upon each other. In other words, for every action there is an equal and opposite reaction. According to Newton's another law of physics, force is directly proportional to the mass and the acceleration. Hence impact of large vehicle is always greater than that of a small vehicle and higher the speed greater the damage.

Another accident near Devprayag on May 8 resulted in tragic deaths of five members of a family in which the father, mother, son, daughter and niece died while returning from marriage shopping from Meerut to Vann village of Chamoli. The girl who was among the five dead was to get married four days later.

A patient admitted currently with us who is a truck driver ferries a truck between Rishikesh and Indore. The distance between Rishikesh and Indore is 1,046 kms. He told us that sometimes he drives almost 18 to 24 hours without any sleep, only having breaks for lunch and dinner. On April 18, he met with an accident in the early morning just before reaching Indore. One presumes that if he had taken proper rest and sleep then probably the accident could have been prevented.

A study conducted in 2020 by Save Life Foundation Mahindra revealed that truck drivers in India drive 12 hours a day covering around 417 kms with almost 50 per cent of them admitting that they feel sleepy or tired while driving. Clearly these drowsy drivers can cause fatal accidents on the road. Sleep deprived drivers are responsible for 40 per cent of road accidents according to a police report from Kerala. There should be an attempt to educate the drivers about the importance of sleep-seven to eight hours of sleep is necessary for good health.

A scientific study conducted in USA revealed that you are three times more likely to be in car crash if you are fatigued. Driving for more than 20 hours without sleep is equivalent to driving with a blood alcohol concentration of 0.08 per cent i.e. the US legal limit. However, in India the permissible blood alcohol concentration (BAC) is 0.03 per cent. The unfortunate part is that a driver might not even know when he is fatigued because signs of fatigue are hard to identify. Some people may also experience narcolepsy – short, involuntary period of inattention. If a vehicle is moving at 60 km/h in five seconds the vehicle will travel almost 80 metres which is equal to the length of football field.

Here it should be mentioned that the practice of consuming alcohol to reduce body fatigue is a common practice in India. According to Motor Vehicles (Amendment) Act the permissible limit of alcohol is 0.03 per cent i.e., 30 mg of alcohol per 100 ml of blood. It may be less risky to drink one peg of whisky, two glasses of wine or two cans of beer an hour before going on the wheel.

On May 17 an accident occurred in which one person died and four were injured while they were returning from Kedarnath. The alleged cause of the accident was that the driver dozed off on that ill-fated night. On April 19 three brothers out of four died in an accident on Saturday night-two on the spot and two on route to the hospital.

Incidence of drunken driving reported in media is just the tip of the iceberg. It is reported only when accidents happen and are known. A scientific study revealed that even with a small amount of alcohol consumption, drivers are twice likely to be involved in traffic accident than sober drivers. Many studies show that alcohol affects drivers' reaction time, impairs their judgement and increases risk taking behaviour like over speeding and abrupt lane changing. An incident reported in the media revealed that a police checking team caught a bus driver who was drunk and was carrying 35 passengers on Char DhamYatra. It is worth mentioning that a fatal accident is probably prevented by routine practices of police checking.

BAC machines or breathalysers estimate indirectly by measuring the amount of alcohol in one's breath. Breath analyser usually costs about Rs 1,000. It is a simple, cheap and fast screening test of BAC. It is suggested that all vehicles should be checked at all check posts not only for DL, RC, PUC certificate and insurance etc. but for indulgence of alcohol too. The police checking team should be equipped with breath analyser to determine the amount of blood in the system of persons suspected of being intoxicated presuming that every driver is vulnerable to alcohol intoxication.

According to WHO report, five lakh accidents are happening in India and nearly 1.5 lakh people are being killed in these accidents while according to a police report of Uttarakhand, in 2018 there were 1,468 accidents recorded which resulted in 1,047 deaths. In comparison to the national data where fatality is 30 per cent, in Uttarakhand it is more than double (71 per cent). It is attributed partially to the terrain. The accidents at night are usually fatal because of driver fatigue, lack of sleep and influence of alcohol. Driver fatigue is one of the top five causes of road traffic accidents. Driver fatigue is commonly referred when driver is tired, drowsy and sleepy. Driver fatigue can impair reaction time and decision making when behind the wheel.

It is advised that the drivers should avoid all-night driving. Accidents occur in a split second and a split second narcolepsy can cause fatal accidents in general but particularly in hilly areas. We all should always keep in mind that prevention is better than cure.

https://www.pioneeredge.in/guest-column-increasing-number-of-road-accidents-a-cause-for-concern%ef%bf%bc%ef%bf%bc/

70

Yoga the Great Unifier

– Dr BKS Sanjay,
Tuesday, 21 June 2022

The International Day of Yoga has been celebrated annually on June 21 since 2015. The theme for this year- 'Yoga for Humanity' perfectly portrays how during the peak of COVID-19 pandemic, Yoga served humanity in reducing suffering. The theme also aims at highlighting how even in the post-COVID geopolitical scenario Yoga can play a major role in bringing people together with compassion, kindness, build resilience among people and foster a sense of unity.

Yoga is a group of physical, mental and spiritual practices or discipline which originated in ancient India and aim to control the mind. There is a wide variety of schools of Yoga practices and goals in Hinduism, Buddhism and Jainism. Traditional and modern Yoga is practiced worldwide. Yoga is first mentioned in the Rig Veda and is referred to in a number of Upanishads.

The term Yoga in the western world often denotes a modern form of Hatha Yoga and a posture-based physical fitness, stress-relief and relaxation technique consisting largely of Asanas. This differs from the traditional Yoga which focuses on meditation and release from worldly attachments. The ultimate goals of Yoga are stilling the mind and gaining insight, resting in detached awareness and Moksha from Samsara and Dukkha.

The word Yoga is derived from the Sanskrit root 'Yuj' meaning "to join" or 'to yoke' or 'to unite'. As per Yogic scriptures the practice of Yoga leads to the union of the individual consciousness with that of the universal consciousness, indicating a perfect harmony between the mind and body, man and nature. Yoga has five principal meanings- a disciplined method for attaining a goal, techniques of controlling the body and mind, a name of a school or system of philosophy, "Hatha", "Mantra" and "Laya", tradition specialising in particular Yoga techniques.

Health, as defined by the WHO, is "a state of complete physical, mental and social wellbeing and not merely the absence of disease or infirmity." Yoga is a physical, mental and spiritual practice which can be done to maintain good health.

Everybody knows that eating a balanced diet, exercising and getting plenty of rest are key to maintaining good health. Physical and mental wellbeing start with access to fresh air, nutritious food and the security of a stable home. People also need healthy relationships and a life free from violence, injury and toxic stress. Access to routine and critical health care is also an important factor to maintaining health and wellbeing.

The philosophy of Yoga tells us that the root cause of all our sorrows and suffering is loss of contact with our true self. This self is called by various names, such as Atman, Purusha and God. Our loss of contact with the self is due to our ignorance of the self as the only reality. Ignorance creates spiritual blindness and subjects us to a world of delusion and desire. This world becomes governed by the seemingly unending rounds of birth and death, pain and pleasure, and happiness and suffering.

Stress is a new health problem. Stress is a constant factor in today's fast paced life that can jeopardise our health if left unchecked. It reduces the body immunity. Stress is a common conditional response to a physical threat or psychological distress that generates a host of chemical and hormonal reactions in the body. As a part of the adaptive response to stress various body systems such as the autonomic, cardiovascular, gastrointestinal, and immune systems may be affected.

Around 70 per cent of the diseases are stress related. Breathing exercise and meditation have proved to reduce this stress, which has been proved by many bio feedback studies. Ample researches have shown that just 20 minutes of meditation a day increases endorphins, decreases cortisol levels and fosters positive states of mind to promote better health. Yoga helps lower stress hormones that compromise the immune system, while also conditioning the lungs and respiratory tract, stimulating the lymphatic system to oust toxins from the body and bringing oxygenated blood to the various organs to ensure their optimal function.

Yoga is known to promote good physical and mental health. Practicing Yoga can help one to calm the body and mind that would in turn, help us with our overall day-to-day performance in every field. Yoga helps in reducing any sort of physical pain, improves all physiological functions, reduces anxiety and any symptoms of depression, improve strength, balance and flexibility of muscles, better sleep and help to relief the symptoms of menopause in women.

There are different kinds of Yoga and it is vital that we identify the right Yoga style for us. Yoga is a good routine activity for those who have high cholesterol, high blood pressure, diabetes. Just as we consider it important to have nutritious food and stay disease free to keep our body healthy, in the same way Yoga also plays an important role in making our daily life healthy and fit.

The habit of Yoga, breathing and meditation should be the part of one's day-to-day activity to maintain his physical, mental, social, psychological and spiritual health. Yoga needs only a little bit of time and is to be done at regular intervals to improve the general health of an individual. Yoga practice of half an hour to one hour on a daily basis is enough to maintain good health.

I believe that we should include Yoga in our daily routine. Yoga needs only little time and is to be done at regular intervals to improve the general health of an individual. It is preferable to teach the Yoga in school so that the habit of Yoga can be developed childhood. As it is said, it is easy to make any habit in childhood but difficult to leave that habit in adulthood. Therefore, the goal should be to target the children to give them good habits.

https://www.pioneeredge.in/yoga-the-great-unifier/

❑

71

Use and Abuse of the Title Doctor

– Dr BKS Sanjay & Dr Gaurav Sanjay,
Friday, 1 July 2022

'Doctor' is an academic degree awarded by a university or an institution, which is used to refer to a person with a doctorate. To obtain the degree, people need to pass a special exam to be called a doctorate or by writing a thesis. A doctorate is usually regarded as a higher degree above a bachelor degree. People who have a doctorate degree may use the title doctor, though in practice it is often and most commonly used by medical doctors. Medical doctors examine, diagnose and treat patients. The word doctor in modern English is most often used to refer to a person who knows the healing art and who is trained and licensed to use the art of healing.

The word doctor comes from the Latin word for "teacher," itself from docēre, meaning "to teach". Only university professors with a doctoral degree, normally teach at university. By the 14th century, the word doctor was being applied not just to a select few theologians but also to qualified and/or accomplished academics and medical practitioners. Historically speaking, eminent scholars whose name had the prefix doctor were usually accorded a lot of respect. Because of that most of the people who are involved or working in medical care are known to use prefix doctor in their name.

Everybody desires to gain respect and prestige which is usually earned by the virtues of hard work, sincerity, loyalty, honesty, compassion, care, selflessness and aesthetic sensitivity. Currently, many other people in the society are interested in gaining respect and prestige which the dedicated doctors have earned by being in this profession but these other people who had not been able to become doctors by qualification due to lack of merit and money use the title "doctor" before their name to earn the same social privileges.

The authors have seen the abuse of the prefix doctor by many paramedics. There is rampant demand for the doctor prefix among the paramedics like physiotherapist, lab technician and many other medical technicians who are working in big hospitals. Now the practice of abuse of the doctor title is so rampant in our society that not only paramedics but even the ward boys and ward ayas are using the title before their name after gaining some superfluous medical knowledge by the means of observation.

The other problem of prefixing doctor is not limited to the name but now it has become a common practice to use doctor stickers in front and back of vehicles to gain the same advantage while travelling on the roads as well.

Unfortunately, there is an uncontrolled rampant use of this prefix in the society, any person who is having little knowledge of medicine and even dispensing any medicine in the rural and remote areas is using the prefix doctor. India has millions of uneducated poor who cannot differentiate between a qualified medical doctor and the unqualified doctors because of their ignorance and poor education. Now the unqualified people who are abusing the prefix doctor give the general perception to the public that they are medical doctors and in due course of time the public continues to call them doctors even though they know that they are not qualified doctors because they are the only available skilled person in the remote areas.

Considering the non-availability of uniform and universal health care services everywhere in the country, the people prefer to take any care which is available in their vicinity irrespective of the quality of care particularly in emergency cases.

Many people know that behaviour, knowledge and skill are the key to success and the unqualified people who are practicing and prefixing the title doctor, know that they lack the required qualifications, knowledge and skill but they give a lot of importance to develop and practice good behaviour, knowing very well that behaviour precedes anyone in exhibiting their knowledge and skill.

Earlier, the Medical Council of India and Indian Medical Association demanded that the prefix doctor be restricted to only allopathic practitioners but according to new amendment all practitioners of the modern medicine, Indian system of medicine – Bachelor of Ayurveda Medicine Surgery (BAMS), Bachelor of Homoeopathic Medicine and Surgery (BHMS), Bachelor of Unani Medicine and Surgery (BUMS),Bachelor of Siddha Medicine and Surgery (BSMS), Bachelor of Naturopathy and Yogic Sciences (BNYS) and Bachelor of Dental Surgery (BDS) who are recognised by the central government of India, can use the prefix doctor in the country. Anyone, who has a doctorate in any field can also legally use the doctor prefix, in addition to the honorary doctorate degree usually DLitt, DSC and DPhil conferred by any university.

One would like to cite a story told by one of the professors of an esteemed university in the USA where one was invited to deliver a lecture. In fact, the host professor who sent the invitation to deliver a lecture asked whether I was a doctor

(Dr) or a mister (Mr). I told him that I am a doctor and he again asked me whether I was a professor. Then I said, "Of course, I am not only a professor of orthopaedic surgery but also the chairman of the department." Then he replied "You cannot be a doctor". Then he politely explained to me that you are no more a doctor but you are a mister.

He narrated the story of misters in the Middle Ages. In case a cut/incision had to be made in the body, if needed, a barber was called to do the same after which they used to complete the surgical procedure. In those days only the barber used to have sharp tools like scissors and knife. In addition to the tools, they had some knowledge and skill in where to cut and not to cut.

Male surgeons are always addressed as Mr in the United Kingdom because physicians were by definition doctors who possessed a university medical degree (MD) while surgeons seldom had any formal qualification before 1800. The growth of voluntary hospitals in 18th century brought high status to surgeons and surgeons became so proud to be distinguished from physicians that the title of Mr became a badge of honour. That's why there is still a practice in England to address senior professors and surgeons as mister followed by his name. And these practices are still going on and they don't intend to change it because English people feel pride in carrying their older tradition.

The National Medical Commission (NMC), in its code of conduct has introduced a major change, proposing the use of "Med Dr" as a prefix for those registered under the NMC Act, 2019 as practitioners of modern medicine. The draft regulations also propose allowing medical practitioners to refuse treatment in case of abusive and violent patients and/ or relatives.

The draft regulations have been put in the public domain by the NMC ethics and medical registration board (EMRB), inviting comments from the stakeholders by June 22, 2022.

Only those RMPs who are registered under the NMC Act 2019 can use medical doctor as a prefix before their names. Every self-employed RMP must self-display the unique registration ID assigned to him or her by the EMRB in his or her prescription, certificate and money receipt given to the patients. As we all know that MD is usually a degree conferred to non-surgical branches in Allopathic Medicine. So this is bound to create more confusion among the ignorant and illiterate as they have to choose who is the real doctor going to cure him or her.

https://www.pioneeredge.in/guest-column-use-and-abuse-of-the-title-doctor/

❑

72

Overpopulation Is the Root Cause of All Ills

– Dr BKS Sanjay,
Tuesday, 12 July 2022

The world population day was observed on July 11 as in past years to raise awareness on various population issues like importance of family planning, removal of poverty, improving the general health particularly maternal and child health and human rights issues. At the turn of the 18th century the world population was almost a billion but in the last just over two centuries, the population has grown to almost eight billion.

India and our neighbouring country China comprise just over a third of the world population. Currently, China is the most populous in the world but India is going to take over that spot and will be the most populous nation by the end of this year if the population in India grows at the current pace. There is need to introspect about the exponential increase and we collectively need to find a solution to the growing population issues. The major causes of population explosion are many but the main is the decreasing death rate due to technical and medical advancement, particularly in the last century.

One believes that human resource is the greatest resource on the earth and health is not only an asset but a resource which must be nurtured by all. Considering this, people should be a part of the solution and not the problem but there is significant demographic difference in different countries of the world. There are the countries which have older people contrary to countries where more than half the population is aged below 35 years. The latter is seen in many South East Asian countries including India.

The situation is quite alarming, as a billion people are increasing every 12 years on our planet which distributes the entire eco system among the humans and billions of other species. The ever-growing population is competing for all resources of the planet which are shared by the all micro, macro and gigantic species. The human race has taken over other species by its innovative scientific technology and application of research.

Whatever humans are doing is mainly for their advantage, but the indirect cost is being paid by other species and our environment which is being seen with the recent drastic climate change and increased number of natural disasters occurring all over the world very frequently nowadays. Natural disasters are not new to mankind but what is new is the frequency and seriousness of these disasters. The author believes that population is a serious and an urgent issue which should not be left to the government alone. We all should come together whether it is non-government, social and public organisations should all come together and should find a solution together. This should be the duty of all citizens irrespective of caste, creed, religion, gender, area and country to make efforts to control the population because the ill-effect of over population is affecting each and every one of us. We are all interconnected not only with humans but all species living together on earth.

In 2011, the world reached a population of seven billion and this year the number will hit eight billion. To reduce the population surge we need solution among ourselves and no other species can contribute or control the influx of human population. There can be many means to control the population but an important one is to increase the awareness about the ill-effect of overpopulation which is the root cause of all ills.

I believe that if any change is needed to change the society, then we have to change the thinking process of the individual. As it is rightly said in Buddhist philosophy, our life is shaped by our minds, we become what we think. The religious, spiritual and political leaders have great control over millions of minds across the world and they have immense power to influence their followers. They can emphasise the ill-effect of overpopulation. Overpopulation is depleting all the resources of the planet which is under so much stress which it has never been in the past.

The ground water level is falling gradually in most parts of the country which is more marked in the summer season due to increased demand. Similarly, because of overpopulation and pollution the quality of air is deteriorating across the country but mainly in the metros and big cities which is quite visible in the winter season in northern India as seen in the form of smog and increasing number of pulmonary diseases during that time. Food is becoming scarce. A recent report suggested that a third of the world population is not having even two meals a day.

Procuring this food is becoming tug of war for many countries because of their geographical location as they are not able to produce food grains and other food items and are dependent on imports. However, any geopolitical change in the exporting countries can disturb the food chain supply as seen in the past during conflicts between countries and recently during the Russia- Ukraine conflict. It is said that

Ukraine was the second largest exporter of wheat and many countries in Africa and Middle East which were dependent on it have been badly affected. Overpopulation is one of the main causes of contamination of air, water and food which are vital for every living creature.

Overpopulation is fuelling climate change and ultimately affecting not only the longevity and existence of the human being but of every creature on the planet. India is suffering a serious decline of freshwater due to over use of water for its agriculture and industrial demands. The situation is so alarming that none of the cities in the country has a continuous 24 hours safe drinking water supply. Overpopulation is leading to undue stress with increasing competition and conflict. Overpopulation in India is an urgent and important issue which should be noted by all but definitely by the policy makers.

The main cause of overpopulation in India is poverty and illiteracy which are leading to ignorance of health, education and nutrition or in other words the quality of life. It is suggested that to control the population, we must have awareness about the overall deterioration in quality of life for all due to an increased need to compete with all-natural resources and manmade resources among humans. This rat race which we are running needs a serious thought and we should spread this message among all stakeholders.

We need to educate the underprivileged, downtrodden and ignorant population that if one is divided by more than one then quotient will be less than one. The easiest and simplest way to control the population is to give quality education and health to all, preferably free or at subsidised rate to all. If this is done the results will be long lasting.

https://www.pioneeredge.in/overpopulation-is-the-root-cause-of-all-ills/

❑

73

Need of the Hour: Quality Healthcare for All, Everywhere

– Dr BKS Sanjay,
Monday, 18 July 2022

Health, education and nutrition are the fundamental needs of every individual but healthcare services have not been given the prime importance they merit in our country. The healthcare services gradually started deteriorating in the last decade of the last century and kept on deteriorating till there was change in leadership of the central government. The services at these centres should be improved- the sooner the better.

There is a concept of establishment of at least a primary health centre (PHC) in each block of the district covering every 20,000-30,000 of the population. The first PHC was established in 1952 and there are 23,391 by 2021. The PHC has played a significant role in improving the healthcare services significantly since independence, particularly in earlier times when there were not many qualified doctors available, especially in rural and remote areas. The maternal mortality rate (MMR) and infant mortality rate (IMR) was quite high at the time of independence in 1947. MMR and IMR are good indicators of the healthcare services of any country.

The system of PHC has also improved the delivery of universal immunisation programme. In addition to the many other programmes related to public health like TB, malaria, leprosy, encephalitis etc. Primary healthcare has also helped and propagated the concept of family planning programme to control the overpopulation in our country. The author remembers many instances as a child when a health worker used to visit every house during the small pox immunisation programme and as an adult for counselling of family planning, methods and distributing free contraceptive pills and condoms to the reproductive age group people.

It is not only my experience but I am sure it may be your experience as well, that in India, the health needs of most of the people are competing with the basic human needs like food, shelter and education. In India, we are still not realising the importance of good health and the government is still figuring out how to keep our fellow countrymen healthy. The WHO asserts, following countless studies, that nations which invest well in universal healthcare makes a sound investment in their human resource.

Access to affordable healthcare will not only truly improve someone's health and life expectancy, but also will reduce poverty, create jobs and drive the economic growth of the nation. The current government under the leadership of Prime Minister Narendra Modi has introduced Universal Health Coverage which is showing fruitful results which I can say for sure for a number of patients who were not getting free or subsidised healthcare services in private hospitals and were coming to the government healthcare services provider but after the introduction of Ayushman Bharat Yojana these people are getting free healthcare, not only in the government hospitals but in thousands of private hospitals.

The Government of India has started Ayushman Bharat Yojana, Pradhan Mantri Jan Arogya Yojana or National

Health Protection Scheme which will cover 10 crore poor families or approximately 50 crore beneficiaries providing coverage up to Rs five lakh per family per year for secondary and tertiary care hospitalisation. This scheme provides cashless benefits from any public or private empanelled hospitals across the country. This is a great relief especially to the poor and needy people.

According to a government report since the inception of Ayushman Bharat Yojana more than three crore people have been benefited and I am sure if the patients and doctors honestly take the advantage of this scheme then it will really be a turning point in the improvement of healthcare services in India. After implementation of this scheme, the cost of treatment which usually deprives the poor patients of good affordable healthcare will not be a problem if the situation arises. This scheme is redistributing the pattern of healthcare services in India and the results are visible.

To achieve the goal of quality healthcare for everyone everywhere, PM Modi announced the schemes for establishment of 17 new AIIMS and a medical college in every district. The implementation of these schemes will also change the scenario of current healthcare services. It will augment the quality of healthcare services which are lacking in many rural, remote and tribal areas significantly. Many of my colleagues have a different view about this scheme.

They say there are nearly six hundred (606) medical colleges and nearly one lakh (92,065) MBBS seats available as on March 16, 2022 cumulatively both in the private and government medical colleges. They say there are already so many doctors in the private sector, who are either having less work than their expectation and many of them are having the apprehension of unemployment even in the private sector. But, I have a very different opinion about the establishment of government medical colleges in every district. These government colleges will not only augment the healthcare services in the respective areas but will also reduce the number of patients in the tertiary care centres especially from surrounding areas.

Overall the quality healthcare services will be more accessible, better and cheaper. First, these government medical colleges will work as a benchmark in healthcare services and they will also work as a role model for the medical and paramedical staff of that area. Second, the younger generation doctors will not only gain exposure and experience from the senior and experienced doctors of these medical colleges but many of them will emulate these senior doctors. Thirdly many of the senior and experienced doctors would like to settle in those areas where they were living for many years. It will also change the demography of the remote and rural areas. In my opinion, the impact of these new medical colleges will be long lasting in terms of bringing the changes socially, economically, geographically and demographically.

When schemes like Ayushman Bharat Yojana 2018, Ayushman Bharat Health Infrastructure Yojana 2021 and Atmanirbhar Swasth Bharat Yojana, will be implemented sincerely then the scenario of healthcare services in India will be changed. Though initially, it may not equal that of developed nations, it will be a step closer to them. Chinese philosopher Lao Tzu said that a journey of a thousand miles begins with one step. Indian Nobel laureate Rabindranath Tagore rightly said that it is never too late to be what you might have been. I would like to pray for all "Sarve bhawantu sukhinaha sarve santu niramaya" meaning may everyone be happy, may everyone be free from disease.

https://www.pioneeredge.in/need-of-the-hour-quality-healthcare-for-all-everywhere/?doing_wp_cron=1658656551.3001298904418945312500

❑

74

Care for Your Liver to Live Well

– Dr Gaurav Sanjay,
Saturday, 30 July 2022

As in past years, World Hepatitis Day was observed on July 28 to bring the world together to raise awareness of the global burden of viral hepatitis. Hepatitis is an infection of the liver which can be self-limiting or progress to liver cirrhosis or liver cancer. Hepatitis is a major public health disease which affects the liver—a body organ important for maintaining almost all metabolic activities. One cannot lead a healthy life without normal liver function. Viral hepatitis is the commonest cause of liver infection. Hepatitis virus is of five types- hepatitis A virus (HAV), B virus (HBV), C virus (HCV), D virus (HDV) and E virus (HEV).

Hepatitis A and E spread mainly through contaminated food and water or hepatitis B and C that spread by body fluids, blood transfusion, use of infected needle and syringe, and through mother to child transmission during early childhood. Outbreak of acute and fulminant hepatitis B still occur mainly due to inadequately sterilised needles and syringes which is demonstrated by the recent outbreak of hepatitis B in Gujarat. It is more in Asian and African countries probably due to prevailing low socioeconomic conditions leading to poor hygiene and sanitation.

Population prevalence of chronic HCV infection in India is about one per cent.

According to the National Centre for Disease Control, the population prevalence of chronic HBV infection in India is about 3-4 per cent, which constitutes approximately 11 per cent of the estimated global burden. HBV infection accounts for 40-50 per cent of the hepatocellular carcinoma and 10-20 per cent cases of cirrhosis in India. HAV is the most common cause of acute hepatitis in the world. HBV and HCV are chronic viral infection.

Needle stick injury is not that common but there are many reports of the needle stick injuries. HBV is the most stable of blood borne viruses and can be transmitted by a minute amount of blood. The risk of acquiring HBV from an occupational needle stick injury of HBV antigen varies from 2-40 per cent depending open the source of level of viremia. The risk of acquiring HCV varies from 3-10 per cent. HCV is thought to be a fragile virus which would be unlikely to survive in the environment. There is no effective post exposure prophylaxis at present. Therefore, all health workers should keep in mind while dealing with blood, any blood products, needle and any sharp instrument that prevention is better than cure. More than 40 per cent of subjects had markers for all three viruses.

A quarter of subjects had silent HBV infection. These subjects should be considered infectious and they pose a public health risk. The transmission of hepatitis infection through injection has been recognised for more than 50 years. Many studies have proved that 90 per cent of drug addicts had at least one serological positive marker HBV or HCV. Compared to HBV and HCV, the risk of getting HIV from a needle stick from a known HIV seropositive source is between 0.2 per cent and 0.5 per cent based on prospective studies of occupational needle stick injuries.

The risk is directly related with higher viral inoculation which is related to the amount of blood introduction, concentration of virus, the size of the needle and depth of penetration. HCV like HIV is a relatively fragile virus and is susceptible to drying. Hepatitis B virus (HBV) is 100 times more infectious than HIV/AIDS. About 37 per cent of HBV, 39 per cent HCV and four per cent of HIV in healthcare workers around the world are due to needle stick injury. A study by a French surgeon estimated that general surgeons have seven per cent lifetime risk of contracting HCV and 0.15 per cent lifetime risk of contracting HIV. I presume the risk for orthopaedic surgeons could be more.

Occupational hazards in hepatitis depend on the task he/she performs. Any healthcare worker may be at high risk for hepatitis infection. Hepatitis B and C are common health hazards among healthcare workers which includes doctors, nurses, paramedics and the trainees who have direct contact with patients, their blood, body fluid and their surrounding environment and the surgeons who deal with sharp instruments during various intervention and surgeries. Being an orthopaedic surgeon, I can say for sure that orthopaedic surgeons are more vulnerable to unintentional injury due to metal sharps than any other surgeon because orthopaedic surgeons deal with many sharp tipped instruments and implants in addition to general instruments.

The fracture ends are often sharp and surgeon or assistant are at greater risk of an injury during reduction of fracture even after wearing thick gloves. Occupationally acquired hepatitis C viral infection is an important issue in surgery since there are no known vaccines or effective prophylaxis. Orthopaedic surgeons are mostly unaware of the true prevalence of hepatitis C. They routinely operate without glasses or double gloving and if double gloving then not needle puncture proof gloves. Needle stick or sharps injury can be prevented by using safe practice during work and getting vaccinated against infection. All health workers need safe working environment, personal protection equipment (PPE) like clothing, gloves, shoes, goggles and face masks etc.

All surgeons should continue to use highest standard of infection control, universal safety precaution and accepted measure to prevent blood exposure. The patients who are suffering with the viral hepatitis are already having disturb liver function but if they consume alcohol and certain other drugs which are mainly metabolised in the liver compromise the already disturbed liver functions. Considering the toxic effects of drug and alcohol, such patients should avoid alcohol and drug consumption.

I would like to cite an example which was narrated by my senior teacher that a 60-year-old patient who was a regular drinker of alcohol developed TB infection which was treated with anti-tubercular treatment. After a start of anti-tubercular treatment, the patient went into pre-hepatic coma due to that patient landed up in the ICU but recovered after withdrawing the anti-tubercular medication.

https://www.pioneeredge.in/care-for-your-liver-to-live-well/?doing_wp_cron=1661520394.5051279067993164062500

❑

75

Calcium and Vitamin D Deficiency in Young Adults in India

– Dr BKS Sanjay,
Friday, 05 August 2022

Calcium is a mineral like sodium and potassium, a micro nutrient which is needed to build strong bones and teeth. It has an important role to play in muscle contraction, blood coagulation, regulating normal cardiac rhythm and nerve functions. Children who do not get the required dietary calcium may not grow tall or gain the potential height they should. Everybody should fulfil the recommended dietary allowance (RDA) of calcium to maintain good health. This can be done preferably with a calcium rich balanced diet or by calcium supplements in the form of medicine.

There are many causes of deficiency of calcium and the commonest is dietary deficiency of calcium and vitamin D in infancy. This may occur also in childhood, adolescence and adult age as well. The symptoms and signs of deficiency of calcium and vitamin D are usually muscle pain, delayed teething and bowing of the legs, rachitic rosary (nodular bump in anterior chest wall) and broadening of the wrist and knee joints in growing children. Deficiency of calcium and vitamin D can be tackled by increasing the amount of dietary calcium and supplementation of calcium and vitamin D in the form of medicine. The correction of deformities can often occur with the splint and plaster manipulation at early stages.

Other causes of calcium and vitamin D deficiency are diarrhoea, dysentery and malabsorption syndrome especially in poor families living in remote areas with poor hygiene. Adolescents and the youth are nowadays obsessed with the physical fitness but do not like to consume natural dairy products which are the best source of calcium, phosphorus and vitamin D. To avoid weight gain and increase muscle bulk they prefer to take energy drinks and foods which are sometimes fortified or mixed with the anabolic steroids, lead, arsenic, bisphenol A, high caffeine etc. The long-term use of steroid is injurious to the health.

Being an orthopaedic surgeon, I have an extensive experience of dealing with the patients having the hip problem which is medically known as an Avascular Necrosis (AVN) of femoral head. If AVN occurs then it is difficult to revert the ischaemia of femoral head and if it is not treated well and in time, then it can be a very disabling problem for the patient. Nowadays the end stage AVN is being usually treated with the total hip replacement surgery which is not easily available and affordable in India to most of the people. One therefore suggests that these adolescent and young patients should prefer to do sports activities and other natural physical activities in from of brisk walking, jogging, skipping, hopping, push ups etc. I am sure these activities will not only maintain the physical fitness but will also save the time and money which is spent on the gym activities.

I would like to mention if you prefer to go to the gym, then all activities should be done under the supervision of a well-trained certified physical instructor and at any cost you should not exert beyond your body's threshold. In the author's observation, 10% of the gym goer land up in orthopaedic clinics because of injury sustained while doing gym specially trying to lift too heavy weights too soon or unsupervised techniques. The common gym related injuries occur in the shoulder, back muscles, groin muscles pull and slip disc.

Another problem which I would like to mention here is about the problem of hypothyroidism and Poly Cystic Ovarian Disorder (PCOD) which are also common in young and adult women who usually present with menstrual disorders, obesity and infertility. It is observed that PCOD is usually due to bad dietary habits of fast food, sedentary lifestyle and frequent use of medicines like emergency pills. Other lifestyle causes are smoking, drinking, lack of physical exertion or intensive physical training as required by athletes and dancers.

Certain patients are also having and obsession to reduce their weight and remain very thin or having the habit of compulsive sliming which are known causes of amenorrhea which leads to poor bone density and a fragile skeleton. It is only in our youth, when our body provides us the biological opportunity to establish a Peak Bone Mass by the age of 30 years. If that opportunity is missed, the deficit cannot be made up later in life but contrary to that we all gradually tend too loose this peak bone mass which we individually achieve. Women start losing this peak bone mass after menopause and men usually start losing it after 60 year.

The unique opportunities for prevention of osteoporosis later in life which is bound to occur is frequently missed before 30 years in our country due to ignorance, lack of awareness, and lack of availability of a balanced nutritious diet in poor families or poverty-stricken society in India which is still very prevalent according to recent government data. Nearly 20% of the population is still living below the poverty line and they cannot afford three times meals a day. We should start building up a strong skeleton early in life by engaging in sports activities. The emphasis should be given to both sexes but more in women because their peak bones mass is 25% lower on an average than that in men. So, what women need is precisely the opposite, a larger skeletal reserve of calcium than men to meet to greater future demand particularly after the menopause.

To develop the bones, in gestation, we need protein (amino acids), calcium, phosphate and vitamin D which go through the placenta from mother to the foetus. If the mother's diet is deficient in any of these essential's nutrients, then the developing foetus is bound to suffer with the deficiency of bone mass because even though the mother is having a deficiency but because her oestrogen level is high and the calcium homeostasis will be maintained in her but the foetus will suffer the most due to mother's ignorance about this fact. Therefore, all pregnant women should take balanced and nutritious diet with extra milk, calcium and vitamin D supplement which is needed for the growth of the foetus in addition to normal need of any women during pregnancy.

The new born baby's bone architecture has relatively more bone matrix and less mineral than those of adults. The human skeleton contributes to little 1% of the average body weight at birth. This becomes nearly 10-15% in adult male. The growth of the bone and the proportionate height of the body increase more at the age of 1 year, then around 5 years and lastly the spurt is at adolescent age. Once the growth plates are fused then any amount of increase calcium, phosphorous and Vitamin D intake will not increase the height of the individual.

I would like to write few words about the advantage of cow's milk over the other animal milk. Cow's milk provides readily absorbable raw material for growing bones. Like other ruminants, cows have a digestive system specially designed for extracting calcium and synthesising first class protein from large volume of vegetable matter which our human digestive system is not capable of doing. The milk and other dairy products therefore provide a source of readily absorbed calcium together with protein, fat, carbohydrate and vitamin D first to mother during pregnancy and then breast feeding for her growing child.

In the first year of birth, the child tolerates breast milk/ cow milk which is almost non- substitutable by any other form of food which is easily digested and readily provide calcium and other ingredients in sufficient quantities to satisfy the demands of growth of an infant. The adequate amount of calcium, phosphorus and vitamin D in diet not only will prevent the rickets but will help to ensure that growing skeleton develops good genetic potential and maintain the calcium phosphorous till the end of the life. We must achieve a good Peak Bone Mass to prevent early osteoporosis which is usually complicated by fractures even with trivial injury.

https://www.pioneeredge.in/calcium-vitamin-d-deficiency-in-young-adults-in-india/

❑

76

Channelise the Energy of Youth Towards Constructive Goals

– Dr Gaurav Sanjay,
Thursday, 11 August 2022

International Youth Day is an awareness day designated by the United Nations. The first International Youth Day was observed in 1999 after the UN General Assembly (UNGA) passed the resolution accepting the recommendation made by the world conference of ministers responsible for youth. According to the United Nations the youth fall between the age of 15 and 24 years. The purpose of the day is to draw attention towards cultural and legal issues surrounding the youth. International Youth Day is observed annually on August 12. It recognises and celebrates the contribution of young volunteers and activists who are dreaming of a positive change around the world. The youth serve as catalysts for peace and prosperity not only in their local communities but also on the global stage. To achieve the SDGs, the world needs to harness and leverage the full potential of all generations particularly the youth.

There is a need to provide quality education and health to the younger generation which will lead to employment and empowerment of the youth. This will result in the development of not only the youth but also of the other generations and the nation as a whole. The objective of this year's International Youth Day theme is inter-generational solidarity-creating a world for all ages. Equitable integration and partnership across all generations is also needed to achieve the SDGs and leave no one behind. Ageism affects everyone in all aspect of life. The concept of ageism should be minimised by rational policy changes, educational activities and inter-generational interventions. If we want to bring any change in the society then we need a change in the thinking process of the society including all strata and groups of the society. The youth are the powerhouse of all kinds of energy whether physical, mental and spiritual. What is needed is to channelise their energy towards constructive goals. Unfortunately, currently the youth power of the whole world and particularly that of India is being wasted or is being channelised in destructive activities.

According to a police report, 16 per cent of the youth are drug addicts in Uttarakhand. Drug addiction is the worst kind of addiction. Though both alcohol and drug addictions are bad for the younger generation, drug addiction is considered much worse. The author has the personal experience of three family friends whose children became drug addicts. Because of the addiction, not only are they suffering but their families are suffering as well. Two of the friends were good in their studies. However, after indulging in drug addiction not only have they ruined their lives but have also ruined their families. The families are putting a lot of efforts for de-addiction but in vain. The habit of drug abuse and addiction or for that matter every habit is formed in late childhood and/or early adulthood because this age is most vulnerable. Therefore, the parents, family and friends should be very cautious and all their activities should be supervised if possible.

An environment of isolation, depression, lack of any constructive hobby and unsupervised activities of youth are likely to increase their chances of coming across bad company which are precursor of such undesirable activities like the drug addiction. There should be a facility of counselling in the house and provision of awareness programme from the outside. This counselling and awareness programme should be given by well experienced person of the society, those who have respect and command in the society in addition to knowledge and experience. Such counselling and awareness programme should be carried out regularly in the schools and colleges among the students of the vulnerable age.

Most of the changes in the world have been brought by the support and participation of young people. Most of the leaders are achieving their goals all over the world with the support of the youth population. In India, there had been many youth movements in the past. One of them was the JP movement in the early seventies and anti-reservation movement in the late eighties. Both these movements have changed the political scenario of our nation. The youth population has been the guiding force in changing the society. The impact of the youth on our society is the largest in the history and it holds true in our country too. Bhagat Singh (23), Sukhdev (23), Rajguru (22) and Chandra Shekhar Azad (24) were the youth who had changed the path of the independence movement of India. All of them were in the prime of their youth. These Indian youth have not only changed the social and political scenario of our country but of the whole world. There are many such stories of freedom fighters of our country. Swami Vivekanand suggested rebuilding the Indian society. Education is the primary means for empowering the people. Real education is that which enables one to stand on their own legs. If education does not bring out strength of character and a spirit of philanthropy, then it is worth the name only. The philosophy of Vivekanand could be a great source of inspiration for the Indian youth. He once said, whatever you think, that you will be. There is a common wisdom that there is significant linear relationship between the age and work performance. This has also been proved by many scientific studies. Metabolic rate of the body is influenced by age and hormonal levels in the body which ultimately influence the amount of physical and mental activities. Younger the age more the hormonal level in the body. The youth can take greater risk and participate in more adventurous activities.

It is observed that "my life, my rules" is the motto of the current generation which should rather be "my life, my nation" which has been shown in the past by the iconic youth leaders like Bhagat Singh, Sukhdev, Rajguru etc. The nation should provide high moral value education and a conducive environment to develop their personality and to harness their potential which can be used for the nation building. The policies and effort should be made by the nation and the society to improve the quality of youth. The nation will benefit from the results if this is done effectively.

https://www.pioneeredge.in/channelise-the-energy-of-youth-towards-constructive-goals/

❑

77

Patient Safety: A Global Public Health Issue

– Dr BKS Sanjay & Dr Gaurav Sanjay,
Thursday, 22 September 2022

With an objective of promoting patient safety which has become a global public health issue, the WHO observed the world patient safety day recently (September 17). The day aims to promote patient safety by increasing public awareness and enhancing the knowledge and working of the healthcare workers. Patient safety should be the goal of all stakeholders- patients, health care workers and the healthcare industry. The patient safety can be improved by setting up the health priorities, developing guidelines and tools for health care workers.

Every year millions of patients suffer injuries or die because of unsafe and poor quality health care. Many medical practices and risks associated with health care are emerging as major challenges for patient safety. Few of the medical errors like hospital acquired infections, unsafe surgical procedures, diagnostic errors, unsafe transfusion practices, radiation errors, surgical procedure in the wrong limb or site are the common errors in medical practices not only in developing countries but also in developed countries as well.

Because of these errors in practices, the nation is losing crores of rupees every year. This burden is more marked in the rural or remote areas where the health care facilities are not as at par with metropolitan cities of our country. The healthcare system should take care of the increasing complexities in healthcare settings that make doctors and health care professionals prone to mistakes. It is a well-known fact that all humans err. The mix-up of the medicine and distribution of the medicine to different patients are well-known in our country. Many times, the patients identify the medicine with the colour of the medicine and if they forget about the colour, then there is a problem. To add to the problem many medicines are having the more or less similar colour and the similar packaging.

To err is human and expecting flawless performance from human beings working in a busy, complex and high stress environment is unrealistic especially in our country where many patients are illiterate and ignorant and healthcare workers are not as experienced as they should be. In addition to that, in our country, perfection is not the goal of most of the people and people are adventurous. Having this attitude, most of the time they end up in the problem. We would also like to share that certain patients do not take the doctor's advice as seriously as they should. We would like to quote an example of one of our patient who was advised anti tubercular treatment initially for first six weeks which should have been revised after six weeks on the next visit but patient continued the same medicine in the same doses for nine months which led to liver toxicity and ophthalmological toxicity. When asked, the excuse they had was that you said the ATT would continue for nine months to a year so we thought why re-consult you. Another instance we would like to mention is that people repeat the prescription for the same problem even after the gap of years or even for the different problem. These are not the only instances but there are many such instances in our country. We presume it is attributed to illiteracy, ignorance and poverty.

Diagnostic error is seen in about 5 to 10 per cent of the cases even in experienced professionals particularly in lack of proper investigation. Here we would like to mention a case where a patient in his eighties developed dorsal back pain that was investigated with MRI in addition to blood investigation. The treating doctor suspected that the patient may be having TB infection because TB infection in orthopaedic practice is rampant in our country hence patient was prescribed anti tubercular treatment but during the course of treatment there was no improvement however patient neurological condition deteriorated. At this time his family consulted one of us for the same problem. After thorough history, clinical examination, review of blood and imaging investigation records, it was suspected that the patient was having distant spread of cancer (metastasis) in the bone which was confirmed later by the biopsy. We believe that if the culprit is to be killed then first he should be identified and for identification of any person, the photo of the individual is needed. Similarly for the identification of any disease the photo of disease is needed i.e., the histological picture of tissue which is the biopsy.

In spite of all precautions, drug reactions can occur. The true incidence of drug reaction is unknown but it varies 1-2 per cent in the world literature. Reaction could be minor to fatal. Minor reactions include skin rashes, hives, itching, perspiration, shortness of breath etc. Authors recall an incidence of drug reaction with an antibiotic cefuroxime which is a second-generation cephalosporin. This injectable antibiotic is widely used as a prophylactic antibiotic for all surgeries throughout the world. The patient who was a doctor himself had already been given the first dose of the injectable antibiotic without any problem. However, when a second dose was given to him after six hours, the patient developed an anaphylactic reaction leading to coma. The patient remained in a coma for 10 years before his death. The error in cross matching is not a common practice but it can happen during labelling of the blood sample, not properly reading the details of the donor pack especially in emergency situations which are overcrowded, under-staffed in chaotic situations. This is not a blood reaction but purely a clerical human error.

WHO works on many issues of patient safety and hence WHO started initiatives like Cleaner Care is Safer Care (2005) for reducing health care associated infection; Safe Surgery, Saves Lives (2008) which is dedicated to reducing risk associated with surgery and Medication Without Harm (2017) to reduce medication related harm. The WHO Surgical Safety Checklist (2009) used in the operation theatre can reduce the errors and improve safety in the surgical patients. Considering the impact of patient safety, all government, non-government and World Health Organization should interact and engage not only with health care workers but also with the patients, their friends and their families. Patient safety should be a fundamental component of the healthcare system. It is important to recognise the impact of patient safety for reducing the harm to the patients and in reducing the healthcare cost. The patient safety will also increase mutual trust and the faith of the patient towards the health care system and the health care workers. It will also increase the quality of human resources in our country.

https://www.pioneeredge.in/guest-column-5/

❑

78

Education: An Antidote for All Social Ills

– Dr BKS Sanjay,
Sunday, 9 October 2022

The way MK Gandhi worked for political freedom by running a non-violent movement in our country, BR Ambedkar, through the constitution he headed the drafting of, provided us with political and social freedom. I believe that many people have contributed a lot in nation building but Ambedkar has contributed immensely. I had an opportunity to attend the release of the book "Ambedkar & Modi – Reformer's Ideas, Performer's Implementation" by former President of India Ram Nath Kovind recently. Being an academician and an orthopaedic surgeon, I would like to confine my views to education.

Considered the main architect of the Indian constitution, Ambedkar gave prime importance to education. He understood well with his experience and gave his key message of "educate, organise and agitate" to the masses. According to him, it is education which will enlighten the human beings and fulfil the dream of every Indian. Prime Minister Narendra Modi said during Dr Ambedkar Memorial lecture in 2016, "If anyone found the antidote to all social ills, it is Babasaheb. If anyone provided a permanent solution, it was Babasaheb who gave the message to the society—to get educated. The solution to all problems lies in education".

The goal of primary education should be to enable children to read, write, speak, calculate and express their feelings through their eyes, hands and other parts of the body. National Education Policy (NEP) 2020, under the leadership of PM Modi is a landmark step to make a radical change in the Indian education system. The goal of education must be to develop interest in the child in reading, writing and learning. The medium of instruction in school plays an important role in guiding and modifying a child's personality because language is one of the basic needs for communication.

The learning process for all children should be in the language which he or she can understand and easily comprehend. Every child learns his first word spoken in his mother tongue. In childhood whatever is taught, the child usually grasps it easily and retains it forever. NEP 2020 has given due importance to the mother tongue. The provision of a three-language formula in primary education in NEP 2020 will give long lasting benefits not only to the children but to the society and the nation. Books play an important role in shaping the life of all citizens. Knowledge has been passed on from one generation to the next through these books. The preservation of the books and construction of libraries has been a part of Indian society since centuries. The ruins of universities of Nalanda near Rajgir, Vikramshila near Bhagalpur in Bihar and Takshashila in what is now Pakistan and their grand libraries are testimony to the past. The programme Padhe Bharat Badhe Bharat is a unique initiative taken by Modi to inculcate the habit of reading among students of all ages. To fulfil the dream of Padhe Bharat Badhe Bharat, the earlier guidelines given in 2021on library grants were also boosted to enhance the habit of reading as a whole.

Ambedkar had said, "Humans are mortal. So are the ideas. An idea needs propagation as much as a plant needs watering. Otherwise, both will wither and die." Books are a good, cheap and permanent medium for propagating any idea. I am sure, like many books, this book 'Ambedkar & Modi' will also fulfil its duty for the same. Ambedkar had the experience of getting his higher education at a young age and hence understood the value of higher education. He was the one who had earned doctorate in political science from the Columbia University of New York, USA and in economics from London School of Economics. He wrote, "Education is something which ought to be brought within the reach of everyone. The policy therefore ought to be to make higher education as cheap as possible to the under privileged classes. If all these communities are to be brought to the level of equality, then the only remedy is to adopt the principle of equality and to give favourable treatment to those who are below level".

PM Modi is putting all efforts on making higher education as inexpensive as possible for the under privileged which is based on the principle of social justice and empowerment as I can see as a medical doctor and an academician. Under the leadership of PM Modi there has been tremendous change. According to a published report, there are 612 medical colleges in India having 92,927 MBBS seats and around 42,182 PG seats which are many times more than earlier. In my opinion the decision taken by PM Modi to reduce the fee structure of medical education such that 50 per cent of all seats in all private medical colleges will be at the fee in state government medical college, another to increase the network of AIIMS across the country and third decision to develop one medical college in each district is not only commendable but if they are correctly implemented and executed it will bring unprecedented changes in the healthcare sector in India.

Whatever Ambedkar did, he always thought about welfare and equality of citizens. Our visionary PM Modi is following his footsteps for the same goal. This could be because both were born and brought up in their contemporary time against all odds prevailing in the society. That is the reason Modi can feel the pain and can aspire to alleviate the pain of millions of those who are living in the same circumstances as he did. Modi is putting all out efforts by making the changes in government policies to make a better India not for the few but for all as it can be seen in his motto of "Sabka Sath, Sabka Vikas".

https://www.pioneeredge.in/guest-column-education-an-antidote-for-all-social-ills/

❑

79

Food Wastage in Undernourished India: A Big Problem

– Dr BKS Sanjay,
Thursday, 20 October 2022

The International Day of Awareness of Food Loss and Waste (IDAFLW) is observed on September 29. This year's theme is "Stop Food Waste! For People and Planet". It is a day to call to action for both the public and private sectors to prioritise actions and innovations to reduce food loss and waste in the world to mitigate climate change, and support food security and nutrition. The Food and Agriculture Organization (FAO) defines food waste as "wholesome edible material intended for human consumption, arising at any point in the Food Supply Chain (FSC) that is instead discarded, lost or degrade".

In 1903, Thomas Edison stated, 'The doctor of the future will give no medicine but will interest his patient in the care of the human frame, diet and in the cause of prevention of the disease. Prime Minister Narendra Modi recalled the maxim 'Yatha Annam Tatha Mannam' which means mental development is directly related to the quality of food.

India is the world's second largest producer of rice, wheat, sugarcane, groundnut, vegetables and fruits as per the Food and Agriculture Organization of the United States. However, according to the Food Security and Nutrition in the world 2022 report, 14 per cent (nearly 200 million) of India's population is undernourished, 20 per cent of the Indian children are underweight and nearly 35 per cent of the children below 5 years in India are stunted. In contrast, according to the National Family Health Survey about 20 per cent people in UP are overweight.

An estimated 14 per cent of the world's food is lost between harvest and retail, and an estimated 17 per cent is wasted in retail and at the consumption level. This comes at a time when 811 million people go hungry. All of this means there is an urgent need to accelerate action to reduce food loss and waste. The 2030 Agenda for SDG calls for halving per capita global food waste at the retail and consumer levels and reducing food losses along production and supply chains.

Although India ranks second in the world in the agricultural sector, at the same time India stands 97th in Oxfam's Food Availability Index, and 103rd in the 2018 Global Hunger Index. There has been a report in mass media that millions of tonnes of wheat are kept on the roads in open after the harvesting because there is not enough storage capacity in FCI warehouses. A country can be called self-sufficient only when it produces enough to meet its domestic needs. Every year in India, about 67 million tonnes of food is wasted, which has been estimated to be worth around Rs 92,000 crores. National capital Delhi produces about 9,000 metric tonnes of waste per day, with East Delhi being the largest landfill in the region.

People involved in the cooking especially in the celebration party like marriage parties cook the food on a hit and trial basis especially in rural and remote areas.

People serve a lot more on their plates than they can eat. Recent trend of having the maid to cook the food is also a newly created household problem because the maid does not think in the same way as the master of the house thinks about the wastage. There is common practice in houses to cook more food than needed.

Food wastage is causing not only the social problems but economic and ecological problems. Nation is producing more food grains by draining more groundwater because of that the water level is going down creating the scarcity of water. Though we are producing more food grains for that we are using more fertilisers and pesticides which are proportionately contaminating the soil and water and creating many health and ecological issues. Food loss and wastage is the third largest emitter of greenhouse gases. This is becoming a vicious cycle.

Food grains are not like the other natural resources like the stones and minerals. All food grains have an expiry date which is usually for a few days to a few months. Nowadays, grains like wheat, rice, pulses can be stored in a proper environment and warehouses for years. If it is not used in that stipulated period then it is going to be rotten or wasted. The wastage can be prevented if the raw or cooked food is sold or consumed at the right time at the same places.

In Indian circumstances the concept of weekly haat or bazaar for vegetables, fruits and other perishable items should be encouraged all over the country at a reasonable distance which will be profitable to both sellers and buyers. It will reduce the storage problem, wastage of perishable items, reduce the inflation and will give a boost to the economy of small and marginal farmers. There should be a provision of cold storage for vegetables and fruits at a reasonable cost and accessible distance. There should be a facility of fridge and deep freezer for both processed and cooked food at all food outlets irrespective of place and size.

One can understand the value of body weight to perform any physical work with a scientific formula, "force is directly proportional to mass". As the body mass increases so does the individual's force to do any work. In simple words, the output of physical work of the stunted person will be less than an average person.

Annam Vai Pranam means food is life. Improving the nutritional status of the citizens is imperative for nation building. The Poshan Abhiyan 2018-22 has set goals to reduce under nutrition, low birth weight and anaemia across all age groups. India needs a mass movement for good nutrition in the country because nutrition is one of the three basic foundation stones (health, education and nutrition) for nation building. All citizens should do their end to achieve the goal "Stop Food Waste! For People and Planet".

https://www.pioneeredge.in/food-wastage-in-undernourished-india-a-big-problem/

❑

80

Limb Health As Important As Health of the Heart

– Dr BKS Sanjay & Dr Gaurav Sanjay,
Thursday, 03 November 2022

Locomotion is important at every stage of life; however, it is more important in childhood. Normal walking contributes a lot for the overall development of any child. Locomotor disability means a problem in moving from one place to another, that is, disability in the legs. According to the 2011 census, 26.8 million people in our country were disabled and 20.30 per cent had locomotor disability. We believe that the health of the limbs is as important as that of the heart and the lungs. Whatever mankind has achieved so far is mainly due to its ability of locomotion. If all of us had not walked on our feet, we would not have reached where we are today. A healthy and educated person not only can do his work but he can also help others because help is the basis of our life.

Strong bones, strong muscles and flexible joints form the iron triangle that carries the most important load i.e. the human body. Interestingly, 50 per cent of a person's bones and the muscles are in the two legs. Both the legs together have 50 per cent of the nerves and blood vessels of the human body and 50 per cent of the blood flows through them. It is the largest circulatory network that connects the body. 70% of the human activities in one's life are done by two feet. The foot is the centre of body locomotion. Only when the feet are healthy then the conventional current of blood flows smoothly so people who have strong legs will definitely have a strong heart.

Overall physical, mental, social and economic development of any individual takes place only by locomotion. Ageing starts from the feet upwards. As a person gets older, the accuracy and speed of transmission of instructions between the brain and the legs decreases, unlike when a person is young.

Cerebral palsy, polio, club foot are the main causes of limb deformities and orthopaedic disabilities in children. Cerebral Palsy (CP) means paralysis of the brain. CP is caused due to obstruction in breathing during or after the birth due to any reason. The CP patients present commonly with scissoring gait and with deformed feet and hands. As the deformity increases so does the difficulty in walking. In certain cases, the child becomes bedridden. CP a lifelong problem which is a permanent condition caused due to damage to the brain. If the deformity is not corrected in childhood, then not only the physical problems increase but also the social and mental problems. This thing should be understood and explained to the family very well. Therefore, treatment should be done in such a way that disability and the related problems of the individual, family and society can be reduced as much as possible. There is a need for a team to achieve this goal and such a team requires a neurologist, physiotherapist, occupational therapist, rehabilitation expert, paediatrician, psychologist, sociologist and counsellor in addition to orthopaedic surgeon.

Any type of disability causes not only physical harm but also mental, economic and social loss. The needs of people with disabilities are the same as those of a capable person. Disability caused due to deformity can be reduced significantly with exercises, manipulation and orthosis and/ or after undergoing various surgeries. When the deformity is minimal, it can usually be corrected with exercises and splints, but when the deformity is severe, it requires surgery. There are several types of operations. In which muscle operations and bone operations are mostly done. To correct any deformity, there is only one principle of surgery that if one muscle is weak and the other is strong then either the strength of the weak muscle is increased or the strength of the strong muscle is decreased. In simple words the muscle strength is balanced. And if the bone or joint becomes crooked, then first break or cut that part of the bone with the operation, then straighten it and then keep it in a corrected position for one and a half to three months. To fix the bone, plaster bars, plates or fixators are applied after discussion between the patient and the doctor.

Flexible deformities can be corrected with soft tissue surgeries and rigid bony deformities can be corrected with Ilizarov external fixator. Our surgical results revealed what surgery can achieve often in an hour, physiotherapy cannot in a year. Sooner the better, the surgery is. Here we do not mean to say that physiotherapy is not required in such patients, rather we say that surgery and other therapies are complementary to each other in treatment.

Patients who have only one hand or one leg problem get better results, in comparison to the children who have the multiple deformities. Problem gets more complicated if there is involvement of the brain as well. Most of the patients become better after operation but some patients get worse, mainly due to either over correction or under correction of the deformities. In patients who have athetoid CP, the outcome of surgery is not good.

The correction of deformities should be done as soon as possible. The perception of the common people is that children should be operated only when they become mature but sooner the correction, better the result. Development of any child depends upon locomotion. If he can walk well and do his work with his hands. Only then will he be able to go to school and get education and by which he will not only do his work but will also contribute smoothly in the work of others. This will make the future bright not only for them but for all of us.

We all need a conducive environment to grow and develop in existing environments and circumstances but disabled people need more. The longer the disability lasts, its ill-effect increases proportionally. Government, non-government organisations and society should try to prevent any kind of disability. Deformity and disability due to any reason should be rectified as soon as possible because the plants can be straightened easily, not the trees.

https://www.pioneeredge.in/limb-health-as-important-as-health-of-the-he%ef%bf%bcart/

❑

81

Time to Really Curb Road Traffic Accidents

– Dr BKS Sanjay & Dr Gaurav Sanjay,
Monday, 21 November 2022

The World Day of Remembrance for Road Traffic Victims (WDoR) was observed, as every year, on the third Sunday of November. Fatal road traffic accidents in India are a common scenario. About 90 per cent of the accidents are due to drivers' negligence. The main causes of accidents are over speeding, overtaking, overloading, lack of sleep, driver fatigue, drunken driving and recently the use of mobile phones while driving. The important factors affecting the speed of the vehicle are driver related aspects like age, gender, alcohol intake, fatigue, number of people in the vehicle, concomitant use of mobile phone etc. Over speeding is fatal at any time but it is more fatal at night time. A road traffic accident in the daytime killed one of the important persons of the country which also grabbed the headlines. On September 4, 2022, former Tata group chairman Cyrus Mistry (54) and his co-passenger Jahangir Pandole (49) were killed and two other family friends were seriously injured.

The road traffic accident which killed Cyrus Mistry along with his friend was a tragic accident for several reasons. Mistry was travelling in a Mercedes GLC SUV which hit a road divider at the Surya River bridge which was the part of Mumbai Ahmedabad national highway. This tragic accident would have been avoided if there were warning signs at the various points before the start of the bridge. A police report revealed that Mistry who was seated in the backseat of the vehicle was not wearing a seat belt at the time of accident.

In a four-wheeler the wearing of seat belt can reduce the fatality of the accident significantly but the lack of awareness about the importance of seat belt and ineffective enforcement of the traffic rules by the traffic police are two major reasons for not wearing the seat belt. After the highlight of the death of Cyrus Mistry, the minister of Road Transport and Highways Nitin Gadkari has passed an order. It has become mandatory to wear the seat belt for all passengers including those who are sitting in the backseat, failing which a penalty will be imposed.

The technical reports released by Palghar police revealed that the speed of the car at the time of the crash was 89 kmph and it seems that the speed of the car before the crash must have been around 100 kmph. Though the permitted speed limit had been fixed 80 kmph on national highways but it was 40kmph particularly in that stretch due to high density of traffic and bifurcation of the road at the Surya River bridge. The Mercedes Benz technical report revealed that the car brakes were applied just five seconds before crash. If the car was driven at 90 kmph before the crash that means the car was running 1.5 km (1,500 metres) in a minute or 25 metres in a second which is too less time for the brake mechanism to reduce the speed of any vehicle of any make. On analysing this fact, it is right to say that "higher the speed, greater the risk and higher the fatalities".

The average longevity of humans in India is currently 74 years and we are sure this will further increase in the near future if we take care. Mistry would have had at least

20 years of his life and that too working life to look forward to.

Another eye opening tragic accident happened on Purvanchal Expressway on October 16 where four young people were killed in their BMW car which collided against a truck in which all four people died on the spot. The four friends, all in their thirties, were travelling from Bihar to Delhi. One of the four was the only child of his parents and he also had a four-year-old son, another left two children and the third was married only last year. A Facebook live video shared by one of the passengers just before the accident showed that the car touched a speed of 230 kmph while the maximum speed limit on the expressway is 100 kmph. The photos of the accident on social media revealed that the vehicle was absolutely battered and nearly unrecognisable under the truck. That indicates the severity of the impact of the accident.

Facebook live video captured before the actual accident revealed that one of the co-passengers was not only repeatedly boasting that Rs 50,000 was spent on the vehicle's servicing for this ride but also urging the driver to increase the speed up to 300 kmph to get more thrill. Speed thrills, but also kills. Considering the age and background of deceased, it is not only the loss of the deceased family but also a loss to society and the nation. The second Decade of Action for Road Safety 2021-2030 was proclaimed by UN with a target to reduce 50 per cent road deaths and serious injuries by 2030. India is signatory to this. All stakeholders should understand that 90 per cent of the accidents are due to the driver's negligence and all should act in that direction. Therefore, the public should learn and follow the traffic rules and the government should educate and enforce the traffic rules. Only then will the aforementioned target be achieved otherwise it will remain only a dream.

https://www.pioneeredge.in/time-to-really-crub-road-traffic-accident

❑

82

Challenges and Means to Better Address Disability

– Dr Gaurav Sanjay & Dr BKS Sanjay,
Monday, 05 December 2022

The United Nation General Assembly had proclaimed December 3 in 1992 as the International Day of Persons with Disability (IDPD). As done annually, it was observed recently to promote an understanding of disability issues and to mobilise support for the dignity, rights and wellbeing of persons with disabilities.

Disability is an umbrella term which covers an impairment in body function or structure. Such people face difficulty in executing certain tasks and have difficulty as an individual to deal with day-to-day activities. Being orthopaedic surgeons, we will confine our discussion to orthopaedic disabilities related with locomotion. According to a 2011 census, 20 per cent of all the disabilities are of orthopaedic nature. We believe that the health of the limbs is as important as the health of the heart. Whatever mankind has achieved by now, is mainly due to locomotion, be it in war or in peace.

The main causes of orthopaedic disabilities are club foot (CTEV), cerebral palsy (CP), congenital dislocation of hip (CDH), scoliosis, myopathies, myelomeningocele and rickets. In certain myopathies there is genetic transmission. The patients suffering from these diseases should get counselling preferably pre-conception. In the last 30 years, a lot of work has been done by governments, non-governmental organisations and communities all over the world. This has been made possible by their social commitment and improvements in techniques and medical advancement. In our experience, 40 years ago the patients of myelomeningocele rarely survived after birth and even if they survived, the infection and septicaemia usually led to their death sooner or later. But nowadays, many of these new born are not only surviving but after medical or surgical intervention they are leading a reasonably good life. The incidence of infection in children has been reduced due to judicious use of antibiotics and surgical intervention. The deformities related to infection have been significantly reduced in the last 40 years. However, the deformities and disabilities have increased proportionately after traumatic injuries especially after road traffic accidents particularly the open joint injuries.

Polio had been the main cause of deformities and disabilities in the past. However, India has become polio free since March 2014. There are no new cases of polio, but millions of patients suffering from polio in the past continue to suffer from post-polio residual deformities and still lead a hard life. These patients require braces and multiple surgical correction and reconstruction to make them lead a reasonably normal life.

In spite of the improvement in medical and technical fields, the incidence of deformities and disabilities due to congenital anomalies are not decreasing proportionately but rather increasing because of increased birth rate and decreased IMR. IMR has improved significantly since the independence of our country. According to a Government of India report, incidence of IMR was 145 per thousand live births in 1947 but as of now the IMR has reduced to 27 per thousand live births by 2022. Management of deformities and disabilities have significantly improved after early detection, early treatment including surgical intervention and better follow up of the patient. Recent social, economic, medical and technical developments have spread awareness about the diseases in general. Hence, the scenario of management of congenital deformities including club foot has changed.

The senior author remembers in his early days of orthopaedic training, the multiple visits of club foot patients in club foot clinic with a prolonged waiting list for club foot surgery being the common scenario. The incidence of only serial plaster application in club foot as a modality of treatment has reduced and also changed though the incidence of club foot surgeries has increased significantly in the past two decades. Hundreds of patients of club foot surgeries have been operated by us with significantly improved results. In certain properly selected cases, quality surgery and a regular follow up of these patients have given such good results that after 5-10 years of surgery it has become difficult to say if these particular children ever had any deformity in the past.

Posterior medial soft tissue release (PMSTR) was a common surgical technique performed about 40 years ago which has been replaced by Ponseti technique with tenotomy lately. In the authors' experience, reconstructive surgery with soft tissue release, Ilizarov fixator and tendon transfer give excellent results in properly selected, cooperative patients particularly those who understand the problem of deformity and disability and value of the surgery.

The results of treatment in CTEV have improved significantly but the scenario is not the same in Congenital Dislocation of Hip (CDH) and in scoliosis surgery. The principle of surgery in CDH and scoliosis are the same as in club foot. The sooner the correction, the better are the results.

Myopathies do not need surgical intervention though scoliosis usually needs surgical correction particularly for aesthetic reasons when the curve is large. Scoliosis is an abnormal sideways bending deformity of the spine which is usually seen near puberty but can also be detected earlier by observant friends and parents. Scoliosis patients mostly lead a normal life and can do almost all activities. Scoliotic patients develop early degenerative changes in the spine in comparison to the normal population.

Road traffic accidents are causing havoc and producing significant disabilities in the society. Road traffic accidents have taken over the deformities caused by other reasons. Nowadays these road traffic accidents are high energy injuries which are fatal and usually involve multiple bones. In such a condition, it is very difficult in general, to give pre-injury functional outcomes in these injuries in spite of the best possible treatment available in the country. The growth and development of an individual depends on locomotion, which is important in every stage of life. Locomotion depends upon strength of bone, joints and muscles which are controlled by various neuro-vascular structures. Injury to any of these structures can give rise to deformity and disability. Deformity and disability caused due to any reason affects the individual, family, community and the nation. Therefore, the goal is to enable the individual with a disability to live a life with the least impediment. The correction of deformities and disabilities requires a multidisciplinary approach. The needs of people with disabilities are the same as those of a non-disabled person. Deformity and disability due to any reason should be rectified as soon as possible, because "plants can be straightened easily, not the trees".

https://www.pioneeredge.in/challenges-and-means-to-better-address-disability/

❑

83

Health Should Be the Highest Priority of All Governments

– Dr BKS Sanjay & Dr Gaurav Sanjay,
Monday, 12 December 2022

The Universal Health Coverage Day is commemorated each year on December 12. Universal health coverage is promoted as an instrument to help advance the more broadly conceived human right to health, which is based upon a number of international agreements, or widely affirmed international documents. Under the United Nations Sustainable Development Goals, all UN member States have agreed to try to achieve universal health coverage by 2030.

Universal Health Coverage (UHC) entails ensuring all people have access to quality health services including prevention, promotion, treatment, rehabilitation and palliation without incurring financial hardship. The concept covers three key elements of access, quality and financial protection. The theme of Universal Health Coverage Day this year is "Build the world we want: A healthy future for all". The day is celebrated and is promoted by the World Health Organisation to provide financial risk protection, access to safe, effective, quality and affordable essential health care services including essential medicines and vaccines by all nations to their citizens. Every person irrespective of caste, creed, race, region and religion needs health, education and nutrition for his or her growth. Even ancient Indian scriptures mention that all humans should be healthy and disease free and none should suffer in any way. According to an Arabian proverb where there is health, there is hope and where there is hope, there is everything. We believe that health is not only an asset but a resource too. Hence, good health for one and all should be the highest priority of all governments. Although progress is being made by all countries of the world, millions of people still have no access at all to affordable quality health care. As the governments around the world are working towards providing good quality health care to the people even the Indian government is doing its bit to achieve UHC. The authorities are taking measures for the welfare of the citizens from time-to-time. These include awareness about medical issues, ensuring adequate infrastructure and promoting health insurance facilities. Universal health care services enable people to develop their potential and to achieve their goals to help not only themselves but to help others as well.

Human resources are the greatest resource on planet earth. Health, education and nutrition are the basic foundation stones for the growth and development of humans. Supporting the health care services is a foundational investment to develop our human resource. The President Droupadi Murmu during her address at the convocation in the Doon University recently said that the progress of any country depends on the quality of its human resources which in turn depend on the quality of the education. Education is the only tool to bring about a change in society. Being orthopaedic surgeons, we can say for sure that quality health care services will significantly reduce the burden of deformity and disability not only in the family and the community but at the national level as well. Currently, about 2.1 per cent of the Indian population is suffering from some or the other kind of disability with 20 per cent of them having orthopaedic disability which is mainly related to locomotion. We would like to suggest to all policy makers to give additional attention towards gathering solutions to these problems related to locomotion because if a person is healthy and mobile then only one can contribute his or her share in nation building.

Although medical treatment is very expensive in developed nations, even in India it is becoming more expensive and some treatments are still out of the reach of the poor people. In our country most of the people are getting the treatment after selling their assets like jewellery, land, vehicle, animals and property etc. The amount spent on universal health coverage can also be reduced by increasing the awareness about the value of their health. In addition to the Central Government Health Scheme (CGHS) and Employees State Insurance scheme (ESI), the current Government of India under the leadership of Prime Minister Narendra Modi has started several new health insurance schemes to improve the health care services in India. One of the schemes Ayushman Bharat Yojana which was launched on September 23, 2018 is working as a milestone to extend the health care services to 10 crore poor families or approximately 50 crore beneficiaries providing coverage of up to Rs five lakh per family per year for secondary and tertiary care hospitalisation.

This scheme provides cashless benefits from any public or private empanelled hospital across the country. The status of implementation of Ayushman Bharat Yojana as on September 2020 has been impressive. Under this scheme 12.13 crore families have benefited all over the country. Over six lakh hospital admissions have been done under Ayushman Yojana in Uttarakhand alone till date. Ayushman Bharat Health Wellness Centres (AB-HWCs) are aimed at transforming 1.5 lakh sub-centres and primary health centres into Health and Wellness Centres to provide affordable and quality primary care to the last mile. There are other schemes like Pradhan Mantri Jan Arogya Yojana or National Health Protection Scheme, Pradhan Mantri Suraksha Bima Yojana, Aam Aadmi Bima Yojana (AABY), Janshree Bima Yojana, Universal Health Insurance Scheme (UHIS) etc. There are four public sector general insurance providers who have implemented Universal Health Insurance Scheme (UHIS) with the intention of enhancing people's access to health care especially for people at or below the poverty line. This not only includes individuals but groups or families also.

As the WHO is focusing on universal health coverage, so is our government. The WHO asserts following countless studies that nations which invest in universal health care make a sound investment in their human resource. Access to affordable health care will not only truly improve someone's health and life expectancy, but will also reduce poverty, create jobs and drive economic growth of the nation in a sustainable way in the due course of time.

https://www.pioneeredge.in/health-should-be-the-highest-priority-of-all-governments/

❑

83

The Manmade Epidemic of Road Traffic Accidents

– Dr BKS Sanjay & Dr Gaurav Sanjay,
Wednesday, 28 December 2022

The great epidemics in the past were infections like small pox, plague, cholera, yellow fever, influenza and others with a devastating impact on human life, wreaking havoc and long-term effects on social and economic development. Today, these have largely been replaced by new epidemics like road traffic accidents and lifestyle diseases like diabetes, hypertension, hypercholesterolemia, obesity, alcoholism and smoking etc.

Road traffic accidents are a manmade epidemic, threatening the already over stressed health systems around the world and causing a disproportionate devastation of the livelihood of all- especially the most vulnerable individuals and the developing countries. There is an urgent need to have a resilient and robust health system to protect them.

There is great need for raising awareness to prevent road traffic accidents and even if these accidents happen then there is an urgent need to provide affordable transportation in the golden hour to reach the nearby hospitals which are easily accessible and have affordable treatment for all, particularly for the poor and vulnerable. The interdisciplinary cooperation among police, local administration, hospital managers, health care workers, patients and their relatives is paramount to deal with such an epidemic. There is a need for a nodal agency which can play a pivotal role and coordinate with all these individuals and agencies.

We need to recognise the primary role of regional transport offices where driving licences are issued, traffic police who control the traffic on the roads and the hospital health care workers who treat the patient with the help of various specialists and non-medical specialists in the hospital. The results of any surgery or treatment in case of a road traffic accident should be judged only after considering the pre-injury status of an individual. This should be assessed in terms of economic, social, mental and psychological status and ultimately the physical activities which he or she was doing before the accident. International days and weeks are occasions to educate the public on issues of concern, to mobilise political will to celebrate and reinforce achievements of humanity. The United Nations General Assembly designated December 27 as the International Day of Epidemic Preparedness in its resolution on Dec 7, 2020.

The commonly asked question is—what is meant by epidemic preparedness? It is defined as a country's sustained investment on prioritisation of the preparedness for disease threats and readiness to act, when an outbreak strike can fundamentally alter the trajectory of an epidemic and determine the number of lives, jobs and money saved. Society at large is in dire need of more awareness, exchange of scientific knowledge of information which can serve as effective measures to protect against epidemic and response to their emergence. In our opinion, road traffic accidents should have been declared as an epidemic by the health authorities all over the world, particularly by the WHO, because road traffic accidents are taking a heavy toll on earning members of the society which is wreaking havoc in the society. In other epidemics like COVID-19 pandemic, the fatalities are mainly the geriatric age group which is usually sedentary and has multiple comorbidities. However, people who usually meet with accidents and are injured or killed are young, healthy and productive. In comparison to the COVID deaths, two-thirds of road traffic accident deaths in India are reported in the age group of 15-44 years which is the prime age for any individual according to the usual parameters. Road traffic accidents cause immense loss to the family, society and ultimately to the nation.

We believe human resource is the greatest resource on earth and we should all collectively take care of it particularly as we follow the dictum of "vasudhaiv kutumbakam" which means that the world is one family. Any physical loss of an individual is not only the loss of an individual but a loss to the whole of mankind. It should not only be the duty but the responsibility of all governments, non-governmental organisations and other social organisations to prevent such an epidemic and to ascertain how to deal with it efficiently and effectively so that we can save the greatest resource in the world- the individual human.

The medical dictionary defines a pandemic as a disease which spreads throughout the whole country or the world, affecting an exceptionally high proportion of the population. Road accidents killed 1.55 lakh individuals in India in 2021 which is the highest death figure recorded in any calendar year so far, according to National Crime Records Bureau (NCRB) data. Besides the deaths, 3.7 lakh people were also injured in 4.03 lakh road accidents across the country. While the number of deaths has reached its peak, the number of road accidents and persons injured has come down compared to the previous year. A research conducted by us revealed that 90 per cent of the traffic accidents occurred due to the drivers' negligence. This is a behavioural problem which should be tackled to prevent the menace of road traffic accidents. Our country has about one per cent of vehicles in the world but it has 11 per cent of the total accidents. If we want to reduce the number of accidents then we have to first reduce the number of vehicles and simultaneously invest to develop an efficient mass public transportation.

The golden hour is a crucial period for an injured patient to have immediate attention. If he reaches a well-equipped hospital within the first hour of injury, then his chances of survival can increase many folds. To achieve the goal to reach the hospital within the golden hour, there is need for an immediate transportation of the patient and accessibility to well-equipped hospital where all super specialty services are available. It is suggested that there should be a provision of a well-equipped trauma centre at the intervening distance of 50 to 100 kilometres on all existing and proposed highways and expressways.

We all should always remember and remind others that prevention is better than cure. A national programme should be launched to spread awareness in general public about road safety. The public should learn and follow, and the government should educate and enforce traffic rules.

https://www.pioneeredge.in/the-man-made-epidemic-of-road-traffic-accidents/

❑

85

Time to Tap the Real Potential of Education

– Dr BKS Sanjay & Dr Gaurav Sanjay,
Saturday, 28 January 2023

Education is one of the human rights. It plays an important role in the development and peace of all human beings. One of the universal declarations of human rights is the right to education. The declaration calls for free and compulsory elementary education and it further goes on to stipulate that all countries shall make higher education accessible to all.

The 2030 agenda for sustainable development aims at ensuring and stipulating quality education for all. Education empowers people with knowledge and skill which leads to employment and employment leads to empowerment of everyone irrespective of caste, creed, religion, region and gender. Noted reformer BR Ambedkar also credited for his role in drafting of the Indian constitution had said that the progress of any society depends on the progress of education in that society. He also said, "Education is what makes a person fearless, teaches him the lesson of unity, makes him aware of his rights and inspires him to struggle for his rights." He believed that education is a movement. If it does not fulfil its objectives, it is useless. Education enhances self-esteem which is the primary force for any act.

Without education the individual, society and nation will not succeed in achieving their desired goals. Unfulfilled goals result in frustration and disturbance in the peace of mind. Though the Government of India has guaranteed education as a constitutional right we personally feel that emphasis should be laid not only on the right to education but also on the quality of the teachers as well. It is rightly said that only the learned can teach. Education is an asset which can be understood with an Indian shloka that means education gives you discipline, discipline comes from worthiness, from worthiness one can get wealth and from wealth one can do good deeds, and the combination of all these things can make you feel pleasant and joyful.

Education broadens the horizon of an individual brain. As we go higher our thinking broadens and so does our compassion for society. Education needs the least investment compared to the returns. Education enhances the creative and innovative ideas which are the primary source of all kinds of evolution and development. Good education not only helps to enhance the strength of the individual but also helps an individual understand one's weaknesses. The strength of any individual depends upon strength whether physical or mental. Education gives the opportunities to explore yourself, your environment and surroundings which help one to understand how to live in those surroundings. Education opens up new avenues and new opportunities to evaluate and enhance your knowledge and skill to deal routine and future problems.

The countries which have invested in education are taking the advantage of available natural resources and transforming their resources through their knowledge and skill. If you analyse the current global scenario the countries which have invested a lot are developed and rich, the countries which are ignoring the value of education are underdeveloped and poor.

We can say for sure that none of the countries are devoid of natural resources. In fact, nature has given something important and valuable to every nation but the poor nations are unable to take advantage of the resources. Take the example of Gulf countries- about half a century ago these countries were the poorest in the world and were inhabitable but after the discovery of crude oil the socioeconomic status of these countries has changed drastically. The hosting of the FIFA world cup is a recent example of the drastic change the region has undergone.

Our constitution in its preamble gives the guarantee of justice, liberty, equality and fraternity. The equality of all citizens can be achieved if education is given to all. Education will give equality not only in terms of political and social aspects but the economical aspect as well. Education is the simplest, easiest and cheapest tool to achieve the concept of equality among all citizens. It can transform and is transforming the lives of millions of poor in our country and in other countries. The credit for whatever development has been achieved all over the world since the medieval times goes to education. After the advent of the era of digital technology not only has the quality of the education, training and teaching been changed, the propagation and dissemination of the education has increased manifolds. The invention and later on use of digital technology in education has narrowed the gap between the rich and the poor countries.

There are still some issues due to the use of multiple languages in the different countries of the world. Can one imagine the exponential changes in society when the whole world speaks, writes or uses only one language.

If there is any ideal meaning of education and moral lesson to learn from democracy, then opportunities should be given to all citizens to develop the unique potential of an individual at every step and to produce disciplined and dedicated citizens so that all can contribute something for the welfare of the nation.

https://www.pioneeredge.in/time-to-tap-the-real-potential-of-education/?doing_wp_cron=1679126167.8189599514007568359375

❑

86

Increasing Prevalence of Cancer, A Major Public Health concern

– Dr BKS Sanjay & Dr Gaurav Sanjay,
Thursday, 16 February 2023

Cancer, in simple words is defined as the uncontrolled growth of the cells, having a tendency of recurrence and which may distally spread to the other organs. Cancer is not new to humans as it is perceived today. Its presence has been recorded in the ancient Egyptian and Indian medical scriptures dating back to about 5000 years.

The most significant factors for aetiology of cancer are prolonged longevity, adulteration of food and water, pollution of air; in addition to lifestyle changes like poor diet, lack of physical activity and being overweight. The important lifestyle factors which are known to cause cancer are use of tobacco and smoking. Tobacco chewing can cause oral cancer whereas smoking can cause lung cancer. The consumption of alcohol is linked with liver, stomach and breast cancer. It has been found that there is a synergetic impact of smoking and drinking alcohol in the development of several types of cancer.

It has been estimated that 30 per cent of all cancer in developed nations and 20 per cent in the developing nations are linked to the diet we consume. It is rightly said that we are what we eat. Our diet plays a vital role in maintaining good health. Tea is rich in polyphenols and green tea has 30 per cent polyphenols by weight. Polyphenols reduce the formation of free radicals in the body which can damage the normal cells and can increase the growth of cancer cells. We should avoid consumption of alcohol and tobacco in any form; rather, we should make the habit of consuming fresh fruits and green vegetables.

In our opinion, patients should know the early symptoms of cancer. The common early warning symptoms are abnormal lumps or bumps, unexplained fever, sudden weight loss, fatigue and pain which cannot be controlled with ordinary painkillers. If there is any suspicion of cancer growth then one should report to the local healthcare facilities at the earliest. Sooner the detection better the results.

Investigations like CT, MRI, PET and bone scans of suspected organs give an idea about the local and distal spread of the cancer. The health care worker should make the effort to have the definitive diagnosis of cancer which can be made with tissue biopsy only. The tissue diagnosis not only tells the origin of cancer but it also grades its invasiveness to the surrounding tissue. Many patients consult the doctors with delayed presentation of cancer due to lack of awareness about the problem, non-availability of the healthcare services and poverty. Once the diagnosis is confirmed then treatment should be started. Approach of the treatments and cure depends upon the type, size and spread of the tumour in the surrounding part and in distal part of the body.

As we know that if the cancer cells are not removed in time or are missed during removal then these remaining cells will not only grow in that area but may spread to the other parts of the body. As there are various means to treat the cancer like local removal of the cancer, reconstruction of the removed part, chemotherapy and radiotherapy to kill the cancerous cells in the local part and in distal parts of the body. Sometimes the cancer spreads in multiple organs then whole-body radiation therapy is given to control the growth and spread of cancer cells. The treatment modalities in the cancer patients are based mainly on whether it is palliative or curative.

The most important factor which influences the outcome of the treatment depends upon the age, comorbidities of the patient, type, size, stage and quality of surgery. Most patients consult the doctor with a delayed presentation. In rare cases, it may be missed by a doctor also, especially in areas with poor health infrastructure setup. Cancer awareness and early detection should be a priority for all. It will be worthwhile to spread the message that prevention is better than cure and realise the importance of early detection. This year's theme of the World Cancer Day was to "close the care gap" which is about understanding the inequalities in cancer care and taking actions to make the necessary progress to deal with them.

Cancer treatment is nowadays done with a multidisciplinary approach because cancer is such a disease which affects not only the one organ but can involve other organs as well like lung, liver, brain and bones etc. Cancer is the second leading cause of death in the world. The common cause of death in the cancer patients are infection, recurrence of cancer and distal spread to other organs mainly chest and brain etc. The distal spread leads to lung, liver, kidney, heart failure leading ultimately to multi-organ failure.

Health, education and nutrition are the fundamental needs for the growth of any person. If we analyse the human development index report of 2021-2022 released by the

United Nations development programme, it revealed that India ranks 132 out of 190 countries and territories. India has improved its ranking but not too significantly.

Budget spending on health is also increasing and it is deemed to rise to 2.5 per cent by 2025. The Government of India is trying very hard to raise the standard of living by providing free, subsidised food grains and housing to the underprivileged people but despite the efforts nearly 20 per cent of the Indian population still lives below the poverty line. Though India is growing, the growth story reveals that 40 per cent of the wealth of the nation is in the hands of the 1 per cent population and only 3 per cent of wealth is in the hands of the poorest 50 per cent of the population. If we analyse more about the richest people of our country then ten of them are having more than 10 per cent (USD 380 billion) of the wealth of the nation.

The treatment of cancer is very expensive in India especially for the people living below the poverty line. It is reported that certain cancer treatments can go up to Rs 20 lakhs. In such a scenario, it is better to follow the dictum, "prevention is better than cure". If India wants to become health conscious, then it has to make changes in its policies so that good quality health, education and nutrition are accessible at subsidised rates to all.

https://www.pioneeredge.in/increasing-prevalence-of-cancer-a-major-public-health-concern/

❑

87

Need of Scientific Community to Find Solutions to Manmade Problems

– Dr BKS Sanjay & Dr Gaurav Sanjay,
Friday, 03 March 2023

On the National Science Day observed recently, we remember the discovery of the "Raman Effect" by Indian scientist and Nobel laureate C V Raman. Chandrasekhara Venkata Raman was recognised for his research on transmission of light which revealed that whenever light passes through a transparent medium, part of the redirected light alters the spectrum and intensity which is known as Raman light scattering effect, in short "Raman effect". This was a significant discovery that opened the stage to a plethora of future scientific breakthroughs.

The purpose of commemorating the National Science Day is to recognise the value and importance of science in people's daily life and to raise awareness of eradicating taboos and rituals which are prevalent in many countries through science. Accepting the fact that the environment is mostly about science, hence, scientific research is done mostly about the environment.

Basically, everything in our environment is based on science. Science pushes us to our limits. Humans are the greatest resource on the planet earth. It is science which has increased our horizon of thinking and stimulated our human brains to think further. Everyday humans are excelling in their scientific endeavours and have gone from Earth to the Moon and now planning expeditions to Mars and they are going to explore other galaxies possibly in the future.

This year's theme of National Science Day 2023 was "Global Science for Global wellbeing". Our national leadership has realised the importance of science and its effects. India as a nation is emerging as a global leader and it is willing to play a more important role for shaping the global scenario. Currently, India is chairing the G20 summit under the leadership of Prime Minister Narendra Modi and this is the right time to harness the potential of the Indian scientist community involved with both government and non-government organisations by collaborating with the global scientists to address the global challenges like climate changes, pollution, future security of food and fuel for the whole global population which is currently at 8.04 billion and is estimated to increase to 9.7 billion by the end of 2050.

If we want to solve the future global problems, including those in our country, the nation should invest to develop the interest of the current young generation in reading and writing science. There should be an increase in the application of the scientific principle for the better survival not only of homosapiens but also of the other 8.7 million species of plants and animals of the universe. The goal of science, scientists and their scientific studies should be the wellbeing of the whole mankind. To achieve that goal, there is need that our current research should go from lab to land, from classes to home and from local to global.

We are in a new era to provide opportunities to common people. For that scientific fraternity in the country and abroad should come together, work together for the wellbeing of mankind; keeping in the mind the G20 summit motto – One Earth, One Family, One Future and Indian dictum of "Vasudhaiva kutumbakam" that means the whole world is one family.

India is bringing together scientists and administrators through international cooperation to discuss research and innovation for an equitable society. One of such meetings was held last week in Kolkata and many more such meetings will be held in the near future in various cities of India. Innovation has always been a cornerstone of progress in all aspects of life – health, education and nutrition which are the fundamental needs of every individual of each and every nation. These scientific innovations will benefit our people and our nations.

It is a challenge for mankind to deal with the major global issues like contamination of food and water, pollution of the air, climate change, poverty, over population, emergence of newer fatal microorganism, war and territorial conflict resulting into displacement of millions of people every year. It is not the duty and responsibility of a few individuals but it is the duty of all of us to contribute to checking climate change. If we all follow the simple principle of reduce, reuse and recycle then everyone can contribute to reducing global warming and can check the climate change.

However, some of the rich influential people are ignoring the above fact. According to media report, a family member of one of the richest persons of our country takes pride in not following the above sustainable principles while refusing to wear the newly purchased clothes even for the second time. In addition to that, they advertise and show their richness by spreading this message in mass media. Many current global problems have also been created by the scientific innovations. Now there is need that our scientific communities should find out the solution for these manmade problems. We make an appeal the researchers to do something not only to increase the longevity but to give longevity with purpose and action, so that the person not only lives longer but remains healthier and active. The person who lives longer should not only be active and do all his activities of daily living but should also contribute in activities which should be beneficial to the society at large with his learned experiences.

https://www.pioneeredge.in/need-for-scientific-community-to-find-solutions-to-man-made-problems/

❑

88

The Way to Achieving Gender Equality

– Dr BKS Sanjay,
Friday, 10 March 2023

As done annually, the International Women's Day was celebrated on March 8. Various events like seminars, marches and concerts are organised worldwide to highlight the issues related to women. According to the United Nations, though the world has made unprecedented advances, no country has achieved gender equality. The UN has set a goal for gender equality by 2030.

International Women's Day is a public holiday in many countries but not in India. We have many public holidays and the policy makers could declare this day too as one. That will be a tribute to the women who make up half of the country's population. The Government of India recognises women's achievements and honours selected women with Nari Shakti Puraskar which is given on International Women's Day by the president of India in New Delhi every year since 1999. This award was started by the Women Development and Child Welfare ministry for individual women and institutions working for the cause of women empowerment. This award carries Rs two lakh and a citation. The purpose of this award is to recognise the achievements of the women and to make them self-reliant. It is a general perception in Indian society that women are not equal to males and this award is given to the women to exemplify that women can also contribute in nation building like the men.

India is a country where women are given the status of a goddess. However, the problems they have to face just show the opposite of this concept. Various social evils like no remarriage of widows and child marriages prevail in India. Such treatment makes the women feel inferior and hinder the growth of a country. Things have changed tremendously after independence especially after accessibility to education for all particularly the girls. I personally feel that education has brought tremendous change in society. It has changed the mindset of both the genders. In modern India women face gender discrimination, dowry demand, dowry-related harassment and death, molestation, rape, domestic violence, workplace harassment and sexual abuse. Most of the time some female members of the family are also involved along with men in such discriminatory acts.

Violence against women is one of the biggest issues facing Indian women today. In a study done in India, 26 per cent of the women reported having experienced physical violence from spouses during their lifetime. Violence against women, especially domestic violence, often goes unreported. Gender discrimination is another major challenge which needs to be addressed in India. India's under-5 mortality of girls exceeds that of boys, unlike the global trend, according to an UN report. Uttarakhand showed the largest gender gap in under-5 mortality. Part of these deaths includes infant girls, as there is a preference for sons in Indian society. It is not an uncommon practice in India for girls to be deprived of proper healthcare, education, nutrition and vaccinations unlike the treatment given to males.

Every citizen and government must try to make it a safe place for women. Governments must make more stringent laws against people who commit crimes against women. The law must also be implemented properly to ensure everyone takes them seriously. Furthermore, opportunities must be provided equally for men and women. Education must be stressed upon and it must be made compulsory to educate every girl and woman for a better future. Therefore, each one of us must be ready to treat women as equal counterparts. We must help them at every stage and more than that empower them to make their own decisions.

A healthy and educated person can do not only his work but the works of others as well. One calls them dabang men full of confidence as he is healthy and educated. I will add here that our country needs dabang men and women. According to the Oxford language dictionary 'Dabang' means one who is not pushed down, fearless and influential. In my view it means healthy and educated men or women. Education is important in shaping the life of everyone. Education gives employment and employment gives empowerment to individuals.

https://www.pioneeredge.in/the-way-to-achieving-gender-equality/

❑

89

Inadequate Dose & Inadequate Duration, Main Causes of Drug Resistant TB

– Dr Gaurav Sanjay,
Monday, 27 March 2023

Tuberculosis bacilli (TB) have lived in symbiosis with mankind since prehistoric times. TB is recorded in Indian, Egyptian, Greek and Roman civilisation as far as 5,000 years ago. As done annually, the World Tuberculosis Day was held recently on March 24 to raise public awareness about the devastating health, social and economic consequences of TB and to step up efforts to end the global TB epidemic. The date marks the day in 1882 when German physician Dr Robert Koch had discovered the bacteria that causes TB. For that he was awarded the Nobel Prize in 1905.

Tuberculosis is preventable and curable. It is time to act, to find, treat and end this disease at a time when a quarter of the world's tuberculosis patients live in India. According to a WHO report of 2021, diagnosis of TB and drug resistant TB remains a challenge with a third of people with TB and more than a half of people with drug resistant TB not receiving quality diagnosis and care globally. The situation is worse in India due to poor socioeconomic status of the patients and under developed health care services in the country particularly in rural and remote areas of the nation. The services are relatively better in metropolitan cities due to high end health care services provided by both government and private sectors.

Due to better socioeconomic conditions in the cities there is better awareness about the causes of spread of infections and about the measures for preventing the infections. If TB infection is diagnosed early then the infection can be controlled early and easily even in cases of multi-resistant infections. The multi-drug resistant (MDR) infection is quite common in chest TB but it is also being seen in skeleton tuberculosis. The author has the experience of encountering MDR TB infection of the spine. Bone tuberculosis usually presents mild to moderate pain, stiffness of affected area, swelling and restriction of the movement of the affected joint and area. Earlier most of the spinal infection used to present with the huge paravertebral abscess and neurological deficit in limbs and rarely with loss of bladder and bowel control but nowadays people are usually experiencing back pain and stiffness which can be easily diagnosed with MRI of the affected area. Spinal tuberculosis is usually treated in early stage with conservative treatment which includes rest to the part, nutritious diet and non-steroidal anti-inflammatory and anti-tubercular drugs. The patients usually start responding to the treatment within 3-6 weeks and if they do not respond then one should analyse the cause of the lack of response to the treatment. In my opinion inadequate investigation, delayed or wrong diagnosis and improper and inadequate treatment are the main causes of the failure of treatment. The doctor can be blamed for empirical treatment/wrong diagnosis but patients are to be blamed for irregular and inadequate duration of treatment.

India is facing the highest burden of drug resistant (DR) TB worldwide. If we look deeply at the problem of MDR, it is a big problem in our country though the government is giving free medicines in government hospitals. Despite this, these patients are either borrowing money or selling their property to treat it especially in surgical and complex TB cases. Drug resistance is a formidable obstacle to TB care and prevention globally, making it harder and longer to treat, often with poorer outcomes for patients. It becomes somewhat difficult to treat TB infection, especially when it is MDR, extensively drug resistant (XDR), total drug resistant (TDR) tuberculosis. TDR TB is defined as a form in which none of the drugs available till date is effective against it.

I believe that lack of awareness about TB still exists today, which is making it very difficult for the society and country to control TB. The principle of prevention is better than cure should be understood very well in order to prevent any infection but particularly in case of TB infection. Inadequate dose for inadequate duration is the main cause for MDR-TB or XDR-TB. MDR/XDR-TB is a major problem not only in our country but in the whole world. This is a manmade catastrophe. The reason for the inadequate dose could be poverty, non-availability of TB drugs, non-availability of trained paramedical and medical staff and dis-continuation of TB drugs abruptly. It is seen because early results of anti-tubercular treatment are very effective. The patients within 3-6 weeks become not only asymptomatic but also think that they have become disease free. Therefore, they discontinue the treatment.

Delayed response to the treatment is usually due to poor immunity of the patients. The immunity is usually reduced if patients are on steroid therapy for any other medical problem or suffering with HIV infections or having associated lifestyle disease like diabetes or have already got DRTB infection.

The National Tuberculosis Elimination Programme, previously known as Revised National Tuberculosis Control Programme, aims to strategically reduce TB burden in India by 2025, five years ahead of the Sustainable Development Goals. The programme has a vision of achieving a "TB free India" with strategies to provide various free of cost, quality diagnosis and treatment services across the country through the government health system. Typically, the drug regimen consists of four drugs in an intensive phase of about two to six months and three drugs in a continuation phase of four to 18 months. To get the better result the immunity of the patients can be improved but drug resistant TB is difficult to treat easily because the drugs used to treat drug resistant TB are not easily available and if so they are costly and more toxic than primary line drugs. At later stage when infection does not respond to the treatment or during treatment patients develop neurological deficit like loss of sensory, motor power, bladder and bowel control, then surgical intervention is needed usually in the form of decompression of pressure on the spinal cord, correction and fixation of deformity and bone graft to enhance the fusion. Irrespective of the type of surgery, patients need anti tubercular drugs and other supportive therapy.

https://www.pioneeredge.in/inadequate-dose-inadequate-duration-main-causes-of-drug-resistant-tb/

❑

90

Resurgence of COVID-19 Infection – A Matter of Concern for All

– Dr BKS Sanjay,
Monday, 10 April 2023

Resurgence of COVID-19 infection is not a nightmare at this stage but considering the experience of the past COVID waves who knows when it may turn out to be so. In that case, it could be disastrous. I would suggest that all stakeholders should keep in mind the dictum of prevention is better than cure. I would appeal to the people to avoid unnecessary gathering, travelling and any other recreational activities in the coming time till the government issues certain guidelines.

Any viral infection including COVID-19 presents with fever, fatigue, headache, body ache, sore throat and running nose. These are the common features but recent loss of taste and smell, nausea, vomiting and diarrhoea are considered to be among the symptoms of COVID-19 infection. In general, we should take measures to prevent the spread of infection by frequent washing of hands with soap and water or rubbing the hands with commercially available sanitisers. The habit of hand hygiene should be observed in homes and in schools. It should be an essential part of the primary education curriculum. Once any habit is formed it is difficult to change. The importance of hand hygiene and technique of hand washing should be taught to children in simple words and simple ways. If the cleaning of hands is done in a group and in a play mode then children will acquire it faster.

As we have seen in the earlier COVID waves, the fatality has been more in the patients who were suffering with the comorbidities like diabetes, hypertension, coronary heart disease, hyperlipidemia, hypothyroidism, obesity and having other lifestyle habits of sedentary life, smoking and alcohol abuse. All of these conditions are known to reduce immunity and make the sufferers prone to increased chances of infection. Gradual changes should be made in the lifestyle habits so as to reduce the chances of developing these lifestyle diseases.

Another observation which was made during the earlier COVID waves was that urban people were more affected than the rural population. It could be attributed to the adulteration of food and pollution of the air. Considering the above fact, not only the policy makers but all stakeholders should make sincere attempts to reduce adulteration and pollution.

As the resurgence of COVID-19 infections in the country entered the eight weeks, India recorded 6,050 new cases of COVID-19 on April 6 which is the highest daily tally since September 15 last year. The Government of India has taken the resurgence seriously. The Union Health minister held a review meeting to assess the current situation with top officials including the health ministers of all States and Union Territories of the country. The Union Health minister has instructed that the share of RT- PCR should be increased all over the country. The positivity rate on the current date is 6.4 per cent which is not alarming. The Union Health minister has requested all the State Health ministers to personally monitor and review the preparedness to deal with the resurgence of the COVID-19 at the earliest.

The health officials can have the control of logistics and medicines but have no control on the behaviour of the virus. How the virus behaves in an individual body is an important and urgent issue. The severity of the infection and the development of the new variants are more serious issues. Every new variant is presenting with more fatalities as has been seen in the past particularly in the second and third wave. It has been more difficult to deal with the emergence of new variants. This is not specific to COVID-19 but is the character of all viruses.

New variants of the COVID-19 viruses are still emerging and spreading even among vaccinated people. New variants may be more transmissible and more fatal than existing ones. It is a matter of concern for all policy makers.

As I mentioned earlier humans do not have much control on the emergence of new variants. However, we all can take precautions. First, one should not get infected and if anyhow one gets infected then one should make all effort to prevent the spread of the infection first to the near and dear then to the others.

In my opinion, first, the whole nation should start again a mass movement to spread awareness to prevent the spread of COVID-19 infection. Second, focus should be laid on increasing the body's immunity by taking balanced and nutritious diet. Thirdly, there is no harm in continuing or restarting the trend of taking (kadha) or concoction of various medicinal herbs as was suggested by the AYUSH ministry.

The vaccine made against COVID-19 does not give a lifelong protection similar to influenza infection. I think as we need re-vaccination for prevention of influenza virus similarly, we need re-vaccination for COVID-19 virus infection. The influenza vaccine is generally given yearly to prevent seasonal influenza. Learning from the influenza vaccine, I think the concept of re-vaccinations should be considered. The pros and cons of re-vaccinations should be considered and discussed thoroughly by all policy makers keeping in mind the dictum of prevention is better than cu re.

It is appealed to all stakeholders to act once again accordingly as we all did during the peak of COVID-19 pandemic in the past. I am sure that with the efforts of all stakeholders under the guidance of our Prime Minister Narendra Modi, the nation will once again win the war against the resurgence of COVID-19 infection as it did in the past.

https://www.pioneeredge.in/resurgence-of-covid-19-infection-a-matter-of-concern-for-all/

❑

91

BR Ambedkar - A Great Reformer

– Dr BKS Sanjay,
Monday, 17 April 2023

BR Ambedkar's 132nd birth anniversary was recently observed on April 14. I have reached where I am because of two reasons- because of Ambedkar's mantra- "be educated" and because of the mantra in the Geeta- "action is superior to inaction".

According to my understanding, Ambedkar's biggest contribution in the making of modern India is that he gave such a detailed and written constitution to our country. Our constitution is based on harmony and equality and is the pivot of nation building. It has guaranteed every adult the right to vote. If this provision was not there in the constitution, most of the people of our country would have been demanding the right to vote and things like equality and justice would have been a far cry. Speaking for myself, I can definitely say that according to my geographical, economic, social and family background, I would not have reached where I have reached and probably many of you too. On Ambedkar's birth anniversary in parliament in 2015, our Prime Minister Narendra Modi had said in his address that it is because of our constitution that today a Dalit is the

President of the country, a farmer's son is the Vice President and a tea seller is the Prime Minister.

I believe that the way MK Gandhi gave political freedom in our country by running a non-violent movement, Ambedkar gave not only political but also social and economic freedom to all of us by running a non-violent movement through the constitution. He was able to do this only because he took education and received education not only from the highest institutions of the country but also from the world-famous Columbia University of America and London School of Economics in Britain.

I think no other national or international leader had received as much respect as he earned through his intelligence and duties. It is a matter of great pride for our country that Ambedkar was given first place in the list of contemporary100 intelligent students of the world. Some years ago, his 125th birth anniversary was celebrated for the first time at the United Nations in New York. He is such a person whose birth anniversary is celebrated every year in about 65 countries of the world. The then US President Barack Obama, while addressing the Indian parliament in 2010, referred to Ambedkar as the architect of India's constitution and a great human rights champion of the world.

His statutes are installed not only in different parts of the country but also in many countries of the world as in the Columbia University in America and London School of Economics in Britain. Ambedkar was not only the architect of our constitution but was a true social reformer for the entire humanity. This is the reason why all the main political parties of the country honoured him in their own way, such as installing his statue in the premises of the parliament, conferring the country's highest civilian honour Bharat Ratna, building a grand and unique government park in his name, naming dozens of universities, hundreds of institutions and places in the country, constructing

Ambedkar memorial in Lucknow and Noida, creating Ambedkar Pratishthan in Delhi, declaring a public holiday on his birthday and making Ambedkar memorial in London which was inaugurated in 2015 by Prime Minister Modi.

Ambedkar was a man of many talents. If you look closely at the Indian constitution it will be clear that he has taken care of every person, class, caste, region and religion of the country. In my opinion he is not the leader of our country alone but one of the few leaders of the whole world, whose ideas have become ideal for the entire humanity today. In my understanding, whatever Ambedkar achieved in his life and even after life, he achieved only through education. The event of reaching America at the age of 22 to study at the prestigious Columbia University with the financial help from the Raja Gaikwad of Baroda acted as a catalyst in his life. He gave the slogan of "be educated", but how to become educated in today's system? Today money is needed to get education with money and education becoming synonymous. Those who have money have education and those who have education have money. Our governments have given the right to education but not the right to qualified teachers. I believe that education leads to employment and employment leads to empowerment. If governments want to give something to the poor, then it should be education and that too quality education, free of cost or at least at subsidised rates.

It is only through knowledge that a person takes second birth and becomes another person. Ambedkar proved this well with his knowledge. The type of knowledge one has decides what type of person he or she becomes. I would say that what is written in Manusmriti proves this fact. "Janmana Jayate Shudrah Karmana Dwij Uchyate" which means every person is a Shudra by birth and becomes a Dwij (twice born) by his actions. Ambedkar is proof of this.

Many examples of this will be found in modern India as well. Our President Droupadi Murmu, Prime Minister

Modi and all of us are also living examples of this. Our scriptures are full of such examples like Vedvyas, the author of Mahabharata, Valmiki, the author of Ramayana, and Vidura, the son of Satyakama who became different by their knowledge and their deeds. Our society should accept the universal fact that there is a need to bring change in individual, society and country and change is a universal truth. To bring any change thoughts need to be changed. It is written in our scriptures, "Vicharam Param Gyanam" which means thought is the ultimate knowledge and it is also written "Gyanam Param Balam" which means knowledge is the greatest strength but certain people are not able to digest the change that is taking place in the society. They are opposing this change in every way, by hook or by crook. This is because of politics or ideology but the root cause of all this is the social system which has been going on for a long time.

Buddhist philosophy states that our life is shaped by our mind, we become what we think. Ambedkar had said that the development of intelligence should be an important part of human existence. This goal can be achieved only through education, so we all should follow the basic mantra of Bhimrao Ambedkar and be educated because knowledge is the basis of every person's life.

I believe that when every child will get a good education, then many Ambedkars, Murmus, Modis, Karnas, Vidurs and Satyakams will be born. In my opinion we all should be identified only by work and not by caste, creed, religion, gender or region. If this happens it will fulfil the dream of Prime Minister Modi and all the citizens in the real sense. Then our nation will become self-reliant and ultimately a Vishwaguru and a developed nation.

https://www.pioneeredge.in/br-ambedkar-a-great-reformer/

❑

92

Nurses are As Important As Doctors in Keeping Health Services Healthy

– Dr BKS Sanjay & Dr Gaurav Sanjay,
Thursday, 11 May 2023

The International Nurses Day is celebrated every year on May 12, the birth anniversary of Florence Nightingale. It was first proposed by the US Department of Health, Education and Welfare in 1953. The International Nurses Council celebrated this day for the first time in the year 1965. It was decided in 1974 to celebrate May 12 as International Nurses Day.

Nightingale was an English social reformer who is called the mother of modern nursing. She rendered outstanding services to the wounded soldiers, opened the way for nursing and opened the first nursing school in 1860. She exemplified how one person can make a change in the whole world. International Nurses Day is celebrated to recognise and to appreciate the hard work, dedication and contribution of nurses in health services, to honour them, to educate and train nurses for the welfare of patients and to discuss various issues related to nurses.

The theme of this year's International Nurses Day is "Our Nurses, Our Future". Nurses play an essential role in our medical institutions. They cater not only to the medical needs but also the physical rehabilitation and mental needs of the patients. They give medicines and injections as per the doctor's instructions, but they also measure their vitals, help in their feed, urination and defecation and maintaining medical records. We think if there is one person who is more important than the doctor in the treatment of patients, it is the nurse. Today, nurses are not only helping in the investigation and treatment of patients but also advising patients and their relatives to avoid other diseases. As a surgeon, we would also say that if the surgeon and anaesthetist are important in the success of an operation, the nurses who assist in the operation theatre and maintain the patient in the ward are equally important. Nowadays, the number of hazards in the operation has increased but the number of hazards after the operation has not decreased as much as it should have, especially in countries like ours.

Infection is the most dangerous risk after an operation, which is a deciding factor after a surgery. It is a huge responsibility of nurses to keep the patient clean for the sanitation workers, the patient and their relatives to know about the importance of cleanliness.

In our understanding, not many doctors are close to the patients but many nurses have closer bonds with the patient. It has been seen many times that the patient does not talk openly or tell all problems to the doctor or surgeon like he or she does to the nurse. A scientific study has proved that when the doctor visits or talks to the patient, the patient's blood pressure increases more than before and on the contrary, when the nurse visits or talks to the patient, the blood pressure decreases relatively due to her/his arrival. If you assess it in simple terms, the patient's intimacy with the doctor is not as much as it is with the nurse. In our opinion, the nurses are not getting as much respect from the society and system as they deserve. In addition to the qualifications for nursing, they also require sensitivity towards the patient and society. We think it's not just a job, it's also a selfless service to society. Nurses do not discriminate against any kind of patients as was seen during the recent COVID pandemic and earlier with patients of AIDS, leprosy, cholera and plague.

Today, like doctors, there is a shortage of nurses in our country. If we look at the norms of the WHO, there is a shortage of about 40 lakh nurses in the country today. Today, there are 1.7 nurses per 1,000 population in the country, while according to the WHO there should be three nurses per 1,000 people. To some extent, nursing schools and colleges are opening in the country, due to which proportionately the number of nurses is increasing, but the quality of nurses is not improving correspondingly as desired. We have seen that nurses who are well behaved with professional and communication skills look for a better opportunity abroad. Trained nurses from India are serving all over the world today.

The quality of the work depends on the quality of the worker and the quality of the worker depends upon the worker's behaviour, knowledge and skill. As mentioned earlier, nurses are as important as doctors in keeping our health services healthy. It would be better if the policy makers focus on increasing not only the quantity of nurses but enhancing their quality also with a good rigorous patient-oriented curriculum.

https://www.pioneeredge.in/nurses-are-as-important-as-doctors-in-keeping-health-services-healthy/

❑

93

The Deadly Behavioural Problem of Road Rage

– Dr BKS Sanjay & Dr Gaurav Sanjay,
Monday, 22 May 2023

The topic of road rage has become a matter of concern from both the social and political points of view. Road rage is defined as an uncontrolled anger of a motorist that is usually provoked by another motorist's irritating act of driving rashly or against the driving rules and regulations which is expressed in aggressive or violent behaviour.

The recent incident involving cabinet minister Prem Chand Agarwal in which he is seen engaging in a fist fight with a man on a congested road in Rishikesh town has highlighted the issue of road rage in the State. The cases of road rage are continuing to increase with the increasing traffic congestion on the roads.

This kind of behaviour is observed all over the world but it is very prevalent in South East Asian countries including India. The incidence of road rage of cricketer turned politician Navjot Singh Sidhu is well-known in our country. Sidhu hit an old man's skull with his fist in a road rage incident and the old man ultimately died. He was convicted which also resulted in the loss of his seat in the parliament. Though he was re-elected but his case was reviewed by a higher court which sent him to jail for a year. He was recently released from jail. Another case of road rage has been reported from the national capital where a man was carried on the bonnet of a car. The issue was honking from behind the vehicle of the accused while asking for space to overtake.

The extreme condition of weather, over congestion on the roads and the behaviour of the drivers are the common factors to provoke the road rage. The chances of incidence of road rage increase in early and the late hours of the day. In early hours drivers wish to reach the office or any work place in time and late at night the drivers want to reach home or destination before it's late. In such a situation, the influence of alcohol works as "the fuel in the fire".

In our opinion, the habit of following the traffic rules and tendency of road rage are basically developed in childhood period when they are driven by parents or by other adults. Another usual factor is when the accused thinks that other person is weaker than him in any aspect like status, gender, education, physical built, financially poor, social and political status.

Even after the implementation of Motor Vehicle (Amendment) Act 2019, the incidence of road rage has increased instead of decreasing. The Union Road Transport minister Nitin Gadkari informed Lok Sabha that the total number of road rage, rash driving cases had jumped from 1.55 lakh in 2019 to 2.15 lakh in 2021. According to him, the government authorities had issued nearly two crore challan and collected nearly Rs 2,000 crore fine from traffic violators in 2021 across the country.

In our opinion, road rage is not just due to the ignorance of the traffic rules but also due to the hostile behaviour of the drivers. We Indians are known to have aggressive behaviour as it is commonly observed that Indian people do not take pride in following the rules and regulations in general while taking pride in breaking the rules. The common observations made are- first, the drivers are not on the designated lane, second- they are habituated to crisscrossing the lane without use of indicator and try to get into every inch of empty space in the other lanes which irritates the fellow drivers and sometimes may hit and/or damage the other vehicle specially the window rear mirror in case of crisscrossing or the bumper of the other vehicle in tailgating. It often leads to incidence of shouting, yelling, abusing, fist fighting and more violence.

Anger, aggression and impatience among the commuters are manifested in increasing road rage. Teenagers are the ones especially displaying their anger and frustration openly on the road. Over bearing personality, lack of tolerance and absence of discipline in these people are the reasons for increasing road rage. In our opinion 90 per cent of road rage cases are due to driver's behaviour and 10 per cent are due to traffic congestion and other issues which can be understood by just bringing change in our thinking.

In a road rage incident, it will be best if it can be ignored by any of the conflicting parties rather than becoming more aggressive or more competitive knowing very well that it may take a dangerous turn which may lead to further damage of the vehicle or even physical injuries or death of an individual. It is better if such incidences can be reported to the traffic police with video evidence through the cameras installed in the vehicles and appropriate and prompt action is taken by authorities in such cases. Often, the mindset in road rage is to settle the incident on the spot, knowing well that the authorities will take forever to bring justice to the incident.

Repeated honking, flashing of head light and crisscrossing on the road are considered as initial warning signs of road rage. Avoid confrontation during road rage situations. It is important to avoid engaging with aggressive or angry drivers. Try to distance yourself from the situation or find a way to de-escalate it. Offering an apology is the best idea and, in any way, avoid eye contact during road rage situations. There is a need to control this menace. Remember that if a situation is escalated instead of being controlled then road rage can be dangerous and can lead to serious consequences for all stakeholders.

Road accidents may not be considered as wilful acts but road rage is definitely a wilful and a criminal act. The incidence of road rage can be prevented by addressing the behavioural issues of the drivers which matters the most. To overcome this, people must undergo good counselling and make Yoga part of their regular routine.

This year, the seventh edition of UN Global Road Safety Week focused on sustainable transport and in particular the need to shift to walking, cycling and use of public transport. The WHO invited all road safety and sustainable mobility partners to spread the awareness for road safety by organising events, activities, sharing messages and materials through social media platforms.

https://www.pioneeredge.in/the-deadly-behavioural-problem-of-road-rage/

❑

94

Those Who Read, They Grow and Become What They Read

– Dr BKS Sanjay,
Thursday, 25 May 2023

British philosopher and prolific writer Roger Scruton once said, "Stress presents with different feelings in different people and a book can reduce them." A study revealed that only 30 minutes of reading a book can reduce your blood pressure, heart rate, psychological stress and pain. It also ascertained that book reading is as beneficial as Yoga, reading a comic book or laughing. Physicians based in Mayo Clinic, USA also advise people to regularly read a printed book before sleeping to avoid computer and mobile screen reading.

It is better to read a preferred book but children should be supervised while reading. Parents should set the example of book reading for their children to increase their knowledge and skills. Books are the simplest, cheapest, easiest and permanent means to learning. We believe that those who read grow and become what they read.

The habit of reading books is not a new one but one imbibed from childhood. Those who didn't become habituated to reading during childhood generally struggle to reach greater heights in their careers. In our opinion, instead of just reading books we should try to read good books.

Our ancestors had realised the importance of books in development of society, for gaining and transmitting knowledge from one generation to the next. Our epic scriptures like Ramayana, Geeta, Guru Granth and others have played an important role in developing the character and culture of our society. There were multitudes of libraries across the country in the past. The grand libraries of Nalanda and Takshila are examples of such rich libraries which were unfortunately destroyed by invaders in the past. The Nalanda university library was the grandest in the world at that time which was built in the 5th century. The library building had nine floors, 2,000 teachers and 10,000 students from across the world.

BR Ambedkar said that cultivation of the mind should be the ultimate aim of human existence. Writers die but their books remain immortal. When we read a book, it seems that we are having a personal connection with the author and this feeling is what makes the authors immortal.

Our thought is the primary source of all actions. Books play an important role in transforming society. We believe if there is a need to bring change in the individual, society and our country then there is a need to change the thoughts. It is written in our scriptures that "Vicharh Param Gyanam, Gyanam Param Balam" -which means that thought is the ultimate knowledge and knowledge is the greatest power. Ambedkar had said that just as a plant needs water, an idea needs propagation or else both die. Books are a good, cheap and permanent medium for propagation of any idea.

The importance of education and books was understood by many of our wise men, politicians and enlightened people. Ambedkar understood the importance of education and gave it due importance in the framework of the constitution. Going further, the habit of sharing books makes one a medium of sharing knowledge. Cultivate the habit of buying, reading, distributing and gifting books so that you inspire others to do the same. Gifting a book costing a few hundred rupees can bring a big change in some person's life. Based on our experience, we believe that books are better friends than individuals.

https://www.pioneeredge.in/those-who-read-grow-and-become-what-they-read/

❑

95

Past, Present and Future of Healthcare Services in India

– Dr BKS Sanjay & Dr Gaurav Sanjay,
Monday, 12 June 2023

Being universal and inevitable, change has also been seen in the healthcare services in India. The senior author had entered medical college at Kanpur in 1974 while the second author joined medical college at Dehradun in 2003.

At the first author's medical college the lecture halls were huge and could accommodate nearly 400 students, usually two batches of about 200 students each. The back benchers could hardly understand the words written on the blackboard and could barely hear the spoken words most of the time, particularly if the teacher was soft spoken with a low tone of voice. But nowadays the methodology of teaching has changed drastically not only in the higher education institutes but also in the primary schools.

Similarly, the clinical teaching five decades ago was mainly patient based. It was difficult to even see the involved part of the body and learning clinical examination was a distant dream in front of the professor. However, there was a well-established tradition of interactive evening teaching in the wards by the PG students, usually demonstrators and registrars. Ward round-based teaching was a good, convenient and beneficial method of teaching because it was an interactive method-based teaching. There wasn't a huge age difference among the postgraduates/demonstrators and the MBBS students, therefore, they were very friendly and helpful. Students were not hesitant in clearing their doubts and asking questions. We personally feel this kind of interactive clinical teaching should be continued and should be started if it's not being done.

In clinical practice there was a lot of physical work in those days which was required by junior residents or PG students like collection of blood samples, arranging other investigations, blood donors and blood units, part preparation of the surgical site, cleaning and painting of the part before the surgery, assisting the surgeon by just holding the re-tractors, application and removal of the plaster cast, transporting the patient between recovery and OT which were a part of the duty of the residents. Now, things have changed drastically because of computerisation and automation of the laboratories and more investment in healthcare professionals such as phlebotomist, ward attendants, various technicians and paramedics etc and other specialised healthcare services.

Being orthopaedic surgeons, we would like to mention a few things from a surgeon's perspective. Though the hospital wards and operation theatres were cleaner than our homes, they were never sterile because there was no concept of sterilisation of OT air. The usual protocol was to clean the operating table and to autoclave the gloves, syringes, needles, OT drapes, linen and the operating instruments. When the senior author started his MS (Orthopaedic) training in PGI Chandigarh in 1981, he saw for the first time that the operating theatres were being fumigated every day in the night before the start of any surgery. Even a premier institute like PGI Chandigarh was lacking the facility of fluoroscopy or image intensifier in operation theatre.

Although fracture of neck femur was not a very common surgery it needed an image intensifier or X- ray control to check the position of fracture reduction and the position of screws within the bone. The only facility we had at that time was a mobile X-ray machine in the operation theatre complex which was being shared among many surgical specialties which could be requested on call. The technician from the X-ray department would take the radiographic exposure in the operation theatre after shifting the heavy machine and return to the department's darkroom to develop the film manually. The whole process used to take a minimum of 20-30 minutes. During that time, the surgery would be put on hold, which may increase the risk of bleeding and infection. Currently almost all orthopaedic operation theatres have an image intensifier which can give the X-ray image with just a click. Images can also be stored permanently and can be retrieved instantly as it is all computerised.

Advancement in fracture treatment is another aspect we will like to mention here. Fifty years ago, all difficult fractures were reduced after opening the skin and then fixing it. The drilling of the bone was done manually which was usually very tiring and at times surgeons would reduce the number of screws ideally required for fixation due to surgeon fatigue. Most of the time the reduction and fixation were accepted even though it was not satisfactory or perfect. The availability of the preferred type, size and quality of the implants, electric and pneumatic (air) drill and saw, and image intensifier in operation theatre has improved the quality of fracture treatment. Even surgeons with average surgical skills are now able to give excellent results. In certain cases, it becomes difficult to say if the patient had any fracture earlier.

There has been tremendous improvement in cancer surgery. Initially in orthopaedic surgery, the usual treatment of bone and soft tissue tumours used to be amputations of affected limbs which caused permanent disabilities. The invention of CT, MRI, PET and bone scan has improved the quality of surgery, postoperative prognosis and quality of post cancer therapy survival. Nowadays the limb salvage surgery is a norm.

A 15-year-old girl was suffering from bone cancer of the leg bone and was treated 17 years ago by the authors in Dehradun. The bone tumour had been removed, the defect had been reconstructed by recycling the same bone and was used as bone graft and reconstruction with a nail was done. This patient was treated post-surgery with chemotherapy in PGI, Chandigarh. After 17 years of the surgery, she has a near normal personal and social life while working as a teacher. In her case the credit goes to the quality of surgery, chemotherapy and faith of the family in the doctors. This is not an isolated case but many limbs and lives are being saved nowadays due to technological and surgical advancement.

Total joint replacement surgery is another major development. Fifty years ago, a patient with any kind of arthritis had to rely mainly on painkillers. When the first author was in Kanpur Medical College, he never saw any surgery for arthritis but PGI Chandigarh was one of the few centres in the country where joint replacement surgery was started in 1981. The hip and knee joint replacement surgeries changed the lives of not only the patients but the professional lives of orthopaedic surgeons too. Similarly, spine surgery which was a rare and risky surgery is nowadays a common and simple surgery which gives gratifying results. When the first author joined orthopaedic surgery, it was not a very popular branch. The most sought speciality used to be internal medicine and paediatrics but three decades later when the second author joined his PG training, orthopaedic surgery was one of the most desired specialities among male doctors. It is just behind radiology which was the least preferred speciality for post-graduation 50 years ago.

The major developments which have occurred in radiology, especially in imaging- CT, MRI, PET, bone scan, interventional radiology and availability of the various isotopes etc have occurred in the last 50 years. Minimally invasive surgery, interventional surgery, navigation and robotic surgery have made tremendous contributions in both medical and surgical fields. CAD (computer aided design) software has facilitated the manufacturing of implants. Nowadays, 3D printed models give a better understanding of complex pathology and anatomy of the patient which helps to do reconstruction and plan the surgeries with patient tailored implants for perfect results. 3D printed patient specific models in cardiothoracic surgery, kidney and other organs transplantation including bone transplantation are the newer advancement in healthcare services. Artificial intelligence (AI) in our opinion has the potential to change medical practice in the future.

Technology has made the life of doctors, technicians, engineers easier and it has improved the quality of life of many patients. The smart watch is a small and relatively cheap and simple tool to monitor the vital parameters of the body. In the earlier days one had to go to a clinic to know the current BP, temperature, blood sugar etc. but nowadays a smart watch or certain portable devices can give you 24 hours continuous monitoring of the vital parameters which can help in prevention of serious complications of the various health issues.

https://www.pioneeredge.in/past-present-future-of-healthcare-services-in-india/

❑

96

Millets Not Poor Man's Food Anymore, Better Than Wheat & Rice

– Dr BKS Sanjay,
Monday, 19 June 2023,

Based on India's proposal the year 2023 was declared as International Year of Millets (IYM) by the United Nations General Assembly. Under the leadership of Prime Minister Narendra Modi, the celebration of IYM 2023 has become a people's movement and has positioned India as the global hub for millets.

The author was born in a village of Bundelkhand which has a dry and arid climate. Bundelkhand is historically known as a drought prone region of the country but as the climate is changing, the frequency and intensity of drought has increased in the past two decades. The incidence of recurrent drought is well-known in the region where the ground water level goes further deep down. The ponds, hand pump, borewells and tube wells- all have become dry. The region is a gently sloping upland distinguished by barren hilly terrain with sparse vegetation especially in river ravine areas where the climate is dry and arid.

Usually, two crops- kharif and rabi are harvested in a year and these are dependent on rain fed water. Crops like rice do not survive in drought prone areas. The millets like jowar and bajra are the common crops in kharif, pulses and mustard are the common crops in rabi in Bundelkhand. Jowar-bajra porridge and flatbread are cooked in most of the houses. They are the staple food of the people. The porridge is usually eaten with milk or butter milk and flatbread with dal and vegetables.

Millets are grouped in cereals that commonly come under the grass family. Millets grow in harsh climate and survive in less fertile soil, that is why millet crops do not need much water, fertiliser and pesticide because of their genetic composition and physical structures like small size and hard outer coat. The millets are divided into two categories-large and small size. Large millets are popular and commonly cultivated and consumed. Large millets, which are the most popular include sorghum (jowar), pearl millets (bajra) and finger millets (ragi, mandua). Small millets are barnyard millets (jhangora), proso or broomcorn millets (barri, chena), buckwheat millets (Kuttu), kodo millets (kodra), foxtail millets (kangni) and amaranthus (chaulai). Millets are coarse grains that have been traditionally grown and consumed in the Indian subcontinent for about 5,000 years. They are tagged as "poor man's food grains" because they are grown in underdeveloped areas and were usually eaten by poor people as a staple food. The author himself consumes porridge or flatbread made of one of the millets (jowar, bajra, ragi) by rotation six days a week.

Here one would like to narrate a story. I have worked and lived in Riyadh, Saudi Arabia for many years. One day when I went to buy wheat flour, I saw sacks of jowar in a shop. When I showed interest in buying jowar, the shopkeeper asked me if I had camels. I questioned why he asked that and he replied that this is camel feed. When I told him that I had eaten porridge and flatbread of jowar in my childhood till I lived in my village the shopkeeper could not believe it and was amazed to know that jowar is eaten by humans in India. He thought that jowar is used only as cattle fodder.

The consumption of millets can help in maintaining good health of the individuals and its production can help in increasing the earning of farmers especially in drought prone areas of Uttar Pradesh, Madhya Pradesh, Uttarakhand, Rajasthan, Gujarat, Karnataka, Maharashtra, Tamil Nadu and Andhra Pradesh. Traditionally, these States have been producing the maximum quantity of millets (98%). India is the largest producer of millets which accounts for more than half of the world production. African countries are the other producers and consumers of the millets. The areas which are not developed in the agriculture sector are still producing and consuming the millets.

The troika of health, education and nutrition (HEN) is the basic pillars of an individual and of the nation. Health is not only an asset but also a resource which must be nurtured by all. It is a fundamental need of any individual and everybody should be health conscious. One should always take care of themselves in order to remain healthy. To achieve good health one can follow the acronym DEWS: Diet, Exercise, Work and Sleep.

It is said in our scriptures, Annam Vai Pranam which means food is life. Diet plays a vital role in maintaining good health. Most lifestyle diseases like diabetes, hypertension, coronary artery disease, atherosclerosis, hyperlipidaemia and many other diseases are linked with bad food habits. Millets are a good source of energy, protein, fibre, minerals like copper, magnesium, manganese, potassium, zinc, selenium, many other micro nutrients and antioxidants. Consumption of millets can not only supply energy but also the essential micro nutrients needed for maintaining good health by improving the immunity. Overall millets are better than wheat, rice and maize.

It is a well-known fact that fruits like berries and cherries which are grown in harsh environments like extreme cold are good for health. The millets from dry and arid land also give the same advantages as berries and cherries. Millets are considerably cheaper than berries and cherries.

A food festival organised by MCD in New Delhi at Talkatora Stadium had food made with millets and was a success story, similar to the Millets Festival held in Mumbai in February 2023. According to an official report the popularity of the millet delicacies was more than expected. Similar food festivals will be held during G20 summit 2023 during September 9-10 at Pragati Maidan. Traditionally, porridge and flatbread are cooked with the millets but new recipes are coming up in this International Year of Millets which was evident in the global millets (Shri Anna) conference in Delhi in March this year.

Once tagged as the poor man's food, millets are increasingly finding their way into dinner plates across the world. Regular consumption of millets will not only help to maintain the physical health of the individuals but more production will help to improve the financial health of the farmers particularly of marginal farmers living in under developed dry and arid areas. This initiative will be a game changer in the future not only in health, food and agriculture sectors but in other related sectors as well as all over the world because 97 per cent of millet production happens in developing countries.

https://www.pioneeredge.in/millets-not-poor-mans-food-anymore-better-than-wheat-rice/

❑

97

No Cost Health Booster: Yoga, Exercise and Sleep

– Dr BKS Sanjay & Dr Gaurav Sanjay,
Thursday, 22 June 2023

Health is not only an asset but a resource too which should be nurtured by all. Whatever we achieve whether natural or manmade can only be used and enjoyed when we are healthy. Hence, everybody should strive to remain as healthy as possible. But, how can we achieve this good health is the pertinent question. Stress is the new health problem and around 70 per cent of diseases are stress related. Most of these diseases are self-created, which are caused due to change in lifestyle. These acquired lifestyles are not difficult to change but strong conviction is needed to change our mindset. By changing our lifestyle, we can change our health and ultimately our life.

Yoga is a group of physical, mental and spiritual practices or discipline which originated in ancient India and aims to control the mind. The practice of Yoga not only helps to maintain better physical health but can also be used as a tool for stress management which has been further proved by many biofeedback studies. The habit of Yoga, regulated breathing and meditation should be the part of one's day-to-day activity to maintain his physical, mental, social, psychological and spiritual health. Yoga needs only a little bit of time and is to be done at regular intervals to improve the general health of an individual. Yoga practice of half an hour to one hour on a daily basis is enough to maintain good health.

Regular physical activity is one of the most important things one can do for good health. Being physically active can improve your brain health, manage weight issues, reduce the risk of diseases, strengthen bones and muscles and improve your ability to do all day-to-day activities. As other organs of the body need exercise, so does our heart. The heart cannot do any voluntary exercise itself but any physical exercise of the body will force the heart muscles to work more proportionately. Walking, jogging and running are good exercises which indirectly help to boost the health of the heart. As our limbs become stronger with exercise, so does the heart. If one does his or her household work and avoids sedentary work, does Yoga exercise and takes a balanced diet then there is a fair chance that one will have a healthy and longer life. In addition to Yoga and exercise, if an individual can abstain from the habit of alcoholism and smoking, then he will be much healthier.

Sleep plays a vital role in maintaining good health both physically and mentally throughout our life. Contrary to the quiet physical stage, the brain is very active and carries out many important functions of the body during sleep. Sleep rejuvenates the body, improves the ability of the body to fight diseases and increases immunity. In fact, sleep is an essential to every process in the body, whether physical or mental.

The body has the circadian rhythm which is the 24-hour internal clock in our brain that regulates the cycles of alertness and sleepiness by responding to light changes in our environment which control physiological and metabolic activities. Sleep and mental health go hand in hand. A person needs seven to nine hours of sleep. It is a common observation that children sleep more. It has been observed in Europe that when the clock is adjusted as a measure for daylight saving the time in which the clock is pushed forward, people lose one hour of sleep. In general, this universal time change creates significant public health problems like increased incidence of heart attack and road traffic injuries increase due to disturbed or lack of sleep.

Poor quality sleep or lack of sleep is associated with lethargic and irritable behaviour, poor learning and retaining capacity for new information. Though poor sleep is known to reduce appetite at the same time it increases weight gain. One cannot be deprived of sleep for more than 48 hours. If one does so, the brain goes into a state of narcolepsy. Narcolepsy is defined as a condition characterised by an extreme tendency to fall asleep without warning. Narcolepsy causes sudden loss of muscle tone of the whole-body including hands and feet which disturb the control on the steering and accelerator. In addition to that a person experiences hallucination. If the tired driver is used to relieve the tiredness with consumption of alcohol, the alcohol may help to relieve tiredness but increases the tendency to fall asleep which further increases the chances of road traffic injuries. In our experience, lack of sleep and the influence of alcohol are common causes of road traffic injuries in India.

The senior author wishes to share his own experience of episodic increased levels of serum uric acid. The basic cause of rise of uric acid in blood is either due to increased production of uric acid or decreased excretion of uric acid or both. Uric acid is a byproduct of protein metabolism. Decreased intake of protein in diet and increased intake of fluid have brought the uric acid of the author to within normal limits in a couple of months. With this precaution there is no more gout attack. Similarly, one was experiencing raised blood sugar level leading to initially pre-diabetic and then diabetic stage. Changing the diet from wheat grain to coarse grain like jowar, bajra, barley, maize and mandua and undertaking half an hour to an hour of brisk walking daily have brought down the blood sugar to within normal limits in only three week's time. Authors suggest that everyone should have a limited diet and unlimited work for a healthy and happy life. An American professor of Harvard Medical School, Dr David Sinclair advised that we should eat plants that have been stressed and grow under harsh conditions.

It is found that those who eat less and work more, live a healthy and longer life. We can be healthy only when we eat nutritious food. For better health, we should eat only when we are hungry and we should keep in mind to eat only a nutritious and balanced diet. If we are healthy then we can achieve our desirable goal and enjoy our life, as it is said by an ancient Indian Rishi Bhrighu that we all are products of pleasure and to achieve pleasure is the goal of every individual. In our opinion, Yoga, exercise and sleep are no cost health boosters. One should always take care of themselves in order to remain healthy.

https://www.pioneeredge.in/no-cost-health-booster-yoga-exercise-and-sleep/

❑

98

Relation of Cleanliness and Health Services in India

– Dr Gaurav Sanjay,
Monday, 26 June 2023

Cleanliness is the most important habit one can possess, as cleanliness and health are directly interrelated. A habitually clean person can fight off and avoid many diseases, especially communicable diseases. Moreover, cleanliness enhances physical, mental and spiritual health.

If one reviews the health problems of India in the last few centuries one will find that in ancient times, infection was one of the main health problems. The epidemics of plague, cholera, smallpox, polio etc killed millions of people in the last century. In the recent decades infections like smallpox and polio have been controlled. India has been free from smallpox since 1977 and from polio since 2011. Other bacterial infections were a great cause of mortality in the past but now some of them have been controlled after the invention of antibiotics. If one reviews the cause of infection in the current scenario then it is found that individual body hygiene and cleanliness of the environment are the common factors in the spread of disease.

As far as body hygiene is concerned, it is the duty and the responsibility of an individual. However, the responsibility of cleanliness of the surrounding area is that of the entire civil society and that of the municipal administration. Regular washing of hands, brushing of teeth, bathing daily, wearing clean clothes and trimming of nails are the few basic precautions to maintain our personal hygiene. Hand washing with the soap and water should be done before consuming food and after using the toilet. It is a common observation in India that people involved in cooking and serving food at roadside eateries are not as careful in maintaining hygienic practices as they should be.

In the author's own experience, it has been seen that there are eateries where there is no provision of clean water supply and proper drainage. Food is being cooked in an open area surrounded by hundreds of flies and insects. Many eateries and restaurants are located along or around open drainage areas. Similarly, the utensils are cleaned with contaminated water and wiped with the same contaminated cloths which are used to wipe the tables. If food is consumed in such places one is bound to get a gut infection. It is suggested that such eateries should be licensed. A license should be issued only after fulfilling the norms and standard followed by the Food Safety and Standards Authority of India (FSSAI), with regular checks of hygienic practices by such vendors.

In my opinion, because of consuming unhygienic foods, the people are not only losing the money in treatment but also losing their valuable time. I would like to give an example of a person who is going for a holiday with his family. If anyone in the family gets any health issue, then it not only disturbs the physical health of that person but spoils the mood and the whole trip. It is suggested that all roadside eateries should have adequate supply of clean drinking water, clean toilet facility, safe food supply chain and facilities to maintain the personal hygiene of staff and customers.

India has many seasons but particular seasons like monsoon and summer are known for fast rotting of food.

It is suggested that all eateries and restaurants should have the facility of fridge and deep freezer which will not only maintain the quality of food but will avoid the wastage of cooked food and raw materials like fresh green vegetables and fresh fruits. Vegetables and fruits carry dust, pesticides, germs and unwanted residues on their surfaces. Preservative and ripening agents are commonly used so they should be thoroughly washed.

The current government under the leadership of Prime Minister Narendra Modi realised the importance of the relation of cleanliness and the health of citizens. In 2014, Prime Minister Modi initiated Swachh Bharat Mission which is a country wide campaign to eliminate open defecation and to improve solid waste management. The government aimed to achieve an Open Defecation Free (ODF) status throughout the country by constructing over 11 crore toilets all over the country. In addition to that the government also started a programme to improve the management of solid waste which will not only improve the health of the citizens but improve the health and lives of all sanitation workers. It is the largest cleanliness drive by any government in the world. This mission is working to achieve the United Nations Sustainable Development Goals.

Here, I would like to inform you about the importance of hand washing. Hands carry the pathogenic organisms from one place to another, from a contaminated surface or object to the mouth. In a scientific study, it was found that if proper hand washing is done then 50 per cent of gut infection and the 25 per cent of lung infection can be reduced. Nail beds are the main harbour of these bacterial infections. Those involved in the food and beverage industry, especially the restaurants, should take care of their nails regularly.

The washing of the hands with soap and water for a minute is enough to kill most of the germs and if water is not available then one can rub hands with commercially available hand sanitiser for a half a minute. The habit of hand washing before each meal and after using the toilet should be taught to everyone in early childhood.

Even a simple bath with soap and water removes the dirt, dust, body secretions and microorganisms. Cavity in the teeth is the most common dental problem. Food particles get deposited in these cavities which become a den for these bacteria. Whenever the patient's immunity decreases, these microorganisms settle in other parts of the body, especially if having a foreign body like implants. In orthopaedic practice if patients need total joint replacement for any problem, then they are advised to consult a dentist in the pre-operative checkup.

If we all, in general, practice to maintain our personal hygiene and the cleanliness in the environment, the chances of infection can be reduced significantly. On the contrary if infections occur, patients are losing not only their time and money but sometimes valuable lives as well. Our country is losing billions of rupees just on the treatment of infections. However, if we all follow the simple principles of maintaining personal hygiene and a clean environment then we will save time and money which can be used for the other better work. We all should follow the dictum "prevention is better than cure".

https://www.pioneeredge.in/relation-of-cleanliness-and-health-services-in-india/

99

Curb Overpopulation – It is Important and Urgent

– Dr BKS Sanjay,
Monday, 10 July 2023

Overpopulation is creating a lot of problems not only for the humans but also for other animals and the environment. The current world population is estimated to be just over eight billion. India's population is currently estimated to be 1.4 billion and is expected to be 1.5 billion by 2030 and two billion by 2050. India has 17 per cent of the global population in 2.4 per cent of the world's land area.

Rapid growth of population results in the creation of personal stress, social, economic and boundary conflicts. The war between neighbouring countries is not only for economic interest but also for increasing their land area. These conflicts further lead to migration of people who usually prefer to settle in cities and urban areas which are developed but are already congested and where the civil resources are under strain. Here, I would like to confine myself to the Indian problems. The population in India has already surpassed the population of China. China has not suffered as much in the past due to overpopulation and will not suffer as much as India in the future also because the area of the China is three times that of India. The sustainability of any population depends mainly on natural resources. Having more area, China also has more resources. Its land area is 9.6 million square kilometres compared to India's 3.2 million square kilometres.

In addition to that, India and China have two different political and administrative systems. China has a one party and almost a dictatorial system while India has a multi-party democratic system. In China, anything can be implemented easily as they did with one child policy for population control in 1980. The pace of population control in India is very slow because of diversity and democratic system. I think these are the reasons that India could not control the population even though the population control programme was implemented in India as early as 1952, nearly 70 years ago. If the programme was implemented honestly and at a fast pace with the help of citizens, things could have been very different from social, economic and political point of view.

In my opinion it is still not too late. I still think the sooner the better because about 65 per cent of Indian population is still aged below 35 years. The change in demography is going to be another challenge for the policymakers to deal with. I would suggest that a law should be enacted and strictly enforced to control the over growing population because voluntary approach of population control is not working among all regions and religions. In my opinion, the cause of overpopulation in our country is ignorance due to illiteracy and poverty which are interrelated hence the all policymakers should think about illiteracy before making any policy aimed at population control.

There is urgent need for population control otherwise the results would be disastrous not only for humans but also for other species. Many species have become extinct and many more are going to be extinct in the near future and somehow it will be attributed to overpopulation of the human species. The main cause of population explosion in India is increasing birth rate and decreasing mortality rate. Rapid population growth is depleting all resources whether natural or manmade. It is suggested that the general public should be given the message that if one is divided by more than one then quotient will be less than one which applies to all resources.

The nation should follow two-baby norm per family, preferably one male and one female baby because if this is followed then there will be no future gender ratio problem. It will also fulfil the aim of this year's World Population Day theme which is focusing on gender equality. Most couples can support a couple of babies comfortably. There will be no personal, social and economic suffering. In addition to that when these children get married then the girl from one house will go to another house and the other girl will move to the first house so there will not be any problem for need of expansion of parental home. I presume that irrespective of economic status in general, every parent must be having at least some kind of shelter. Only three bedrooms per family will be sufficient for almost every generation.

Hence there will be no shelter problem for future generation for most families who wish to stay together. Similarly, if children don't get their desirable work, till then, they can continue at least the parental vocation or profession with the parent's tools and equipment for their survival. Therefore, I presume that there will be decreased stress on the younger generation or newly-wed couples for arranging or procuring the tools and find a new shelter to carry on with their new lives. When the family will be limited, then their needs will be limited and can be easily fulfilled hence there will be no undue stress, competition or conflict. In fact, all three generations—grandparents, parents and children will have happy, healthy and comfortable life.

Overpopulation is the leading cause of malnutrition, starvation and famine especially in poor families of underdeveloped areas. It is also depleting the earth's already strained natural resources. Media reports state that groundwater is depleting, air is being heavily polluted and food products are being adulterated which is affecting the general health of all citizens. Overpopulation is the leading cause of industrialisation resulting into pollution and exploitation of the natural resources. Pollution and global warming are resulting in natural disasters in the form of drought, flooding, glacier melting, deforestation, wildfires and rise of sea water level. The problems related to overpopulation are not confined to our country alone but affecting the whole world. According to Maslow's hierarchy of needs, five categories of human needs dictate an individual's behaviour. At the bottom of the pyramid are the physiological needs and self-actualisation is at the top. Maslow states that basic physiological needs must be addressed before humans move onto the next level of fulfilment.

I believe that human resource is the greatest resource on earth but due to non-fulfilment of their physiological and basic needs, the human resource is rather becoming a liability on the others. Though it is a herculean task for the Indian government to deal with issues related to overpopulation, all policymakers should look into them and act to make a law and enforce it strictly to control the population. If it is done, then it will be proved that whatever Indians say, they mean it. Indian scriptures- the Upanishads say that may all be happy, may no one suffer from illness, may all see goodness, may no one suffer sorrow.

https://www.pioneeredge.in/curb-overpopulation-it-is-important-urgent/

❑

100

Medical Negligence: A Matter to Ponder

– Dr BKS Sanjay & Dr Gaurav Sanjay,
Friday, 21 July 2023

Medical negligence under the IPC Section 304A reads as, "Whoever causes the death of any person by doing any rash or negligent act not amounting to culpable homicide shall be punished with imprisonment of either description for a term which may extend to two years, or with fine, or with both."

The doctor is not liable for every injury or complication suffered by a patient. Bolam test states that when a doctor accepts standard practice, then he is not doing a breach of his duty. In case there is no breach or the breach did not cause the damage, the doctor will not be liable. Normally, the liability arises only when the plaintiff is able to discharge the burden on him of proving the negligence. However, in some cases like a swab left inside the abdomen of a patient or the wrong side operated, the principle of 'res ipsa loquitur' (the thing speaks for itself) might come into play.

In our opinion, it is difficult for a lay man to evaluate the quality of a product or a service given by any professional. In our country, where significant number of people are illiterate and there is a hostile atmosphere among the general society it seems that the cause may not actually be medical negligence but the difference of perception in certain services which leads to discord in doctor-patient relation and communication which may lead to an altercation and ultimately the issue may land up in the court.

It is seen that some patients usually hide the actual cause of injury, history of alcoholism and the pre-existing comorbidity to avoid non-settlement through insurance companies. They hide comorbidities because many healthcare providers either refuse to take up such high risk patients or if they do then the financial liabilities of the treatment increases. Diseases like HIV and hepatitis B/C infections are usually hidden due to social stigma or the fear of refusal of medical services to them.

The National Consumer Disputes Redressal Commission (NCDRC) dismissed a case filed by the wife and two daughters of former Chief Justice of India (CJI) JS Verma alleging that medical negligence led to his death. The plaintiff was seeking exemplary damage and compensation of Rs 10 crore by the treating doctors and hospitals. The commission observed that "as long as a doctor acts in a manner which is acceptable to the medical profession, and the court finds that he has attended on the patient with due care skill and diligence and if the patient still does not survive or suffer a permanent ailment, it would be difficult to hold the doctor to be guilty of negligence". The commission observed that Justice Verma, 80, suffered from multiple comorbidities which contributed to his death.

It is also said that Delhi Medical Council (DMC) and Medical Council of India (MCI) had considered it twice and found there was no negligence on the part of the treating doctor at any stage. The commission also held that "...a medical practitioner is not to be held liable simply because things went wrong from mischance or misadventure or through an error of judgement in choosing one reasonable course of treatment in preference to another."

We would like to share another incident of a patient who had a dubious history since presentation when his friend admitted him to the hospital with the history of an alleged injury at home but when his father was asked, he gave a history of an adventure sports injury and later on of a road traffic injury in a police complaint. Although this was overlooked initially, the chain of falsification continued. On asking for the medical and personal history he did not give any history of alcohol or any substance abuse. It was known only after routine blood investigations done routinely before the surgery which revealed that his GGTP -589 IU/L which was much higher than the normal range of 10-45 IU/L which is a marker of alcohol intake. Further it was also observed that his serum Bilirubin was 3.3 mg % which is a marker of liver disease.

The surgery of the patient was hence postponed as his coagulation profile report was awaited and delayed till his parameters were optimised to be fit for surgery. The patient was known to have a long-standing alcohol and drug abuse issue which was known to all his neighbours, local chemists and local police but the patient's father did not divulge these facts at the time of admission. The patient died in the hospital due to sudden spontaneous internal bleeding due to his pre-existing alcohol and drug addiction complication and other comorbidities.

The patient's father brought this matter to the police and local administration. The CMO inquiry committee did not find any medical negligence. In spite of that, the patient's father approached the local state medical council. With the connivance of the patient's father and a certain member of the committee, the state medical council debarred the doctor from medical practice for six months. The doctor appealed to the MCI. After a thorough investigation and adequate deliberations, the doctor was exonerated from all charges. In fact, the MCI stated, "The MCI is unable to understand from the records supplied by the state medical council that on what ground the state medical council debarred the doctor?"

The incident which was cited here is a glaring example of the nexus between the fraudulent behaviour of the certain relatives and certain doctors of the medical authorities who are harassing the majority of the honest and sincere medical doctors and healthcare providers. This is just the tip of the iceberg in the hundreds of thousands of cases which are pending in various courts in India. The courts should think over about the patients who behave fraudulently and have the habit of manipulating facts with their malafide intention to blackmail and to extort money from doctors and the healthcare service providers.

Many a time due to professional rivalry, state medical councils in connivance with their committee members have not looked into the facts but have passed vindictive judgements to settle their own scores by misusing their power. It is a matter of concern for all medical professionals and for the policymakers to amend the act to safeguard the interest of the doctors and the other healthcare providers because this is not only in the interest of the medical profession, but that of the society and of the nation.

Humans err and doctors are human and hence they are also prone to make mistakes but the incidence of mistakes by well qualified experienced doctors are minimal. In India, just about over 52 lakh medical errors happen every year, according to medical negligence statistics in India. In a recent study by a state government in India, it was found that of the 112 cases of medical negligence in a year and only 14 per cent of the patients were real victims of medical negligence. Certain patients and their family and friends are always on the hunt for mistakes and shortcomings in the treatment and services and are regularly inciting the staff and doctors by indulging in verbal abuse, brawl and vandalism among other means.

Health is one of the basic needs of all individuals. The medical profession is a noble profession and the basic foundation of the medical profession is the faith and trust between doctors and patients and their friends and family. But considering these incidents, the younger generation is least interested in opting for the medical profession. This is a matter to ponder.

https://www.pioneeredge.in/medical-negligence-a-matter-to-ponder/

❑

101

Stronger Bones, Stronger Nation

– Dr BKS Sanjay & Dr Gaurav Sanjay,
Thursday, 10 August 2023

Bones support our body and allow us to move. They protect our brain, heart and other organs from injury. Nowadays, the younger generation has weak bones due to its lifestyle that lacks physical activity. Besides, their indulgence in smoking and intake of alcohol and steroids interferes with calcium absorption in the body which weakens the bones. Bones start forming as early as six months in the body and remain till the end of life. We need to provide a substantial amount of calcium, protein, vitamins and minerals for their proper growth and development. To develop the bones, in gestation, we need protein (amino acids), calcium, phosphate and vitamin D which go through the placenta from the mother to the foetus.

If the mother's diet is deficient in any of these essential nutrients the developing foetus is bound to suffer from the deficiency of bone mass Therefore, all pregnant women should take balanced and nutritious diet with extra milk, calcium and vitamin D supplement which is needed for the growth of the foetus in addition to normal need of any woman during pregnancy. Children who do not get the required dietary calcium may not grow tall or gain their potential height. Everybody should fulfil the recommended dietary allowance (RDA) of calcium to maintain good health. Always take a combination of calcium and Vitamin D to strengthen the bones throughout your life. This can be done preferably with a calcium rich balanced diet or with calcium supplements in the form of medicine.

Strong bones, strong muscles and flexible joints form the iron triangle that carries the most important load – the human body. Interestingly, 50 per cent of a person's bones and the muscles are in the two legs. Both the legs together have 50 percent of the nerves and blood vessels of the human body and 50 per cent of the blood flows through them. It is the largest circulatory network that connects the body. About 70 per cent of the human activities in one's life are done by two feet. The foot is the centre of the body's locomotion. Only when the feet are healthy then the conventional current of blood flows smoothly so people who have strong legs will definitely have a strong heart. Locomotion is important at every stage of life though it is more important in childhood. Overall physical, mental, social and economic development of any individual takes place only by locomotion. Ageing starts from the feet upwards. As a person gets older, the accuracy and speed of transmission of instructions between the brain and the legs decreases, unlike when a person is young.

Normal walking contributes a lot to the overall development of any child. Cerebral palsy, polio, club foot are the main causes of limb deformities and orthopaedic disabilities in children but currently road traffic injuries in young age and osteoporosis in old age. The deformities and disabilities caused due to traffic injuries are manmade while osteoporosis is mainly a physiological and metabolic disease. We all can exert control to reduce the incidence of road traffic injuries but the same can't be done for osteoporosis in a similar manner. Loss of bone strength can lead to osteoporosis-a disorder in which bones become very fragile and more likely to break. Older adults with osteoporosis are most vulnerable to breaks in the wrist, hip and spine. These fractures can seriously limit mobility and independence.

Osteoporosis is such a serious health issue that affects both men and women of all races but Asian women especially postmenopausal are at high risk. Certain medications like steroid and anti-epileptic drugs and certain conditions like hyperthyroidism, diabetes, unhealthy diet and sedentary work increase the probability of osteoporosis. Osteoporosis can be diagnosed by taking medical history, physical examination along with blood, urine and x-rays. But the gold standard test nowadays, is to measure the Bone Mineral Density, which can be measured by DEXA Scan and can help to confirm the diagnosis of osteoporosis.

The vitamins and minerals are needed irrespective of age in addition to protein to strengthen bones. As it has been seen, there is no deficiency in bone structure in rickets and osteomalacia, but such patients are deficient in vitamin D in addition to calcium and phosphorus. Minerals such as calcium, phosphorus, iron, magnesium, potassium, copper, selenium and zinc are very important for strengthening the bones. Milk, milk products and eggs are very good, cheap and natural sources of minerals.

The consumption of coarse grains should be increased as they are a good source of energy and the nutrients beneficial for the health of the bones while also supplying energy to the body. Millets are a good, cheap and accessible way to strengthen bones. We should make a habit of eating coarse grains and doing regular exercise not only when we are growing or becoming older but also from childhood.

https://www.pioneeredge.in/stronger-bones-stronger-nation/

❑

102

The Need for Driving Schools and Awareness of Traffic Rules

– Dr Gaurav Sanjay,
Monday, 31 July 2023

The purpose of schools is to give us strong basic fundamentals which can be worked upon to build better skills in the future by well-trained and certified teachers. This is important for every profession but many times it is more important for the driving profession because the lives of many passengers remain in the hands of drivers.

As of 2023, India is the third largest automotive industry in terms of sales but a contrasting statistic is that only eight per cent of Indian households own an automobile. It contributes to 6.4% of India's GDP. The NCRB data of 2021 shows that highways in India constitute just two per cent of the length of roads but are responsible for 30 per cent of accidents, 36 per cent of deaths and three per cent loss of GDP. With almost five lakh accidents annually and 1.5 lakh deaths it is a high time for the policy makers and the public at large to rethink about what is going wrong in our country as far as these road traffic accidents are concerned.

A clinical study done by us revealed that 90 per cent of the accidents are caused due to negligence of the drivers.

A well-made course for driving could be a major change which would help India to decrease these accidents and deaths which are hurting the youth of the country majorly. Road traffic safety and rules must be inculcated as part of school curriculum and we must have government driving schools in which we should be mandatorily made to spend a few weeks before we give a driving test and it must be strictly and fairly conducted.

About 30 per cent driving licences in India are fake, Road Transport and Highways minister Nitin Gadkari informed in the Lok Sabha in July 2019. The government is still not very strict about how these driving licences are issued as it will need a major revamp of the entire process. Driving schools per se are not advertised well enough in our newspapers and mass media. Maruti Suzuki has the largest chain of driving schools in India with about 520 driving schools in 250 cities in India. The average fees there is about Rs 7,000-8,000. The government should invest in driving schools and make them state of the art so that other State governments can take them as a model and reduce these accidents by the means of a well-structured programme at an affordable rate.

China has a theory test which has 100 questions and two practical exams to get a driving license. In Croatia, you have to attend 70-100 hours of mandatory driving school before you attempt the driving test and in Australia it is 120 hours. In France you must clock in 3,000 kilometres behind the wheels with an instructor before you apply for a driving test. In Montenegro, you can make only three mistakes in the test and it's a straight fail then. Apart from that an ophthalmologist and psychiatrist assess you for your fitness to drive as well. Learners in Japan are expected to attend a mandatory driving camp for 26 hours. They also need to take a theory exam, five-day driving practice and finally a practical exam which makes it one of the toughest driving tests in the world. But in India according to data, it is one of the easiest exams to pass. You just have to learn to drive in a straight line and turn left/right and stop after 50 yards to pass. Drivers aren't tested in the true sense to ascertain if it is safe to give them the licence for driving.

India has one per cent of the number of the vehicles in the world with 11 per cent of the total accidents. The role of the government should not only be to boot the economy by selling these cars at high tax which is around 28 per cent GST and 22 per cent CES totalling to an effective tax rate of 50 per cent, but also to have a pool of safe drivers on the roads so that they can avoid these traffic mishaps and accidents. In many countries driving license tests cost hundreds of thousands but in India it costs under Rs 1,000 and the drivers often feel that even if they fail in the test, which they often don't, they will again pay this nominal fee and reappear. They are not serious regarding the test as they won't be losing a lot of money. Although the pricing should not be too high seeing the average wages in the country but the cost should not be taken for granted.

Making a habit from school time will inculcate good driving values among the children who will become responsible drivers in the future. A small exam in every grade can help the nation's children learn it gradually and effectively over the time we spend on primary education. Driving is required almost by each one of us later in our life when we drive ourselves to our coaching centres, colleges, offices or drive our loved ones in time of vacation or injury. The number of driving schools should be increased proportionately to the sale of vehicles. Schools should have mandatory school bus facilities. It will save the time and money which can be utilised by the parents and guardians for other important works.

E-challans are currently being issued by most state governments but it was found in a report in 2022 by nearly eight lakh motorists were challaned out of whom over five lakh had not paid their penalty in the stipulated time. This shows poor enforcement by the authorities. Offenders must be effectively dealt with by a fast process and their licenses must be suspended if they fail to pay within a stipulated time.

Most motorists created an uproar on news channels and social media after the Central government imposed higher fines for breaking these rules, alleging that the government had found a way to earn money. I fail to understand the need to pay the fines if you follow these traffic rules religiously. The youths often throw away Rs 500 for minor offences like not wearing a helmet. Because it doesn◎t burn a hole in their pocket so they are not serious and instead of changing their behaviour to follow the rules they often wait till the next time they are caught and then are again willing to give the money or try to bribe the traffic police.

If punishment is not painful, how can it be punishment? If punishment is not monetarily painful it cannot alter the mindset of such drivers. If they have to pay a hefty sum which is actually difficult for them to pay then most of them will definitely be careful to avoid repeating the offence.

It is a shame to see that the public doesn◎t realise the importance of safe driving. We often disregard the importance of our and other lives by violating the traffic rules. The government should educate and enforce the traffic rules for all. India is striving for UCC but when it is unable to deal even with issues like traffic violation effectively, we have a long way to go.

https://www.pioneeredge.in/the-need-for-driving-schools-and-awareness-of-traffic-rules/

❑

